THE
SCYTHIAN
TRIALS

OTHER BOOKS BY ELIZABETH ISAACS

The Light of Asteria
The Secret of the Keepers
The Heart of the Ancients

THE SCYTHIAN TRIALS

ELIZABETH ISAACS

The Scythian Trials

Copyright © 2018 Elizabeth Isaacs
All rights reserved.

Cover Credit: Original Illustration by Justin Paul

ISBN: 978-1-944109-30-1

VESUVIAN BOOKS

Published by Vesuvian Books
www.vesuvianbooks.com

Printed in the United States of America

10 9 8 7 6 5 4 3 2 1

For everyone who still holds hope that humanity will rise above itself and finally embrace peace.

Strength through Equality.
Power through Knowledge.

CHAPTER ONE

Nya knelt, her fingertips grazing the embedded paw print in the dark soil. Deep grooves on one side revealed the mountain lion had been favoring its right flank. The impressions were fresh, which meant they were closing ground.

Her prey had led her deep into the heart of the dense forest.

She slowly rose from her crouched position. The bright moon's light broke through the thick clouds, casting a soft glow on the path ahead. The cat's lopsided tracks wove between the trees, skirting dangerously close to the mountain's ledge.

She glanced over her shoulder, watching Jax weave through the trees. He chose to stay a few hundred yards back. She had mixed feelings about the gesture. Tomorrow was her last challenge before graduating from the academy, and Jax was giving her the rare gift of space, which she appreciated. But he also insisted she lead, which made her leery.

In her culture, being treated as an equal was a dangerous thing.

Nya picked up the pace, following the path until it ended at the edge of a bluff. She stopped for a moment to watch the brooding mist that crept along the valley's floor. From this vantage point, the streetlights looked like fireflies trapped under frosted glass.

The average human, or Allos as her people called them, knew little of her kind. They stayed on the forest's fringe, consumed with the newest technology, choosing instead to take in the mountain's beauty through windows and distant porches. Most Allos lacked the physical stamina to reach her compound, and those foolish enough to venture too close never came back.

Her stomach flipped as the hair on the back of her neck prickled. Even though Jax hadn't made a sound, she knew he was behind her.

"Do you think the cat fell to his death?" His deep voice, always so calm, muttered in her ear.

She shivered. Jax officially was the academy's weapons expert, but he also carried a Ph.D. in psychology and had been her counselor since her first year. He knew she hated people getting in her space. Until a few weeks ago he'd always respected the boundary. Now, he seemed to go out of his way to cross it.

Her brow lowered. "What do you think?"

"You're the tracker. You tell me."

The tension eased as she stepped closer to the ridge, putting some distance between them. She looked at the steep angle leading to the small town below. "I don't think it's down there."

"And why not, Vtachi?"

Nya scowled, hating the nickname only he used. He'd given it to her the first time she snuck out of the compound. It meant 'little bird' in her native language, Dacian, and it made her feel small and weak. "Stop calling me that. I have more in common with that mountain lion than I do a helpless vtachi."

Jax's perceptive eyes held her gaze. He sighed. "Sadly, that may be true. But it's become my priority to help you change that. Now, how do you know the cat has not fallen to his death? Answer the question, please."

The stubborn part of her wanted to stay silent, but knowing Jax, he'd keep her there all night discussing the finer points of tracking. Or worse, he'd delve into the significance of her having more in common with a wounded predator than an animal gifted with flight.

Better to just answer the question and get it out of the way.

"Fine." She pointed to the slope of dark green foliage and black soil. "See that? Nothing's been disturbed. If the puma had slipped off the ledge, we would see signs of it—somewhere along here, or here." Motioning for him to follow, she turned and walked a few yards back. "And look at the way her tracks are growing heavy, particularly this last half mile or so. See how she's dragging her back paw?" Nya pointed to the deep print and then and dark smear along the right side. "She's smart enough to try and throw us off by going close to the edge and then jumping back inland, but she's too weak to have gone far."

"She?" Jax grinned. "Why do you think the cat's female?"

Nya shrugged. "Makes sense. She's wounded, and yet she is making her way here. I believe she's protecting something."

"And where do you think she's gone?"

His calm voice usually soothed her. Tonight, it grated on her nerves.

"How the hell should I know?" she snapped.

Jax's eyes flashed. "Language, Vtachi."

Scythians, as barbaric as they were, rarely used obscenities. Their high intelligence allowed little tolerance for such crudity. Of course, the fact that the Allos tossed around vulgarity like candy at Mardi Gras proved the theory that only dull-minded, unimaginative people used foul language.

Words were to be chosen carefully. They were the instrument of scholars, philosophers, and lovers.

Personally, Nya couldn't give a shit.

She looked away. "If you're tired of being around me, why did you come? Wasn't like I asked you to."

Jax spread his feet apart and rocked back on his heels. "You volunteered to track some mountain lion two days before the championships."

She hated it when he turned into a shrink. "So?"

"You don't find it odd the top contender in her class would choose to hunt instead of rest before a challenge that will decide her future?"

Nya squared her shoulders and forced herself to meet his gaze. "Not at all. Hunting relaxes me."

He smirked. "Nice try. But I know you, Vtachi. Whether you admit it or not, you're afraid. On the one hand, your mind craves seclusion, wanting only to be left alone. But your heart." He stepped forward. "Your heart wants to win the challenge and choose what is rightfully yours. An equal. A rovni. A mate." His eyes, always so astute, watched her like a hawk.

She stepped back. "You're wrong. My heart wants to be left the hell alone."

Jax's expression cooled. "I'd hoped after four years you would finally trust me and explain why you're so opposed to love."

"I do trust you. And I'm not *opposed to* love, I just don't want to claim an equal."

"Ah." Jax smiled. "So, you would take a lover but not a rovni?"

Nya scowled. "Why is it so outrageous that a Scythian female may not want to become a breeding factory? What if I don't want young? Maybe I don't like sex. What if I'm a lesbian, ever think of that?"

"You're deflecting, Nya." Jax ran his finger down her arm, watching her shiver. "We've had too many sessions together. I've seen you play with those little brutes in the village; I know you like *vahna*. And I think once you have sex, you'll enjoy it enough to want it again."

She blushed, trying to suppress the humiliating memory of the in-depth physical she'd gotten when she first arrived. She didn't find out until later that Jax had access to her records. Virginity wasn't something Scythians coveted, but it embarrassed her that Jax knew something so personal. It made her feel weak like he thought she couldn't handle allowing a male inside her body.

The ugly truth was, she couldn't.

He stepped closer, watching emotions flash in her eyes. His voice grew soft. "As for you being sexually attracted to females, as long as you continue your line by bearing a few offspring, no one will care who warms your bed at night."

Nya shivered as his fingers traced the line of her collar.

He smiled at the reaction. "But I don't think your predilections run in that direction. I can prove it if you'd like."

She clasped her hands together. Her right thumb rubbed across her left palm, like the center of the thing was a worry stone.

Jax glanced down at the movement, and his eyes lost their heat. "Unfortunately, now is not the time to test the theory. Let's find this cat and head home."

Relieved at his sudden change in tack, Nya turned on her heel and jogged up the path, her heart settling as she put some distance between them. It wasn't a minute or two until she found the puma's tracks again. She followed them to a small gorge. Massive evergreen trunks lay scattered like matchsticks along the belly of the ravine, evidence of a rare tornado that ripped through last year.

She held up a fist, signaling Jax to stop.

A deep purr rumbled in the darkness, and Nya pulled her bow off her shoulder. She drew an arrow from the quiver resting on her back. Situating the string between the arrow's nock, she straightened her left arm as her right pulled the bowstring taut.

The moon's light caught two round reflections in the dark forest floor. The cat let out a warning growl.

Nya cleared her mind, took a steadying breath, aimed between the reflections, and released the arrow.

The sickening thud of metal shattering bone sliced through the night.

Light illumined behind her as Jax turned on his flashlight, stepping ahead and walking toward the fallen trees. Numbly, she followed his lead.

The puma's lifeless body slumped over a log, an arrow embedded between her eyes. Her back paw, mangled and twisted, looked as if the poor animal had tried to chew it off before managing to escape.

Tears threatened, but Nya fought them back. She closed the short distance between her and the cat and squatted down beside it. She grabbed the arrow and pulled it from the skull, wiping the blood and brain matter her on pants. Regret bit deep into her belly. The Allos should've tranquilized the mountain lion then taken her to higher ground, away from the general population. But they didn't know how to track like Scythians did, and so they resorted to traps.

Cruel as it was, Nya didn't blame them. They were doing what they thought necessary to protect their children. God knew she understood the importance of safeguarding *vahna*.

Still, as she ran her fingers through the cat's golden fur, the words she'd spoken to Jax echoed in her mind. *I have more in common with that mountain lion than I do a vtachi.* This cat embodied the spirit of a warrior. It was a predator, cunning, fast, and intelligent. And yet, something had wounded it so badly it was irreparably damaged and had to be put down while still in its prime.

And wasn't that a depressing thought?

Jax's large palm rested on her shoulder. "Perfect shot, Nya. The mountain lion never saw it coming." His voice warmed like he knew what was bothering her.

"She didn't have to die this way." Nya wiped her nose with her sleeve. "I could have let her fight."

"True. But then the lion's last moments would have been full of panic and suffering. You saved her from dying in the agony of defeat. And that has to count for something."

Nya kept her eyes on the lifeless cat, understanding precisely what Jax meant. Scythians were the secret warriors of the human race. The cat would have struggled until it was overpowered, being forced to submit to the enemy until her heart finally stopped beating.

The only thing worse would be to submit and then live.

At least wherever the mountain lion was now, whether it be Heaven, Hell, or just a black hole of nothingness, she knew her fate and no longer struggled.

Part of Nya thought that might not be such a bad thing. A feeble snarl sounded from the left.

"Did you hear that?" Jax stood, turning the flashlight's beam toward the base of the uprooted tree. Two smaller reflections glimmered in the light.

"Oh, hell." Dread washed over her. "I was right. The puma was making her way back to her young."

Nya ran ahead and fell to her knees. Two cubs were there, one dead the other barely alive. "Why would she go so far from them?"

Jax rubbed the back of his neck. "I'm not sure. But she must have had a good reason."

The cub scratched and growled in a feeble attempt to ward Nya off, but she picked him up and placed him in her hoodie, zipping him securely to her chest.

Jax shook his head. "What are you doing?"

"I can't leave him."

"And you can't bring him to the compound either. It's best to let nature take its course."

She scowled. "Says who? Is it best for the cub, who will starve to death or be eaten by another predator? Is it best for me, who will agonize over the fact that I've left him here?" She placed her hand on the lump under her jacket. The little cub purred. "*Vahna* should be safeguarded until they can protect themselves. Tell me, Jax. Why do you think it's best to leave something so helpless undefended?"

Amusement threaded through his tone. "Apparently, we don't need to worry about your maternal instincts."

She closed her eyes and counted to ten. Most of the time Nya knew when Jax was baiting her with his psycho-babble bullshit. But this time she stepped into it with both feet.

A warm palm touched her cheek, and her eyes flew open. Jax's fingertips grazed her neck before slowly unzipping her jacket until triangular ears and a small muzzle peeked out. Nya blushed as he rubbed the cub's head, which happened to be nestled between her breasts.

"And you're right," he muttered. "No young should ever be left defenseless."

"We still talking about the cat?"

Jax's eyes warmed. "Perceptive, aren't you?" He stroked the cub's head a few times. "If you want this little one to survive we can't keep him in the compound. Cassius will feed him until he's big enough to use in a challenge. And we both know that won't end well."

"But we won't have to keep him that long. I'll teach him how to hunt. In a few weeks, we'll ask the forest reserve to take him north and release him in the wild."

"You'll be on a plane to Carpathia soon, remember? If you want to save him, I'll have to take him to the ranger station when we get back."

Dread washed over her at the mention of the Scythian homeland. "Can't you take care of him until I get back? I'll be home soon."

Jax's fingers swept under the cub's jaw, coming dangerously close to Nya's soft flesh. "I know you think of Montana as home, but your rovni might want to live elsewhere. Besides, I won't be here. I'm taking personal leave."

Nya frowned. Jax never took time off. Sure, when she first got here he was gone on missions for weeks at a time. But the Society hadn't called on him since then.

"Why?" she blurted out.

Jax raised a brow. "They call it personal time for a reason."

"Oh. Sorry." She blushed. Maybe he was finally ready to settle down with that female he'd been seeing in the valley.

And didn't that thought feel like hot coals sitting in her gut?

Jax stroked the cub's muzzle, smiling when it tried to suckle his thumb. He slowly zipped up Nya's hoodie, grazing his fingers along the edge of her jaw as he pulled his hand away. "Time to go."

He bent down and picked up the bloody arrow. The shaft had cracked from the impact, and he snapped it in two before taking the razor-sharp tip and putting it in his pocket.

"You led here, so I'll take point on the way back." His voice darkened as he started across the field.

Streaks of pink and yellow stretched across the horizon, waking the birds to another crisp, autumn day. Nya followed Jax, watching his long stride eat up the distance.

Jax had several doctorate degrees, including one in psychology and another in cross-cultural studies. At just twenty-nine, his sharp mind and infallible logic already had given him the reputation as one of the world's best negotiators.

Yes, everyone knew that Jax was amazing. Between his lineage, incredible mind, and physical strength, most female warriors thought he would make an excellent rovni.

But when Nya looked at him she only saw a threat. Her senses heightened when he was around, and her body tingled at his touch. She'd never physically bested him in the arena, and his hyper-intelligence about the human psyche put her on edge. She didn't like anyone messing with her head. Like this morning. How the hell did he get so close to the truth?

She hated to admit it, but Jax was right. A part of her longed for someone who understood her completely. Someone who knew of her past and yet respected her anyway. A true equal.

Snowball's chance in hell of finding it, though.

Jax stopped and waited for her to catch up.

A breeze drifted across her face, pulling a few strands of hair over her lips. Nya tucked them back in her hood and started closing the distance between them.

Most equals settled for friendship and intimacy, which hopefully developed into love. But rarely, equals became something more, something almost sacred—and they developed an *Intima* bond. It was the most profound connection that allowed mates to form a sixth sense about their partner.

Personally, Nya thought the *Intima* bond was a wagonload of horseshit. Only Scythian Empaths had the ability to feel another's emotions or pain. Besides, intimacy in any form scared the hell out of her.

Jax stopped in a clearing, waiting for her, his eyes not leaving hers as she drew near.

"Need a break?" Nya smirked. Scythians could run for miles without stopping, and they both knew it.

He chuckled. "If it makes you feel better, we'll go with that." His eyes lost their humorous spark. "Listen, tonight when you enter the arena, you'll have two choices: win the challenge and earn your right to choose a rovni or lose and hope your mother lets you stay for the Claiming Season. Win or lose, your life's about to change."

"I know." She started to turn away, but he stepped closer.

"Vtachi." His eyes warmed as his large palm cupped her face. "You have to trust me on this. You're ready. No more running."

Nya jerked from his touch and squared her shoulders. Honestly, the only thing that had kept her at the Academy these past few weeks was knowing that if she took off, Jax would hunt her down. And then she would forfeit her chance of winning the championships, which would leave her saddled with a male she didn't know. Worse, one of her mother's choosing.

And didn't that make a female want to stand and fight?

Even if she didn't want what she was fighting for.

CHAPTER TWO

Cassius stepped from her desk and stood in front of the window. The dawn's early light filtered through the dense woods surrounding the arena, barracks, and guest quarters, but her eyes stayed on the road leading into the compound. They'd been gone for two days. Two. Days.

She hoped to hell Jax knew what he was doing.

Anya Thalestris, or Nya as her friends called her, hadn't run since her first year, but if she tried it again, there wouldn't be much anyone could do. She'd be at the mercy of the council. And the only thing keeping them from taking a more aggressive approach to getting the information they needed was the fact that Nya's father, Ike, was a direct descendant of the first Amazonian queen, Otrera, and the first Scythian leader, Ares.

Of course, it didn't hurt that Ike and the Madame Executive Chancellor had been friends since their Trials, even if that friendship was shrouded in scandal.

A knock sounded at the door.

Cassius turned from the window. "Come in."

"I thought I heard you in here. What is it that has you up so early the day of the championship?" Silver hair gleamed in the morning light as a middle-aged warrior stepped through the threshold, closing the door behind him.

"Good morning, Cyrus. Coffee?"

"I'd love some."

Cassius walked to the coffee pot and flipped a switch. "Championship days always start early. The contestants' families were arriving at three this morning."

Cyrus grunted. "We have people in place for that."

"Yes, but with Anya participating, the media is already here, and we're expecting a record turnout."

He crossed the room and sat in a plush chair, which faced an oversized mahogany desk. "They'll hound her, you know."

The robust scent of Arabica beans permeated the air, and Cassius opened a sideboard and pulled out two mugs. "Already taken care of. I've forbidden the media to approach any of the females participating until the championships are over."

She poured the coffee and set the pot back in its place. "Heard from Jax yet?"

Cyrus shook his head. "No. But he knows what he's doing. They'll be back."

"When are Ike and Gia Thalestris due?" Steam rose from the mugs as she picked them up and crossed the room.

"Sometime this afternoon. Thanks." Cyrus took the coffee cup. "I spoke with Ike yesterday. He's coming straight from Carpathia, Gia's flying in from Ireland. They're scheduled to land within an hour of each other, so we're sending just one car."

"Good." She took a seat behind her desk. "That gives us a little time. If Jax doesn't show before they arrive, we'll have some explaining to do."

Cyrus took a sip. "Whether they're back or not, Ike will demand to know what you were thinking letting them go off together in the first place."

Cassius wrapped her hands around her mug. "I've got it covered."

He sat back in his chair, his gaze thoughtful. "These past four years I've watched Anya Thalestris go from a sullen terrified young female to an extraordinary warrior. Just doesn't seem fair that she still suffers from the shock of what happened so long ago. Why we decided to involve *vahna* in matters of war is beyond me. It just isn't right."

Cassius raised a brow. "Her father commanded the operation, and Gia is one of the best in her field. They knew the risks. Yet, they thought they could both protect her and still help the Society."

His gaze fell to the window. "Then they thought wrong, didn't they?"

Sweat trickled down Nya's back as she kept Jax's steady pace, eating up the miles that distanced them from the compound. She normally took two strides for every one of his to accommodate his long legs, but today she let the gap between them stretch. With the upcoming championship, her mind wandered to places she'd rather not go.

Places like Ireland.

Nya's family had moved every few years until she turned ten. Even though she had lived in various parts of the world, when her parents took an assignment in Ireland, she couldn't have been happier. Lush didn't begin to describe the place. She missed the vibrant green, the people in the village.

But most of all, she missed Penn.

They hadn't been there a month before she met him. Penn, no more than twelve or thirteen, stood on a step-ladder, washing storefront windows. It was apparent he lived in poverty. His sunken eyes held such hopeless misery; she wanted to protect him, even then. When her mother suggested they invite him over to play, Nya readily agreed. That afternoon, somewhere between sketching the meadow together and playing tag, she and Penn became the best of friends.

Accepting—Penn was the definition of the word. Scythians were mentally and physically stronger than Allos, and so Nya could think circles around him, out run and jump him easily. Most boys his age would resent it, but Penn didn't care. His gentle spirit and artist's heart never envied her abilities. Through their youth, he encouraged her, listened to her, even when she said something silly. He was the epitome of a true friend.

A few years passed with Penn coming to their house in the afternoon. They were thick as thieves. He started calling her by her full name, Anya, and after a while he shortened it to Ana, loving that only he called her that.

Eventually, Penn confessed that his mother had taken him in the dead of night and fled from an abusive father. Nya swore she wouldn't tell a soul. When Penn showed up one afternoon, ashen-faced and scared, mumbling that he might have to go because his father had found them,

Nya took him to an abandoned cottage she'd discovered on the edge of their property, right next to the creek. Even though it was nothing more than a one-room shack, Penn loved it. They spent weeks repairing the walls and thatched roof so that he would have a place to hide. Nya even fixed the crude fireplace to protect him against Ireland's harsh winters. They planted wild vines around the small dwelling, so it was almost impossible to see from the road.

As autumn grew colder, Penn waited at their fort every day after school for her. She always came, if only for a few minutes just to say hello.

That was the last time in her life she remembered feeling whole.

A hawk screeched overhead, and Jax slowed, finally stopping at a small stream. Sunlight filtered through the fir trees, streaking across the forest like shards of hope, and Nya unzipped her hoodie and took the cub from her jacket.

"You remember this place?" he asked.

She nodded. "You brought me here after I needed some alone time."

Jax smiled. "If by 'alone time' you mean after you went missing and I was called back from a mission to find you, then yes, this is the place."

Nya bent down and swirled her fingers in the clear, icy water. "I wasn't missing. And I still think it's pretty sad the other instructors couldn't track a twenty-year-old a few miles away."

"It wasn't their responsibility."

"It wasn't yours either."

His eyes locked on her. "Yes, Vtachi. It was."

Subtle heat rippled through her, like sunshine passing through water. She set the cub down by the stream; the poor thing desperately lapped as its front paws sank into fresh silt.

"Hungry?" Jax asked.

Nya shrugged as she stood, watching the cub settle on its haunches. "Not really."

"Suit yourself." He pulled out a breakfast bar, peeled back the wrapper and took a bite before throwing a bit of it on the ground.

The cub pounced.

"Here." He tossed another bar to Nya, grinning as her hand shot up and she caught it reflexively. "Keep it for later."

She put the bar in her pocket.

"So." The shrink voice was back. "We should discuss the championships."

Nya tensed. "Don't start. I still don't see what's so wrong with wanting to stay single. Scythian males do it all the time."

His voice became soft. "Males can't carry the future in a womb. And you more than anyone, sweet Nya, need a rovni."

She scowled. "Bullshit. I've dreaded being forced to find a mate for years, Jax. *Years.* And I've got news for you. I'm more than a walking uterus. I speak ten languages, and I am just as good as you when it comes to hand-to-hand combat. I can contribute to future generations in a lot of ways. Why do I need to be a broodmare too?"

Understanding deepened his dark eyes. "That's fear talking."

"No, Jax. That's me talking. It's how I feel."

He stood for a moment, taking in her words, his gaze darting to the thumb rubbing her palm. "Tell me about your scar."

She dropped her hands to her side. "You've heard this story a hundred times. I cut my palm on a rock when I was a kid."

"You were with Penn."

She pulled her jacket's hood over her head and shoved her hands in her pockets. "I never said I was with Penn."

"You never said you weren't."

Frustrated, Nya scowled. She hadn't told Jax about Penn, but after she'd gone missing her first year, dear old mom was happy to fill in the blanks. "Why do you always bring him up? He was a village boy. The leader of our compound didn't like me hanging around him, and so I never saw him again."

"Why would your *Suveran* care if you were hanging out with an Allos boy?"

Nya looked away. "I don't know. I guess for the same reason you keep bringing him up. Why is Penn such a big deal?"

His expression turned serious, intense. "I believe your relationship with him is the root of several issues."

"Like what?"

"Like your aggression, your need to keep people at bay, and your fear of males, for example."

Nya scoffed. "You're delusional. And I'm not afraid of males."

"You're afraid of intimacy."

Nya met his eyes. "Just because I don't jump into bed with everyone that looks my way doesn't mean I'm scared to have sex."

"There's more to intimacy than sex, Vtachi."

"I know that," she snapped. "Why am I a freak because I don't want what everyone thinks I should? Whatever happened to individuality?"

He stepped closer. "Individuality is too broad a term for this discussion. And I've never used the word freak."

Nya held her ground, refusing to step back. "That's just semantics, and you know it. Tell me. Why am I the only warrior who has a shrink? I don't see you bugging Xari about her hair or Myrina about her obnoxious need to put everyone down. And what about Rissa's obsession with stupid Allos erotica novels? Why not help her see that all those hot and steamy men with their I-have-to-have-you-now are just bullshit. Personally, out of all of us, Rissa's the one I worry about most. Why not get in her head and leave me alone?"

"You're deflecting again."

"And you're annoying the shit out of me."

Jax crossed his arms and leaned against a tree. "Have you heard of Maslow's hierarchy of needs?"

She crossed her arms, mirroring him. "No, but I'm sure you'll enlighten me."

Jax smiled. "It states that all humans, including Scythians, need certain things to thrive. Food, shelter, and clothing are the first level, as they are required for survival. But the needs get more complex the further up you go, and each one must be mastered before we achieve the next on the list."

Her eyes fell on the small puma. "What's at the top? Some internal utopia, I'm sure."

"Self-actualization, actually. Utopia in any form is an impossibility."

Despite her frustration, Nya smiled. She and Jax often verbally sparred about if it were possible to create a perfect society. According to Jax, if it were obtained it wouldn't last long.

"What's so great about self-actualization?"

He bent down and petted the cub. "It's where one meets their full potential so they may thrive and live life to the fullest."

Nya frowned. "What's your point, Jax?"

"I'm merely making an observation."

"Which is what, exactly?" Her voice trailed away as he stepped closer.

"Simply put, your needs aren't being met. And until they are, you'll never reach your full potential, which would be one of the world's greatest tragedies."

She scoffed, trying to make light of the subject. "Yeah … me not meeting my potential is right up there with Stalin, the Christian Crusades, and World War II. And just what are these needs that I'm woefully neglecting?"

Jax kept his eyes on her as he switched to Dacian.

"A restful night's sleep, little bird. A sense of belonging. Safety in your environment to express yourself honestly and freely. A healthy self-esteem that anchors you, allowing you to see how truly rare and valuable you are. And most of all, love." He ran his finger along her jaw. "All humans, especially Scythians, need love."

Nya took her hands from her pockets, her thumb once again polishing her palm.

She hadn't got a good night's sleep in years, her frequent nightmares wreaking havoc with her mind. Her experience with Penn left her feeling like an outsider with her own kind, much less his. Her self-esteem swirled the bowl about half the time. And, while part of her secretly yearned for it, in her heart Nya knew she'd never be loved. She didn't deserve it.

How the hell did Jax know?

"Why, after all this time, are you just now getting around to telling me this?"

Jax cupped her face with both his hands, and she flinched.

He kept her gaze. "We've been busy working on other things."

Yeah. Like her no-touch policy and the fact that she had a helluva temper.

His expression became that unreadable mask that always made her leery. Nya shifted her weight, trying to back up, but Jax wouldn't allow it.

"No more pulling away. You've made such progress over the past few years. But we're out of time." His nose grazed against hers as he tilted his head. He paused for a moment, soaking in her reaction before he leaned in, brushing his lips against hers in a soft, chaste kiss.

Her breath caught.

His voice deepened as he kept her gaze. "Vtachi, the secret you carry is slowly killing you. It haunts your dreams. It keeps you from embracing your future. But I can help you get past this pain. I can make sure your needs are met. Trust me, Vtachi. Trust and let go."

She whimpered as his warm breath tickled her face. His long fingers circled the back of her neck, and heat followed his touch. Her blood raced with strange new feelings, and Nya placed her hands on his chest, trying to understand what was happening between them.

He brought her head to his chest, resting her cheek on his heart. They stood there, his fingertips making gentle patterns on her back while she marveled at the feel of his touch, the warmth of his skin. It had been forever since she'd allowed anyone to come near her, much less hold her in their arms.

Actually, she couldn't remember anyone ever holding her like this.

She trembled as she leaned back and looked at him. "Why?" Was all she managed to say.

Jax's coffee brown eyes grew tender. "The next few weeks are going to be trying. You've learned to control the impulse to fight when touched, but there are still issues that need to be worked out. I've spoken with the Chancellor, and we've found a way to help you through."

Her heart dropped. "So, this is another form of therapy?"

Jax smiled. "In a manner of speaking. We will work on touch desensitization, but I still would like to get to the root of the problem before you declare your mate."

Defeated, she slumped, her forehead resting on his chest. So, this reaction wasn't Jax the male wanting her as a female. This was Jax the shrink helping his patient. She pulled away from him.

"Who knows about this?" She could endure many things, but humiliation wasn't one of them. Warriors would see her as weak, and she'd die before that happened.

"No one other than my colleague at the consulate. And I plan to keep it that way."

"How's that going to work? I mean, I'm supposed to be spending time with male warriors who best match my personality profile, not talking with a shrink."

His voice returned to that calm, impersonal tone. "We'll discuss it later, but I think you'll like Dr. Ramova. He'll be your official psychologist during the trials."

Shocked, her gaze flew to his. "What? I don't want another counselor."

"He's just taking the lead, and it can't be helped. Now, if I'm to take the cub to the park ranger we'll have to hurry."

He slipped the small mountain lion under his coat.

Nya stared at the water rushing over rock. Why did everything have to be so complicated?

Jax's hand brushed across her face, startling her.

"Hey. Don't worry so much. We got this." He smiled before taking off.

Nya blindly followed, her mind trying to wrap around what just happened.

We got this. It was a saying that Jax loved, particularly in hard sessions. The fact that he'd said it now both calmed her and made her wary at the same time.

Just what, exactly, did they have? One minute, Jax's touch almost had her in tears, and the next he was telling her this was some weird counseling session.

Nya knew the rest of the world viewed a simple hug and kiss as no big deal. Maybe less so to Jax because she was sure he touched and kissed that female who lived in the valley—a lot. When she first arrived, knowing he had someone else put her at ease. But for Nya, well, the fact that she had allowed him to touch her at all, much less kiss her, was huge. And Jax knew it. Her mouth still tingled, and she reached up and grazed her thumb over her lower lip.

She'd never physically reacted to any male like she did Jax, and didn't that scare the hell out of her?

The sun blazed high in the sky as Nya slowed her steps again, allowing the distance between them to grow. The road forked ahead, and Jax cut to the left, heading for the guard station at the front of the compound.

For a split second, she imagined herself heading to the right, running until the gravel met asphalt—not stopping until she made it past the state line. She had a small window of opportunity to create a new identity and disappear. She'd have to live like a hermit, but at least she'd be in control of her life.

Jax stopped just inside the main gate, and Nya sadly sighed. That wouldn't be possible, though, would it? Her father and mother would search until they found her, and then Jax would probably have her committed.

"You coming?" he yelled.

"I'll be there in a minute," she hollered back.

Jax looked torn, but the cub squirmed, and one of the warriors guarding the entrance jogged to the gate. The male handed Jax something before jogging away. Whatever was in the message must not have been good because Jax scowled as he wadded up the paper and shoved it into his jacket pocket.

"I have to go. Don't be long, and get something to eat," he shouted.

Nya waved as if to comply, and Jax walked through the gates. She looked back down the road, the temptation to take off hitting her again.

What would be the point? She wasn't sure what the future held, but she knew she didn't want to live it alone. And she would never consider trying to find Penn. It had been over four years since she'd seen him. He probably had married a sweet Allos girl that matched his gentle heart. Nya's stomach churned as she envisioned him coming home after a long day at the office, slipping off his shoes at the front door, his children running to him with open arms. He'd put them to bed and then make love to his wife before sleeping soundly, unaware the Scythians were the ones that blanketed his family in safety and peace.

Her father's words rang in her ears.

It's for the best, Pumpkin.

Funny. It didn't feel that way to her.

CHAPTER THREE

Nya's father leaped from his chair as Jax entered Cassius's office. "Where the hell is she?"

"Calm down, Ike." Gia Thalestris rubbed her temples. "How is my daughter, Dr. Nickius?"

Jax closed the door behind him and clutched the squirming cub beneath his jacket. "She's well."

"Did it work?"

Ike's gruff voice grated on Jax's nerves. He took a deep breath, allowing the room to settle. "In a way. I was right to think that Nya needed space before tonight. She's starting to see that she can trust me, but she needs more time."

Ike glared. "That's not possible, and you know it."

The cub growled, and Jax unzipped his jacket.

Cassius sat on the edge of her desk. "Brought back a souvenir?"

Jax set the cub on the loveseat, watching it paw at the soft material before settling down. "Nya insisted we bring the little thing back when she realized she'd just killed its mother. I promised her I'd take it to the ranger station."

Cassius waved her hand, dismissing the idea. "We'll keep it here. Next fall, it'll be big enough to use in the opening ceremonies for the new recruits."

"No." Jax's voice held a thread of steel. "I promised Nya I'd take it to the station, and that's what I intend to do. I'll not lose her trust over an orphaned cub."

Ike tilted his head, studying Jax. "And what other promises have you made, Doctor? What else did you do with the last of Otrera's line while you were playing guide?"

Jax crossed his arms over his chest. "I don't appreciate the implication, Commander."

"Just answer the question."

"What Nya and I discuss in a counseling session is confidential." Jax's expression remained calm.

"Awfully damn convenient, don't you think?"

"Oh, for God's sake. Knock it off," Gia snapped.

Ike's gaze darted to his mate. Something in her expression weakened his anger, and he turned to the window. "Will she be ready for Carpathia?"

"I believe so." Jax half smiled. "Hunting relaxes her."

Nya waited until Jax was out of sight before turning and heading the other way. One of the guards shouted for her to come back, but she ignored him.

Birds chirped overhead as the path grew narrow, and she quickened her pace. Her favorite spot lay just beyond the hill, and she needed a moment alone before she faced the stupidity waiting for her at the compound.

By now, every female within a five-mile radius knew where she and Jax had been. It was rare the academy allowed male warriors on the premises, much less alone in the woods with a female. Except for Jax and a few mated instructors, the whole place was nothing but one big estrogen fest.

The reason? Amazonian warriors accepted to the academy were highly sought after. Scythian males had been known to force a claim by impregnating young warriors before their trials. If a female of great potential was taken by a male less than she, the future suffered.

Nya's stomach growled. She pulled out the breakfast bar Jax had given her. By tomorrow, her fate would be set, and Nya couldn't help wishing she had a real mother-daughter relationship to lean on. She wanted to ask her mom what the championships were like. And then there was the very personal conversation about the marking ceremony and the claiming night. But Gia Thalestris was an expert in chemical and biological warfare, not exactly the warm-and-fuzzy-heart-to-heart kind of female.

Besides, Nya had never relied on her parents before, why start now?

Sunlight slanted through the trees as she hiked on, a sure sign the day was slipping away. A chilly breeze brushed her face as the ground leveled off, leading her to the ridge which overlooked Bitterroot's Valley.

If this were her last day of freedom, she didn't want to spend it in the compound avoiding Myrina's bitch squad. She'd rather stay in nature surrounded by nothing but peace and quiet.

"There you are." The bright lilt of a familiar voice came from behind, and Nya silently cursed. Her best friend had a knack for showing up when Nya just wanted to be alone.

Pasting on a smile, she turned around. "Hey, Xari. How'd you find me?"

"I saw Jax come from the guard shack, but you never followed. Figured you needed some time, and as this is your favorite spot, I thought I'd look here first."

Xari and Nya were opposite in almost every way. Nya's long stick-straight black hair held a blue sheen in the sunshine. Few saw it sway to the end of her spine because she always kept it in a tight bun. Xari, on the other hand, had short blond hair that brushed her jawline. Her favorite hobby was coloring the tips to match her mood. Extroverted and optimistic, she accepted Nya's reserved personality, which often bordered on pessimistic and cynical.

No, they shouldn't have gotten along at all, and yet they trusted each other implicitly.

Well, as much as Nya could trust anyone.

"By the way, the guard said Jax was checking in every fifteen minutes." Bright blue tips swung whimsically around Xari's cheek, and thick eyeliner and mascara rimmed her eyes. Amazonian warriors never wore makeup, viewing the Allos emphasis on outward beauty as shallow and ridiculous. Xari, however, used it as some weird form of artistic self-expression. "He's livid, you know."

"The guard?"

Xari rolled her eyes. "No, Doofus. Jax."

Silence.

Xari plucked a dandelion from the ground and blew the seeds from its stem. "So, what happened out there?"

Nya watched the flower's floss float and dance on the breeze. "We found the mountain lion. I shot her between the eyes. She had a cub, so Jax is taking it to the park ranger."

"That's not what I meant."

Nya grimaced. "It's Jax. What do you think happened?"

Xari's eyes got as big as saucers. "So, you and he—"

"Of course not." She aggressively exhaled and took a seat on a nearby boulder. "He's in a relationship with some female in the valley, remember? Not to mention he's my shrink. Sheesh."

"I think he likes you."

"And I think you're full of shit."

Xari sat down next to Nya. "I hate it when you use foul language."

"Then don't piss me off."

The two friends shared a smile. They'd been bantering like that since their first night at the Academy.

Nya leaned forward, resting her elbows in her knees. "It wasn't a coincidence you were by the front gates, was it? You were waiting for me."

She sighed. "The press started arriving yesterday, and your absence has been noticed. Cassius ordered a moratorium on reporters interviewing candidates, but they can still film you coming in. I didn't want them to get a good shot of you and Jax walking through the front gates together."

Nya nudged her friend's shoulder. "Thanks for having my back."

"Anytime. But if we don't leave soon, it'll only get worse."

Shit. Jax was right—she was out of time.

Thunder rumbled in the distance as she stood and started across the field.

Leaves crunched under Xari's feet as she came alongside her. "You should know that everyone thinks Jax is staking his claim on Otrera's descendant."

"That's ridiculous."

"Why else would the two of you be gone for days?"

Two lines creased between Nya's eyes. "It wasn't like that."

"Yeah, well maybe not if he were a regular warrior. But Jax is a Tova, and they take what they want."

The Tovaris were elite warriors. Practically a new breed among their own. Bigger, stronger, meaner, their missions dealt with the worst of humanity.

"He might have been a Tovaris at one point, but he's now an instructor and a counselor. That's all."

Xari shook her head. "Once a Tova, always a Tova. And sometimes you just don't see what's in front of your face."

Nya's stomach flipped at those words. She hadn't heard them since her big fight with her father.

Xari's blue tips swung around her face as she started down the hill, and Nya followed behind, her mind racing with memories. After Penn had taken a job on the docks, he'd show up at the fort covered in bruises. Nya wanted him to quit, but when he refused she promised to show him defensive moves. The only problem was her father had expressly forbidden it years before, so they wouldn't be able to use her backyard and they couldn't practice in the village for fear of being seen. When her parents announced they were needed on a mission and had to leave for a few days, Nya asked Penn to come over.

"Come on. Give me your best shot."

"What?" Penn's voice rose as he stumbled back. "No way."

She rolled her eyes and stood up straight. "You can't hurt me. Besides, who's gonna know? Now, are we doing this or what?"

Penn started to walk away, but then he lunged. Nya ducked, easily catching his wrist, twisting, and throwing him on the ground.

"Gotcha again."

"Not quite." Penn rolled, surprising her, and she lost her balance, landing on top of him.

She smacked his arm. "Cheater."

"You know what they say ... All's fair in love and war ..."

She started to get up, but one of Penn's hands stayed in the middle of her back, while the other disappeared under her long hair, finding its way to the nape of her neck.

Nya grinned. "You're getting better."

"Yeah." He grinned and settled her close, like he planned on staying a while. "I am."

"Anya Thalestris." A deep booming voice came from the patio, and Nya and Penn scrambled to their feet.

A hulk of a man stormed across the lawn. His bulky muscles flexing beneath his tight shirt as he clenched and unclenched his fists, his expression promising pain and death.

"Hi, Dad. You're home early." Nya's voice came out high, over-bright. She cleared her throat.

"Apparently, I'm just in time."

Heat warmed her face as she mentally played back the last few moments. "I was teaching Penn a few defensive moves, that's all."

Penn's brow rose. "And you know I'd never disrespect Ana that way."

"Her name is Anya." Nya's father took a step closer, his chest barreling out. "Go home, Penn."

Penn's jaw clenched as he openly glared.

Nya patted his shoulder. "I'll call you later."

He grabbed his jacket off the ground and stormed away.

She waited until Penn had left the yard before turning on her father like a rabid animal. "I can't believe you just did that."

"What were you thinking?" Her father's thunderous voice echoed off the trees.

"I know he's just an Allos." Nya's voice hitched. "But that's never mattered to me. He's still my best friend."

Ike softened his tone and put his arm around her. "I've never minded you having an Allos for a friend. But the way he looked at you today was the way a man looks at a woman when he wants her for his own."

"It's not like that."

"You can't see what's in front of you. Penn is falling in love with you, Pumpkin. If you care anything for this boy, you'll realize it's time to let him go."

A kestrel cried overhead, bringing Nya's mind back to the present. Everything changed after that day, and not for the better. Her mother became strangely attentive, and her father upped her training, which took every spare second of free time.

She resented her parents keeping her and Penn apart, but she couldn't help acknowledging her father was right about one thing. No Scythian female could ever live as Allos women did.

The problem was, she wasn't sure she could live this way either.

CHAPTER FOUR

Gravel crunched under their feet as Nya and Xari made their way to the Academy's open gates. The low murmur of a crowd filtered from the distance, and tendrils of anxiety surged through Nya's veins. She took a deep breath and fixed her eyes on the buildings ahead. The place was a weird mix of modern and ancient architecture. The lush forest served as a timeless backdrop to a Roman style coliseum surrounded by modern looking buildings and rustic cabins. Anyone who stumbled on it would find the combination strange—that is, if they made it past the state-of-the-art cloaking and security systems.

Scythians had technology so encrypted it made the Allos' dark web look like child's play.

They neared the guard station, and Xari linked her arm through Nya's.

They sped up once they noticed the camera crews under the arena's easement, scrambling to zoom in on them.

Nya pulled up her hood. "I hate this. I really do."

"We are the way we are because of our traditions. No way around it."

Recorded Scythian history dated well before Allos languages were set to paper, when Amazon warriors ruled. Fierce and loyal, the females lived among their own kind. Wanting *vahna*, every spring they'd visit Scythia, a region well known for virile, intelligent males. They'd spend a week assessing potential mates, and anyone deemed worthy was invited to their bed. After the females became pregnant, they would head home. Soon, rumors spread like wildfire—Scythia had sexually uninhibited females like no other. Better lovers than the most experienced consort, they were also intelligent, witty, and incredibly strong.

For centuries, males from all over the known world flocked to Scythia in hopes of experiencing such a phenomenon. Over time, the strongest females bred the most dominant males until a new species of humans evolved. Allos tried to make sense of their differences by creating myths and legends of gods and demigods. How it was that Scythians managed genetic mutations in a few thousand years when other species took a few hundred millennia was still a mystery—something the intellects had been researching for centuries.

Xari's eyes sparkled with mischief. "I should probably thank you. If it wasn't for your dear old ancestor, Ares, deciding that he wanted Otrera always at his side, we might still be stuck in an all-female village on the outskirts of the Black Sea."

According to legend, once the males claimed a female they didn't want to let her go, demanding the Amazons become their wives. The females were ready to battle over the issue, but Otrera offered a compromise, for she and Ares had formed an *Intima* bond. The females would stay if they were treated as true equals.

Ares demanded monogamy as a concession.

"Yeah. Lucky us." Sarcasm dripped from Nya's tone. She looked over her shoulder at the cameras still pointed their way. Thunder rumbled in the distance. "At least they're not following us."

"Well, that's something, isn't it?" Xari looked at the sky. "I had hoped the rain would hold off. Hey, you bringing your sword tonight?"

Nya rubbed her temple. "No. Bow."

"You sure? The challenge is in the arena, not the woods."

She shrugged. "Doesn't matter. If I need a sword, I'll take one from one of the weaker contestants. If we head to the woods, I'll have my bow. Either way, I'll win."

"Ah, that's the Ny I know and love." Xari grinned.

Trees dipped and swayed as the wind picked up speed, and they quickened their steps.

They rounded the bend, and Nya stopped when she saw Jax pacing at the crossroads that led to her cabin.

"You had three minutes left before I came for you, Vtachi." His usually calm voice held a tinge of annoyance.

Her eyes narrowed. "I really hate it when you call me that."

"Then quit trying to fly away."

Her fingernails dug into her palms, but she kept her temper in check and started past him.

His hand caught her wrist as she passed by. He dipped his thumb between her fingers, soothing the little grooves her nails had left. His deep brown eyes grew intense as he leaned in, his lips touching her ear. "Quit worrying so much. We got this."

Nya froze as he pressed his thumb into the scar marring her palm.

"I'll see you tonight." His voice grew husky as he let her go and walked away.

Wide-eyed, Xari waited until he was out of earshot before speaking. "What was that about? And if he's part of the challenge, we're as good as toast."

The drizzle became a steady rain, washing muddy rivulets across the newly graveled road.

"We're not toast. And you shouldn't let him mess with your head."

Xari bristled. "I'm not."

Nya ducked under the last cabin's overhang and stomped her feet on the welcome mat. "Sure you are."

She opened the door. Worn leather furniture sat in front of a large screen television, just above the fireplace. A refrigerator stood in one corner, in the other a microwave stand. Other than that, the place was bare. She shuffled her feet out of her boots and set her soaked jacket on a hook by the door. "Like right now. I can see your pulse trying to jump out of your neck, and your hands are trembling. What is it about him that makes you freak out?"

"I'll admit, I'm a little intimidated. He said some things in our first year ... well, let's just say I didn't like it." Xari tossed her jacket on the floor, next to her shoes.

"He's full of shit, and we both know it." Nya started across the living room.

Xari smiled as they passed the bathrooms and custodial closet. The place was set up like army barracks. No privacy. Multiple showers and toilet stalls in one area, while bunks cordoned off another. Putting warriors that sparred in such close quarters often meant a few skirmishes off the field. Nya didn't care. She enjoyed kicking the other females' asses.

Which, of course, made Myrina and her crew hate Nya that much more.

As soon as they opened the door to the bunkroom, she knew she was in trouble. All six of her cabin mates stood shoulder-to-shoulder like they were ready to pounce.

This couldn't be good.

"So," Myrina was the first to speak. "Tell us. Is Jax as good between the sheets as he is in the arena?"

"Don't you have someone else to hate on?" Nya slammed her shoulder into Myrina, forcing her way through. She went to the corner of the room, where she and Xari had hung sheets around their bunks to create the illusion of privacy. As soon as Nya scooted back the curtain, she froze. On top of the standard issue blanket and pillow sat a little blue box.

"We brought you a gift." Myrina's sickeningly sweet voice rang over the giggles. "It's obviously too early, but we thought we'd save you the trouble of going to the infirmary. So you can check. You know, after you lose. When I send back potential candidates for the Claiming Season, they'll be wondering if you're carrying another warrior's *vahna*."

"Wow. It took you two days to come up with this, didn't it?" Nya smiled, although her eyes were nothing but chips of blue ice.

Myrina tilted her head, her eyes to the ceiling. "On second thought, I'm sure it won't matter. No male of worth would be willing to fight for you in the first place."

"Shut up, Myrina." Xari pushed the girl back. "You're just jealous. Jax wouldn't look at you twice, much less want you in that way."

Myrina threw her wild, curly red hair over one shoulder. "I can't believe you're defending an instructor's *suka*."

A collective intake of breath let Myrina know that calling Nya the Dacian equivalent of a whore was going too far.

Xari started for her, but Nya put her hand on her friend's shoulder.

"Fighting in the barracks means no weapon in the next contest. Myrina's not worth losing your sword. Not tonight."

As soon as she brought up the championship, reality smothered any interest in Myrina's drama, and everyone started toward their bunks to get ready.

Nya tossed the pregnancy test in the trash like it didn't affect her, but inside she was seething. Damn Jax. He should've let her go hunting alone. And if she were honest, she shouldn't have volunteered to track the stupid mountain lion in the first place.

None of that mattered now. The damage was done. Everyone thought she and Jax had been in the woods having wild carnal sex, which was ridiculous. Anyone who knew her understood she could barely stand a handshake, much less full on body contact.

Proving yet again that irony did exist.

She grabbed her shower caddie and headed down the hall. The room buzzed as soon as she closed the door. She didn't give a shit what they were saying, but her parents would. She hadn't spoken to either of them in eighteen months, and the last thing she needed was for them to hear that she'd been on a two-day romp in the woods with the weapons instructor.

Wouldn't that just prove her father right?

She stripped, turned on the shower and jumped in, not waiting for hot water to make its way through the pipes. Icy spray pelted her skin, and Nya shivered as she grabbed the soap.

Maybe her father wouldn't mind so much this time. At least she'd been with a Scythian. The last time she'd been caught, she was with Penn.

Moonlight arced over meadow as she snuck away from their home. She crouched low as she ran across the field and headed toward their fort. As soon as she opened the door, Penn pulled her into his arms and kicked the door closed with his foot. She leaned back, searching his eyes.

"I've missed you," he whispered, running his thumb down her cheek. He slid his fingers through her hair, cupping the back of her head in his palm, and then he kissed her.

Heat rushed through her as he shuffled them closer to the small cot that lay near the fireplace. His lips nipped and nuzzled in a flurry of soft caresses as he gently lay her down. In a confused haze of new sensations, Nya found herself on the cot in a tangle of blanket and limbs. Penn's warm breath brushed across her face, his tender eyes never leaving hers as he unbuttoned her shirt and ran his palm down her bare side.

"My Ana." His voice became husky. "I love that I'm the only one who calls you that." He slid his palm across her torso, finding the snap of her jeans. "And after tonight, you'll be mine forever."

Nya froze as reality splashed over her like ice water. This was so wrong. She didn't love Penn, not the way he needed. Her father was right. This would destroy him.

"Penn ... no."

He pulled his hand away. "I'm sorry, Ana. I shouldn't have pushed you. We can wait if that's what you need."

The door burst open, and Ike took up the entire threshold, his gaze raking over her disheveled state.

Nya sprang to her feet. Her breath caught as she looked into his eyes, so disappointed and worried.

"Penn texted me and needed to talk." She rushed to explain. "This was the only time we could meet."

"Since when have you needed to unbutton your shirt to talk?"

Mortified, Nya's fingers shook as she fumbled, trying to shove the bits of round plastic back through their holes.

Penn started forward, but she stepped in front of him, making sure he was out of her father's reach.

Ike's voice rumbled in Dacian. "Even now, the protection you offer makes him feel weak."

Tears rolled down Nya's cheeks as she glanced at the surly young man behind her. "I know."

"What's he saying?" Penn's voice became hard, bitter. "He doesn't think I'm good enough, is that it?"

Nya's father kept her gaze, his eyes full of pity. "Already his feelings for you make him desperate. And desperate men do foolish things. You must let him go, Pumpkin. He's no longer the boy who was your friend."

Sorrow ached through her. She closed her eyes and forced the words from her lips. "Penn, I'm sorry. I can't love you. Not the way you want me to." Before he could respond, she bolted to her father. He wrapped her in his arms, and they shuffled out the door.

"Ana!" Penn's voice screeched across the meadow. "When I come for you, your father won't be able to stop me. You're mine, and you always will be!"

Steam cascaded around her as tears stung Nya's throat. That night had gone wrong in so many ways. She should have stopped Penn as soon as he took her into his arms—should have tried to explain that she'd snuck out because she was worried about him. She'd never wanted more than friendship from him, and yet that night the feeling that someone wanted her, needed her, swayed her decisions more than anything.

At least, Penn survived. It would have been so easy for her father to have gone back and killed him with his bare hands. In their Society, no one would have thought a thing of it. Penn had openly challenged a warrior when he threatened to take her away. Yet, Ike never even looked back—he kept his arms around his *nata* and took her home.

Nya always suspected her father regretted leaving Penn alive. What bothered her most was she didn't know why.

CHAPTER FIVE

Jax grumbled as he wove his Ducati through the cars and shuttle buses cluttering the road. Scythians had been arriving for hours, some coming from as far away as Canada and Mexico. Everyone wanted to see the top female warriors compete.

On edge, he parked his motorcycle by the arena. He scanned the gathering crowd. Dammit. Security wasn't tight enough.

If what he suspected was true, Sarkov, the leader of their enemy the Drahzda, would be getting desperate. But who would be stupid enough to go into an arena full of Scythians?

A deranged, sick bastard, that's who.

The thought almost sent Jax into a tailspin, but he took a few deep breaths and headed toward the contestants' entrance. The visitors milling around gave him a wide berth.

Cyrus smiled. "Evening, Jax. Before you ask, she hasn't come to the stadium yet."

If Nya had taken off again, he'd spend however long it took to hunt her down, the council be damned.

Blond hair wove through the masses as Xari sprinted across the compound.

"Where in the hell is Nya?"

She backed away, stammering over her words. "She ... she said she needed a minute."

"One job, Toxaris," Jax furiously rumbled in Dacian as he stepped toward her. "Your one job was to get her to the stadium on time. This will not go well for you if she doesn't show. I can promise you that."

Nya stood in the barracks and looked around, wondering why she felt nothing. This was the only place she'd ever thought of as home, and yet she didn't have any remorse about leaving. Surely, she should be a little nostalgic, or maybe melancholy … or something?

It was times like this she knew that disconnected, empty feeling wasn't healthy. She was tired of not getting a decent night's sleep. Tired of constantly feeling like she was missing part of her life and tired of being an emotional zombie.

She slipped her long-sleeved shirt over her tight-fitting camisole before taking the leather pants out of her footlocker. She told Xari she needed a minute, but there was another reason she waited until she was alone to dress. If Xari stayed, she would have seen that Nya planned on bringing extra protection with her.

And who needed that kind of drama?

She tucked the shirt into her pants and put on a belt. Next came bracings around her palms and wrists, followed by a leather jacket that fit her like a glove.

Nya reached into her footlocker and pulled out a few knives. The first was a large hunting blade sheathed in leather, and she tucked it at the small of her back. Next, she attached a black Velcro band that housed her favorite serrated blade under her pants just below the knee. But the smallest and sharpest was already hidden in a pocket attached to her inseam. The design was one of her own; the thin knife's blade followed the curve of her inner leg while the handle tucked neatly at the juncture of her hip and thigh. She had worked for hours getting the handle just right before sewing the sheath next to the zipper of her leathers. Most females in the compound chose to wear tight, light clothing, swearing that it gave them the edge of speed and endurance. But not Nya. Leather had saved her ass too many times to count. And while her pants fit, the thick material was enough to cover a multitude of sins—like knives and stones. She didn't need specialized clothing, anyway. She got her speed by training with weights. She worked on endurance by fighting through sweat and pain. The past year every practice ended with some part of her either bruised or bloody. And still, it all came down to tonight. Scythians weren't given second chances. If she didn't win, her future would be in the hands of dear old mom.

Nya clutched the outside of her left hidden pocket, just below the rise of her hip, making sure the handful of dirt hadn't spilled. No helping the rain. If she had to resort to using it, she'd have to admit bringing it into the stadium instead of reasoning that she had grabbed it from the ground. The other hidden pocket on the right held several round stones.

If they discovered either, it would be considered contraband. While it would not disqualify Nya from the competition, her primary weapon, her bow, would be confiscated as punishment for not following the rules.

A siren wailed through the compound, signaling the Trials were starting in fifteen minutes. Nya took the quiver hanging by her bunk and looped the strap over her shoulder, the worn leather easily finding its place across her chest. She grabbed the modern composite bow, specially tailored for her, and took off at a full sprint. The arena's front gates remained open, and Scythians poured in, slowing her down. She growled as she wove through the crowd, veering right where the contestants' entrance lay.

Her stomach dropped as soon as she saw Jax pacing in front of the archway. He ran his hand through his hair, searching the crowd. His eyes narrowed to slits as they landed on her.

She swallowed and jogged the rest of the way.

"Late. Tonight of all nights, why are you late?" He grabbed her arm and pulled her to the side.

"I've been late before. That's nothing new."

Jax's large palms landed on her shoulders, forcing her to face him. "What are you up to, Vtachi?"

"I took too long in the shower. You can ask Xari."

"I'm sure you did. The question is, why?"

Nya's frustration grew. "Really, Jax? Must we go into my subconscious motivation on long showers? As you've pointed out, I'm late. So, get on with it. My parents are here."

For once, his emotions bled through his expression, making his handsome features menacing. "Which is even more puzzling, isn't it? It's the championship, and yet you chose to be late." His hands made his way to the small of her back, and Nya's shoulders dropped.

He pulled the knife from its hidden place. "You know the rules. Only one weapon."

Nya took a calm breath and brought her eyes to his, struggling to keep her expression blank. "Can't blame a female for trying."

Jax studied her for a moment. She shifted under the weight of his gaze.

"You were counting on waiting until the last minute so you wouldn't be searched, which isn't like you. And why hide contraband in such a ridiculously obvious place? What are you up to?"

She shrugged. The ten-minute warning blared overhead. "Maybe you're right. Maybe I'd hoped the enforcers would've let me pass because Cassius would be pissed if I were late. You done?"

"Not by a longshot."

"Jax, I have to go."

He glanced down at her feet, noting the shift in weight. He dropped to one knee, then gripped her left ankle. Edging his fingers around the rim of her boot, he huffed before snaking them up her pant leg and wrapping them around her upper calf.

Nya's breath caught as heat trailed his touch.

Jax shook his head as he ripped off the Velcro strap. "I'm disappointed."

"Why?" Anger flushed across her cheeks. "I've brought a little help with me before. Never bothered you then."

Jax rose to his full height with the knife in hand. "I'm not disappointed that you brought it. Only that you chose such poor hiding places. That's not like you, Vtachi." His gaze ran slowly down her form, and she didn't dare breathe. "Unless I was meant to find them, yes?"

Nya scoffed. "I had no idea you'd be the one searching. Usually, it's Cyrus and Teagan."

"The championships are the start of the Rovni Trials. Cassius wanted the best."

"Did you search Xari?"

Jax shook his head. "No, Cyrus did. He's the other enforcer tonight."

"So why isn't he searching me?"

Jax kept her gaze. "Because it's my responsibility."

"Stop saying that." That was the second time he'd claimed to be responsible for something involving her.

His eyes cooled. "It's true. The day Cassius assigned me as your lead instructor, you became my responsibility."

The first week in the academy, Tina, the trainer in hand-to-hand combat, thought it a good idea to scare the new recruits so they could test their reaction time. Nya broke two of the warrior's ribs and gave her a concussion before Jax got between them. From then on, when it came to combat training, the headmistress ordered Jax to instruct Nya.

He reached up and pulled her hair from its tie. Her long braid swept down her back.

"You are not responsible for me. And what are you doing?"

"Making sure you don't have another throwing star hidden in this mane. Last time we were in the arena, you almost took out Myrina's eye."

"I wish I had," Nya grumbled, remembering the pregnancy test on her bunk. "Is this necessary?" She smacked his hand as he unraveled her braid. Her hair fell around her shoulders in disheveled waves. "Happy now?"

"Not yet." He gently raked his fingers through her hair. When he grazed the base of her spine, she stepped back.

"See? Nothing to hide." She held up her hands. "And nothing up my sleeves. Now can I go?"

"No."

Nya's heart sped, and she took a deep breath, trying to calm down. If Jax stripped her of all her weapons, she'd have to fight twice. Once to get what she needed from the other warriors, another trying to defend against whatever Cassius had in store.

"Raise your arms over your head."

Nya's attention snapped back to him. "What? Why?"

Jax's hands gripped her waist, his fingers so long they almost touched at the small of her back. "You heard me."

She blindly stared ahead and complied. Jax's impassive gaze flicked down her body before he focused on his task. He let go of her waist and reached overhead for her hands, running his fingers down her arms and her sides until his thumbs rested below her breast. "Your personality profile is one of an introvert. You shy away from touch, and you are extremely private. It only makes sense that you would hide a weapon in a place you were sure no one would dare search, especially one who is about to start her championship. You're betting that no warrior, male or female, would dare touch an innocent, a *novo*. No one but Cassius that is. And that's why you waited until the headmistress was in the top box before making your way to the stadium." His hands swept up while his thumbs stayed put, completely cupping her full breasts from the sides. Nya's breath caught as Jax's fingers tightened and then roved over her chest until they centered on her breastbone. With a final sweep, his fingers ran down her midriff before dropping to his side.

He cleared his throat. "You may put your hands down now."

Nya scowled as her arms fell to her sides. Even though being touched in a public setting was a nightmare, this was worse because Jax's touch always did something to her.

His deep brown eyes, so perceptive, searched her face. "Nothing personal, Vtachi. I was ordered to make sure."

Her heart picked up speed as it occurred to her that this was the reason he searched her instead of Cyrus. He knew how touch affected her, but with Jax, it didn't send her over the edge—yet another way he was trying to help her.

"Thanks," she mumbled. "That would've thrown me had Cyrus or Teagan put their hands … there."

Sadly, Jax smiled. "I know, Vtachi. I know."

She started to walk away, but he reached for her bow.

Nya groaned. "Come on, Jax. No one knows I had the knives but you. Let me keep the bow."

He shook his head and grabbed the top of the limb. With one solid tug, he pulled the bow off her shoulder and down her arm. "Sorry. Can't. Rules are rules."

Jax reached for her quiver, but Nya grabbed the strap across her chest.

"Fine. Take the bow. But I'd like to keep the arrows."

"I'm sure you would. But that would leave you with a weapon, now wouldn't it? And you did bring contraband into the stadium."

He started for her again. She backed away, her gaze darting toward the inner corridor of the Coliseum.

Jax wearily scrubbed the back of his neck with his hand. "You run, you know what happens. Don't make me take them from you. You didn't get much sleep last night, which already puts you at a disadvantage. Fighting me now would needlessly tire you further, and the championship is about to begin. Believe me. Tonight, you're going to need your strength."

Nya frowned. "How do you know I didn't get any rest? I like sleeping in the woods."

Jax's piercing gaze shot straight through her. "I was there, remember? You tossed and turned all night like your dreams tortured you." He stepped closer and lowered his voice. "And Penn was on your mind. You kept calling for him."

For years, she'd dreamt of being alone in their field, waiting for Penn, calling his name. But just as he appeared she exploded into flames. Excruciating pain usually woke her from her nightmare, like every nerve had been scorched.

It was humiliating to think that Jax knew.

"My nightmares are none of your business." Nya grabbed the leather strap across her body and jerked it over her head. She threw her quiver on the ground, and arrows skittered across the floor. "Here. You want them, take them."

"Vtachi."

Regret deepened Jax's tone, but she kept her head high and stormed away.

The five-minute warning rang overhead.

She came to the last checkpoint in front of the entrance to the arena floor. Teagan took in Nya's hair swinging behind her back and her empty hands and motioned her forward. The tension in her shoulders eased and she quickened her stride. Xari and the other candidates had gone through several searches before getting into the stadium. But the warrior must have assumed that Jax had already found what she had hidden.

Rain pelted her face as she stepped onto the muddy arena floor. Hundreds cheered and took to their feet as the trumpets sounded overhead.

"Where the devil have you been, and where's your bow?" Xari grabbed Nya's hand and marched her toward the center of the ring.

Nya shrugged. "Jax took it."

Xari snapped a band from her wrist and handed it to her. "Here. Tie your hair back before Myrina grabs hold and doesn't let go. You really should get that mess cut."

"Thanks." Nya took the elastic tie and pulled her hair into a high ponytail before braiding it and winding it into a tight ball at the top of her head.

"What are you going to do now?" Xari glanced at her before facing the crowd.

"Don't worry. I've got what I need."

Fifteen pedestals stood in the center of the arena, arranged in a circle. A brightly colored scarf hung from their edge. One by one, the loudspeaker blared overhead, introducing each warrior. They hopped up to their small dais, taking their scarf and tying it somewhere on their body.

Nya looked at the other females, each one built just like her—tall, broad-shouldered, and big chested. Their tapered waists gracefully flared into strong hips and muscular thighs. They kept their heads high, shoulders back, their eyes alight with anticipation of the upcoming challenge. Strong. Able. Confident. Nya realized that even though she'd kept her distance from everyone but Xari, she felt a strange kinship with these females. The experiences they'd shared over the past four years had bonded them.

Her name echoed across the field, and the crowd went wild. Nya tied the scarf around her neck, tucking the ends securely in her jacket.

They stood, feet apart, hands behind their backs and heads bowed as Cassius's voice replaced the announcer's. She touted each of the warriors' accomplishments before going over the guidelines of the tournament. Per usual, the rules were pretty much cut and dried. The only thing strictly forbidden was deadly force, which was understandable. After all, the entire point of the process was for the champions to find their equal and create future generations. Females wishing to disqualify themselves need only climb back up on their platform or if they were injured and unable to make it that far, they were to drop the scarf on the ground. Trainers and medics would then come to their aid.

Of course, if the challenge was hand-to-hand combat, another warrior could forcibly take the scarf, and the candidate would be defeated as well.

There were three rounds, and the tournament ended when only three warriors remained. Those females would be declared champions and then head to the Rovni Trials in Romania.

Nya took one last look around. Half of these warriors wouldn't last an hour, and judging from their expressions, they knew it. A few had a chance as long as everything went their way—which it never did. That left Xari, the fastest, Nya, the most cunning, and Myrina, the annoying.

Cassius droned on and on about what an honor it was to serve, protect, and assure their noble race continued. Nya kept her head down, glancing out of the corner of her eyes. Where were her parents? Maybe their flight was delayed.

The trumpets sounded overhead, signaling the end of Cassius's speech, and Nya finally had a chance to look up. She scanned the crowd, row after row until her eyes made their way to the top box. Silhouetted against the stadium lights were the Chancellor, a broad-shouldered male, and the slightly smaller frame of a female. The lights shifted to the arena wall, and Nya's heart jumped into her throat.

What in the hell were her mother and father doing in the top box with the headmistress?

A horn blared, signaling the start of the first round and she was engulfed in a deafening roar as the crowd stood and cheered. Nya jumped from her dais and crouched, using the column and platform to help guard her back. The dull clatter of chains grinding against gears chinked above the noise as small sections of the arena's perimeter wall opened.

Distracted, she glanced up. Her parents in the top box were to be expected. They were part of the Society's elite, and God knew her father would have wanted to avoid the press. Her mother leaned against the railing, her expression grim.

Shit. What if control freak Gia Thalestris was here to claim her right as Nya's guardian? The law was clear. If Nya didn't win, it would be up to Gia to decide if her daughter participated in the Claiming Season. Hell, she probably had some male in mind—maybe someone from her or Ike's unit. Someone that would keep tabs on her and report back.

Nya growled and focused on the wall, determined to take out whatever came her way. She might not want any of this, but she'd be the one to control who she claimed as an equal. Not mommy dearest.

The chains ground to a stop, and silver orbs the size of basketballs rolled onto the field. Hundreds of tiny red lights flashed, a sure sign of infrared sensors. Each sphere came within a few meters of a female as if they had been programmed to take them on individually.

Nya knew better. As the warriors fell, the bots would move on to the next. If this weren't the first round of the championships, Cassius would probably let the challenge continue until one warrior was left to fight them all.

The rain didn't seem to affect them, but it could help her get through this round.

Someone screamed to the left, and Nya glanced at Dianne doubling over in pain. A blue bolt shot from the orb, and she dropped where she stood. Light flashed from Nya's periphery, and she jumped behind her pedestal. The jolt of energy landed on the column, just above her head, leaving a scorched mark in its wake. Her mind raced with possibilities.

Silver gleamed from her right, and Nya shifted, her foot slipping on the mud-slick floor. A bolt of blue missed her leg by mere inches. The machine hissed, quieted, and then a high-pitched sound started as a whistle and grew into a scream. A blue bolt shot from it again.

Nya scrambled around the column. One lesson Jax had drilled into her time and again was to observe the enemy before engaging. She allowed the bot to fire a few more times, counting between the hiss and through the crescendoing pitch until the thing shot again.

She had just under a minute between strikes, which would have been plenty of time if she had kept her bow. The only way past this challenge was to take down the bots, but how?

The silver ball rolled toward her, and she realized the outer rim of the sensors were raised. The thing fired, nearly hitting Nya's shoulder and she slipped as she darted to the left.

Mud. That was the answer. The bot couldn't aim if its sensors were blocked. She fell to her knees, scooping up as much muck as possible. Shifting around the column, she then waited. Blue streamed, missing her yet again, and Nya charged.

Electricity shot through her palms as soon as she touched metal, but she gritted her teeth and powered through, reaching over and grabbing more sludge, slathering the sphere, filling every eyelet until she held nothing but a dark, muck-covered ball. She dove, barely making it behind the pillar before the ball blindly shot a stream of electricity.

"Watch out!" Nya screamed.

Xari fell to the ground.

CHAPTER SIX

"Thanks for the heads up, Ny," Xari shouted, as the blue bolt shot overhead.

As soon as the energy fired, Nya charged the ball again, grabbing her hidden knife from its sheath. She flipped the bot over, finding its seam.

The structure was a spherical hexapod, meaning she could section the thing like an orange, but she'd have to do it quickly. The curve of her blade served as an advantage, and Nya plunged through the metal shell, allowing the sharp edge to arc along its outer perimeter.

She dropped the ball and ducked again as another bolt shot from one of its sensors. Luckily, the blue streaked toward the sky this time. Determined to find the timing mechanism before it ended up shocking the hell out of her, Nya charged, prying apart the metal shell and shoving her hands through the tangle of wire.

Her fingers wrapped around a small, black box, and she smiled. Grabbing the sensor, she cut the timing wire cleanly with her knife. The high-pitched squeal stopped.

"Nya!" Xari screamed.

Blue shot from the left. Nya dove, but the bolt grazed her arm. White hot pain streamed, and she shook as she crawled, dragging the disemboweled orb with her. Aggressively taking deep breaths and exhaling, she accepted the pain coursing through her. She'd found early on that fighting pain split her focus. Better to accept it and concentrate on the problem at hand.

Xari scrambled next to Nya as two more orbs rolled their way. "I followed your lead and buried mine in mud, but my sword is too damn big to do much at disarming it."

Nya pulled the wiring from the ball, following the red wire to its end. "You ever play baseball or golf?"

Xari just looked at her like she'd lost her mind, but Nya kept her eyes focused on the nest of wiring, finally finding the small taser mechanism in the center.

"Take your sword in its sheath and swing ... preferably toward Myrina. I need another minute, and then we'll give these things a taste of their own medicine."

Xari's eyes lit up. "Got it."

They both ducked as four orbs closed in, the high-pitched mechanical drone eerily drowning out the cheers of the spectators.

Xari unbuckled her belt; the sword and casing fell to the ground. She grabbed the hilt with both hands and swung. One of the orbs sailed across the way. She turned to the other just as a blue bolt shot out of it, hitting her square in the chest.

"Damn it!" Nya yelled, dodging the third and fourth orb while scrambling to Xari's side. "Breathe, and don't you dare reach for that scarf."

Xari clutched her chest, while Nya dragged her behind the column and covered her.

"Hang on, let's hope this works." Nya twisted two severed ends together, causing the tangle of wires to hiss and then scream like the thing was in pain. The other orbs rolled closer, all eyes aimed at the two females by the column.

Where the hell was everyone else?

A series of hisses followed by squeals sounded around them, getting higher with each passing breath.

"Stay behind me!" Nya yelled as the tangle of wires grew hot; she grabbed the small taser mechanism and aimed.

Blue shot out of the metal prongs in Nya's hand, her muddy leather gloves doing little to keep the residual shock from firing up her arms. She let out a deep-throated yell, her fingers digging in, as she turned wildly from side to side, aiming from one ball to the next.

The bots glowed an unholy red as each of the eyelets exploded, quickly followed by the acrid scent of hot wiring and burning plastic.

A horn blared overhead, signaling the end of the first round. Nya fell to her knees and crawled toward Xari. "You okay?"

"I feel like someone hit me with a two-by-four, but yeah. Other than that, I'm all right. You?"

"Peachy."

Xari chuckled.

Nya threw down the eviscerated orb, noticing the burned tips of her gloves and fresh blisters covering the pads of her forefinger and thumb. She blew on her fingers to soothe the sting.

Xari moaned. "Great."

Trainers walked on the field, and Jax headed straight for them.

Nya turned away from him, quickly sheathing her knife back in its hidden spot.

Jax lowered to his haunches. "You should know, Myrina is complaining to the head judge that Xari should be disqualified."

"Nowhere in the rules does it say you can't help another candidate." Nya's voice held a quiet reason, and Jax smiled.

"That's because no other warrior has done it before. And how did you get the hexapod apart, Vtachi?"

Nya forced her eyes to stay on his, knowing if she looked away he'd know she was hiding something.

"I found a design flaw along the bottom seam, where all the sections converge."

"Hmmmm …" Jax picked up the broken sphere, noting the knife groove along the edge. "Seems you have strong fingers."

"Seems so."

"That's my sword mark," Xari blurted out. "I used my sword."

He smirked, obviously not believing her. "You aren't the best liar, Toxaris. Haven't we discussed this before?"

Xari looked away, her face flaming bright red.

"Don't be an ass," Nya hissed as the five-minute warning sounded overhead. "And get out of here. The second challenge is about to begin."

Jax's hard eyes fell on hers before he glanced at the top box. "By the way, your parents say hello."

Nya blanched. "You've spoken to them?"

"Well, they did want an explanation of our little hunting trip and a detailed report of everything that happened." Jax's finger traced down Nya's arm, and it felt like every eye in the place was focused on them.

"Stop that." Nya slapped his hand away. "What is it with you? You know nothing happened."

Jax leaned forward. "You let me touch you, hold you … kiss you. And that's something, isn't it?"

The second horn blared overhead.

"Shit," Nya grumbled, hating feeling vulnerable, especially in front of a crowd.

Jax's eyes sparked. "I have to go. And quit helping the competition."

He glanced back and waved as his athletic build gracefully jogged across the arena.

"You let him kiss you?" Xari's eyes were round as saucers again. "Where? And just how much holding went on between you two?"

"He hugged me and kissed me once. That's all."

Xari's eyes warmed. "Well, he's right. It is something."

"No, it's not." Nya rolled her head from side to side and stood. "Enough about Jax. Let's just get through this, all right?"

"Together." Xari held up her pinky, and Nya linked hers with it.

"Together."

Xari let go, and they both jogged toward their platforms.

Nya looked at the others, noticing seven of the fifteen were now empty, which meant those stupid bots had cut the field in half. Sadly, Myrina took her place on her dais.

Nya took off the gloves, leaving the leather bracings underneath. Her fingers would be exposed, but at least her palms were still protected, and the burnt tips no longer rubbed against her blisters.

The horn sounded; this time guards opened the center doors.

Roars and bellows thundered across the arena, and a collective groan came from the pedestals.

Nya's heart sank. She hated when they brought in wild animals. She never understood the needless loss of life. At least after tonight, she wouldn't have to kill something other than the Drahzda.

Odd that she had more compassion for wild predators than she did for other humans.

The familiar sound of a growl echoed in the arena, and Nya groaned as the large cats padded in.

Oh, God. Not again.

So that explained why Cassius wanted a volunteer. She'd brought the mountain lions here to be part of the championship round, but one of them escaped, hurting her leg in the process.

It wasn't the fault of the townsfolk and their archaic trapping practices. It was the Scythian's archaic practice of warrior-versus-wild.

Nya glared at the top box.

And Scythians were so pious about how they'd evolved into a higher thinking species. They'd been doing this shit since Nero and the gladiator days.

A wide panel slid open from either end of the arena, followed by the sharp crack of whips. A dozen or so pumas charged onto the floor.

This time, the pedestals lowered into the ground, and Nya crouched, cursing Cassius again.

The animals attacked, and Xari dove, sword in hand. Myrina and the others did the same. Nya stood in the middle of the field, briefly shielded by the fighting warriors.

She knew these animals were not natural enemies of humans. But when they were this enraged, they'd take it out on the first thing they saw. A mountain lion's instinct was to attack from behind, snapping its prey's spine at the base of the skull, and so she'd have to watch her back.

Nya untied her scarf, and a collective gasp ran through the crowd.

Xari glanced back; her eyes widened in disbelief. "What are you doing?"

"Watch it!" Nya hollered, and Xari pivoted and thrust her sword, nearly impaling the cat in the chest. Her blade caused the animal to shift, and the massive beast roared in frustration, backing away.

"I'm not quitting. Pay attention to what you're doing!" Nya shouted back. She took the opposite ends of the large bandana in each hand, whipping them around until the fabric wrapped around itself. She adjusted the middle and created pocket. In one fluid motion, she bent down, one hand grazing the ground while the other dug into the secret compartment on the rise of her hip. Nya pulled out a few smooth stones from her pocket as she stood. She placed one of the rocks in the middle of the scarf. The crowd jumped to their feet as she swung the makeshift sling overhead, allowing the stone to gain momentum. With a flick of her wrist, she released one end of the bandana, and the rock sailed through the air.

The mountain lion roared as the stone found its mark. Crimson seeped down his fur, and he changed direction, turning from Xari toward her. Cursing, Nya lunged to the side, but the Puma's massive paw swiped, leaving three deep gashes in the top of her thigh. She jumped on his back, grabbing the fur at the base of his ears.

Frantic, the puma's deep growl became a feral scream as he bucked, whipping his head from side to side, his canines bared in hopes of finding flesh. Nya's fingers dug into the sides of his throat, squeezing, hoping like hell that pressure points worked on animals as well as they did on humans. The last thing she wanted to do was kill the beast with her bare hands.

The cat finally stumbled, then fell forward in a heap, taking Nya with him.

A horn blared overhead, and handlers rushed to haul away dead carcasses and cage the cats that were still alive.

Nya stayed down, keeping her puma secure until one of the handlers made their way to her.

"This one's still alive, and I want to keep it that way."

The male smirked and waved toward two instructors carrying a cage.

Nya glared. "I mean it. This cat's earned his freedom."

"We'll see what the headmistress says." He turned back.

Nya searched the arena floor. Xari stood next to a fallen cat while Myrina brushed the dirt off her pants.

And, surprisingly, Rissa was still with them.

"And then there were four," Xari grumbled, coming to help Nya to her feet. She glanced at the cat stirring behind the bars as they took him away. "You know. It's weird how you'll risk your life to save a cat, but when you spar another Scythian, you turn deadly. I wonder what that says about you. We should ask Jax."

"Shut up."

Xari's eyes mischievously twinkled as she held up her hands. "No need getting defensive. I won't tell anyone your animal-loving weakness."

Nya shrugged. "Whatever."

The horn blasted overhead, signaling the start of the third round.

Several warriors ran onto the field, rolling out large partitions. They sectioned off the arena floor into four spaces. As soon as the dividers were secured, the top extended, creating a curved overhang. To Nya, the place looked like a campground amphitheater they'd gone to when she was young.

"What's the next challenge, show tunes?" Xari grinned.

Guards jogged into the arena, taking a position between each section, assuring the contenders couldn't leave their area.

Nya looked at the top box. "Think Cassius thought of the guards before today, or are we the reason they're here?"

Xari shook her head. "No clue. But you'd better take care of that before you bleed out."

Nya looked down. Dark crimson ran down her leather pants, pooling on the mud at her feet. She sighed and took her scarf, wrapping it tightly around her thigh before tying it off. "That'll leave a scar."

Xari laughed. "Probably. But it's a great story for the *grandvahna*."

Nya flinched as the pain finally registered. "Thanks for the reminder."

Xari's smile fell. "Ny, I promise, this won't be as bad as you think. I …" her voice trailed away as she looked across the arena. "Well, swell."

Nya looked up to see Jax jogging across the field. Three other instructors followed him, breaking off into different directions, heading for the paneled structures.

"Xari, you're with Cyrus," Jax called as he grew near.

Relieved, Xari sighed. She held up her pinky. "*Staratsa.*"

Nya's eyes watered at the Dacian endearment. The word was only meant for family and was a plea for their loved one to stay safe until they were together again. She linked her pinky for a quick squeeze before dropping her hand.

"*Staratsa.*"

Xari took off across the arena, and Nya finally turned and faced the one male that could ruin it all.

Jax's eyes became counselor calm like he was getting ready to talk her off a ledge or something.

She hated that look. "Just spit it out. What do I have to do?"

He stepped toward her, not missing the fact that she stepped back.

"Listen, Vtachi. This is a holodome. Everyone in the arena can see you, but you won't be able to see them. Think of it as a one-way mirror."

"All right. But I can't punch an illusion. Just who, or what, am I fighting?"

He held her gaze. "Me."

Nya stilled. In four years, no one had defeated Jax. The only reason she held an undefeated record was that he never participated in challenges. His job was conditioning and training. She glanced around the arena, noting that Xari had Cyrus, Rissa had Melani, and Myrina had Pheobe.

"I want to lodge a complaint. Myrina has already beaten Pheobe, and Rissa took down Melani just last month. That's not fair."

Jax smiled. "If it makes you feel better, Xari's never beaten Cyrus."

"But both Rissa and Myrina have proven they are stronger than their opponent," she insisted. "Cassius should have given me Teagen or Knox, someone closer to the other trainer's abilities. You're a Tova. You've been undefeated for four years. Why are you my final challenge?"

Jax's eyes pierced hers. "Because it's my responsibility."

"Damn it, Jax. Stop that. I don't know where you get your sense of obligation. I'm not some helpless Allos girl. And after tonight, I'm on a plane to Carpathia, so you don't owe me anything. My future is my responsibility, not yours."

"We'll see, Vtachi." He frowned as he glanced at her leg. "You're still bleeding."

She looked at the soaked scarf. "I'll live."

"Do you have a long-sleeved shirt under that jacket?"

Confused, Nya nodded. "Yes."

Jax's jaw clenched as he looked at the top box. "Good. Rip off your sleeve and tie it again."

Nya froze. Jax wasn't allowed to help her, and they both knew it.

"I'll be fine."

"Vtachi," he rumbled.

"For the love of God, stop calling me a fucking bird!"

The horn blared overhead.

Jax crossed his arms, settling his weight on the back of his heels, his expression aloof.

"Your mother has requested you not stay for the Claiming Season, should you lose the championship, that is. She already has a rovni in mind that she feels would be better than any candidate the champions could choose. I know him from my days in the academy. He's not exactly a conversationalist, but—"

"Oh, shut up." Nya ripped off her jacket. She tore off her shirtsleeve and put the jacket back on. Grumbling a stream of obscenities that would make a sailor blush, she tied the extra material around her thigh.

"Tighter," Jax ordered.

She grumbled some more, straining to pull the material as tight as it would go. Her leg screamed in pain.

"There. Happy?"

"Not quite." Jax stepped forward, his eyes never leaving hers. He put his hand on her hip, his fingers resting on the rise of her backside. His thumb grazed her hipbones as his palms moved down. His knuckles swept across her lower abdomen, trailing downward until his fingers grazed her sex, finally resting on her inner thigh.

Nya gasped as he pressed the soft flesh there, quickly finding the hidden knife. Tucking his thumb and forefinger beneath the hidden pocket, he unsheathed the blade.

Leaning in, he whispered as his lips grazed her ear, "Sorry, Vtachi. No weapons allowed this round."

Jax tossed the curved knife to the trainer on the side, who seemed to be enjoying the Jax and Nya show.

She groaned. "Great. Now Knox thinks we've done it, too."

"Done what?" Jax's innocent expression did nothing to hide the twinkle in his eyes.

"You know what. And it's not funny." Nya double-checked the knot on the torn shirtsleeve. "You weren't the one with a pregnancy test waiting on your bunk. And you didn't have to deal with the after-effects of Myrina announcing to your classmates that you've become the instructor's whore."

Jax's eyes hardened to stone. He glared at the redhead on the other side of the arena. "She said that."

"I believe the term she used was *suka*, but yeah, she did, so why don't you switch places with Pheobe and teach her a lesson."

Jax kept his eyes on Myrina like he was considering it. He finally looked back at Nya. "As much as I'd love to, I can't."

"Figures."

The third horn sounded, and the stadium lights faded to black. Fog rolled in from the edge of the arena, blanketing the muddy ground like a cloud of despair. Jax nudged Nya to the center of the partitioned space as trainers closed in. They extended the partitions until it felt like they were the only two left in the arena.

"Jax," Nya looked around. "What is this?" The overhang was larger than Nya thought. The screens surrounding them glowed white as the arena's noise fell away.

How were the panels blocking sound?

She started to ask, but Nya couldn't find her voice when she realized that she was now alone with Jax in a colorless world of quiet.

He came forward and put his hands on her shoulders, his eyes grave. "In order to win tonight's challenge, you must fight while being overstimulated."

She pushed his hands away. "What?"

He wearily rubbed the back of his neck. "The final challenge is exploring how you fight when your senses are kicked into overdrive, including fear."

"Fan-fucking-tastic."

The fog became thigh high, and lights flashed as the panels and overhang came to life. Thunderclouds and lightning streaked across the dome as a series of images streamed along the makeshift corridor. Pictures of things she feared when she was young—clowns, vans with no windows, a lone field next to a stream.

Distracted, Jax's eyes flitted from one screen to the next as if he were studying a case. Nya took advantage and attacked, sweeping her good leg from behind and knocking him off balance.

Jax stumbled to the ground and emerged from the fog grinning. He crouched in a defensive stance. "I guess I deserved that."

"Yes, you did. Quit trying to get in my head."

Nya jumped as screams rent the air. The pictures were bad enough, but sounds added a whole new dimension.

The images flashed faster, as horrific cries of human suffering came at her from all sides. Third world villages being tortured, children with swollen bellies dying of hunger. A lone field next to a stream.

Jax kept his fists up, ducking and weaving against her assault, all the while his eyes darting from panel to panel.

The sounds crescendoed as the pictures flashed faster and faster until they took on a strobe light effect. The rancid odor of death filtered in and Nya gagged before breathing through her mouth.

Her anxiety ramped up as the scents, sights, and sounds sent her adrenaline into overdrive. Her ears popped as the pressure in the place seemed to close in, like they were several meters under water. Heat caused sweat to bead on her forehead. Nya shook her head, trying to keep her focus. Jax sprang, but she dodged him easily, elbowing his ribs as he fell past her.

He disappeared below the fog, and Nya froze. A white cloud settled around her, oddly tranquil among the images and sounds. Without Jax, there were no distractions, and Nya was alone, trapped in suffering. She froze, seeing if the fog would shift as Jax moved. An unseen adversary was a dangerous one, and Jax could be anywhere.

Wind gusted in, swirling the fog as the temperature plummeted. Her breath became ragged, showing in little tufts of air as she tried to contain her panic.

Oh, God. What if Jax wasn't the worst thing crawling around. What if Cassius had something else under there?

She wouldn't put it past her. Nya's mind raced with endless possibilities … spiders, snakes, scorpions, rats.

Oh, good sweet Lord—anything but rats.

Something grazed her ankle, and Nya squealed. Instinct kicked in, and she flew toward the partition. Pain shot down her thigh as she jumped, her fingers latching onto the top of the paneling. Something grabbed her ankle, but Nya brought her other foot down blindly kicking, causing whatever it was to let go. She scaled the makeshift wall and sat, precariously balancing her weight on the top of the thin barrier.

Jax emerged like some sick apparition, slowly making his way toward her. His eyes darted around the room, searching for the best way to get to her while images of people jumping from burning ships flashed across the screen. He paced in front of her, studying the way she balanced on the thin panel, his eyes resting on the torn shirtsleeve, now saturated in red. For a moment, Nya allowed a sliver of hope to run through her. Maybe she could just stay perched on her panel. It couldn't be long before someone else went down.

But the determination in Jax's eyes let her know she wouldn't have the luxury of waiting. He inched closer with each pass, his body subtly shifting forward. Just as he lunged, Nya pushed off the wall, diving over his broad shoulders. She rolled as she sailed through the air, but terror struck when she realized that she had no guide to judge the distance to the floor. Afraid she'd over-correct and land on her face, Nya extended her legs, allowing them to take the brunt of her weight. Pain ripped through her thigh, and she cursed as she fell beneath the fog. Her back hit the ground, knocking the wind out of her. The idea of hiding in the fog was quickly dispelled as her other senses naturally heightened. Being surrounded by sounds of gunshots and sloshing water was strangely terrifying.

She scrambled to her feet. Warmth seeped down her thigh, her leg nearly giving out. Her panic eased as her eyes found Jax's. The screens went dark. Nya hobbled to the middle of the enclosure, distracted by the lack of light.

The noise stopped, and relief flooded her.

Here's hoping that Myrina got her ass kicked.

The screens flashed back to life, and Nya groaned. She shifted her feet into a defensive stance and brought her fists up to protect her face.

Quiet.

Bile rose in her throat as a haunting Russian melody filled the space. Instead of pictures flashing across the screens—a panoramic view of the docks from her home blazed around her.

Gunshots rang amidst the music, the scent of gunpowder, blood, and tobacco scented the air, and the scene turned into horror as warriors removed bodies from the water. Nya dropped her arms; her eyes became empty pools of despair.

That music. God, someone make it stop. Penn ... how could he do this? No. It wasn't Penn. Penn didn't do anything.

Jax dove, wrapping his arms around her torso, and they both disappeared under a cloud of white.

CHAPTER SEVEN

"Nya." Jax's calm voice echoed in the distance. He lay on top of her, shifting his hips, trying to avoid her injured leg while his forearms bore the brunt of his weight. "Are you all right?"

She kept still, gazing over his shoulder.

Jax's brow lowered. "Anya Thalestris. Answer me."

Nothing.

Jax settled his weight into hers, his hands digging into her hair, his entire body swathing her in warmth. He lowered his forehead to hers. "You're safe. Nothing is going to happen to you. I'm here."

She stirred, closing her eyes. "I can protect myself, Penn. You know that."

Jax hesitated. "Penn's not here, Vtachi." He rubbed his thumb along her cheek. "Breathe, sweet Nya. Come back to me. Penn's gone."

Her blank gaze turned fuzzy at the mention of Penn's name. "Jax? Where's ... where did he go? Where's Penn?" Her voice barely made it past her lips.

Jax kissed her forehead and sighed. "I don't know. You tell me."

She closed her eyes as a tear streaked down the side of her face. "He left after ... I wasn't strong enough. I mean, I thought I could fight it, but I couldn't ... they died. They all died, because of me. Penn. He ..." She tensed as she realized that Jax's body was touching every part of her.

"Tell me about your scar, Vtachi."

Nya closed her eyes. "You'll think less of me if you know."

"No, I won't. I promise."

"Are you going to ask that female in town to be your romni?" Nya asked, her random question shocking them both.

A flush ran across Jax's cheeks. "You're deflecting, Nya. Tell me about your scar."

"No."

Cool air brushed across them as the sounds switched back to children suffering.

Jax sighed. "I'll make a deal with you. I promise I'll stay below the fog line and let you declare victory, but you have to do something for me in return."

She froze. "What?"

"Tell me the truth."

"And if I don't?"

"Then I'll win the challenge by staying right here. When the fog clears, everyone will see me completely subduing you. You'll come in fourth place and head home to live a life in Ireland with some ruddy-cheeked warrior."

Nya scowled. "That's blackmail."

"Call it what you will. Make your decision."

Nya became uncomfortably aware of a myriad of sensations. The way Jax's fingers rubbed small circles on her scalp, how his swollen biceps flexed on either side of her, making her feel small. The way his hips settled between her thighs—his warm breath brushing across her chin.

The light bleeding through the smoky cloud faded to nothing. The screaming stopped. The arena burst into applause.

"You're out of time. What'll it be?"

"Fine. I was with Penn. We were on the docks. We weren't supposed to be there. I fell. That's when I got the scar."

Jax studied her. "Is that all you remember of that night?"

"I remember falling off something because I'd cut my palm. I tried to get out of the water, but I couldn't. My father was there. He helped me out and carried me home. Now let me up."

"And why would I think less of you for that?"

The stadium roared as Cassius announced the end of the trials.

Nya's voice became nothing more than an aggressive hiss. "It was my fault. Warriors died because I disobeyed the Suveran, and my father ordered his team to find me. Something happened, and they died."

"What happened, Vtachi?"

Her eyes squeezed closed as her heart sped. "I can't remember, but I know it was my fault."

Jax rolled to his side, and Nya scrambled to her feet, finally relieved to be free.

"You promised. Stay down."

He placed his hands behind his head. "I never break my promises. Remember that."

She'd just cleared the fog when the stadium lights flooded the arena. Squinting, she held her hand over her eyes and watched the trainers roll the partitions away. The fog settled, easing downward until Jax's long frame appeared, making it seem like he was floating on a cloud.

Cassius's voice rang overhead. "Our three champions are Anya Thalestris, Toxaris Romaine, and Myrina Pisto!"

Nya groaned when she heard the last name. "I so hoped Rissa would've won."

Jax smiled, apparently following her lead for normal conversation. "Myrina's not so bad."

"Yeah, you try living with her, and then we'll see how you feel."

"I'd rather not." Jax and Nya shared a smile, one born of the common bonds of friendship and time. His expression subtly changed as he stepped forward. "Vtachi, I—"

She backed away. "Thanks for making me bandage the thigh. I'm not sure I'd have been able to get back up after the jump off the partition." She stretched out her hand and forced herself to smile.

He sandwiched her scarred palm between both of his. "You'll do well in the trials." He spoke in Dacian as he gently raised her hand to his lips, kissing the rise of her knuckles. "Keep an open mind, all right? Any warrior would be honored to call you his romni."

And with that, he strolled away.

Disappointment twisted through her. After four years of endless walks in the woods, hard therapy sessions, hours of hunting and sparring together, Nya had come to depend on having Jax around. As she watched him disappear into the crowd, her chest ached. Even if she did see him again, things would be different. After today, their relationship would change.

And what in the hell do you say to something like that?

Xari ran up and wrapped Nya in a tight hug. "We did it. Although I wish Rissa were the third instead of Myrina."

Nya half smiled. "I said that very thing to Jax."

Xari stopped, like something had just occurred to her. "Wait a minute. Did you beat Jax, or did you run out of time?"

Nya blushed. "Technically I defeated him, but—"

"Don't start." Xari chucked her on the shoulder "You officially won, and that's all that matters."

"How did you get past Cyrus?"

"Apparently, he hates the overstimulation thing. He got distracted, and I put him in a chokehold." Xari smirked.

"And Myrina?"

"Oh, Myrina didn't win. She just made it longer than Rissa, who got knocked out when she hit the deck."

"I hate that fog."

Xari tilted her head. "I thought it was kind of cool, being surrounded by white. It's peaceful."

"It never occurred to you that Cassius might have let loose spiders, rats, or scorpions?" Nya glared at the floor like it was the arena's fault.

"God no. Glad you didn't share that little nugget of paranoia with me. I'd have freaked out."

"Even after I figured that nothing was there, I still hated it. Made me feel suffocated."

Xari grinned. "I wonder what that says about us, all that white calmed me while choking you. We should ask Jax."

Nya kept her eyes forward. "I'd rather not."

Xari laughed. "Come on, Gimp. Let's get you stitched up." She wrapped her arm around Nya's waist, taking the brunt of her weight as they hobbled toward the exit.

The stadium had cleared considerably by the time they found the small triage room, which held an examining table and glass cabinets full of supplies. Nya waved at one of the EMTs.

"How much longer is this going to take?" Myrina's whine was like an icepick in Nya's ear.

"What happened to her?" Nya mumbled, watching the physician take a pre-formed mold, which looked more like thick spider webs in the shape of a cast. He placed the form around her arm and passed a UV light over the structure. The webbing shrunk around her like a second skin.

Xari smiled. "She took a bad spill after Pheobe put her on her ass."

Nya's brow disappeared under her bangs. "Xari, I'm kind of proud."

"What can I say? It's celebratory vulgarity, which makes it okay."

The doctor gave Myrina a set of instructions and mumbled something about the cast disintegrating once it sensed she had healed.

Her cat green eyes flashed as soon as she saw Nya and Xari standing by the door. She winced as she hopped off the table and headed in their direction, waiting until she was within arm's reach before speaking to either of them.

"Congratulations," she purred, reaching out to pat Nya's stomach. "Let's just hope you didn't hurt the unborn."

Everyone stopped in their tracks, the EMTs openly stared, and Myrina grinned.

"Go to hell," Nya said, shoving her hand away.

Myrina's smile grew, her voice getting louder. "Maybe Rissa should accompany us. You know, as backup."

Nya started toward her, but Xari stepped in her way.

Myrina sweetly smiled. "See you later."

"She's so not worth it," Xari whispered. "Besides, you can't go after her now. You're leaking like a sieve."

Nya looked at the blood running down her boot.

"Fine," she grumbled, allowing Xari to help her to the examining table.

The doctor glared at them, his thick glasses making his eyes seem too large for his face. He grumbled under his breath while ripping the scarf and torn sleeve from Nya's thigh.

"Stay still," he ordered, taking scissors from his white coat pocket. He started at the bottom of Nya's pant leg, slicing through the leather until he reached her hip.

"This may sting." Being less than gentle, he rubbed antiseptic over her thigh.

Nya hissed in pain as she assessed the damage. A testament to her Scythian heritage, the bottom of the laceration had already started closing. But the top was still a mass of angry, swollen flesh.

"That doesn't look good," Xari commented as blood oozed, dripping down her leg.

"She'll need stitches." He took a large gauze cloth, covering the spot while his thumb dug into her thigh.

Nya whimpered. At this rate, he'd hit bone soon. "Really." She pried his hand off the bloody gauze. "I'm fine. I'll just bandage it up."

"Suit yourself."

Jax passed by the door and stopped, watching the physician snap off his gloves and throw them in the trash.

The doctor started through the threshold, but Jax held him back, mumbling something. They both cut their eyes to Nya, the physician nodded and then left.

Jax came in the room.

"Vtachi, the physician is right. You won't heal in time unless you get stitched up." Jax leaned against the door frame, his eyes sweeping down, resting on her exposed leg.

Nya gently lifted the gauze pad and winced. The jagged, inflamed flesh oozed with puss and blood.

"Benson!" Jax barked as he started toward her.

Nya jumped, and Xari shuffled against the wall, giving him ample room.

The doctor came back in. "Yes, Jax?"

"Did you debride her thigh?"

Dr. Benson seemed offended. "Of course."

Jax picked up a sterile gauze pad and saturated it with an antiseptic solution. He swung a blue light around, muttering at whatever he saw.

"What are you doing?" Nya blushed as his large hand palmed her knee, keeping her still.

"Don't move." He grabbed a pair of tweezers.

Nya whimpered as Jax dug into inflamed muscle tissue, but she refused to let him know how much it hurt.

He leaned closer, his breath brushing against her bare leg, and she couldn't help but squirm.

"Stay still." He glanced up. "I almost had it." One more painful jab and he pulled the tweezers away with a thin shard of something black.

"What is that?"

"Part of the puma's claw, which Dr. Benson would have seen *had he done his job.*" Jax's voice got louder with every word as he glared across the room.

The doctor rubbed his face. "It's been a long day."

Jax dropped the tweezers into a metal bowl and swung the lamp back into place. "I don't care if you've triaged the entire Scythian army. There's no excuse leaving her in that condition."

"Is there a problem?" Cassius stood in the doorway, followed closely by Nya's mother and father.

Nya feebly smiled. "It's nothing. We're just finishing up. I'll be done soon."

Jax glared at Nya before turning to Cassius. "If I hadn't walked by, Nya would be going to Carpathia with part of a puma's claw embedded in her thigh."

Cassius turned to the doctor. "Is this true?"

The male sputtered a few excuses until Cassius held up her hand.

"I've heard enough. You are relieved of your duty." The headmistress turned to one of her guards. "Send for my physician, and tell him I want a report in my hands tonight."

Dr. Benson stopped as he passed Cassius. "Have him do a blood test. The others say she's with young."

Her mother gasped while her father's expression turned ruthless.

Mortified, Nya covered her face with her hands, but Jax laughed, startling them all.

"I'm sure that's Myrina's doing. Test her blood if you want, but there's no doubt in my mind Nya's still a *novo.*"

Nya blushed, livid with Jax for acting like her virginity was up for discussion with anyone, much less the headmistress and her parents.

Cassius waved a dismissive hand, seeming as blasé about the subject as Jax. "As you are the only male she's been alone with, I'm sure you're right." Her brows lowered. "But what interests me is whether the doctor had been aware of the gossip before he tended her wound."

Xari stepped forward. "Myrina said something nasty as she left, making sure everyone heard her."

"Ah." Cassius turned to the guards. "That changes things. Have Dr. Benson whipped before you send him away. And alert the other compounds. He will be confined to treating only those foolish enough to go to him."

Dr. Benson blanched as the guards escorted him out of the room.

Cassius turned to Ike. "The press is waiting for a statement from each of the champions, but as Nya isn't finished here, would it be possible for you to escort Toxaris to the front and then give a short statement in Nya's stead?"

"Absolutely." Ike glanced at Nya, taking in her pallid features and tense frame. "And your mom and I will make sure the media is gone before we come and get you."

Relieved, she smiled. "Thanks, Dad." One thing she and her father agreed on—they both hated the press.

His eyes twinkled. "You're welcome, Pumpkin."

Ike led Gia and Xari out the door.

"Could this day get any worse?" Nya put her hands over her face.

Cassius warmly chuckled. "I think it's a matter of perspective, Anya Thalestris." She switched to Dacian. "Most would see this day as a good one. You've beaten an opponent of intellect, one of strength, not to mention a Tova. You are a champion, earning the right to meet the best warriors of our kind. And yet, you act as if you're about to go the way of the doctor and be whipped in the square." Her voice gentled as she came forward. "Why?"

Nya sat up straight and bared her teeth in what she hoped was a smile. "It's been a long day. That's all."

Cassius took in Nya's too-tight expression and Jax's frown.

"Address the issue, counselor," was all she had said before she walked out the door.

Jax flipped a blade on the counter next to her. "Here. I got it back from Knox."

"Thanks." Nya reached over and grabbed it before flopping back on the bed. "What in the hell was that about? Exactly what are you addressing?"

"We need to talk."

Cassius' doctor knocked on the doorframe, saving Nya from having to respond. He took his time to re-assess her thigh, making sure no bits of claw remained. Nya closed her eyes as he brought out a hypodermic and started numbing the area along the deep tear. He hummed as he stitched, oblivious to the tension in the room.

Finally, he finished up, slathering the stitches with some unguent that smelled of black walnuts and coconut oil.

"The bottom should heal within a day, but the top is rather nasty. Still, it shouldn't be a problem, and the stitches will dissolve within a week. Until then, avoid sparring." He handed her a jar of salve. "And put this on it twice a day."

"That will be all." Jax's calm voice held a subtle undercurrent of impatience. The physician gathered his things and left.

Awkward silence bloomed between the two of them.

"So, I guess this is goodbye," Nya muttered, struggling to sit up.

Jax came over to help. "Not by a long shot. Remember, I'm consulting with Dr. Ramova during the trials."

"Dr. Who?"

"My colleague that we discussed this morning."

"He's the other shrink, right?"

Jax's eyes grew wary. "Yes, and he's aware of your situation." He ran his hand along her bare leg, skirting around the bandage. "He agrees with me that it would be best if you had someone to help get you through. With the press and meeting so many males, your stress levels will already be high. You'll need help decompressing."

"Oh, God." Nya pulled away, her eyes resting on her feet. "And how's that supposed to work? I can see it now. 'Excuse me, warriors, but I've got a session with my shrink. See, I'm just learning how to stomach being touched by you. Don't worry, though. If all goes according to plan, I should be ready by the time our claiming night rolls around. But hey, don't hold it against me if I kill you in your sleep.' Yeah. That'll go over, I'm sure."

Jax took a deep breath and let it out slowly. He stepped between her knees and pulled her into his arms. "You haven't flown off the handle in three years, so no more talk of killing anyone in their sleep. And someone touching you is getting easier. You've said so yourself."

"Yes, but social touch is a helluva lot different than sexual touching, isn't it?"

Jax's eyes held a strange gleam. "Vtachi, this is between you and me. No one else needs to know."

"How? I'm sure the place is already swarming with media. They'll be filming every minute of my life, and unless I've heard wrong, the activities in the first and second rounds are nothing more than glorified dates designed to help Amazonian warriors find their equal."

"You let me handle the details, all right?"

She looked away. Weird as it seemed, she wasn't sure which would be more difficult—letting a stranger "desensitize" her to sexual touch or letting Jax do it. Seemed wrong when he had someone else that he cared about.

"Why are you doing this?"

"Because you're my responsibility."

Her brow lowered. "No, I'm not."

He rested his hand on either side of her hips. "Yes, you are. You still need me, Vtachi. I don't give up, and I don't walk away. You know that."

She looked away. He might be able to keep his emotions out of this, but that gaping hole in her chest only eased when Jax was around. What if she started to develop feelings for him? Shit.

He touched her nose with his. "I know you're holding back. Talk to me."

Nya groaned. Oh hell, no. She so wasn't going there right now. "Jax, I've lost a ton of blood, I'm battered and bruised, both emotionally and physically. My leg hurts like a mother. The brutal reality that I'm getting ready to choose a rovni is hitting me like a two-by-four. You've just informed me that you'll be coming to Carpathia for some bizarre intensive therapy, which is supposed to help me tolerate sex. And to make matters worse, the next four hours I'll be spending with my parents pretending that everything's peachy when all I want to do is scream and run the other way.

Can we *please* not do this now?"

Jax stared at her long and hard. "You're right. Now's not the time." He leaned in until his lips brushed her ear. Nya's pulse raced as his warm breath tickled her neck. "However, sweet Vtachi, there will come a time when you won't be allowed to deflect, evade, or fly away. And then we *will* have this discussion; I can promise you that."

Nya's thumb found its way to her palm, circling the scar over and over.

Jax's hand landed on top of hers, stilling their motion. He leaned in, his lips nudging hers in a gentle kiss.

"Relax," he whispered in Dacian. "We got this."

Nya's eyes glittered with unshed tears as she looked at him. "I hate to admit it, but that last challenge threw me. I need some time."

Jax's deep brown eyes warmed as he squeezed her hands. His touch caused too much sensation, and she tugged her hands from his, tucking them beneath her thighs.

"Answer me one question," she prodded as Jax took a step back.

"All right."

"Really?" Every time she'd asked about his life, he refused to answer, explaining that it was counterproductive to spend their sessions talking about him when they were trying to get to the root of her issues.

Jax stepped forward. "Really."

"Why go to all this trouble? I mean, you've got a life beyond being a weapons instructor and a shrink. Surely you'd rather spend your leave time doing something other than counseling a nutcase with a temper?"

"Nya, your self-deprecation is concerning at times." Jax studied her for a moment like he was deciding how best to answer. "If it helps you feel less guilty, my leave extends through the summer, and I promise I'll concentrate on my personal life after the trials."

"Oh." Nya's heart sank as she remembered his female in the valley. "That's good. That's really good."

Jax smiled. "I think so. I'm looking forward to it, actually. But let's focus on you first, all right?"

She fiddled with the torn leather hanging from her leg, unaware that she'd switched to Dacian. "This female, the one you plan to spend the summer with, I hope she's your true equal, my friend. And in her arms, I hope you find more happiness and love than you can imagine."

Jax's finger nudged her chin up until her gaze met his. "I'm sure I will, my little bird," his deep voice seemed to caress the rhythmic sounds of their native tongue. "I'm sure I will. And I wish the same for you."

Nya tried to smile, but her eyes became empty, haunted. "That's not in the cards for me, and we both know it."

A soft knock on the door had Nya pulling away.

Her father stood in the threshold, fiddling with something he held in his hands. "Press is taken care of. And Xari ran by the barracks and brought these for you." He held up a hoodie and some yoga pants.

Nya took a deep breath. "She's a lifesaver."

"The headmistress has approved our request to go into town. Your mother made reservations for the seafood place. Xari said she'd join us."

Nya pasted on a smile. "Sounds great." She hopped off the table, embracing the burning sensation that lashed through her leg. Pain always centered her. And how sad was that? "Just let me get changed."

"If you'll excuse me." Jax's eyes latched on to hers. He leaned close so her father couldn't hear, his eyes piercing hers. "I'll be seeing you."

"Goodbye, Jax." Tears flooded as she turned away.

He crossed the room, shook her father's hand, and walked out the door.

The silence became oppressive, and Nya hobbled behind a partition that served as a makeshift changing area. She shucked off her jacket.

"Jax is a worthy opponent," her father commented as she stripped down to her cami.

She glared at the partition before donning her sweatshirt. "Yes, he is. But he's in love with a female who lives in town, and he's taking personal time off to be with her. So, don't get any ideas, all right? Jax is my counselor. And a friend." She peeked her head out, watching her father look oddly relieved.

"Then why is his name on the list?"

Nya ducked behind the partition again and shucked off her ruined leathers, replacing them with the yoga pants. "Rumor has it his name's been on the list for years, but he never participates."

This seemed to satisfy his curiosity because he didn't say anything else. Nya limped from behind the screen and grabbed the fresh pair of socks and sneakers her father had dropped on the examining table.

"You must be hungry."

Relief flooded her as they hit neutral ground. "I'm starving. And just so you know, Xari can pack away enough food to feed a family of four."

Her father chuckled. "We're in luck, then. I think tonight's the buffet."

She grabbed her leathers and knife, and Ike took her arm, helping her keep the weight off her leg. Together, they made their way down the open corridors to the front of the arena.

That hollow feeling pounded through her chest as they started toward the front gates. The past few weeks the sensation had grown so much she wondered if there was a black hole consuming her from the inside out.

She had hoped seeing her parents again might help, but it hadn't.

She couldn't help wondering if the instincts were right. Maybe she should just run while she could.

CHAPTER EIGHT

Heavy black curtains hid large arched windows lining the bedroom's far wall. The soothing scent of jasmine and sage wafted through the air, the orange glow from the incense the only real light in the room. An enormous four-poster bed overwhelmed the space, its stacked wine-colored pillows cradling someone in comfort.

"Sir?" A deep voice, soft and cautious, muttered in the darkness.

"What is it, Stephan?" Penn rolled to his side, grabbing one of the pillows and tucking it to his chest. Days like this weren't worth getting out of bed.

"We have news."

Penn wearily sat up, throwing the pillow to the ground. "What's the status?"

"The championship is tonight, and then your Ana should be back in Romania, as you predicted."

Penn pressed his thumbs against his temples. "Do we have a confirmation on her flight?"

"If she wins, she'll be flying commercial first class in two days. We will not be able to access her once she reaches the Scythian Capitol."

Penn stood, grabbing the mahogany bedpost. "We have people in place to intercept her before then?"

"Yes," Stephan muttered as he snatched a robe from the wingback chair and tossed it on the bed.

"And what of her condition?" Penn shrugged into the velvety robe before knotting the sash.

"Everything we've learned confirms there is no change. She still doesn't remember."

Penn smiled. "This is good news. When do the Carpathian Trials end?"

Stephan cleared this throat. "We don't know."

Penn's expression turned deadly, and Stephan backed up, rushing over his words. "Our informant isn't a Scythian, and they've locked down the consulate for this event. She's attempting to find out as we speak."

Penn turned his head to the side, popping his neck. "We better have the information soon, or I'll have her skinned alive."

Stephan shuddered. "As you wish."

"Have you secured the area around our new home?"

Stephan swallowed. "Drones show the parcel of land to the south, a wildlife refuge, which is completely uninhabited. The rest of the area has several villages—two of the four are cooperating. The transition team is working on persuading the others. We should have the region under our control before we arrive, and then renovations start soon after."

"Good. Now leave me."

Stephan backed out of the room. Penn made his way to the window and pulled back the heavy, velvet curtains, wincing as overcast light streamed into the room. The large courtyard and sprawling hills beyond had been in his family for a hundred years. The Astana Fortress had been a gift from Tsar Nicholas II in gratitude for Penn's great-grandfather's discovery of the Scythian race. For a short time, Nicholas had wanted them to join Russia in stemming the violence in the region. But after seeing their warriors' superior strength and intelligence, the Tsar feared they would eventually take over. He formed a secret sect of the Russian military, gave Sarkov and his men unlimited funds and a fortress, and ordered them to hunt the Scythians to extinction. Known as the Drahzda, Sarkov gave his men a standing order: no matter what, they were to see their mission through. After the Tsar was overthrown, funds for the project dried up, and Penn's grandfather, who had taken over, reached out to the young budding Russian Mafia. Together they embezzled and stole millions, funneling them into bank accounts all over the world. The Second World War had all eyes pointed toward Germany, and it was then that Sarkov Industry was born. No one questioned a Russian corporation hiring scientists and researchers under the pretense of helping defeat Hitler. The country had sustained heavy losses, and the gains made in weapons technology overshadowed any knowledge of the Drahzda or their mission.

By the time Dmitri, Penn's father, had taken over, the Scythians were the only ones aware of the Drahzda existence.

But that was about to change.

Once his Ana was back, he could finally put his plan into place. And then he'd find the peace he once knew in Ireland.

Yes. It was only a matter of time before they entered a new era, one where Drahzda ruthlessness and Scythian strength ruled.

For the past four years, the Americans had worked closely with the Scythians to keep his Ana from him, but the experience of the Trials would unlock her mind once and for all. It grieved Penn to think of someone else touching her. But he'd make sure she was back where she belonged before any of those *males* took what was his.

He slowly sank back into the plush bedding, tucking a pillow beneath his head.

Nya might find it difficult at first, but eventually she would find herself Ana kneeling at his feet, where she was meant to be.

The restaurant grew quiet as Nya and Xari stepped inside. Ike nudged them forward and motioned for the hostess. The young girl's hands shook as she grabbed four menus.

"You must be from the training facility." She smiled a little too wide.

For years, the Allos in the valley believed the Scythian Academy was a renowned sports training facility for international athletes. Cassius made sure only a few warriors visited the town at a time, but even then, their tall frames and thick muscles made it impossible to blend in.

Ike kept his voice gentle. "That's right. We have a reservation for four under the name Thalestris."

"Follow me, please." The Allos woman was a good eight inches shorter than Nya, and her thin frame looked like a stiff wind would blow her away. She wove through the tables, her heels rapidly clicking on the floor like she was trying not to run from the hounds of Hell. Nya sighed as people watched until they drew close, and then their gaze would dart away. Throughout the world, it was the same reaction. Curiosity and extreme intimidation. She suspected it was because Scythians radiated a kind of energy that left most Allos twitchy.

Ike thanked the wisp of a girl, and they took their seats. Gradually the conversation buzzed around them again. The massive jellyfish tank in the center of the restaurant was a great topic of interest—for about five minutes. Xari's Midwest hometown held everyone's attention for the next fifteen. Thank God for the buffet, which, mercifully, was popular among the Allos. A crowd gathered along the walls, where sneeze guards trapped mounds of endless food on heated serving trays. Nya and Xari stood on one side while Ike and Gia took the other, the Allos giving them a wide berth.

Finally, after everyone had settled at the table, the discussion turned to Carpathia. Xari seemed genuinely excited, and Nya sat back, letting her friend take the lead.

"I'd love to meet your parents sometime, Toxaris." Nya's mother adjusted her napkin in her lap.

Xari smiled and grabbed a breadstick. "Please, Mrs. Thalestris, call me Xari. And Mom and Dad have been on a mission in the Middle East for the past twelve months. I'm not sure when they're coming home."

"What are their specialties?" Nya's father leaned back in his chair, coffee cup in hand.

Xari shrugged. "Mom's in cyber warfare; Dad's in communications. You still head of Fourth Gen?"

Nya's father smiled. "Yes, but Gia has taken a break from weaponry to be on the Chancellor's council."

"Niiiiiiiice."

Gia smiled. "What area are you planning on specializing in?"

Xari picked up a crab leg and systematically pulled the meat from its shell. "Mom and Dad always worked as a team. Sometimes I was left with my aunt for months at a time, which stunk, but at least my parents were together. I know it sounds strange, but I always felt better knowing if something awful happened they wouldn't die alone."

Ike reached over and enveloped his wife's hand with his own.

Gia cleared her throat. "So, you're waiting until you find your rovni?"

Xari dipped her crab in butter and took a bite. "Yep. I'm not sure what I want to do yet, and so I thought I'd see what his interests are before deciding."

Ike turned to Nya. "What about you, Pumpkin? Have you thought about what field you'd like to go into?"

"I'm interested in psychology, particularly helping those heal from warfare," she said, picking up her wine glass.

Stunned, her parents froze.

Nya backtracked. "Eventually, though, I'd like to be an instructor."

Her mother carefully set down her fork. "Both are ambitious and require a lot of time and travel. Why not work in linguistics? You speak ten languages, and there's a tremendous need in counterintelligence."

Nya ran her finger along the edge of her wine glass. "Nothing's set in stone, of course. But if I had a choice, I'd like to look into psychology."

Thankfully, the waiter came by with a dessert tray, and Xari's love of all things sweet steered the conversation in a different direction.

It wasn't until Nya's dad signed the bill and put his card back in his wallet Nya's anxiety eased. The last thing she wanted was an in-depth discussion on linguistics being a better career choice.

"Let's take a walk before heading back. The town has changed so much since we were here," Gia said. Ike smiled as he took her hand.

"This was my mother's campus for her academy training," Nya explained to Xari as they walked beside them.

"I didn't know that." She turned to Gia. "So, after you won the championships how long did you stay in Carpathia?"

Nya's mother kept her eyes forward as her shoulders stiffened. "I didn't win. An American Champion defeated Ike in the Trials. He came here for the Claiming Season, and the rest, as they say, is history."

Nya glared at Xari. It wasn't like the media didn't bring her father's scandal up. Every. Single. Year. Why on Earth would she ask her mom about it?

What made it worse was the female that beat him was none other than the current Scythian Chancellor.

Now that Nya was a Champion, the press was bound to walk down memory lane. They'd start with old interviews of the Chancellor claiming that Ike was her top pick. And then they'd follow up with that awful footage from their final round, the one where her dad dove to the ground and stayed there, while Alexandra fell to her knees, pleading with him to get up. The incident had cast a shadow over Nya's entire life.

Xari's face flamed red. "I'm sorry. Of course, I knew that. I'm an idiot."

Ike's eyes warmed. "Don't apologize. It happened long before you were born. And choosing Nya's mother was the best decision I've ever made."

Gia changed the subject and pointed to various places, telling them about stories of her time in the academy. Xari kept the conversation going, asking questions and laughing at the right times, but Nya remained quiet. Her leg ached with every step, but she tried to keep an even pace so no one would notice. This little walking tour down memory lane distracted her parents, and she needed time to think.

According to Scythian law, the first round of the Trials allowed an Amazonian warrior to choose five males that she thought best matched her as an equal. The next round was dedicated to getting to know the males on a personal front. Candidates were encouraged to go beyond the arena and explore other avenues of interest, socially, emotionally, even sexually. The third and final round of the Trials set a challenge in the stadium between the Amazonian warrior and her Chosen. The male that proved his worth became the Amazonian warrior's rovni, while the other four candidates were sent back to their champion's academy. At the start of the Claiming Season, the roles shifted. Males then had time to choose five females that he deemed could be his equal, and the process started again. In both the Carpathian Trials and the Claiming Season, once a mate was chosen there was no going back.

On the rare occasion that someone protested the match, the *Suveran*, or leader of the region, ruled on the dispute. Nya shivered thinking about that. The Suveran over Carpathia was the very female her father had spurned all those years ago, Madame Executive Chancellor Alexandra Vasilica. Ike and Alexandra had managed to remain friends. Still, it would be smart to avoid having her rule on anything.

"Isn't that Jax?"

Nya glanced up, her eyes following her friend's gaze. Broad shoulders and dark hair stood a head taller than those around him. The Allos obsessed over even features and muscular bodies, and so they considered Scythians extraordinarily beautiful. Jax garnered attention every time he went to town with his dark hair, strong jaw, full lips, and muscular build. But his most striking feature was his eyes. Deep brown irises framed with thick lashes hid his thoughts well, although when he was angry, they sparkled like diamonds on dark velvet. At 6'7" he towered over most Allos but was an average height for a Scythian male.

He walked down the street, his hand on the small of a female's back. Her dark eyes twinkled as she laughed at something he said. Her blouse clung to her curves perfectly, and her pants hung just at the end of her high heels, making her legs seem impossibly long. Between her outfit and her layered bob, she had an air of sophistication and polish. She looked to be in her early to mid-thirties, and her bronze complexion, dark eyes, and full lips led Nya to believe that her heritage most likely centered in Persia or India. Nya's stomach churned as Jax leaned in, whispering something that caused the female to lay her hand on his arm. The move could hardly be considered inappropriate, but the way she looked at him made the gesture incredibly intimate.

"That must be the female he's been seeing," Nya said, her voice sounding off.

Xari turned, her gaze thoughtful. "Did Jax tell you about her?"

Nya shrugged not wanting to admit listening to idle gossip. "It doesn't matter. Besides, he said today that he's taken the rest of the summer to concentrate on his personal life." She kicked a rock, watching it bounce across the road. "And she must be the reason why."

Jax and the female reached a small pub on the corner. As he dropped his hand and opened the door, he looked their way.

"So. Mom. Dad." Nya turned to her parents.

Ike kept his eyes on the pub's entrance. "Yes, Pumpkin?"

"We leave tomorrow afternoon for Carpathia. Any idea how long the flight will take? And are you staying to see us off, or are you leaving first thing in the morning?" She kept her tone light.

Xari glanced over with a why-are-you-so-enthusiastic-now look, while Nya's mom sadly smiled. "Your father and I will be saying our goodbyes tonight. We've accepted a mission in Russia for the next six months. We wanted to wait and tell you after the Championship."

Nya glanced at her mother. "Would you still have gone if I didn't win, or would we all be headed back to Ireland?"

The question hung in the air like a lead balloon.

Ike cleared his throat. "You won. That's all that matters."

Obviously, Jax had told her the truth about her parents' backup plan. Awkward silence loomed as they crossed the street.

"Pumpkin, you're limping." Her father stopped in front of the pub's large storefront windows.

"I'm all right."

Gia put her arm around her daughter. "I'm sorry. I didn't think about your injury when I suggested a walk."

Ike patted Xari's back. "I'd love to hear more about your parents. Why don't you go with me to fetch the car?"

Xari glanced at Nya; *I'm sorry* written all over her face. "Sure, Mr. Thalestris."

Gia's frame tensed as she met Ike's gaze. His eyes sparked as he squeezed her hand. "You two stay here. We'll only be a minute."

People milled about as Xari and Ike started down the street. Desperate, Nya looked around for some other place to be. The last thing she needed was Jax looking out the window, seeing her waiting like some pathetic Dickens' orphan.

She spotted a bus stop bench down the street. "Mom, do you mind if we sit?"

Concern deepened the creases around Gia's eyes. "Not at all, sweetheart. Here, let me help." She put her arm around her daughter's waist, taking some of the weight off Nya's leg. "You've overdone it. Why didn't you tell us?"

Nya shook her head. "I'm fine. Just a little worn out. I helped track a mountain lion, and we didn't make it back until right before the trials." She groaned as she sat, keeping her hurt leg straight in front of her.

"Yes, I heard about that."

Nya leaned back and rested her head on the hard-wooden edge. The silence became oppressive.

Gia finally spoke. "Nya, choosing your rovni is one of the most important decisions you'll ever make. Let me help you."

Absolutely not. "I think I can handle it on my own."

The black Range Rover pulled around the corner, and Nya exhaled in relief—until it slowed as the light in front of the pub turned yellow, then red.

Damn.

"Sweetheart, I know we never discussed what happened with Penn, but—"

"We are not talking about that." Nya sat up straight.

"Honey, I'm worried about you."

Nya stared at the light, hoping like hell the thing would turn green. "Don't be. I'm fine, Mom."

"No," Gia's voice grew husky, "you're not. You won the championship, a feat only a few achieve. You should be overjoyed, and yet, you seem lost. Sometimes, it's hard to look at you and see all that pain. It's my fault you met Penn in the first place. I should have never—"

"Mom, stop. It's not your fault, and Penn has nothing to do with how I feel."

Even as she said it, Nya knew that wasn't true.

Gia's breath hitched. "I can't ask you to forgive me, and worse, I'm afraid you may never heal. It breaks my heart."

The last of Gia's words cracked, and Nya scooted closer, putting her arm around her mother's shoulders in a rare display of affection.

"There's nothing to forgive, so stop with the guilt. And I'm doing the best I can," Nya whispered, telling her mother the God's honest truth. "I'll go to Carpathia and pick five warriors, but you're right. Something inside me is broken, and it'll never be whole again. I'm disconnected like my emotions aren't attached to me anymore. How can I be someone's equal when the only thing I can offer them is my body?"

"Oh, Nya." Her mother's voice thickened. "You make it sound hopeless, but I promise, it's not. Try and keep an open mind. I have faith there will be someone strong enough to break through that barrier you've built. And when that happens, you'll find love."

"I don't believe in love. You know that."

Gia's eyes filled with tears. "Love exists, but you must let go of the past. Concentrate on the beauty around you and live in the moment you're in."

Nya just stared, trying to find something to say.

Gia wiped a tear from her cheek. "I sound like a sap, but it's true. You've spent the past four years either worried about the future or trapped in the past. You may not understand right now, but someday I hope you will."

The light finally turned green, and the Range Rover pulled forward.

"Dad's here." White hot pain licked up her leg as she stood. She welcomed it, allowing it to wash over her. A crying Gia Thalestris was an enigma. But pain, that was something she understood.

She started toward the SUV, afraid to look back. Gia finally got off the bench and followed.

The stoplight was headed from yellow to red by the time her father did a U-turn, and they ended up in front of the pub again. Nya couldn't help searching for Jax's dark hair and tall frame.

She found him easily. He and the female were sitting at a table near the front; their chairs scooted close. He looked into her eyes, his gaze intense.

Nya didn't know if it was the constant pain she'd been in since the championship or the fact that her mother had brought up a subject that left her feeling raw.

Whatever the reason, for the first time in years her throat ached with unshed tears.

She kept her face toward the window, watching as Jax's female ran her thumb along the side of his mouth, wiping a crumb from his lips. He smiled and leaned back.

There's more to intimacy than sex, Vtachi.

That hollow ache in her chest intensified as Ike pulled away. Nya closed her eyes, trying to drown out the depressing thought that she would undoubtedly experience sex, but true intimacy, a connection with someone that understood her, was something she would never really know.

CHAPTER NINE

Jax stood outside the main conference room dreading the conversation ahead.

He'd seen Nya in town but couldn't do a damn thing about it because he was in the process of telling Joanna goodbye. And now, as if things weren't complicated enough, Ike Thalestris demanded a meeting. He took a few calming breaths before opening the door.

Ike stood at the windows, his back to him. "Who was that *suka* you were with last night?"

Well, at least he got straight to the point. Jax closed the door behind him and counted to ten. "Her name is Joanna, and she is no whore."

"If she's not your *suka*, then what is she to you?" Ike's soft voice held such intensity he might as well have been screaming.

"With all due respect, Commander, that's none of your business. But if you must know, she's a fellow counselor and a friend."

"I've researched every Scythian psychologist on the North American continent. I would have seen her name before now."

"She an intellect and left the Society a while ago to specialize in Allos diagnosed with Post-Traumatic Stress Disorder."

Ike balled his hands into fists. "Why would you bring a defector and an *Allos lover* into this?"

"Defector is a bit dramatic, don't you think?" Jax leaned against the large table, crossing his feet at the ankles. "Just because she chooses to live outside a compound and use her knowledge to help others doesn't mean she should be drawn and quartered. Like it or not, both Allos and Scythian psychology are the same, and when it comes to Nya's well-being, I'm willing to use whatever means available. Joanna is a wealth of knowledge and has used controversial but hugely successful techniques when dealing with the subject."

"You're sleeping with this female."

"Again, not your business," Jax calmly replied.

"As long as you don't have your sights set on my pumpkin, you're right." Ike's eyes found Jax's. "But I've seen the way you look at Nya, and I know your reputation. It concerns me your name is on the list."

"So, you demanded we meet to, what, warn me that you didn't want a Tovaris claiming rights to your *nata*?"

Ike's eyes flashed. "I've always had the utmost respect for your kind, even if you do skirt around the law. You know that."

"Then what is this about? Why did you demand a meeting?"

Ike turned toward the window again as his voice became weary. "Fourth Gen has been working in conjunction with American counter intel. Last night, someone inquired about flights in the area heading to Romania."

Jax froze at the change in subject. "You think the Drahzda know Nya is a champion?"

"It's too big of a coincidence to assume anything else. We've ordered decoys on the commercial flights we scheduled for the champions, and the Chancellor is sending a private jet."

Jax's shoulders relaxed. "Good."

"By the way, what did Nya say to you in the triage room, when I brought in her clothes?"

Jax smiled and eased away from the table. "It doesn't matter what she said. The point is she's waking up."

Ike frowned. "And what does that mean?"

"That it won't be long until she remembers. And when she does, God help you all."

It took Nya little time to pack her belongings. The Society would provide any clothes and supplies they needed. They were instructed to bring only personal necessities.

But the idea of leaving behind everything made her uneasy, and so she stayed up half the night sewing a hidden sheath into the last of her leathers. By morning, her curved blade had a new home. She also packed her favorite hunting knife, ten arrow tips, a small medical kit, a few of her favorite tops, and three sets of bracings that fit her palms perfectly.

She held onto her pack like it was a lifeline as they got into the large SUV. Xari threw in her headphones, while Myrina stumbled into the very back seat. Thankfully, her broken arm still hurt, so the doctor gave her pain meds for the flight. With any luck, she'd sleep the eighteen hours, which included a layover in Paris. Cyrus was their official chaperone until their feet hit Scythian soil.

The first hour of the trip had Nya playing the "what if" game in her head—what if she wandered off and disappeared in Paris. Or what if she hid in the bathroom and missed her flight. Or what if—

"We'll be at the Scythian airport within the hour," Cyrus announced.

Nya sat ramrod straight. *Wait ... what?*

The sudden movement had Xari glancing over. She took out her earbuds and tucked them into her pocket.

"I thought we were flying out of Missoula." Nya tried to keep the panic from her voice.

Cyrus glanced in the rearview mirror. "Change of plans. The Society sent a plane along with two formal embassy representatives. Good news is we won't be departing the aircraft when they refuel in Paris. Once we reach Carpathia, you and the other regional champions will join the Madame Chancellor for a formal dinner."

Excited, Xari leaned forward. "Ooooh, and then what?"

The male smiled. "It's a bigger event than usual, which has the press out in full force. There will be a meet-and-greet after the formal dinner. There, your guide will introduce you to your candidates. The council has thoroughly vetted these warriors, and they are the best match for you according to the personality profiles we created last summer. But if you don't find them suitable, you have time to dismiss them and choose from the uncommitted, which are the males that made the list but were not matched by the profile data. Know that the decision to discharge a warrior should never be taken lightly. Once a male is released, he cannot be selected again. At the end of the first round, you will officially name five warriors that become your Chosen. And that's when the fun begins."

Nya felt like someone had dumped a cup of sand in her mouth. Her fingernails dug into her palms as she fought the urge to open the door and jump. Luckily, common sense took hold, and she sat back, staring blindly at the forest whizzing by.

"You okay?" Xari whispered.

Ashamed to admit she was scared, Nya said the first thing that popped into her mind. "I've only flown on the big airlines. Little planes freak me out."

Xari patted her arm, but Nya kept her eyes on the window. Her emotions simmered close to the surface, and she didn't want her to see. She hadn't struggled with control in years, yet twice in under twenty-four hours she had the urge to cry. Really cry. Ugly, wailing, can't-catch-your-breath-until-you-do-nothing-but-sob cry.

Cyrus pulled through a tall fence that protected a long strip of asphalt, a small tower, and a hangar. He drove down the runway, stopping within feet of a large plane. The thing wasn't one of those huge jets the president had, but it wasn't a tiny crop duster, either.

Cyrus got out and then opened the back passenger door. "I'll come back for Myrina after we get you settled."

"Or you could just leave her and take her back to the compound," Xari suggested.

He bit back a smile. "I know you've had your differences, but Myrina is a champion of this region, too. And it may make things go easier if you try and get along."

Nya started to suggest that maybe he should give Myrina the same sage advice but decided against it.

The engines stirred as the pilot started the plane.

Oh, God. It's happening.

They walked across the small portable hallway that connected the stairs to the fuselage. Two males in khaki's and white shirts stood in front of the cockpit doors. Nya's heart sped as she noticed the official Scythian emblem embroidered on their shirts. Cyrus followed with an unconscious Myrina draped over his arms.

"Excuse me. There are a few beds in the back. I thought it best if Myrina continues resting."

"I'm sure we're all happy you did," Xari said.

Cyrus smirked as he shuffled past, made his way to the back, and returned alone.

"Now." Cyrus gestured to the hulking warriors still at the doorway. "These are our guides who will see us to Carpathia."

Both males bowed, the taller one, oddly familiar, spoke in Dacian. "It is a pleasure meeting the American Champions, I am Victor, and this is Erik."

A steward came forward and closed the plane's door. Black specks crossed Nya's eyes as she realized there was no hope of escape. Panic, fresh and horrible, flooded through her, and bile rose in her throat.

"Excuse me." Her thick voice barely made it across her lips as she dropped her pack and fled, finding the small bathroom and slamming the door.

Nauseous and faint, she sat on the toilet lid and put her head between her knees, gulping in deep breaths of air.

I'm not dying ... I'm not dying ...

A small knock sounded in the quiet. "Anya Thalestris, are you all right?" Cyrus's muffled voice came from the other side of the door, and Nya tried to pull herself together.

"Just need a minute," she wheezed.

The floor vibrated as the plane taxied to the runway. Nya retched. She stood, flipped up the toilet seat, and her knees hit the floor in one fell swoop. Pain ran up her thigh as she lost her breakfast.

She hadn't had a panic attack in years, not since the months after the incident on the docks.

And didn't that bring back precious memories?

Nya wiped the seat clean and flushed the toilet before stumbling as she stood. Trembling hands fumbled for a small basket above the sink. She sifted through soaps and lotions, whispering a prayer of thanks when she found what she was looking for—a small bottle of mouthwash. Dumping half the thing in her mouth, she let the sting of the alcohol wash away the bitter taste of bile.

"Nya." Xari rattled the handle. "I've seen you pee. Unlock the door."

Nya spit in the sink before dropping the mouthwash back in the basket and placing it on the shelf. She held her breath as her thumb worked furiously over her palm. She couldn't hang out in the bathroom the rest of her life, and she didn't want the Carpathian warriors to think her a coward.

Or a nutcase.

She visualized calm sunsets, laundry dancing in the wind as it hung on the line, buttercups, fucking sunshine sparkling on a lake.

Jax's scowling face flashed in her mind, and she half-smiled. Rolling her head from side to side, she took one last deep breath and turned the lock to "vacant."

"No need to panic. I'm feeling better." Nya nudged Xari into the hall. "Just a little queasy. Ready to go?"

"You're not a little queasy," Xari furiously whispered. "I thought you had a heart attack. What is up with you?"

"Nothing." Nya started down the small corridor. "I'm okay now," she said a little louder as she reached the main cabin and flopped down on the leather recliner closest to the window.

Victor, or was it Erik, came forward and took a seat across from her, but she refused to look at him—or the other one. She couldn't meet their eyes. Not yet.

"You know," Xari piped up. "Nya did say she's only flown on big jets. Smaller planes make her anxious. I'm sure it will be better once we're in the air."

The captain's voice chimed over the intercom, something about a seatbelt, but Nya kept her face toward the window concentrating on the simple act of breathing.

Xari fastened Nya's buckle as the plane accelerated down the runway.

The plane lifted, angling upward, and Nya closed her eyes, her knuckles turned white as her fingers dug into the armrest.

"Look out the window, Vtachi. You're flying," Xari whispered.

Jax's nickname broke through the panic and numbness, and a tear trickled down Nya's cheek. She turned her back toward the cabin and placed her forehead on the glass, watching her old life turn to mottled shapes of muted green.

Loneliness blanketed her in utter sorrow, and she closed her eyes, shutting out everyone around her. Someone, probably Xari, placed a blanket over her shoulder and a pillow beneath her head. Ironic. At this moment, the one person who had accused her of running away was the very person she wanted to fly to.

CHAPTER TEN

The plane jarred as wheels met pavement, rumbling beneath her feet. Nya stirred, noticing that her seatbelt had been refastened. Or had she ever taken it off?

"Welcome back, sleepyhead." Xari smiled. "You look better."

"Then I will call her father and tell him not to schedule a flight." Cyrus's voice came from behind.

That had Nya sitting up straight. "Please tell me you didn't tell him I was sick."

He looked offended. "It was my duty, Anya Thalestris. I was ordered to keep him abreast of every situation involving you."

Erik and Victor seemed amused by the conversation—which pissed Nya off more.

She stiffened as Erik stepped forward and took a seat across from them. It had been so long since she'd seen a strange male, she just sat and stared. He must be only a few years older. His ice-blue eyes, almost white in the middle, made his pupils seem endless. Light skin and black hair brought out his sharp, even features. He studied her, and she studied him back. Nya viewed him as she would an insect she'd never seen, while Xari, on the other hand, sat right next to her practically drooling.

"Anya Thalestris," his deep voice rumbled. "Are you not looking forward to visiting your native land?"

Loaded question. She kept her expression neutral.

"All Scythians look forward to visiting Carpathia," Nya finally hedged.

Xari sat a little straighter. "I've been looking forward to this since our third year."

Erik glanced at her, taking in her swinging blue-tipped hair. "I'm sure you will find the motherland beautiful."

"I'm sure I will, too." Xari blushed as she smiled.

"Is your name on the list?" Nya asked, shocking him a little.

"Yes, Anya. Although my profile does not suit any on this plane, and I'll have to wait until a primary candidate is let go to be considered."

Xari beamed at the news.

"Where are we?" Myrina's natural whine came from the back of the plane, and Nya groaned. Cyrus stood, motioning Myrina to her seat, which, mercifully was across the aisle.

"Have a good rest?" Xari asked sweetly.

"Like you care," Myrina griped. When she noticed Erik, her green eyes flashed from hateful to positively angelic in a microsecond. "Cyrus, please introduce me."

Erik greeted her in the Dacian tradition of placing his fist over his heart. Myrina tossed her obviously just brushed curls away from her face.

But it was Victor's reaction that caught Nya's eye. He hadn't said a word since they'd been airborne. For the first time, Nya looked at him. His skin tone was a few shades darker like he'd been in the sun for a while. His well-groomed short beard covered an angular jaw, and he looked to be mid to late thirties. His cornflower blue eyes held that calm, assessing quality that reminded Nya of Jax. But what had her intrigued about the man was the way he observed Myrina like he was systematically cataloging every weakness the female had.

"I'll go and check with the pilot to see how much longer before we're back in the air." Erik stood and headed toward the front of the plane.

Victor must have felt Nya's gaze because his eyes found hers. She kept still, refusing to look away.

What was it with eye contact? Jax taught her early on not to let anyone rattle her cage, and she wasn't about to start now.

Victor finally smiled. "I never congratulated you on your victory, Anya Thalestris. You must be very proud."

The lead-in. He would analyze her response, everything from her words and tone inflection to her body language. She didn't move a muscle, kept her calm demeanor, and tried not to give anything away. As the seconds ticked, Victor's attention held a fascination that bordered on disturbing.

Nya slowly took a breath and spoke in Dacian. "All the warriors at the American Academy were commendable opponents. It is an honor to be considered their champion."

Victor chuckled. "An answer worthy of a politician." He stood. "If you'll excuse me, I need to visit the restroom."

He headed toward the back of the plane, while Cyrus put in his headphones, typing away on his laptop.

"Yeah, right ... worthy opponents." Myrina rolled her eyes.

"Rissa beat you into the ground last week." Xari leaned forward. "So yeah, I'd say plenty of females could be on this plane instead of us."

Myrina's lips flattened to a thin, ugly line. "Rissa should be here instead of Jax's *suka*."

Xari started to get up, but Nya stopped her. "Don't."

The redhead snorted. "I'm so sick of you, Anya. You're all look-how-humble-I-am when everyone knows you cheated. It's no coincidence that you were alone in the woods for days with the weapons instructor before the championship, and then he mysteriously was assigned as your last challenge."

"Nya had no control over that." Anger deepened Xari's tone.

"Yeah, sure. In four years no one, not even the trainers, could put Jax on the ground. And yet, Anya manages to defeat him with her leg ripped open, bleeding all over the place. I can't believe after she spreads her legs to win the championship that you'd still defend her."

Something slammed behind them, and their eyes shot to the back of the plane.

Victor's heated gaze landed on Myrina. "Are you finished berating your fellow champions, or would you rather I wait in the back until Anya has had enough and kicks your ass."

Myrina blanched.

He calmly walked to his seat, his eyes never leaving Myrina as he switched to Dacian. "You've accused a champion of your region and a Tovaris of cheating. I'm sure you have evidence to back your claim."

Myrina's eyes widened.

Nya cleared her throat. "Myrina broke her arm in the Trials and has been taking pain medicine." She smiled at Victor, ignoring Myrina's glare and Xari's why-the-hell-are-you-defending-her frown. "I'm sure that's the reason for her being so rude."

Victor's eyes warmed with gentle humor. "You've no need to protect her. I've read her personality profile which clearly defines both her good qualities and her shortcomings."

"You're a psychiatrist?" Myrina practically shrieked.

Victor sat back in his chair and crossed his legs. "Yes. I specialize in clinical and cross-cultural psychiatry." He reverted the power of his gaze back to Nya. "But perhaps you are right. We will chalk Myrina's careless accusation up to medication. After all, I'm sure the last thing you want is the Tovaris Suveran meeting us at the airport, demanding a challenge."

Myrina swallowed a few times and looked away.

Erik came from the cockpit. "Looks like we're clear for takeoff."

"I'm not feeling well. If you'll excuse me, I'll go back and lay down." Warily, Myrina stood.

Nya watched her slink to the back of the plane.

Xari leaned over. "You know she'll hide until we get to Romania. Maybe we should thank Victor."

Nya smirked. "Maybe *you* should thank him. I'm not that brave."

CHAPTER ELEVEN

A hot bowl of hearty stew had Nya longing for bed. But after Myrina's little meltdown, she'd rather sleep in a lion's den than be stuck in a room with the witch. Well, that and Victor kept watching her every move, like she was an experimental lab monkey. Even though she was exhausted, and her thigh felt like it was on fire, she'd be damned if she showed any sign of weakness. Xari must have felt the same because after dinner she had her nose in one of Rissa's books, completely unashamed of the writhing, naked bodies on the cover.

Nya shifted, trying to ease the ache in her thigh. She probably should change the bandage. And she needed to pee, but she'd been fighting it, hoping that everyone would be asleep before she moved.

That, apparently, wasn't going to happen. Erik played on an iPad, Cyrus was on his laptop typing away, and Victor sat across the aisle, leafing through a magazine.

"I'll be right back," Nya muttered, grabbing her pack. Her stitches pulled as she stood, and she winced.

Victor glanced up while flipping a page.

Cyrus watched Nya hobble to the aisle, frowning as she limped. He grabbed his phone, his thumbs skittering across the screen.

"Oh, for the love of God," Nya finally snapped. "I haven't moved in hours. My leg is stiff, that's all. No need to sound the alarm."

Cyrus sighed. "He worries."

"Tell my father I'm fine."

The older warrior looked at Nya like he was deciding what to say. "I was texting Jax."

Victor closed his magazine, now openly watching their conversation, but Nya ignored him.

"Tell Jax he's off the clock. And, please, keep my parents out of this, too. They're on a mission, and they don't need the distraction."

She walked away before Cyrus could reply. Shuffling to the bathroom, Nya hustled in and closed the door. Leaning against the sink, she opened her bag and found her toothbrush. Getting the fuzz off her teeth felt like heaven, and after she grabbed a bottled water and did the swish-and-spit routine, she almost felt normal.

Now, to take care of her leg. She washed her hands before unzipping her pants and pulling them down to her knees. Yellow had seeped through the white gauze, bringing with it a foul odor. She peeled off the bandage and groaned. The bottom half of the gash had almost healed, but the top still wept with infection. Nya bit her lip as she squeezed either side; thick liquid oozed from between the stitches. She swiped the old bandage across the wound, gathering the puss before throwing it in the trash. Taking the new padding from her first aid kit, she found the antibiotic cream and slathered it on. If it weren't better by tomorrow night, she'd send for someone. It was rare that Scythians needed help when healing, but the stress she'd been under this past month would be enough to lower anyone's immune system.

She shuffled to the door, stopping when she met her reflection in the mirror over the sink.

God. She looked awful. The dark circles had gotten worse, making her eyes seem too big for her face.

Jax was right. She hadn't been taking care of herself.

That's not what he said, though, is it? He said your needs weren't being met, and that's a different thing.

She grabbed the brush from her bag and ran the bristles through her hair until the tangled mess became a long, glossy mane. The tension in her shoulders eased as she pulled her hair back into a bun.

Finally, feeling more in control, she put her things in her bag and started toward her seat.

"Better, are we?" Victor smiled.

"I brushed my teeth," she blurted out for some odd reason.

"Ah." He said it like she'd just revealed her deepest, darkest secret.

She hated it when Jax did that, much less a stranger. It was on the tip of her tongue to lash out, tell him he didn't know shit about her and to quit acting like he did.

Instead, she settled back, pulled the blanket over her, and watched the plane's wing cut through the clouds. Bone deep loneliness set in. A shiver tickled her skin, and she pulled the covers up to her ears.

Stephan stood outside the palatial meeting room, listening to Penn rage about incompetence. Why couldn't the council at least try to keep him calm? He took a deep breath before opening the door and slipping inside.

"If we don't have control of the South American region soon, I'll have someone's balls!" Penn slammed his drink down.

Twelve men, dressed in formal Drahzdan uniforms, sat at a table, their stoic faces never leaving their leader.

Penn paused as Stephan closed the door.

"Sir." Stephan cleared his throat and made his way across the room, bending so his lips almost touched Penn's ear. "Your Ana's plane is in the air, but she's not on it."

"What?" Penn screeched. The twelve sitting at the table winced.

Stephan rushed on in a hurried whisper. "Word has it the Scythians changed plans at the last minute. There was a private plane that took off shortly after, but its destination was France. I believe it is a layover and the plane will continue to Romania. We have operatives in the airport should they depart and go in, but I fear the Scythians will keep her secure until they reach the consulate."

Penn shot out of his seat so quickly the solid oak chair tipped back, clattering to the floor. "You told me we had a handle on this."

The council remained stock still.

"Get out!" Penn shrieked. "All of you, get out!"

Wood scraping across marble echoed in the vast hall as everyone hurried and shuffled out of the room.

Penn waited until the door closed before throwing his tumbler against the wall. Shattering glass exploded in the room, followed by an ominous silence.

Incompetent fools. All of them. First, the uprising in South America, which considerably slowed the Drahzda's cocaine production. And now his Ana not being on her flight. Someone screwed up, and when he discovered who, there'd be hell to pay.

Penn looked at the hundreds of hand-painted scenes on the ceiling, which housed seven crystal chandeliers. The place was initially a grand ballroom, but his grandfather had declared this the "war room" during World War II. His father hadn't had the balls to change it. Penn's council said they were honored to keep the ridiculous tradition alive, but there were too many memories here—memories of being beat as a child during a meeting, or that dreadful day he and his mother had been brought from Ireland to face his father's wrath. The only thing keeping him from taking the space down to the studs was a small, unassuming corner toward the back.

Penn was across the room before he realized what he was doing. He leaned against the wall, not wanting to get too close, lest he disturb anything. Cordoned off with a velvet rope, the curtains, chair, and sideboard held a thick layer of dust. An empty syringe lay under the chair, next to a tangle of shackles and chains.

His Ana had spent much of her first days here while his father questioned her. Penn missed her so. Had she not been taken, they would be getting ready to celebrate their fifth anniversary. By now, she would have come around, quit fighting her future. She would have enjoyed waking up with him, abiding by his rules and submitting to his will. They may even have found a way for her to carry his child—something he still hoped she would do one day.

God. It had been so long since he had felt her tremble beneath his touch. Most of those times she'd been tied down, either terrified or furious, but once, when they were still in Ireland, she trembled in a good way. It might take a while, but she would do it again.

Penn's blood painfully coursed through his veins, but he closed his eyes anyway, allowing memories of the past to flood through.

Her hair felt like a river of black silk streaming between his fingers. Her eyes, blue as the Caribbean Sea. She had this scent about her, musky yet sweet, and the way she laughed resonated deep within him. He knew he loved her the first day they played together as children, and the night he almost took her was the defining moment in his life.

Memories of her flesh, firm yet soft as it filled his palm, and when he squeezed, she whimpered. God. That sound. In all his dark, twisted life, he'd never felt anything close to what that sound erupted in him. A feeling he could only define as hope.

"My Ana," he muttered, running his nose along her jawline. "I love that I'm the only one who's ever called you by that name." His touch became sure as he slid his palm across her torso, finding the snap of her jeans. "And after tonight, you'll always be mine ... forever."

The gasoline pulsing through his veins exploded into white-hot agony, and his gaze flew open as he stared at the chair.

And then Ike Thalestris had shown up and ruined it all. If things had gone according to plan, Penn would have murdered his father before ever bringing his Ana into their world.

Heat screamed through his blood again. Every nerve became excruciating, and Penn finally turned his mind from the past. After he'd been injected, his father had chosen memories of Ireland as a trigger, creating a firestorm in his body.

He trembled as he took a pillbox from his pocket and snapped open the lid. He popped two tablets under his tongue. The pain eased.

Even though his men had failed to rescue Ana from that dreadful academy, it wouldn't be much longer. Soon, she'd be forced to remember, and when she did, she'd come back to him.

And then Penn would spend the rest of his life atoning for all that had happened to his sweet girl. He would build a new empire for her, one where she submitted fully to him. And then he'd treat her like a queen, coddle and protect her. She would want for nothing. He'd rule the Drahzdan Empire, and together they would make history.

"Stephan." He said the name as if the man were standing mere feet away.

The door across the room opened. "Is there something you need?"

"Ready the plane. It's time we complete the renovation of our new home."

The door quietly clicked closed, but Penn's eyes never left the chair.

His suffering these past four years would all be worth it once his Ana was back in his arms.

"Hey, sleepyhead, quit mumbling and wake up." Xari nudged Nya awake.

Sharp tingles of dread had Nya's eyes flying open. "What did I say?"

Her friend bustled around their space picking up odds and ends and stuffing them in her bag. "I don't know, something about Jax and a cub. We've just landed."

"Wait ... what?" Nya yawned and tried to get her bearings. Her head ached, and chills ran through her body. "We're here?"

"Yes. And Myrina's already off the plane. They're waiting for us."

Nya reached for her bag and followed Xari to the front, her thigh throbbing with every step.

Didn't take a genius to figure out she was in trouble here. Obviously, the wound was infected. She'd pull Cyrus aside and quietly ask for an antibiotic. If things got too bad, she'd pop open the stitches and debride it again. The first week was nothing more than meet-and-greets anyway.

They stopped at the small landing just outside the plane's threshold, and the sun shone brightly as a cold wind whipped around them. Erik and Victor waited at the bottom of the stairs.

"Where's Cyrus?" Nya asked, pulling her light jacket tighter.

"He left."

"What do you mean, 'he left'? Where the hell did he go?"

Xari raised an eyebrow. "Calm down, Ny. He took Myrina to the consulate. We'll see him tonight."

Nya tackled the stairs like an old lady, a death grip on the rail as she tottered down, one step at a time. Victor's eyes held hers, his jaw set, determined.

And didn't that just send her anxiety into a tailspin?

As soon as Xari stepped on even ground, Erik came forward. "You're with me," he grumbled, taking Xari's arm and leading her to the back SUV.

Nya stayed in place, refusing to budge. "What's going on?"

Victor gently took hold of her elbow, ignoring the fact that she stiffened at his touch. "Toxaris and Myrina are settling in at the consulate.

And we, Anya, are going to a medical facility to get this wound straightened out."

Relief washed through her, although she resented him taking charge. "How did you know?"

Victor held up a plastic bag that contained her old bandage. "You left this in the bathroom. There's quite a bit of drainage, which is concerning."

Nya's insides squirmed. Who the hell checked an airplane trashcan?

"Tell me." He took off his coat and put it around her. "Do you always shiver, or are you running a fever?"

Nya flinched as his large hand palmed her shoulder. Her muscles relaxed as the body heat trapped in the coat warmed her.

Victor ignored the bizarre behavior and helped her into the SUV. "You should know, someone is waiting for you at the hospital."

She groaned. "Oh, God. I told Cyrus not to call my parents unless there was an emergency."

Victor raised a brow but didn't say anything.

Nya stared out the window as they rode in stilted silence. She glanced at his profile. She couldn't quite place it, but she had a feeling they'd already met. "Have you ever worked with my father?"

Victor kept his eyes on the road. "I've worked with many warriors."

"You'd remember him. Ike Thalestris. He's the commander of the Fourth Generation division. Or maybe you've worked with my mother, Gia ..." Her voice trailed away as she rubbed her temples. "It's more your voice. I know I've heard it somewhere before."

Victor kept his expression neutral as he pulled up to a modern building surrounded by a tall chain-link fence.

"Where are we?" she asked, fear creeping in.

"Relax, Anya. We're on Scythian soil. The doctor is waiting, and then we'll join the others." He stopped at the front entrance, went around the SUV, and opened her door.

"How come Xari couldn't come with me?"

Victor took hold of her elbow again. She gritted her teeth.

"She wouldn't have made it back in time to meet her official candidates. Speaking of which, I've called the council, and they've agreed to reschedule your introductions until you've been medically cleared."

Her chest tightened at the thought of meeting strange males. And the media. Good Lord. They must be having a field day.

Victor glanced over, one brow raised. "Whether it's tomorrow or a few days from now, you will meet them. You can't avoid it forever."

She hated that he read her so well. "I'm not avoiding anything."

His perceptive eyes rested on her once more. "Of course not. Every champion that comes to Carpathia is exhausted and has the same empty hopelessness in their eyes."

Nya glared ahead, ignoring him.

An attendant opened the door as they made their way up a short ramp. Victor spoke in Romanian to the other male, who then scrambled through a door and came back with a wheelchair.

Oh, hell no. All Nya needed was someone snapping a picture of her in that thing. The press would have a field day.

"No thanks. I'll walk."

"Hospital policy. You must ride."

The attendant cleared his throat. "Is there anything else you need, Dr. Ramova?"

Dr. Ramova? Why did that sound familiar?

"No. I can handle things from here."

Distracted, Nya looked out over the lot, her mind racing. A memory from a few days ago finally clicked into place as Jax's voice echoed in her mind.

"… I think you'll like Dr. Ramova."

Nya froze. "You're the one helping Jax? Is that why you've been touching me?"

She knew she sounded crazy, but at the moment she didn't care.

Victor stepped forward, for the first time getting in her personal space. "No. Your therapy hasn't started, and it's common courtesy to help someone who's injured. Enough of this. Either get in the chair, or I carry you. Your call."

She crossed her arms, her head held high. "I'd like to see you try."

His blue eyes sparked with the challenge, and before she could blink, one arm snaked around her waist as the other buckled the back of her knees. He jerked her hard to his chest.

Panic weighed on her like a ton of bricks, and she struggled to breathe. Familiarity washed over her. Pain. These arms holding her—a wisp of memory flooded her mind.

He was there. That night. On the docks. The night her father's team died.

"You carried me ..." Her breath became nothing but short, shuddered puffs. "Why were you carrying me?"

Hot agony shot through her veins as black dots sparked her vision. Someone hollered in the distance, and the world went black.

CHAPTER TWELVE

Sounds exploded as gunfire blazed over Nya's head, the floor beneath her rocked and swayed. Weak and helpless, she strained to break free. Her body hurt like she'd been beaten for days. The stench of rotting fish hung heavy in the frigid air. Unbearable pain shot up her arm in runnels of white-hot agony.

She glanced down. The handle of a knife stuck out of the center of her palm, the blade running through flesh and bone, securely embedded in the floor beneath. Her fingers curled toward the ceiling, her palm drowning in blood. She strained, reaching with the other hand, trying to grab the handle, but a shackle braced that wrist, the chain just long enough so her fingertips grazed the top of the knife.

Screams came from a distance, growing louder, and Nya struggled to break free. The ship melted into a sterile hospital room, and Jax bolted through the door.

"Vtachi, wake up." His large palm landed on her shoulder. Disoriented, her eyes darted from the door to the window and back. She couldn't get her bearings. Which was the dream? Was she in this strange room or on a boat somewhere?

"Jax?"

He flipped on an overhead lamp. "I was at the nurse's station when I heard you scream."

"The room's spinning."

"That's normal. You've just come from surgery."

"Ugh. What? Why?" Nya tried to sit up.

Jax nudged her back down. "Stay put, or you'll get sick. Your femur had part of a claw embedded in it, which is what caused the infection. They're pumping you full of antibiotics now. You should be better by tomorrow."

She groaned. "Everyone's going to think I'm as weak as an Allos."

"It's not that bad." He smiled. "The Madame Chancellor kept the media busy while we moved you to the consulate's infirmary, which is where we are now. And you're only missing the opening ceremonies. You'll meet your official candidates tomorrow."

Her head fell back. "Do my parents know?"

"I called them as soon as I talked to the surgeon."

"That's good."

Jax's eyes cooled as his expression became blank. "I know it's late, but I'd like to hear about this dream."

She turned away. God, she couldn't take Jax's shrink face. Not now. The pain, the trials, the memories—it was too much, too soon—she was too open. She needed to be alone, to regroup and think.

Jax's calm voice drew her in. "Come on, Vtachi. Talk to me. It might help."

Bile rose in her throat as raw emotions grated like sandpaper over burnt flesh. She sat up and brought her knees in tight, wrapping her arms around her shins, making her thigh burn like hell. She looked into his dark eyes, so sincere, and that empty place inside of her cracked.

"It wasn't a dream," she whispered. "It was a memory."

"Oh?"

Her chest felt like someone had parked a car on it. Rocking back and forth, she kept her eyes cast downward, ignoring the tears blurring her vision. "When we first got here, I remembered Victor was there that night on the docks. And now this ..." her voice trailed off. "I think I'm going crazy, Jax. I really do."

The bed dipped as he sidled in behind her, his broad chest covering her back. He bent his knees, his thick thighs swathing her in body heat. Jax ran his large palms down her arms until they encased her cold hands.

"You're not crazy. Now breathe, Vtachi."

Nya leaned back, turning her head so her ear rested over his heart. Feeling the slow rise and fall of his chest, she forced air in, held it, and let it out, matching his rhythm.

He kept quiet, grazing his thumbs over the backs of her hands, and the pressure eased.

"I was on a boat," she whispered. "There must have been a storm or something because we were rocking back and forth. There was gunfire and shouting."

His hands skated up her arms again, swirling around her shoulders and then back down. "Is that all you remember?"

"No. Before the boat, I remember feeling like a rat in a cage. They drugged me and then hurt me, charting how quickly my skin sealed back together. I was injected and then cut, over and over for days. They discovered the sedatives stayed in my system longer if I had to continually heal. I knew I was going to die—part of me wanted to give in so the pain would stop."

"Tell me about your scar."

Her breath became ragged. "We were getting close to shore, but they didn't trust I wouldn't escape, so they ran a knife through my hand, pegging me to the ship like a damn insect to a board. When they shot me full of whatever juice they were using, I couldn't move. I tried to pull the knife out with my other hand, but they had chained it to the rail. What sick bastard does something like that?"

Jax took a deep breath and let it out. "You were taken by the Drazhda."

Nya's eyes flew open. "Do you think they killed Penn? Is that what I can't remember—that they made me watch him die?"

His arms tightened around hers. "Is that what you think happened?"

Her eyes squinted closed as she concentrated on the memory. "I'm not sure. But Penn would have died trying to save me, I know it."

As soon as she mentioned Penn's name, familiar panic surged through her. She became aware of Jax's warm body, his thighs pressing on hers, his hands making their way up and down her arms.

It was wrong for a male to touch her in this way. No one touched her like that. Ever.

Jax's fingertips grazed up her arm and back down, his breath steady beneath her ear.

But why, though? Why did Penn's name make her freak out about someone touching her? What happened that night on the docks?

Her thoughts churned, and Jax waited patiently, stroking her softly, occasionally muttering the same soothing Dacian phrases he'd used since her first year.

Her heart slowed, but conflict boiled within. Trembling, she took a deep breath and tried to rein in the instinct to fight Jax off and bolt for the door.

"You want me to go?" His voice caressed her like warm honey.

Nya's heart hammered as she leaned back. She allowed her weight to settle on his torso. Her head found a comfortable spot on his shoulder. "No, stay."

"Whatever you need, Vtachi. Whatever you need." His large palms slid down her arms, covering her hands again.

Sheer terror drained away, and something else seeped in—a tinge of something real, something warm and tingly and safe. Jax pulled her close, his palms tenderly circling over the rise of her knuckles. The feeling grew stronger, rushing through the emptiness she'd felt for so long.

"You know, I can't remember the last time someone held me."

Jax's chest rose as he took a deep breath. "Third level of Maslow's needs."

Nya half smiled. "Hey, I'm moving up in the world."

Leaning back, he rested his shoulders against the headboard, settling her between his thighs. She closed her eyes as his feet dipped under hers, nudging them down until her legs straightened out and her body relaxed.

He pulled the discarded covers over them both.

"Why do I remember this now?"

Jax tucked her hair behind her ear. "Often, when we go through traumatic events our mind keeps memories from us until we can handle them. It's a good sign that you're starting to remember, but try not to stress about it. Concentrate on the Trials. Your memory will come in time."

The door opened, and a nurse came in, IV bag in hand. She spoke to Jax in Romanian, something about pain meds and Nya needing to rest.

"They're giving you something to help you sleep."

The nurse changed the bag and plunged the syringe into the line. She left, and the room grew fuzzy.

Nya fought to stay awake. "Wait … I knew you'd be in Carpathia. Just not so soon. Why are you here now?"

Jax sighed. "I told you after the championship. I'm here for you."

Heat warmed her veins, her eyelids drooped. "Yeah—as my shrink. I bet your female had some choice words to say about all that."

Jax tilted her head so he could see her eyes. "What female?"

"Xari and I saw you with her—in town." Nya blinked a few times. "She looked sophisticated, intelligent."

"Joanna's a colleague that's been helping me with some research. Nothing more."

She took a deep breath and sighed. "It's okay, you don't have to lie. I saw the way your hand rested on her back, the way her thumb brushed across your lips. And then she looked at you. Really looked at you. She let you touch her like it was easy as breathin'. I can't imagine it ... someone touchin' me like that, I mean."

"Vtachi." His voice deepened.

Nya turned and settled back in her spot. "An' then she turned and smiled at you like you were the only thing in the world ... all soft and feminine. Intimate. That's what it was. Intimate." She tried to focus on his hands, so large and strong, encompassing hers. "You deserve someone good at the whole intimacy thing."

Why did those words feel like someone was knifing her through the chest?

Jax wrapped her in his arms. "You didn't see what you thought you saw."

"Saw 'nuff to know," she mumbled. "An' it's okay. I know the score. You're my shrink who's helping me, so I don' end up killin' someone when they start touchin' my pink parts. You'll go back to your lil' miss perfect, and I'll try not to shank my rovni in his sleep." Her lips turned up in a sloppy smile. "Shank ... that's a Xari word."

"I'm not going anywhere, and you're not shanking anyone."

"Yeah. My big, badass Tova shrink will make sure of it, huh?" She closed her eyes, her voice barely making it past her lips. "I know what you're gonna say ... We got this."

Jax sighed as her head lolled to the side. He rested his lips on her neck. "Yeah, Vtachi. We got this."

A wall of monitors flickered in a hidden room just beyond the Madame Chancellor's private quarters. Alexandra sat in an upholstered chair that looked like something Igor the 1st might have owned. She usually concentrated on a series of screens to the right, which housed all the cameras around the perimeter. Sometimes she viewed the guest hallways, or even a few quarters if she felt there were cause.

But today, her attention was completely fixed on the top left screens of Jax holding Nya as she cried. She rolled the Turkish cigarette between her thumb and forefinger.

"I understand we've made a breakthrough." Victor's calm voice came from behind.

Alexandra turned the sound down. "Looks more like a breakdown, no thanks to you."

Victor's brow rose. "I thought we were trying to jog Anya's memory, not bury it."

"I still think exposing her to someone she doesn't remember is a risk. Now that she's in the Trials, she must focus on finding her rovni. We'll have to deal with the issue of Penn afterward." Smoke rolled from her mouth as she spoke, making her features harsh, ruthless.

"Would it be better to wait?" Victor took a seat next to the chancellor. "Regardless who she chooses, he'll be a warrior of merit. And he won't be happy that his mate has been put through such an ordeal, much less at the hands of the Society."

Alexandra stilled. "And what do you mean by that?"

"You know what I mean. Before young Nya had entered secondary school, she was allowed to have feelings for the son of one of the worst *Allos* the world has ever known. You shouldn't have sanctioned it, and her parents should never have allowed it."

"Ike had it under control."

Victor kept his eyes on the monitor, watching Jax's body encompass Nya's smaller frame. There was nothing sexual about the move, but protection practically emanated from him. She turned her face, resting her ear on his chest, drawing comfort from him. Jax kissed the top of her head before looking at the camera, his angry bitterness glaring in his eyes.

Victor tapped the monitor. "From the way things turned out, I'd have to disagree."

CHAPTER THIRTEEN

"Sir, you'll need to fasten your belt." Stephan spoke in a hushed whisper as the red light flashed overhead. The window shades had been pulled down throughout the plane's cabin, leaving only rims of dismal light. Penn sat alone in the back, his personal guard in the front as far away as possible. Only Stephan was allowed near him, and he strategically placed himself on the other side of the aisle.

The engine roared to life, and Penn buckled in. His eyes ached from the ride over, but the discomfort started to subside. His best scientists were making great strides in lessening the pain wrought from his father's serum, but so far, the effects of the Phoenix were irreversible.

For a brief time in Ireland, Penn had hoped that he could avoid being conditioned at all. But then his bastard of a father threw him in that hell hole of a camp. His "training" began with a series of tests and then injections. That's when the blood fires started. At least that's the only way he could describe the feeling. One wrong thought or memory and every nerve ending blazed, leaving the sensation of being burned alive from the inside out. Death would have been preferable, but that peace only came to those not strong enough to handle the pain. The Drahzdan doctors made sure Penn survived by monitoring his progress. If his pulse became weak, they combined hypnosis and some form of barbiturate to bring him back from the precipice of death. And then they would begin again. Asking a series of questions, bringing up memories they fused with triggers. Over and over, day after day, blood fires ravaged him until his old consciousness had disintegrated. The Drahzda termed the method "Phoenix Conditioning" because out of ashes came a new, ruthless fighter. One worthy to wear a Drahzdan crest.

Even now, with constant medication, the blood fires never truly ceased. Unfortunate that his Ana had to suffer the same affliction. But in the end, when she came to him, submitted to him, willingly allowed him to take her, he would spend his life making sure she never burned again.

"How long?" Penn muttered.

Stephan stirred in his seat. "A few hours in the air, and then another few on land. We should arrive at the safe house before nightfall."

"And Ana's new home?"

"Supplies are already rolling in. We should begin within forty-eight hours."

Pleased, Penn eased his chair back and closed his eyes.

"Um ... Ny?" Xari's voice gently drifted across the room.

Nya stirred, nuzzling against something that was firm, warm and smelled like heaven. God, she hadn't slept this well in years.

"I don't want to train today, Xari," she grumbled, settling in as warmth tightened around her. "Tell Jax to kiss my ass."

"Language, Vtachi." A dark sleep-scratched voice rumbled under her ear.

Nya's eyes flipped open, taking in Xari's shocked expression. She tried to sit up, but Jax tightened his grip around her torso, pulling her against his chest.

"Morning," he kissed the top of her head.

Xari's eyes were as big as saucers. "I ... uh wanted to make sure you were all right, but I see Jax has everything in hand." Her faced reddened as she realized what she'd implied. "I mean, I'm glad to see you're doing better. I'll ... uh, I'll see you at lunch."

Xari closed the door, and Nya groaned. "Well, that wasn't awkward at all. Let me up."

"Not yet." Jax wove his fingers through hers and pulled her closer. "I told you there would come a day when you wouldn't be able to run. You had a breakthrough last night, and we need to talk about it. We're staying just like this until everything is out in the open."

Of course, he'd want to have a session. She didn't need this shit right now. "Let me up."

"No."

"I need to pee."

Jax huffed in her ear. "Nice try. You have a catheter."

Mortified, Nya's head fell back against his chest.

"Let's start with the obvious. How do you feel?"

"My leg's much better, thanks."

Jax rested his chin on her shoulder. "Let me restate. How do you feel after last night's memory?"

She kept her eyes on the large window across the room, glad she wasn't facing him. It was easier to talk when he couldn't see her.

"I'm not sure. Something happened, and I realized that my instinct is screwed up … like it's been tampered with. I think you've been right all along. This has something to do with Penn. I just don't know what."

The door swung open, and Nya froze as the surgeon and a nurse came in.

"And how are we feeling today?" The doctor smiled, acting like it was completely normal that Jax was in bed with her. She lifted the covers from their legs, bypassing Jax's thick thigh like it was part of the mattress and flipping Nya's cotton gown up to her hips.

Heat rushed across Nya's face. Great. Jax had been holding her all night while she was practically naked.

The surgeon took the bandage off the top of her thigh and smiled. Pink flesh puckered around a series of staples, but the wound looked a hundred times better.

"Seems to be healing nicely," she said. "You're finishing up the third round of antibiotics now, and if all goes well, you'll be discharged before lunch. I'll take the staples out in a few days."

"Thank you," Nya muttered, not sure what else to say.

The doctor smiled and headed for the door. "And no more wrestling with wild animals for a while."

Nya shifted the blanket back to her chest. "Like I was doing it for fun."

Jax chuckled, and silence settled around them once more.

The longer the quiet stretched, the more fidgety she became.

God, she hated his waiting game.

"My father is the head of Fourth Generation warfare," she finally stated like Jax didn't already know this.

"Yes, he is."

"We used to talk about everything at the dinner table."

"Where are you going with this, Vtachi?"

She turned so she could see his face. "He once told me about these innocent Allos who'd been mentally conditioned into becoming suicide bombers. I think something like that has happened to me."

His eyes sparked with interest. "Explain."

"Last night, when I mentioned Penn, memories flooded my mind. When we were kids, he'd say that when we grew up, he'd protect me. It was sweet in a weird Allos kind of way. Anyway, there was a flash of memory. We weren't kids. Penn was a man, and he stood over me, taunting me. Like he wanted me to admit I was helpless without him or something." Nya's voice became desperate. "But that couldn't have been Penn, could it? And is that possible? For something like that to happen?"

Jax settled her legs across his, so she'd be more comfortable. "Only you know if it was Penn or not. And yes, it's possible."

"But how could anyone condition someone's mind in just one night?"

"You can't. They'd need more time."

He traced her jawline, his thumb skating over her bottom lip, and the world fell away. She became acutely aware of his chiseled features. His scent. His eyes. His hard body resting alongside her hip. And for the first time in her life, she wanted to lean in and kiss someone. Touch her lips to theirs. Connect in a sexual way.

His deep brown eyes, fierce yet tender, searched her face. "You'll remember everything eventually."

That calm counselor tone had Nya pulling away. Even though she'd been through some heavy shit the past twenty-four hours, nothing had changed. She'd better remember Jax was here as her shrink—this was a form of therapy, nothing more. After the Trials, she'd be off with her rovni and Jax would be back in the States. With that female.

And wasn't that a depressing thought?

Metal clanging against metal rang in the stadium as hundreds of warriors sparred. A crowd filled the lower deck, watching as champions roamed through the arena, solely focused on potential candidates. Alexandra usually looked forward to the first round, seeing warriors spar with both modern and ancient weaponry. The tradition had furthered their race, and she loved being a part of it. And yet, today her eyes traveled across the arena floor like it was empty, her mind on Anya, and the potential political firestorm she might cause.

Centuries ago, Scythians created a council that presided solely over the mating ritual. This assured that politics would have no bearing on the Trials. The governing Chancellor was strictly forbidden to influence or rule unless called upon by the council.

Which made the situation impossible to control.

Nya winning the championship had sparked international interest. And now, all Scythian eyes had turned to Romania. If the media got wind of what happened, the political fallout would be more disastrous than the Chevnian riots. Worse, if the young warrior was seen as permanently scarred by her past, the Society itself could split into two factions—one following the traditionalist, the other supporting the opposition, most likely led by Zander, the Tovaris *Suveran*.

It didn't help that rumors of her goddaughter's nightmare had already circulated throughout the infirmary.

Maybe it was time Alexandra publicly reached out with love and support. That would eclipse any hint that something was wrong, and it would give her a chance to judge the girl's mental state for herself. After all, she hadn't had the opportunity to officially welcome Nya to the trials.

She reached into her pocket and pulled out her phone. "Claire, call the Rovni Council, I need to speak with the chair."

Nya stuffed her hospital gown in a laundry chute and put on her shirt and jeans, wishing she had something other than the clothes she'd worn on the plane. She'd just slipped on her shoes when the door opened.

"Good, you're dressed." Victor walked in and picked up her chart, flipping it to the front page.

"Where's Jax?"

He closed the chart and set it down. "It's nice to see you, too. Come, your official candidates are waiting."

Nya swallowed a few times as she zipped up her hoodie. "Shouldn't I be in something, I don't know, more than just a hoodie and jeans?"

Victor raised his brow. "What would you suggest?"

All right. That was a stupid thing to say. Scythians didn't give a shit about fashion, but the truth was she wasn't ready to meet the males yet.

"I don't know, maybe something that hasn't been slept in."

He planted his feet shoulder width apart. "Your clothes were laundered while you were in surgery, but if you'd rather, we'll stop by your room so you can change. Of course, if we're late the males might think that you don't want to meet them, and the media, of course, will speculate that you may be afraid."

Nya scowled. "Afraid? You're kidding, right?"

"Then let's go."

She glared as she limped across the room. "I know what you're doing. Keep pushing my buttons, and I'll start pushing back."

"Duly noted." Victor took her arm and wove it through his as if they were going to a formal event. "As your official guide, it's my duty to introduce you to your candidates. You will have a few minutes with each to say hello. From there we'll go to the arena, where you will have an opportunity to watch all the warriors spar. If I may make a suggestion?"

Cautiously, she nodded.

"Allow your instinct to guide you. Release any official candidate you feel can't be your equal. This will give you time to look for someone more suitable as well as give the male a chance to find another champion. Honesty is the key to finding a compatible rovni."

Oh God, she might get sick. Nya kept her shoulders back, head high and lips closed, thankful that her bangs hung to her lashes.

"Do you have any questions?"

She shook her head.

Victor slowed to a stop, his gaze coolly taking inventory. "Are you sure, Anya? Your breathing is shallow, your eyes are dilated, and your jaw is clenched so tightly it's a wonder your molars haven't been ground to dust." His brilliant blue eyes twinkled as his voice warmed. "You're obviously upset. I'm here if you need someone to listen."

The reach out. Nya had seen Jax do it a hundred times to warriors before their first challenge. Ironic Victor used the same technique on her now.

"I'm fine, Dr. Ramova. Now, please tell me about each candidate."

Victor started forward again. "It's Victor. We're going to spend quite a bit of time together these next few weeks. If you start with Dr. Ramova, we won't get past idle pleasantries. And I hate idle pleasantries."

Despite her nerves, a tiny smile escaped her lips. "Me too."

"That's much better." Victor patted her hand as the corridor widened into an upper vestibule. "And it's a little late for summaries. We're here."

They stopped at the top of a grand marble staircase. Reporters and other warriors milled around five males that stood on the Scythian symbol in the middle of the foyer. Each dressed in black pants and a colored shirt, which represented their area of expertise, they glanced restlessly around the room.

Cameras flashed, and all eyes were on her. She focused on the first warrior before her gaze flitted to the next and then on down the line. When she reached the last candidate, she froze.

Glittering like diamonds on brown velvet, Jax's dark eyes stared back at her.

CHAPTER FOURTEEN

Peanut brittle. That's how Nya felt—like peanut brittle. Seeing Jax down there had her so tight just one tap of a rolling pin, and she'd shatter like glass.

Reporters circled the males like a rash, and years of training took hold. Nya kept her shoulders back and clenched her jaw as she smiled.

Why in the hell didn't he say anything?

Victor leaned in. "You should know, the law forbids official candidates from telling anyone they've been selected until they are formally introduced to their champion. It is an archaic custom, but one Jax had to follow. Now, are you ready?"

She glanced at Jax as they started down the steps. She'd spent hours with him at the Academy, but he'd never looked as intimidating as he did right now. Dressed in solid black, indicating his allegiance to the Tovaris, made his shoulders seem broader, his jaw stronger. But the most significant change was the aggressive sparkle that danced in his eyes.

Oh, God. Why didn't she just take off when she had the chance?

"Relax," Victor muttered as they made their way to the foyer.

Nya's gaze shifted to the first warrior in line. His gray eyes stood against stark black hair and deep purple shirt, his stare as intense as Jax's.

"Anya Thalestris, may I present Killian McCrae. Born of Celtic heritage, at twenty-eight years of age he's one of the youngest in the Special Activities Division of the CIA. Known for his linguistics, strength, and tracking skills, he's most useful in counter-intel and has served both the Scythian Society and the United States admirably."

Nya held out her hand, and Killian brought it to his lips, kissing her knuckles. "Anya, it is a pleasure finally meeting you."

"And you as well." She took in his even features and masculine scent. "Have you always lived in the States?"

"No. I was born in Scotland and lived there for most of my childhood, but then we moved through my teenage years. That's how I picked up so many languages."

"Oh, how many do you speak?"

Killian smiled, revealing a dimple that ran alongside his left cheek. "Not as many as you, I'm afraid. But I believe I hold the upper hand when it comes to weaponry."

"Oh? How so?"

"When I have something in my sights, I never miss."

Nya's heart sped. "Is that a challenge? Because you should know better than to challenge a Scythian."

Intrigued, Killian's eyes blazed. "That rule only applies if you're afraid of losing."

She kept his gaze, not sure if the instant connection she felt was friendship or the start of something more. "It would be interesting to see who's better with a bow, Killian McCrae."

He leaned in. "Would you care to make a wager?"

"Depends on if I can find a bow. The Academy shipped mine to Ireland, along with the rest of my gear."

He lowered his voice. "I'm sure I could find something to accommodate the intriguing warrior."

"Time's up." Victor stepped forward and took her elbow, guiding her to the next candidate in line.

"This is Han Ming. Han is twenty-seven and is a freelance warrior from Myanmar and holds doctorates in chemistry, physics, and mechanical engineering."

Han was only an inch or two shorter than Jax. His thick, black hair, almond-shaped eyes and skin tone a few shades darker than hers was attractive, but as they spoke there seemed to be no interest on either of their parts. They exchanged pleasantries, but Nya was relieved when they moved on.

"And this is a true Norsemen, Gunnar Wolff. His male line comes from the original Vikings and serves in the Swedish Special Forces. He's been credited with several technological advances in software development."

Gunner's glossy blond hair gleamed as he bent and kissed her hand. When he looked up, she shivered at the ruthlessness in his eyes.

"I look forward to our time on the field, Anya." His deep voice held a rasp to it like he rarely spoke.

She hoped that her leg had healed by the time they got to the finals. This male didn't want an equal. He thrived on a challenge. They spoke of training habits and local weather before Victor said their time was up. She relaxed and moved to the next candidate.

Amber eyes sparked in anticipation as the male standing next to Jax stepped forward.

"You're a linguist?" Nya asked, noting his white shirt, which stood in sharp contrast to his olive skin.

Victor held out his hand. "Anya, may I present Giovanni Rossi. He serves as a leader in Italy's Special Forces, but his primary focus is in counterintelligence."

Giovanni took Nya's hand in both of his, one thumb circling the tender veins of her wrist while the other swept up to her elbow.

The move was hardly inappropriate, but Nya couldn't help squirm as his thumb found the pulse at the bend of her arm. He rested his lips on her hand far longer than necessary, and when he finally looked up, passion sparked his eyes.

"You are exquisite, *Bellissima Dea*. The world pales to your scent, your strength, your grace."

Nya's eyes widened. No one had ever called her a beautiful goddess before.

Giovanni switched to Italian, his eyes never leaving her. "I wish to bring you the challenge you desire on the field ... and off."

Aggression practically rolled off Jax as he openly glared at the Italian.

She cleared her throat and pulled away. "That was lovely." She answered back in Italian, her voice a little tight.

Victor's smiled widened as he guided Nya to the last of the group. "And you already know Ajax Nickius."

Nya scowled, and Jax took her hand and stepped into her space.

"So, this is your solution to finding time for my sessions?" she whispered, glancing down the line to make sure the others couldn't hear.

Jax sighed. "In a manner of speaking."

"And what if I dismiss you?"

His voice turned gruff. "I would respect your decision, of course. But I am an official candidate, given that right because the council agrees that our personalities and fighting styles are a good match." He lifted her fingers to his lips, but instead of kissing the back of her hand as the others had, he turned it over and kissed the center of her scarred palm.

Nya blushed to her hairline.

Jax leaned in. "Your therapy is vital, and your recovery means everything." His voice became a husked whisper, swirling in the recess of her ear. "But know this. I kept my name on that list because I want to be the one you choose. I want to defeat those who think they are stronger, and I want to claim you as my romni."

"Jax," she muttered, not sure what to think or how to feel.

"You promised you'd try, Vtachi. Don't give up on us before we have a chance to see where this can go."

Victor eased her from Jax's hold, and tension burgeoned through the silence. She looked at the others, every one of them held the same expression.

Jax had thrown down the gauntlet, and they were more than ready to pick it up.

She felt as if they were back in ancient times when warriors died competing to find an Amazonian mate. These males prepared their entire lives for this moment, and each one of them wanted her as their equal.

Which scared the hell out of her.

Victor took her hand and wove it through his arm. They started toward the dining hall, her official candidates falling in behind.

By law, one of these males would prove themselves worthy and take her for his own. And after the tattoo ceremony, he would move into her chamber and began the process of creating the next generation.

Nya looked over her shoulder and shivered. How the hell was she supposed to pick someone to spend the rest of her life with when she'd just met most of them? And Jax ... she didn't even know what to do with the thought of him. The budding attraction between them was confusing enough, add to it the fact that if they mated she'd become a Tova. Her heart jumped as reality struck. One of these warriors would eventually be the father of her *vahna*.

And didn't that make her want to run out of the consulate screaming?

Victor's hand subtly made its way over hers, keeping it sandwiched between his large palm and his arm like he knew what she was thinking. The front door opened, and males poured in, making their way across the foyer.

"The uncommitted," Victor explained. "They are only allowed to mingle with official candidates during formal events and meals."

"Why?"

Victor raised his brow. "You must not have paid much attention in your ritual and ceremonies class. It became law several hundred years ago after an uncommitted sabotaged an official candidate so he couldn't attend the Chosen ritual."

"Why would they do that?"

"A champion cannot call on a warrior who isn't present for the ceremony."

"Oh."

Soft music played as they entered the dining hall. Males milled about as warm light cascaded from crystal chandeliers. Roundtables draped in the Champions' regalia filled the center of the chamber, elegant bouquets serving as splashes of color in their centers. Crisp white linens wrapped long rectangle tables that lined the outer perimeter, the area reserved for the uncommitted.

A hush fell across the hall as soon as Nya crossed the threshold.

"The other candidates have been anxious to meet you as well, it seems," Victor muttered dryly, his palm grazing her lower back.

Nya searched the room, looking for her friend. Xari's pink colored tips grazed her jaw as she tilted her head to the side, listening to something her guide was saying. She looked over and waved.

"Ah, here we are." Victor motioned, finding the table in maroon and gold. Her candidates gathered around the elegant bone china. Servers circled the room, filling one goblet with water, the other with rich, red wine.

Nya sat, and the others joined her. Victor was to her immediate left, but the spot to her right was empty. She looked around. Xari's table had only seven places, and so did Myrina's.

"Why is there an extra setting?" Nya asked Victor.

"A visitor has requested to join us." The entire place grew quiet as everyone stood. "And here she is now."

Nya looked across the room, and her heart sank.

The Madame Chancellor was heading straight toward them.

The SUV dipped and swayed and Ike drove the SUV between Russian spruce and pine. A wall of evergreens shrouded them from view, and they slowed, finally stopping just beyond a dilapidated castle's front gates.

"They're already here." Gia pointed to another Fourth Gen unit parked along the southern wall. Guns drawn, the team surrounded the castle.

He took her hand. "You need a minute?"

"I'm fine."

Her voice sounded wooden, dead. Ike searched Gia's pallid features and hollow eyes. She'd been this way since she'd spoken with their pumpkin. What the hell was he supposed to say—everything would be all right? They'd get through this together? Neither of them knew what was in this godforsaken place. Fear crept in as he kept his eyes on his romni. His Gia had been strong for so long, but if they didn't get answers soon, she might just reach her breaking point.

"We're burning daylight," Gia muttered, getting out of the vehicle. Ike's frown deepened as he scrambled from his side of the SUV. He hoped like hell his intel was wrong, but his gut told him differently. The sound of a lone wren cut through the silence, signaling the all clear, and they ran, crouching below the broken rampart. Ike's team closed in as they made their way up the broad steps and onto the front portico. Warped plywood protected the tall windows. A warrior came forward and ran his hands along its edge.

The high-pitched scream of a cordless screwdriver echoed as he systematically took the particle board from the window's seal. Jagged shards of stained glass jutted from the casing, but the entire center of the window lay open and bare.

Ike turned to his warriors. "You've been given the blueprints. Gia and I start in the basement, the rest of you take the top floors. We sweep to the middle and are out in twenty. And you." He turned back to the warrior with the tools. "Watch our six, and fix that damn window so we don't have to take the thing apart again."

"On it." The warrior tucked the screwdriver under his arm and reached in his cargo pocket, pulling out a small bag that held an assortment of hinges, nuts, bolts, wiring, and screws.

Ike ducked beneath the broken glass and stepped into the room. The place had been a grand ballroom at one time. Peeling hand-painted Trompe-l'œil depicting trees and Greek scenes bled through dingy walls. Overhead, dirt and grime covered smaller paintings, which stood among the coffered ceiling. The gray mahogany floors told the room had been at the mercy of the elements for quite a while before being boarded up.

Gia took small flashlights from her pack and tossed them to the others. Everyone looked at their wrists.

"Time starts now," Ike said. Five consecutive beeps sounded before three warriors made their way to the stairs while Gia and Ike took a path toward the back of the castle.

"Blueprints show an undercroft connected to the kitchen." Gia scrolled across her phone screen. "It's over here."

Making their way past broken cabinets and large weatherworn tables, they headed toward a narrow archway.

Stone steps disappeared into the darkness, and Ike took the lead as they descended to the depths below. Rusted metal streaked from torch sconces, leaving black marks along the jagged walls. Water dripped from leaks in the ceiling; mold grew along the crooks and divots, giving the air a musty smell. Gia's flashlight pointed to the far end of the corridor, illuminating an iron door hanging from its wooden frame. Her steps faltered as she stumbled forward.

Within the crude room, metal restraints dangled from the wall along the side where a filthy mattress lay. A wooden bucket stood in one corner, the faint odor of urine still clung to the stagnant air.

Gia's breath hitched.

"This doesn't prove Pumpkin was held prisoner here." Ike swept his light along the perimeter of the wall.

"No, but that does." Gia's voice broke as she ran forward and dropped to her knees, her hand gently moving along crude scrapes in the wall's stone.

Scratched and chipped in limestone was a letter written in Dacian— an apology to a father for sneaking out at night.

"Oh, God. No," Gia's whimper turned into a sob, becoming louder with each painful breath.

Ike looked at the stained mattress and shackles on the wall, and all he could see was their little girl bleeding at the hands of Sarkov.

Gia blamed herself, but Ike knew it was his fault. Every bit of it. He'd allowed their child to be used by the Society.

Hurried footsteps shuffled along the stone passage behind them, growing louder.

"Commander. There's something you need to see."

CHAPTER FIFTEEN

"**A**nya Thalestris. My how you've grown. I hear you've become quite the warrior." Alexandra Vasilica reached out and gave her a hug. Shutters clicked in stereo around them.

Nya's eyes shifted from table to table. Wasn't bad enough that everyone knew the scandal her father caused when he lost their Trial. Now they had a front row show to her godmother's media blitz. She only hoped her smile looked genuine and not forced like it was because these photos were guaranteed to land on the front page.

"Your father will be thrilled when I tell him how quickly you are recovering." She motioned for Nya to sit, and the rest of the room followed suit. "I had to get special permission from the council to join you, but we never had a chance to visit when you first arrived. How are you finding Carpathia?"

Sweat beaded on Nya's brow as all eyes stayed on her. She kept her back straight as she placed her hands on her lap, her thumb furiously polishing her scarred palm. "Unfortunately, I haven't had a chance to see much of the homeland."

The Chancellor looked at the males sitting at the table. "Perhaps you can persuade some of your candidates to show you around, yes?"

Nya kept her smile firmly in place. "What a splendid idea."

Alexandra turned to Giovanni as servers set appetizers in front of them. "What are your plans for the immediate future? Do you wish to stay in Italy, or are you looking for a change after you've claimed a romni?"

"My heart will always be in Venice." Giovanni's dark eyes glittered. "But I assure you the beauty of Italy is a siren's call few can resist. I'm certain Anya will find it perfect for our family."

Nya focused on her plate as Alexandra posed the same question to Killian, Han, and Gunnar. Each answered the same as Giovanni. They had already established friends and a solid foundation. As Nya was in transition, it only made sense that she move, at least until she decided on a career path.

The waiters came to remove the first course.

"And what about you, Dr. Nickius?" Madame Chancellor asked. "Do you plan on continuing as an instructor? The Tovaris would love nothing more than to have you home in Carpathia."

Jax waited until his plate had been cleared before leaning back in his chair. "I've decided to wait and see what Nya would like to do."

The other warriors grew quiet. Admiration glinted in Alexandra's eyes. "You are a true Tova, I see."

Jax tipped his head in agreement while the others grumbled. The Chancellor turned to Killian, asking him something about the inner workings of America's government.

Nya leaned over to Victor. "What did she mean, 'true Tova?'"

Victor smiled. "The Tovaris rarely take a mate, but when they do nothing is more important than that union—not even the Society or their brotherhood."

Startled, Nya glanced at Jax. His eyes bore into her.

The waiter finished topping off wine glasses, and Alexandra turned to Nya.

"I haven't seen you since your rite of passage. Did you enjoy your time at the academy?"

Nya fidgeted with her napkin. "Of course. The instructors are well versed, Montana is beautiful, and I met my best friend there."

The Chancellor smiled. "Ah, yes. The lovely Toxaris. She's the one you rescued during the trials, am I right?"

Surprise rippled around the table. Nya grew uncomfortable.

"Rescued implies she couldn't do it on her own. Had we not been side by side when the incident happened, Xari still would have gone to the next round."

Gunnar grumbled, and Alexandra looked across the table.

"And what do you think of Nya's decision to help Toxaris?"

The Norseman tapped his finger on the table. "It was the wrong move. Had Anya been eliminated in the process of helping her friend, she would now be waiting at the compound for the leftovers, not taking charge of her life and choosing a rovni for herself."

What an ass.

The table froze, and Nya realized she must have said the words out loud. Jax bit back a smile and picked up his fork, but the Chancellor and Victor both zeroed in on her.

"Elaborate, please," Victor quietly commanded.

Nya gritted her teeth, fighting the urge to knock that arrogant expression off Gunnar's face. "The warriors in this room are the best Scythian males of our generation. But according to you, if they don't defeat a champion they're a failure."

Anger lit Gunnar's eyes. "The strongest males claim their warrior. It stands to reason the ones that don't are inherently weaker than the ones that do. So yes, in my book, they have failed."

Nya's wine glass froze halfway to her lips as she glared at Gunnar, unaware the entire place was listening. "My father met my mother in the Claiming Season. So, I guess *in your book* that makes the last line of Ares and the Commander of Fourth Gen worth less than you, is that right?"

Gunnar's brow rose. "That's not what I said."

"Oh, I misspoke. That makes him inherently weaker than you. Those were your words."

Regret flashed in Gunnar's eyes, "Anya, I—"

"I just want to make sure I understand correctly. According to your black-and-white view of the world, my mother was less of a warrior than the champions of her region, and my father was less of a male because he was defeated in his third round."

Cameras clicked in the silence, but the frustration she'd been feeling finally spilled over.

"Make no mistake, Gunnar Wolff. The only reason we're sitting at this table is because I'm not good at following rules, and you and I marked similar answers on some ridiculous profiling test, which is obviously flawed."

Alexandra glanced from the Norseman to Nya. "So, you feel Gunnar does not possess the qualities to be your equal?"

Nya's back became ramrod straight as she set her glass down, not caring that wine splashed over the lip. "I don't see how, not when he doesn't understand the first thing about friendship or loyalty."

Her voice rang through the quiet, and she became acutely aware the room had gone still.

More shutters clicked as the cameras closed in.

The Chancellor slowly smiled. "I'll say one thing for you, Anya Thalestris. You have your father's spirit." She stood, looking at Victor. "Take Gunnar Wolff of Anya's list."

Mutters rippled across the room as hushed conversations exploded around them. The press followed the Chancellor out of the hall, and an uneasy silence settled over Nya's table.

Gunnar threw his napkin on his plate. "If you will excuse me, I believe I've lost my appetite."

And with that, he stormed away.

The remaining four stared, silent.

Nya leaned over to Victor. "How badly did I screw that up?"

"You're always free to voice your opinion. Only, if I may make a suggestion?" He patted her arm. "The next time the Chancellor visits, let's try and keep the conversation civil, shall we?"

Her shoulders slumped.

"Come now. It's not that bad." Victor smiled. "I've known Alexandra for years, and if it makes you feel better, I'm sure she agrees with you."

Her gaze met his. "So, she thinks I should have helped Xari?"

"Of course not," Victor scoffed. "But Gunnar *is* an ass."

Nya chuckled.

Servers carried the next course out, and Victor took the lead as host. Giovanni, Han, and Killian jumped into the conversation, all pointed toward lighter topics, but Jax was unusually quiet, watching Nya interact with the others.

Finally, after coffee and traditional fruit for dessert, the announcement was made to proceed to the arena.

"We'll see you in a minute," Jax muttered as her official candidates left. Victor waited until the males were out of the room before he nudged her along, veering left and heading to a sitting area behind the stairs.

Nya crossed her arms. "Listen, I know I—"

He held up his hand. "This isn't about your little outburst, as entertaining as it was. This is about choosing your candidates. Is there anyone else you wish to replace? The media attention will only get worse until you officially declare your Chosen. It would be better to cut loose the warriors you know aren't a good match."

Nya ran through her options. Even though it scared the hell out of her, Jax stayed. Giovanni was sweet, Killian was confusing, but Han ...

Frustrated, Nya frowned. "How am I supposed to know?"

"Your ancestors relied heavily on instinct. What does your gut say?"

"Run like hell."

Victor's expression became grave. "That instinct is not intrinsic. Search deeper."

"How do you know my instinct isn't intrinsic?"

"And that discussion is for another day."

She blindly looked across the foyer, her mind racing. "I don't think Han is going to work out. We have so little in common."

Victor placed her hand on his arm, and they headed toward the door. "And what of the others?"

"The others are fine."

"All right. I'll see Han knows to look for another champion." He cleared his throat. "Anya, we should discuss—"

"You know, most people call me Nya," she interrupted.

He raised his brow. "I'm not most people."

Memories of rain splattering across his face, his voice hoarse from screaming as he called her father's name skittered across her mind.

She looked away. "No ... no, you're not."

Frustrated and more than a little pissed, Jax marched down a darkened corridor that led to the Chancellor's private suite. Why in the hell did she summon him when he was supposed to be on the field sparring with Killian? He took a deep breath in an attempt to calm his anger. He'd been struggling through lunch, watching other males touch his Vtachi, flirt with her—want her for their own. God. He never imagined it would be this hard.

And now this. Nya was on her way to the arena, and instead of being there to show her that he was her true equal, Alexandra pulled him away by ordering him to her chambers. What could be so damn important he had to leave the Trials?

He knew he'd shocked Nya when she saw him at the bottom of the stairs. The betrayal in her eyes cut him like a knife. If he lost her trust, she might make good on her threat to dismiss him, and there wouldn't be a damn thing he could do about it. He'd lose her for good.

He should have told her; rules be damned. But there was the problem of her parents. Knowing Ike and Gia, if Jax didn't jump through every hoop possible, they'd have him disqualified.

Zander, the Tovaris' *Suveran*, called Jax a fool for not just taking Nya after they performed the *Zvaz*, an ancient ritual not seen in the Society for centuries. *To hell with the consequences*, Zander said. *When a Tova finds his mate, he takes her. End of.*

But Jax knew he couldn't do that to his Vtachi. Four years ago, she wasn't ready for that kind of commitment, and he'd be damned if he'd jeopardize her recovery that way.

Two guards stood shoulder-to-shoulder, blocking a massive oak door. As soon as they saw Jax, they nodded and stepped aside.

He stood at the Chancellor's private chambers and resisted the urge to rip the door off its hinges. Instead, he knocked.

"Counselor, so happy to see you. Come in, come in." Alexandra stepped back so Jax could cross the threshold. "Whiskey?"

"No, thank you. Too early for me. With all due respect, what was so urgent that you called me away from my champion?"

Alexandra motioned toward the elegant furniture, and reluctantly Jax took a seat by the fireplace.

She went to the liquor cabinet and pulled out a crystal tumbler, pouring herself a drink. "Quite a display at lunch, wasn't it? Anya was magnificent."

"She understands the importance of loyalty." Jax's impatience rang in his tone.

The Chancellor sighed. "Dr. Nickius. Four years ago, the Society asked you to fly to the States and assess a young female who had gone through a traumatic event. When you said she needed extensive therapy and offered to stay as an instructor, I readily approved. You've done well with Anya these past four years, and I want to thank you for your service."

"It was my pleasure. What's your point, Chancellor?"

Alexandra swirled the amber liquid in her glass. "I'll be blunt. After all Anya's been through, Ike and Gia want their *nata* to have a future that isn't riddled with violence and death, something a Tova cannot give her. They feel there is someone better suited for her future."

Jax remained stoic, even though rage bubbled inside. "I won't step down if that's what you're asking."

"Hear me out." Alexandra leaned forward. "You've never expressed interest in my goddaughter until now. She was a warrior that needed your help. It's understandable that you might misconstrue your sense of responsibility for something more. But you needn't worry. Now that she has turned away a candidate, Lucian, Gia's choice had Nya lost the championship, can openly pursue her. And they've found a wonderful counselor in Ireland so she can maintain her therapy."

"Interesting theory, Alexandra." Jax leaned forward, his stance matching hers. "But Nya did become a champion, which makes this discussion pointless. Gia has no say in which warrior Nya picks any more than you or me."

"Jax." Alexandra's expression softened. "They have her best interest at heart."

"I highly doubt that." His voice became gruff as his temper bled through. "This is Ike and Gia's pathetic attempt to ease their guilt, but nothing will change the past. The fact remains they knowingly put Nya in harm's way when she wasn't old enough to defend herself from a flea."

The Chancellor's eyes iced over. "Careful, Dr. Nickius. That order came from me."

Jax stood. "And after the trials, we should take some time to explore how you came to such a reckless decision." He walked toward the door. "We're done here."

"There's one other matter. We need you in Russia."

Jax's eyes narrowed. "Not happening. The law states you cannot order a warrior away from the Trials once it has begun. Not unless there's an act of war against the Society."

"That may yet happen if we can't get the Drahzda under control."

"Which won't be this month. Sorry, Chancellor. I'm not leaving. Not now."

Alexandra stood and headed toward the liquor cabinet. "You'll only be gone a few days. I'll make sure you're back before the second round."

"And if I'm delayed?"

She pulled the stop off the crystal decanter. "Then I'll postpone the trials."

"You cannot do that unless—"

"There is an act of war on the Society. Yes, I know." Whiskey sloshed over the crystal's rim as she poured herself another drink. "I'm not giving you a choice. Unless you want to go before a tribunal, you'll not push this. I'm ordering you to go to Russia. Tonight."

Jax's deep brown eyes furiously glittered, although his voice remained eerily calm. "Four years ago, I openly declared that Anya Thalestris would be my romni. If you're forcing me to leave so that you can try to manipulate the outcome of the trials, I will not stand down. I'll fight for what is mine."

Alexandra smirked. "You didn't demand a *Zvas*, so it doesn't matter what you declared."

"The ritual was performed the week after I tracked Nya her first year. If you need confirmation, every Tova will serve as my witness."

Utter disbelief marred the Chancellor's face. "Why wasn't I informed?"

"It wasn't your concern."

Alexandra glared across the room. The *Zvas* bonded Jax to his word, which meant if he didn't shoulder Nya's mark, his lineage died with him, and he lived the rest of his life alone.

"How could you risk losing your line that way?" Even the Tovaris had a bastard child with a widow or an outcast.

He turned to face her. "That's not what we're discussing. The point is, we both know the weight the *Zvas* carries—the Tovaris already view Nya as mine. They will protect her as one of their own." He paused, allowing her to mull that over. "And so, I ask, do you think it wise to set a tribunal of my peers, my Tovaris comrades, and then allow them to investigate what happened to my future romni, which is why I refused to go?"

Alexandra's hand trembled as she finished her drink.

"That's what I thought." Jax opened the door.

"Ike's found the place they held her."

The words hit him like a ton of bricks, and he closed the door again. The past four years Nya's father had been obsessed, trying to unravel the mystery of her disappearance. They knew the Drahzda had taken her, but they didn't know why, and up until tonight they hadn't a clue where.

He turned, giving her his full attention. "And what did they find?"

"Evidence that changes everything. You know Anya Thalestris better than anyone. And Ike insists there's something you should see."

Jax's knuckles whitened as his hands balled into fists. He glared at the Chancellor. "If it's that important, I'll go. But know this. The Tovaris would have supported me had I taken Nya her first year, but I wanted to honor the traditions of our race. As of tonight, I'm done playing by your rules."

He opened the door and quietly closed it behind him. Heading down the hall and taking the stairs at a quick clip, his smooth stride seemed confident and relaxed. But inside panic ripped through him. Abandonment was a big issue for his Vtachi, even though she hadn't realized it yet.

She'd been so open to him last night, but as soon as she saw him from the top of the stairs, she'd started building emotional walls at an alarming speed.

Of course, he'd fight like hell to knock them back down, but the problem was Nya didn't know her own mind. Her parents had taken that from her when they denied her a healthy upbringing. She should have dated. Figured out what she liked in a male and what traits she couldn't stand, maybe taken a lover or two so she could find out what she wanted in a sexual relationship. But she'd never been allowed to explore that part of herself. And that was the problem, wasn't it?

She must be overwhelmed and confused, and he'd made it worse by keeping it secret that he was one of her candidates. Hell, he didn't say two words at lunch, and he didn't show up to spar with the others, something she was bound to take as rejection.

And now, he wouldn't be in the same country for a few days.

Damn it. For the first time, Jax considered the possibility he might lose his Vtachi.

CHAPTER SIXTEEN

Clouds billowed over the consulate's heavy woodlands, floating in the bright sky, their white tufts peeking through the coliseum's elegant open arches. Nya marveled that such a massive stone structure could seem at home among the infinite flora of dense evergreens and vibrantly flowered meadows. Most Scythian arenas were architectural masterpieces, but the Consulate's stadium outdid them all.

She and Victor stepped beneath the entrance that led to the heart of the arena. As they entered the sun-drenched stadium, Nya stopped to watch the hundreds of warriors sparring.

The males were in the same gear they wore at lunch—black pants and bright jackets, which represented their areas of expertise. White, the hue for linguists, was sprinkled throughout the various colors of the science, technology and several weapons industries. Strangely missing was Tovaris black.

A hulk of a Scythian, skin the color of ebony, stood among the others, his dreadlocks pulled back in a loose ponytail, which hung down his back. His thick thighs strained as he charged, his biceps flexed as he swung a large pole with a double-edged axe on each end. The warrior used a halberd as if it were made of air, creating a clean swath through the others. His black eyes glittered with the joy of the fight, his bright white smile a contrast to his dark complexion.

"Who's that?" Nya asked, admiring his form as he dipped and swayed.

Victor pulled out his tablet and tapped on the warrior's picture. "His name is Aren Maori, and he leads the Scythians that protect parts of Africa."

She strained to see around the growing crowd watching the display.

"He's already their Suveran?"

Victor studied her expression. "Yes. Would you like to meet him?"

Nya swallowed. She had to admit, he was beautiful when he moved. The warrior must have felt her stare because he turned. As soon as he met her gaze, he dropped the weapon and jogged across the field.

"You must be the reason I'm here." He smiled, his black eyes sparkled with a gentleness that contrasted his bulky frame.

"Aren, may I introduce Anya Thalestris?" Victor motioned toward Nya.

"Anya." The warrior spoke slowly as if he was testing the feel of her name on his tongue.

She blushed. "Most people call me Nya."

His large hand engulfed hers as he brought it to his full lips. "Most people call me Aren, but you can call me whatever you want."

Nya's eyes widened, and Victor walked away.

"What's your specialty?" she asked. Aren grasped her hand, gently leading her forward.

"Hand-to-hand combat, but I'm also good at negotiation."

"And why did you choose to participate in the trials?"

Aren squarely met her gaze. "My intended died seven years ago during a Drahzda uprising. After the loss, I thought I would never take a mate. But things grow tense at home, and I've been called to lead. Whether I like it or not, I need an equal who can bear offspring. That's how I find myself here."

Startled at his bluntness, Nya looked away. "I'm sorry for your loss."

Aren stared at the warriors sparring in front of them. "It's taken time, but I'm finally able to see a life without her in it."

Nya cleared her throat, and he glanced over.

"Probably isn't something I should be telling a prospective romni, is it?"

She smiled. "Probably not. But personally, I appreciate the honesty. And I understand loss and Scythian responsibility more than you know."

"Being the last of Ares and Otreras line, I'm sure you do." Aren stopped and looked down at their interlocked fingers, his skin so dark against her pale ivory. He brought the back of her hand to his lips. "I am glad to have met you, Anya. I wish you happiness, and I hope to see you again."

She smiled as he let go of her and walked away.

Victor came to Nya's side. "So, I take it the Moor is on your list?"

"I'm not sure."

He raised his brow but didn't say anything.

The ching of metal against metal rang at one end while hand-to-hand combat stayed in the center. The far end had been set up with an archery range. The soft thud of arrows hitting targets was contrasted by the sharp crack of the Urumi, a thin strip of metal sharply honed on both sides. The thing was flexible as a whip and as deadly as a sword.

They made their way across the field. The loud clack of wood smacking together grew as two warriors dipped and lunged, brandishing tall poles sharpened at each end.

"I haven't seen anyone spar with pikes in ages," Nya said.

The warriors must have heard her because they stopped and stared. She found herself looking into identical sets of light green eyes, so bright against their copper skin and dark curls.

Victor stepped forward, tablet in hand. "May I present Luka and Tor Romano from Greece."

The males made a show of bowing with a flourish, and Nya smiled. Playful. She'd never thought of warriors as such, but the word described these two perfectly.

"You ever fight with real weapons?" She couldn't resist teasing them a bit.

Twin sets of brows disappeared under messy hair, followed by two grins.

"Depends," the one on the left piped up. "Would you like to join us? 'Cause I'm pretty sure I'd like a little hand-to-hand time with you."

Nya smirked. "You couldn't handle me."

The other twin stepped forward. "He probably couldn't, but I'd love to try. I'm Tor, by the way."

Nya's lips twitched as she reached out and shook his hand and then his brother's. "It's nice to meet the both of you."

The twins grinned as they picked up their pikes and started sparring again.

She and Victor started forward when she noticed a lone male standing against the arena's far wall. Older, menacing, a long knife strapped to his hip, his gaze swept across the crowd as if he were searching for someone. A thick rope scar marred the side of his face, starting at his temple and disappearing beneath the collar of his black shirt. His shaved head somehow brought attention to the mark, like he was taunting those around him even to mention it.

His eyes narrowed as soon as he spotted her, and a shiver ran down her spine.

"Who's that?"

The male started jogging towards them.

"We haven't seen the swordsmen. Come." Victor nudged her the other way.

She stayed put. "Why is he wearing black? Is he a Tova?"

The male stopped in front of them, blocking their path. "So, this is Ajax Nickius's pet project."

The sounds of sparring died away as everyone around them grew still.

Victor subtly placed himself in front of her. "Zander, this is neither the time nor the place."

"Of course it is. For the first time in decades, one of ours is in the Trials." His heated gaze raked over her before resting on her face. "From what I've heard she wasn't able to make it through her championship round without getting sliced. What makes Jax think she's strong enough to be a Tova's equal?"

Nya's eyes turned to chips of blue ice.

Victor shifted closer.

"You'll have to ask Jax," his voice remained calm, although he looked ready to attack.

"I would, but Nick is off, cleaning up the mess this one left behind … again."

"Nick?" Nya whispered to Victor.

"Tovaris call most of their kind by some semblance of their last name."

"Nick hasn't shared much with the chit, has he?" Zander scoffed. "I told him he was an idiot for getting into this mess. The Trials are nothing but a dog and pony show. Tovaris don't strut around trying to gain the attention of an Amazonian warrior. When they find one worth keeping, they take her, the consequences be damned." The scar around his eye puckered as he glared at Victor. "And why are you on princess duty anyway? This is a job for one of Alexandra's underlings—unless you're babysitting for Nick."

Outraged, Nya bristled. "I don't need a babysitter. I can take care of myself."

"Like you did when we had to save your tiny ass from the Drahzda? No. I've seen how you take care of yourself, Anya Thalestris." Zander practically spat the last of his sentence at her.

Nya's hands clenched into fists. Tiny was one of the biggest insults to her kind. A warrior was muscular, strong, and capable. The way he spoke you'd have thought she was nothing but a wisp of an Allos. And how in the hell did this jerk save her from the Drahzda?

Wait ...

She blinked several times, trying to keep her head from spinning as bile rose in her throat. Images of a black-eyed warrior pulling a knife from her hand flashed through her mind.

"You were there," she whispered.

He bowed from the waist. "Michael Zandros, at your service. My Tova call me Zander, though. And yeah. I was there. And I have this trophy to prove it." Zander traced his scar with his forefinger. "Tell me, how've you been, Anya? Still crying because we took you from your precious Penn? I've never heard a warrior scream like that. You almost sounded like a helpless Allos *girl*."

Nya's cheeks heated with anger as her eyes darted to the warriors listening around them. "Shut up."

"Oh, that's right. Your subconscious is protecting your weak mind. You don't remember, do you?" His expression matched his malicious tone. "Definitely not Tovaris material. Our kind never forget."

Nya's knuckles whitened as she clenched her fists. She hadn't lost control in two years, she couldn't lose it now. "Shut. Up."

"Jax was perfectly happy with his brothers, and then you came along. Tell me, Princess. Do you know where he was when you decided to play hide and seek your first year in the Academy?"

She ignored the question.

Zander stepped into her personal space, his hot breath brushing her forehead, his voice lowered so no one else could hear. "He was with me. We'd just visited a whorehouse outside of Bosnia. Thanks to Doc, Nick no longer participated like he used to, so he stayed outside and kept watch. Shame that Nick abstained. At least for the females. That warrior can make the most experienced *suka* scream. Apparently, he understands what they need. Guess all those years of studying the female psyche comes in handy now and then." Zander chuckled, watching insecurity flash in her eyes. "Of course, rumor has it you wouldn't know about screaming ... not like that, anyway."

She clenched her jaw and kept quiet, refusing to take the bait.

"Want to know what happened next?" He waited, and when she didn't answer, he continued. "After I had my fill, we started tracking our prey. When we trapped them, I wanted to play with the Drahzda scum a little. After all, we'd trailed them for days. It only seemed fair to draw it out a bit—the entertainment might make the effort of catching them almost worth it. But our Nick, he thought that might be crossing some ethical line, so we slit their throats instead of breaking their bones one at a time. Good thing too, because as soon as he got the call you were missing, he left his Tovas, his brothers, *in the field.*" Zander's voice turned to a snarl. "The bodies weren't even cold, and he left us to clean up the mess while he flew across the globe to find a helpless female lost in the woods. Inconceivable, isn't it? One of ours, leaving his family for *you.*"

Nya's head tingled as blood furiously rushed through her veins. Her teeth clenched as her control started slipping. "I've never been helpless. And my relationship with Jax is none of your business."

"Bullshit." He callously smiled. "I've seen you helpless. And Nick is Tovaris, which makes it my business. He's a good male, our Nick. He deserves an equal, not some fragile thing that constantly needs protecting. Hell, he'd be better off with that *suka* in the valley. At least she's intelligent enough to find her way home."

His words flamed the massive insecurity raging through Nya, but instead of crushing her spirit it stoked her fury. She wouldn't cower in front of this ass. She'd stand proud like her Amazonian heritage demanded.

She tipped her chin up and stared straight in his eyes. "Fuck. You."

Zander smirked. "No thanks. I'm not like Nick. I have no interest in an Allos's leftovers."

Complete rage washed over her, and before she knew what was happening, the heel of her palm struck Zander's throat.

Shocked, he stumbled as she whipped her right foot around, kicking him with surgical precision in his temple, his throat and then his kidney before she round-housed him to the ground. The world narrowed as rage took over, and she vaguely recalled sweeping her perimeter with glancing blows when someone grew too close. With lightning speed, she repeatedly punched and kicked him in soft, vulnerable places. Zander tried to get to his feet, but a swift kick to the groin had him back under her control, and she elbowed his head. Black arms wrapped around her, and she threw her head back, grunting as her skull met a nose.

The warrior didn't lose hold. Instead, he pinned her arms to her torso as he picked her up and trapped her shins between muscular thighs.

Nya's chest heaved as she took deep breaths. Adrenaline pumped through her veins. Her mind raced with scenarios of escape and attack. One more headbutt and her arm almost slipped through his grip.

A warm voice chuckled next to her ear. "Be still. I'm not letting go. But I will subdue you in front of the others if you continue."

She struggled again.

Zander stumbled to find his footing. Blood ran down his face, and a fresh bruise bloomed from his jaw to collarbone.

"Let me go." Nya bucked, trying to break free.

Zander made his way toward her. "Yes, by all means. Let her go."

Nya strained against Aren's too large frame. Her thigh burned as warmth seeped down her leg.

"Anya, enough!" Victor's voice rang as his livid features came into view. "You are not allowed to spar, much less take on the head of the Tovaris." He turned to Zander. "And you. If you've baited her into reinjuring her leg, Jax will have your balls on a stick."

Zander didn't acknowledge he'd heard Victor. He kept his eyes trained on Nya as he spoke in Dacian. "You fight well, Warrior."

She glared at him, hating that she was being contained.

"Understand, I had to see if you were worthy of Ajax Nickius, descendant from Troy. Your loyalty to my Tova is commendable."

Nya stopped struggling, her face flushed with rage. "Again. Fuck. You."

Zander grinned and turned to the crowd. "The Tovaris publicly approve the match of Ajax Nickius and Anya Thalestris."

"Like I give a shit!" Nya screamed, struggling, wanting to punch Zander in the back of the head, but Aren's arms tightened around her.

Zander smirked as he glanced back. "I'm sure we'll be seeing a lot of each other after the Trials."

She gritted her teeth, desperately needing space. "Get. Off. Me. Now."

As soon as Zander was out of sight, Aren loosened his hold, she bolted from his arms.

"You shouldn't have interfered."

He shrugged. "You're not cleared to spar. How's your leg?"

It burned like hell, but she'd be damned if she let anyone know. "Peachy."

She dusted the dirt off her pants, bypassing the warm, wet spot that now rested over her wound.

Aren stopped her hands, trapping them between his. "Please don't hold this against me, the fact that I was the one who finally stopped you."

Nya warily looked around. "What do you mean?"

"You knocked three other warriors down while keeping the Tovaris Suveran on his knees. After today, you'll be the stuff of legend."

Nya groaned. That's all she needed. More notoriety. "Wasn't a big deal. I'm sure it'll blow over in a few days."

"I doubt it." Aren grinned, pointing to a camera in the stands. "Right now it's being broadcast on every Scythian channel. Still, I do regret holding you back. It would have been interesting to see what happened when the Tova found his footing."

Nya shrugged. "I would have fought until one of us went down."

The males around her growled their approval.

Aren's obsidian eyes glittered, and he surprised her by pulling her in for a tight hug.

"Aren, what—"

"Choose me," he whispered in her ear. "Please. Choose me."

Nya blushed as he released her and walked away.

Gia stirred, and Ike wrapped her in his arms, settling her back into sleep. The cloying scent of stale air freshener wafted through the small room, a lumpy mattress reminding him they were in a seedy hotel and not at home.

He'd give anything to be back in Ireland. This region held nothing but bad memories.

And now, that damn castle.

God. If he had a chance to go back, things would be different. For starters, during his Trial, he would have been honest with Alexandra and withdrawn before he became one of her Chosen. Instead, he made fools of them both.

Back then, he'd been nothing but a young buck hell-bent on claiming a champion. Arrogant and full of pride, Ike wanted the best, and Alexandra was it. Already an elite member of the Society and the daughter of the reigning chancellor, she seemed to have it all. As soon as Ike put his name on the list, the media went into a feeding frenzy, calling Ike and Alexandra the "dream team." They were a storybook tale—the stuff of legend. Passion sparked as soon as they met. But as he got to know her, doubt settled in. Other than sexual compatibility, they had little else in common. Worse, she was determined to follow her father's political footsteps and stay in Carpathia, but he loved being on the frontline of the Drahzdan war.

Instinctively, he knew they'd never work. But instead of acting like a male of worth and being honest with Alexandra, he kept quiet and led her on. He'd never forgotten their final round. The way the shadows stretched across the arena floor, like bars on a cage, his name ringing over the thunderous applause. Alexandra charged, and the arena went wild. He ducked at the last moment, her knuckles grazing his cheek. She smiled, saying he was smart to give the crowd a good show—it would boost their ratings.

That's when brutal reality took hold, and he saw a dismal future flash before his eyes. She loved what he hated most— the media attention and political games. He couldn't take a lifetime of being trapped in front of cameras, forever by her side, while his fellow warriors fought to defend their way of life. Alexandra charged again, but this time his hands stayed by his side. She struck him in his chest before spinning, catching the base of his jaw with her heel. His head flew back, and he went down like a sack of rocks.

After all these years, he still remembered the crowd's collective gasp, still smelled the grit of the dirt as it settled around his shoulders, still felt the air cool as the sun disappeared behind the coliseum's stone. But nothing was more embedded in his memory than Alexandra bending over him, her eyes full of shock and betrayal as she demanded he get up.

"After all these years, she's still on your mind, isn't she?" Gia's sleep-scratched voice pulled him out of his thoughts.

Ike kissed her head as he trailed his fingers up and down her bare back. "Nya heading off to Carpathia has stirred memories, that's all."

The silence grew heavy.

"If you could go back, would you do things differently?"

His fingers stilled. "I wouldn't change claiming you. But yes, after Pumpkin was born I would've handled things differently."

After his Trial was over, the media became relentless. Sick of the constant embarrassment and humiliation, Alexandra secretly met with Ike and demanded he find a way to fix the mess he'd made. So, they came up with a plan. Instead of avoiding each other, they were openly seen laughing like old friends at social events. Alexandra promoted Ike to the Commander of Fourth Gen, and Gia went to the consulate at least once a month to have lunch with the Chancellor. God, Gia hated those visits— but she did it anyway. Alexandra made sure that every holiday, every family milestone, was turned into a PR event, showing the three of them as close-knit friends. And through it all, Gia never complained.

Ike's fingers grazed his romni's familiar curves. Her hair spilled across the pillow like spun honey, her beautiful scent, as always, intoxicated him.

"Gia," he whispered, leaning in and nipping the ink he'd placed over her heart.

She tensed. "After today, what we found in the castle, I can't. I need time."

He met her gaze. "And I need you."

She rolled away from him, tucking her hands under her pillow. "You've never needed me, except to create an offspring." Her lifeless voice spilled into the darkness like poison in a stream. "And when Nya needed me, I didn't protect her. I should have left you as soon as she was born. We could have gone anywhere, lived on the fringes of the Society, somewhere far away from Penn."

Ike eased onto his back and looked at the water stain running along the ceiling. "We should have left together."

"You wouldn't have gone against Alexandra and the Society, and we both know it."

"I would have for you."

Gia stayed silent, and Ike leaned in and kissed her shoulder. "We've been up for over forty-eight hours straight. Get some rest. We'll talk later."

Weak afternoon light peeked through the worn curtains, its beam streaming across the floor. Ike watched dust motes float in and out while he listened to his romni's breath ease into a slow, steady rhythm.

Honestly, he wouldn't blame her if she left him. He'd missed too many opportunities to prove that she was the most important thing in his life. There were too many words he'd left unsaid, too many actions not taken. It took time to build an *Intima* bond, but he had done little to nurture their connection, and after a while, Gia stopped trying.

Ike put his arm around his romni, settling her back against his chest. She clutched her pillow tighter, a small crease appeared between her eyes, and his heart ached.

Even in sleep, she kept her distance. And now this. What they'd discovered at the castle had taken its toll. If anything else happened, it would destroy Gia.

And that was the only thing that would destroy him, too.

CHAPTER SEVENTEEN

A horn sounded overhead, and all sparring stopped. Warriors milled out of the arena, some clapping Nya on the back with hearty congratulations for taking down a Tova.

Shit. Aren was right. This wouldn't blow over.

"The three you defeated have been dismissed," Victor said as he took her arm. They followed the others to a narrow path which lead to the consulate. "Now, tell me. How badly did you injure your leg?"

"I think I pulled a few staples, but it doesn't hurt like it did before."

Victor's gaze swept over her. "Are you able to continue?"

"Do I have a choice?"

He ignored the comment. "Tonight's dinner is a formal affair in which the champions will socialize with the uncommitted. Jax, Giovanni, and Killian will dine at the outer tables while you interview other males."

"Swell."

He stopped in the middle of the path, and a few warriors behind them grumbled as they passed by. "There is one other matter. Champions must have five official candidates at all times, although during the first round it is her right to change them as she sees fit. As you have let two of your original warriors go, we must choose two more before tonight's affair. Are you interested in any that you've seen so far?"

"I like the Romano twins."

"Tor's been disqualified."

Nya's brows rose under her bangs. "What? How?"

"He was one of the males you took out when you tried to kill the leader of the Tovaris." Victor nudged her, and they started forward again.

"I didn't know he was their *Suveran*. And I wasn't trying to kill him. I just lost control for a minute. I don't remember Tor coming toward me."

"That's because your eyes never left your target, but you kicked Tor into the crowd, and so he's no longer considered a viable candidate."

Nya sighed. "Poor guy."

That seemed to amuse Victor. "So, the other then? Luka?"

"All right. I'll choose Luka."

"Well, that's settled."

"Wait, what about the fifth?"

"I had assumed you would choose the Moor."

Nya tensed. "I'm not sure …"

"Yes, you are." Victor's voice deepened. "But your loyalty to Jax is clouding your decision."

Nya's face heated, and she kept her gaze pointed forward.

The narrow path wound through dense woods and thickets but eventually opened to a clearing just behind the consulate's courtyard. Old gas torches lined the cobblestone trail that ran alongside the massive stone structure. As soon as they started down the side of the building, Xari came running from the trees.

"What took you so long?" She hugged Nya. "I've been waiting out here since you set that Tova on his ass. I wouldn't have believed it if I hadn't seen it for myself."

Nya groaned, pulling away from her friend. "How bad is it?"

"Let's just say you kicking that male in the balls has been trending for hours."

Nya scrubbed her face with her hand. "I lost my shit out there, Xar. I haven't done that in two years."

She shook her head. "Didn't look that way to me. I saw a warrior being challenged. You did what any Scythian would do, only you did it better."

"Really? I didn't look like a raving lunatic?"

Xari rolled her eyes. "Hardly. You looked like a bad ass."

They started forward again, and the sound of a restless crowd buzzed in the distance. Victor offered each female an arm, and side by side they faced the reporters that had gathered on the consulate steps.

"Anya! Can you tell us what prompted you to spar with the leader of the Tovaris?"

"Have you replaced the two candidates you've dismissed?"

"Toxaris, can you confirm the rumor that you have released a warrior also?"

Xari and Nya smiled, not saying a word while Victor calmly informed the media that neither champion would be answering questions at this time. He opened the door and Xari nudged Nya through.

For some reason, the media stayed at the consulate's steps like scalded dogs.

"Is it true?" Nya asked as they milled through the warriors mingling in the foyer.

"What?"

"That you released one of your candidates."

Xari shrugged. "He and I didn't have much in common."

They stopped by the palatial stairs, and Nya grasped her friend's hand. "I'm sorry. I suck as a friend. I haven't even asked how your Trials are going."

"You don't suck. You've just got a lot on your mind." Xari nudged her shoulder. "I'll see you later."

She smiled at Victor and walked away.

A commotion at the top of the stairs had all eyes collectively looking up. Alexandra peered over the rail, her livid expression etched unforgiving lines along her nose and mouth. She searched the room until she found Nya. Hushed whispers followed her clipped stride as she made her way down the stairs. The warriors backed away, giving her space.

"Chancellor." Victor's calm voice eased Nya's anxiety. "What a pleasant surprise. Your support in these Trials is commendable. I'm sure the Scythian world is eager to hear your take on the Trials this year."

Alexandra stared at Victor, taking in his subtle warning. Warriors gathered around them, openly curious, and she smiled, though her eyes remained hard as stone.

"Yes, I must say the skills of our uncommitted are impressive. I'm sure all the champions are struggling to narrow their choices to just five males." She tipped her head to the uncommitted now crowding around them. "You are a testament to the excellence of our kind. Please, don't let me keep you from getting ready for the festivities."

The warriors bowed en masse, and they started to disperse. Alexandra grabbed Nya by the upper arms, pulling her into an embrace. To the casual observer, the move looked like a godmother showing affection for her charge, but Alexandra's grip bit into Nya's arms, and her whisper was nothing but an angry hiss.

"You listen to me. Your little stunt today has raised a lot of questions. Tell me, what reason should I give the press when they ask why you attacked the *Tovaris Suveran*." Alexandra's fury bled through her tone as she tightened her grip. "I will not have another Thalestris creating a scandal. Be warned, Anya ..."

The pungent aroma of Turkish tobacco overwhelmed Nya's senses, and pain lashed through her head as the Chancellor's words fell away.

"That smell ..." She pushed the Chancellor away, stumbling back, blindly reaching to catch her balance. "I remember that smell ..."

"I beg your pardon? I don't know ..."

Nya's eyes became hollow, blank, as dark memories swept her away.

Snippets of Turkish conversations echoed, bouncing off of metal walls, and Nya lifted her head. Tobacco smoke curled, twisting as it climbed to the ceiling of a cargo hold. Every time she moved, cable laid rope chafed her wrists and ankles until they grew bloody. Thick bars caged her in a makeshift cell, her hands pinned overhead. Pain throbbed in her shoulders from hours of holding her weight. Rats skittered along the edge of the floor, their whiskers and fur tickling the tops of her feet. The heavy chink of a metal lock echoed, and a man stepped into her cage, followed by several others.

"Are you ready to discuss things like an adult?" Penn's deep voice sliced through her heart.

Why? Why was she in a cell suspended against a wall? And why would Penn act like he enjoyed her pain? He was her friend.

"... Anya? Anya, are you all right?" Victor's voice came from behind her, somewhere in the distance.

"Answer me, Ana. Are you ready to submit?"

A band tightened around her chest. Her breath became a rapid tattoo as she fought to distinguish between memory and reality.

Victor's hands landed on Nya's shoulders. He pressed his thumbs along the base of her neck to the point of pain and pulled her back against his chest. Whiskers brushed the top of her ear as he leaned in and whispered. "Focus, Anya. Concentrate on what's in front of you and breathe."

The ship melted away, and she found herself in a foyer with warriors crowded around her. Someone must have alerted her candidates because Jax, Killian, and Giovanni pushed their way through the crowd.

Jax stopped in front of her, blocking everyone else from her sight. He rocked back on his heels, his voice eerily calm. "Talk to me, Vtachi."

Desperate and vulnerable, she focused on the only one who understood. "There were Turks on board ... they smoked ... I remember the smell ..."

He glanced at her thumb furiously rubbing over her scar. "What else do you remember?"

"It was that night ... on the docks. They drugged me when we stepped into the boat, and when I woke up, I was hanging by my wrists. Penn ... he was there."

The room buzzed at the mention of Penn's name, and Nya glanced around.

Oh, God. How many had seen her freak?

"How could a female warrior just days out of training already have experienced the darkest side of war?" Killian furiously turned on the Chancellor. "And Penn—is she speaking of Penn Sarkov, the Drahzdan Tsar? Why was she anywhere near him? As her future rovni, I demand an answer."

"As do I," Giovanni said.

"Wait ... Penn is the leader of the Drahzda?" Nya's legs strained to hold her weight. "I don't understand."

Jax cursed as he stepped forward. "Vtachi, Dmitri Sarkov was Penn's father."

Nya's complexion became pasty white. "But that's impossible."

Aren and Luka made their way through the crowd.

"What is this? Anya was taken by the Drahzda? When?" Aren's black eyes glittered as they bore into the Chancellor.

Alexandra pulled herself to her full height. "Now is not the time."

"I think it's a perfect time," Killian snarled. "Tell us, how is it possible that Nya, the last of Ares and Otrera's line, knew Sarkov in the first place.

And when was she taken? Either she worked for the Society before she went to the academy, which is ludicrous, or something happened while she was at school. Which is it?"

Bile rose in Nya's throat as horrid images flashed in her mind.

"Answer me, Ana. Are you ready to submit?"

Victor's thumb found the pressure point at the base of her neck again, and she sucked in a deep breath through her nose. Pain forced her mind to stay in the present. She trembled, pulling her spine straight until her head rested under his chin.

Warriors pressed in, their questions rose through the hall like a swarm of angry hornets, and the Chancellor held up her hand, waiting for complete silence.

"What happened to Anya Thalestris was tragic, but the information is classified. Let's not lose focus on why you all are here. Concentrate on your Trials, Warriors. Rest assured, the Society is taking care of the situation."

Warriors glared in silent accusation as the Chancellor ascended the stairs and disappeared from sight—and then all eyes turned to Nya.

Oh, God. This was her worst nightmare. Everyone knew. They'd seen her blank. They heard her say that she'd been captured and was defenseless. Mortified, she stared at the floor.

Jax, Killian, Giovanni, Aren, and Luka encircled her as Victor wove through the males, speaking to those he knew, and soon the warriors dispersed.

Blonde hair bobbed in and out of the thinning crowd as Xari hurried over. "You okay?"

"Not really." Nya's voice shook.

Victor stepped close and addressed Nya's candidates. "If you will excuse us, my champion needs time to decompress." He took her arm.

Nya's feet stayed glued to the floor. "Not now."

Victor's brow rose. "Now."

Nya hated admitting it in front of her candidates, but damn it, enough was enough. Between Zander setting her off and now this, she wanted for just one red-hot minute to be alone. Her voice lowered to a resentful, bitter tone. "It's going to be hard enough facing everyone tonight. You screw with my head now, and I'll lose it."

Xari stepped forward. "She's right. Come on, Ny. Let's go to your room and see how much damage you've done to that thigh, and then I'll help you get ready for dinner." She didn't wait for Victor's reply. Instead, she linked her arm through Nya's and whisked her away.

CHAPTER EIGHTEEN

Xari chattered about her candidates all the way to Nya's room, pointedly ignoring the warriors staring as they passed by. They turned down Nya's corridor, which, thankfully, was empty.

"I take it you ripped a staple?" she said, noticing Nya's slight limp.

"Hurts like a mother." Nya groaned.

"Good news is this day is supposed to be over around midnight."

"Smart ass."

Xari slowed their pace. "Seriously, Ny. You all right?"

She stopped at her suite and focused on putting the key in the lock. "Other than a bruised ego, a torn thigh, and wondering if I'm losing my mind, I'm fine."

The hinge creaked as the door swung open, and Nya cringed, hating the over-the-top décor of her room. Bolts of rich fabrics hung in soft arcs from the ceiling's center, stemming to the corners of the chamber. Two-story windows ran along the back, a platform bed stood boldly in the middle of the space. A large flat screen hung along the dark-paneled wall opposite the windows. The place was an amalgam of old world royalty and modern-day technology.

They walked in and Xari closed the door behind them. Nya hobbled past the bed to a small seating area by the closet and lush bathroom. Sitting on one of the chairs, she gritted her teeth and pulled off her shoes.

Xari leaned against the threshold. "I'm not going to pretend that I understand what's going on. But if you need me, you know I'm here."

Nya kept her gaze down, focusing on unbuttoning her pants. "You remember my nightmares?"

"They're not easy to forget."

She shifted her hips and eased her pants down her legs. "I'm beginning to think they really happened."

Thunderstruck, Xari froze. "I hope you're wrong."

"I do, too." Nya ripped the blood-stained bandage from her thigh. Flesh hung from one edge of the top staple, the other side dug a little deeper than the rest. She grabbed hold of the shard sticking up and pulled. Crimson trickled down her thigh as the staple ripped through skin. She fumbled for a washcloth and pressed down on the fresh wound.

Xari cringed and sat in the chair opposite her friend. "I'd put something over it before your lineage team gets here. If they're anything like mine, they'll probably faint at the sight of blood."

"What the hell is a lineage team, anyway?"

Xari smirked. "They're in charge of making sure your instincts are clear."

"English, Xar."

She sighed. "You'll see. Luckily, we only have to deal with them this round. They're supposed to help you clear a path so you can find your Chosen."

Nya pulled the washcloth away. Blood welled, and she found a clean swatch of cloth and pressed in again. "Sounds like a blast."

"It's not that bad, actually. Tonight, we'll be getting to know the uncommitted. From what I understand, each course will not only bring new food but new warriors, too. The good news is your guide is supposed to be taking notes, so you don't get overwhelmed."

"Too late."

Xari grinned. "I know, right? Anyway, it gives the champions a chance to see if they want to choose someone other than their official candidates."

Nya rubbed her forehead. "How awkward is this formal thing? Am I going to hate it?"

"Nah." Xari grinned. "After kicking a Tova's ass, wearing a dress and chatting with males will be a piece of cake."

"I think I'd rather take on the Tova."

"Sicko." Xari chuckled.

Nya pulled the cloth away, pleased that the bleeding had stopped. "In case I didn't say it already, thanks. I needed a few minutes of normal after this afternoon's drama."

"Anytime." Xari stood. "I wish I could stay, but my team will panic if I'm not there to greet them." She walked to the door. "Ny?" She hesitated. "About the nightmares. I've heard what you screamed. We've never talked about it, but those awful dreams ... they can't be true. They just can't." Her voice grew thick, and she walked out the door.

Silence blanketed the room in peaceful quiet, and Nya eased against the back of the chair, grateful for a moment alone. Since she'd lost control in the arena, she'd been wound tighter than a drum. Alexandra's threat and that nasty memory hadn't helped. God. She didn't know if she could take any more shit. Victor was right. She did need to decompress, but that usually meant Jax challenging her to some ridiculous contest in the woods. They'd scale a cliff or run up the mountain until she dropped. And then he'd sit beside her, chipping away at whatever set her off until she finally talked it through.

But here, she had no outlet. And then there was this damn dinner. No way she'd get out of it, not after missing the first one. Her thigh burned as she stood. Most people shied away from pain, but sometimes, like today, when she got lost in her own head, it was the only thing that kept her grounded.

Proving yet again what a freak she was.

Nya grabbed her robe and headed to the bathroom. The shower was a large affair with multiple heads and a marble bench. Sure, it was nice enough, but what she wouldn't give for a good old-fashioned bath. One of her earlier memories was of an old clawfoot tub. She'd soak in the thing until her skin pruned. And then her mother would towel her off and brush her hair. That was before Ireland, though.

Hot water cascaded over her, and she slathered her body with a jasmine scented body scrub. A quick knock startled her as a husky French accent bled through the door. "Anya Thalestris. Quick, please. Finish showering, yes?"

Nya hung her head and turned off the faucet. She dried her body, placed a fresh bandage on her thigh, and put on her robe. Someone knocked again, and the tension she'd managed to wash away came back.

She flung open the door. "I take it you're my team."

Surprised at the sarcasm, the four strangers stared back at her.

"That would be correct." The French female stepped forward. "I am

Brigitte. Now come. We haven't much time." She nudged her toward a chair. Two females knelt at her hands and feet while Brigitte tackled her hair.

A male entered the room carrying a ceramic jar with her family's crest embedded on the lid. As soon as he opened the top, fragrant wisps of something musky yet sweet floated through the air.

"I like that scent. What is it?" Nya's head jerked to the side as Brigitte found a tangle.

He smiled as he handed the container to the female at Nya's feet. "These were the oils Otrera wore the night she chose Ares for her mate. She loved Red Lotus, which honors true authenticity and purity of heart. And all Amazonians wore Jasmine, which is associated with fertility. This cleansing ceremony is designed to give females clarity. The oil is said to wash away the dirt of the past, cleansing the feet to help find the right path. Pummel stones make the palms sensitive to touch. The original Amazon's believed the heart and hands were spiritually connected, and so they kept their palms free from calluses so they would remain sensitive to touch, which helped them to find the right Chosen."

Nya looked at her scarred palm. Sometimes symbolism was a bitch, wasn't it?

As the females pressed, prodded, combed and braided, she realized Jax was right. While she didn't think she'd ever be comfortable with strangers touching her, she also didn't have the urge to punch them in the throat either.

Maybe this wouldn't be as bad as she thought.

The females finally stood. "Your gowns are in the wardrobe. We'll wait for you in the other room."

Hair up in a way-too-complicated mass of jasmine flowers and clips, she stood alone in the small sitting area and opened the wardrobe door. The three gowns that hung to the floor were identical except the first was sapphire blue, the second white, and last dark forest green.

Nya took the sapphire dress from the hanger and slid it over her head. The Grecian design was simple. One thick band rested on her right shoulder. Her left shoulder remained bare, assuring the tattoo trailing under her collarbone and around an empty place on the top of her arm could be seen. The intricate design held every symbol in her lineage dating back thousands of years. After the Trials, Nya's equal would ink his emblem in the blank space at the top of her arm, and she would then wind her mark around his chest and shoulder, leaving them with identical symbols. And when the claiming ceremony was over, they would go into this very bedchamber and place one more tattoo over each other's heart— one of significance, honor, and devotion. It was the most sacred ceremony, seen only by two. The meaning of the symbol was never revealed to anyone other than their mate and rarely seen in public. Marking was an artform honed by time. Scythian *vahna* spent years in drawing and inking classes to prepare for their claiming night. It was said the act of marking your mate was more intimate than sex.

And didn't that scare the shit out of her?

Panic ran through her in sharp, hot tendrils, and Nya tried to contain the pressure building within. After her stunt with Zander and then her freak out in the foyer, she couldn't lose her shit again.

Distracted, she made her way out of the sitting chamber.

Brigitte gasped and clapped her hands together. "Parfait!"

'Perfect' wasn't exactly how Nya felt, but she kept quiet. The male knelt before her, placing her feet in flat sandals with ribbons that crisscrossed up to her knee.

"It's a bit unorthodox, but Dr. Nickius suggested you wear these." Brigitte held up a pair of white opera gloves. Nya swallowed past the lump in her throat as the pressure in her chest eased. The cleansing ceremony had left her scar sensitive, red, and a little swollen. Jax must have known—the gloves protected her hand from curious eyes and a stranger's touch.

The silk hugged her fingers and wrists but allowed her skin to breathe. As soon as the gloves were in place, one of the other females brought over a red box with her heritage mark painted on the top. She opened the lid; nestled between satin covered padding was a coiled upper arm cuff.

"It's beautiful." Nya ran her finger along silver and gold. A fierce dragon baring his teeth started at the top of the coil. Thousands of scales wound around the midsection, creating the body, and the cuff ended in a spiked tail. The intricate design shimmered in the light, giving the piece depth.

"The dragon is meant to protect your lineage through the Trials." The female slipped on the arm cuff, sliding it past Nya's glove until it rested under her tattoo. "Dr. Nickius commissioned the cuff, making sure your dragon's eye was onyx, as black-eyed dragons were the fiercest in Dacian lore. This will remain on your arm until your mate replaces it with his mark."

The team gathered their things and headed out the door.

Nya's vision blurred, and she blinked away the tears. She was so confused. A few days ago, she was nothing more than Jax's patient, and then he became one of her candidates. He said he wanted her—honestly, she hadn't believed him. But as she stared at the glittering eyes of her dragon, a small voice whispered in the back of her mind. Maybe he meant what he said. Maybe he did see her as romni material.

A knock sounded at the door, and Nya shook away her thoughts.

Victor leaned against the wall, relaxed shrink expression firmly in place. He had trimmed his beard and slicked back his hair. His dress blues fit him perfectly, his burgundy sash, the color distinguishing him as an elite in the Society, made him seem more intimidating, if that were possible.

"You clean up well," Nya said as she locked her door.

"And you're on time." He stepped forward and slowly inhaled, taking in her scent. "That is heavenly."

She took his arm, grateful for the silky gloves. "Thank you. Apparently, it's of my ancestry."

"Yes, but it also contains pheromone enhancers which bring out your natural scent as well."

"They didn't tell me that." Nya's voice became thin.

Victor kept their pace leisurely. "Attraction plays a major role in finding an equal. It is imperative you and your mate have sexual chemistry. Pheromone enhancers help the process along."

Fantastic. Now males weren't going to just look at her, maybe touch her. Now they were going to sniff her, too.

Was this day ever going to end?

Furious, Alexandra stormed into her private chambers and slammed the door. Would this day ever end? The footage of Nya taking down Zander played over and over in the media, commentators quick to point out her agility and speed. And then came the questions. Why was the Tovaris' *Suveran* on the field? What had he said to the last of Otrera's line to merit such a response?

The Chancellor had spent a good part of the day in a press conference, explaining that Zander's behavior was nothing more than tradition, even though the word implied it had been done before. She would have been cornered had the video not picked up the leader shouting some nonsense about Nya being worthy of a Tova.

Idiot.

Amber liquid swirled as she grabbed the decanter and poured a tumbler full of whiskey. Being put under the microscope caused her to go off half-cocked, and now that Warriors knew Nya had been taken, Alexandra would be careful. God help her if they knew the circumstances surrounding the young warrior's abduction. If she weren't careful, Anya would end up looking like a victim—or worse, become a Martyr.

She tossed back the last of her whiskey before picking up her phone and making a call she had dreaded all day.

"Is everything all right?" As usual, Ike didn't bother with a hello but got to the heart of the matter.

"Everything is fine, my friend. I'm calling with an update. Dr. Nickius refused the suggestion to step down, rather adamantly I might add. However, he will be on a plane tonight."

"Good. And Pumpkin?"

"Nya released two of her official candidates and went to the arena to watch the others spar."

"Has she met Lucian yet?"

"I'm not sure."

Silence.

"I thought we agreed that you would encourage her toward Savva. He's a good male and has Gia's full approval." Ike's deep voice rumbled.

"Yes, but the consulate is swarming with media coverage. The last thing I need is someone implying that we manipulated the process. Anya is my goddaughter, and Lucian was under your command for the past five years. Someone is bound to notice."

"True." He grunted. "Is there anything else I need to know?"

Alexandra swallowed. "I would steer clear of the news for the next few days."

"It's been more than twenty years. When are they going to stop dredging up our Trial?" Ike quietly cursed. "I'll keep Gia away from the internet."

"I'm diverting the media's attention to the other candidates. I'm hoping it helps."

"Good. Keep me posted. And Alex? Thanks."

The Chancellor hung up the phone and sunk into a chair. She hadn't lied … technically. But the last thing she needed was Ike and Gia barreling in, demanding to know what Zander said to make Anya lose control.

She couldn't afford another public spectacle like the ones they had today. No. She'd have to find a way to smooth things over, and then she'd make sure her goddaughter stayed out of the limelight.

Even if that meant Nya didn't finish the Trials at all.

CHAPTER NINETEEN

Jax kept a tight rein on his emotions as he stood on the other side of the foyer, waiting for his Vtachi to come down. Thank God Victor had agreed to give them a few minutes before dinner. Otherwise, Jax might not have a chance to explain why he was leaving.

His breath caught as Nya appeared at the top landing. She was a vision, her sapphire dress bringing out the sheen from her raven hair and emphasizing her blue eyes. And he loved that his dragon protected her mark. Most females wore a cuff that had been passed down from generation to generation, but when Victor discovered Gia never had one, Jax stepped in. He'd secretly spent months handcrafting the piece, making sure the Tova's Dragon, with its onyx eyes, watched over his Vtachi. No one else knew the significance, of course. But he did, and one day Nya would as well. His eyes skipped from her shoulder to her face, and his stomach dropped at the defensiveness he saw there.

Well, he hoped she would. If she let him go, another warrior's *nata* would wear Jax's dragon.

That thought turned his stomach.

Victor and Nya descended the stairs and mingled with other champions and candidates waiting in front of the dining hall. A chime sounded overhead, she started toward the dining hall, but Victor nudged her across the foyer to the darkened ballroom.

"Where are we …" her voice trailed away as Jax stepped from the shadows.

He stood stock still, letting her take in the medals that hung down his royal blue uniform and the black sash hanging from his shoulder, indicating his allegiance to the Tovaris. Her eyes widened as they met his, and he tried to reign in the intense desire to snatch her up and take her far away from this place.

"No more than ten minutes, and then we have to go." Victor nodded to Jax and then closed the door, taking most of their light with him.

Nya tensed as Jax took her hand, leading her to one of the settees lining the wall.

"Isn't everyone waiting for us?" Her voice caught, and she cleared her throat.

Until he knew she was all right and she understood about him leaving, everyone could damn well wait.

"Victor will hold them off. This afternoon was rough, and I wanted to make sure you're all right. I'm glad you didn't take to the woods."

Nya half smiled. "I was tempted. Although, I think Victor might've been pissed if he had to chase me around."

He'd be damned if another male tracked her. That was his responsibility.

He took a deep breath. There was so much to cover in such little time. "Vtachi, I'm sorry I didn't tell you about Penn. I thought it would be best if you—"

"I don't want to talk about this afternoon."

His heart sunk. Shit. She'd already rebuilt that wall he'd worked so hard to take down. Needing to touch her in some way, he took her hand and brought it to his lap. "All right."

Nya looked at his thumb circling her knuckles. "I guess I should thank you for the gloves. They help."

His deep brown eyes warmed as he smiled. "I'm glad you like them."

"And while I'm at it, thanks for the dragon, too. After my mother lost the American championship, my grandmother took it back and refused to speak to her."

Jax's brow rose. "I would have thought Ike claiming Gia should be enough to smooth things over."

"Not on the heels of the scandal of the century." Nya bitterly smiled. "Dear old grandma viewed it as the icing on the cake."

"Ah." Yet again one more selfish person in her life who valued their pride over his Vtachi.

She pulled her hand away. "I doubt you brought me here to talk about my family. Why are we hiding in the dark?"

He fell silent, scrambling to find the right words. How could he explain that he'd have to leave after he promised he'd stay?

"Is this about your *Suveran*?" She kept her eyes down, smoothing out a wrinkle on her dress.

"Zander?" What the hell had he done now?

"You haven't seen the news, have you?"

Jax's eyes hardened though his voice remained calm. "I've been working on something for Alexandra. Why are you asking about a Tova?"

"I met him today, on the sparring field." Nya's thumb circled her gloved palm as she told him about losing her temper. Jax had a feeling she was doing her best to gloss over what really happened. Needless to say, when he got back from Russia, he was kicking Zander's ass.

"So, the problem wasn't that he pissed me off. It was how I reacted." Her eyes, so vulnerable yet strong, found his. "I lost it, Jax. In front of everyone. And then I lost it again in the foyer." She put her head in her hands. "God. I'm a freak."

He sighed. "You're not a freak. And you didn't lose it. You reacted as any warrior would."

"That's what Xari said. Still doesn't feel that way, though."

Jax glanced at the clock and silently cursed. "Forget about Zander." As much as he wanted to, they didn't have time to ease into the subject. He took her hands again. "Before Victor comes back, I need to know how you feel about me being one of your candidates."

She stayed quiet, eyes down.

"Come on, Vtachi. Talk to me."

She must have felt his desperation, thank God, because she took a deep breath and held it. He'd taught her that technique as a way of gathering courage when she had something difficult to say. She kept her eyes on their hands as she slowly exhaled.

"All this time I thought you had that female in the valley—which made you safe. I could give you that screwed up part of me that I never planned on sharing with anyone. And then I'd go to the Trials and find a rovni. He'd claim my body, maybe we'd be friends, but that would be the only part I shared with him. My colleagues, they'd get a part, while my *vahna* would have another. As long as I was the only one with all my pieces,

I'd be okay. I could survive that way."

She looked up, struggling to meet his gaze.

"But then I saw you waiting with the others, and I wanted to run because I knew if you were my equal, my plan wouldn't work. You wouldn't settle for only a piece or two, you'd want all of me, and I'm not sure that's something I have to give."

He wrapped an arm around her shoulders. "That's self-preservation talking."

"Maybe." She shrugged. "But after a few months in the Academy, when I finally felt like I was home, I realized that a fractured life is better than being alone."

Yes, between her father and that bastard Penn, his Vtachi had learned the hard way to not put all her trust in one person. It would take time, but he'd teach her that not every male was a selfish prick. Although, going on a mission during their Trial was bound to look like he was abandoning her, too. How could he walk away from her now when she was finally opening up?

He grazed his fingers along her jaw, nudging her eyes toward his. "You deserve a whole life, not something that's shattered and broken. And I want to share your pieces, not take them from you."

"You don't understand." Her eyes became haunted. "I can't share what I don't have."

Jax stilled. He hated that after four years of therapy she still didn't remember. "You think you're still missing a piece?"

She looked down. "It feels that way, but I don't think I want it back."

He wasn't sure he wanted her to get it back, either. But the only way forward was to face her demons of the past. And she couldn't do that unless she knew what happened. He kissed the top of her head. "Whatever it is, we'll work through it together. Trust me."

"Wrap it up, Nick." Victor's voice came from the foyer.

Jax watched Nya roll her head from side to side like she was getting ready for battle. His hand tightened around hers. "Listen, Vtachi, I've been ordered to help with a mission in Russia. Believe me when I say I'd rather walk through glass than go."

She frowned. "Why would they order you to leave in the middle of your Trials? Are we going to war?"

Jax swallowed. "Not yet. And it's classified."

Disappointment flashed in her eyes as she slid her hand from his. "I understand."

His chest tightened as he realized she must have heard that same excuse from Ike for years. He snatched her hand back. "No, you don't, and I don't have time to explain." His voice sounded harsher than he intended, and he softly cursed. "Listen, the council has ruled that the night we spent together in the hospital counts. By law, you must spend some time with the others before we can be alone again. I have no choice about going to Russia, but I promise I'll be here before the second round starts."

A commotion in the foyer had both of them looking at the closed door.

Light arced across the floor as Victor peeked in. "We have to go. And Nick, hang back a minute."

Jax watched Nya walk away, back straight, head held high. Anyone else would see a confident, regal warrior in her prime. But the subtle tightening around her eyes, the strain in her shoulders, told Jax she was a hair's breadth from bolting.

And his gut ached knowing it was his fault.

To any passerby, the Drahzdan safe house looked like an abandoned store, but the inside had been constructed to mirror Penn's chamber in the Astana fortress.

"How is he today, Stephan?" Sergei, the leader of Penn's guard, asked.

"Better. But he is anxious to hear about his Ana. Is there any word?"

"Not yet." Sergei walked down the hall toward the door at the end while Stephan went into the kitchen. He returned a moment later with a tray heavily laden with food, a tea kettle, and cup.

Sergei opened the door, and Stephan quietly made his way in. "Sir, I have your breakfast."

Penn sat up, swinging his feet over the edge of the bed. "Put it on the table."

"Yes, sir." Stephan placed the tray on the ornate marble slab and started pouring from the kettle. He spooned out three teaspoons of sugar, added a splash of milk, took a sip and then placed it on the side. Steam rose as he took the silver dome off the plate. He tasted the eggs, mush, and fruit and put them next to the tea.

Stephan and his guard assured that only trusted servants ever prepared the Drahzdan Tsar's food, but Penn insisted on seeing it tested before he ever ingested anything. While it would do little good if someone had laced his meal with a slow acting poison, Penn insisted on the ritual, and Stephan complied.

After all, Sarkov's last assistant tried to get him to see reason, and the next day he was drawn and quartered in the fortress square.

Penn waited three minutes, the time he believed it would take to see any adverse reactions to most poisons, and then sat at the table, picked up the fork and took a bite of eggs.

"Any word of my Ana?"

Stephan sat in a chair across from Penn. "We understand something has jogged a little of her memory, although we do not know what that is. We believe she will remember soon, and then she will find her way home."

Penn started on his mush. "She swore fealty to me, you know."

Stephan's brow rose as he smiled. "That must be a wonderful memory, sir."

In a rare moment, Penn smiled back and set his fork down. "It was. When Father finally located Mother, he was horrified she had chosen a village so close to a Scythian compound. But despite Mother's betrayal, he told her he would allow her to live on the condition that she try and bear him another son. She agreed but only if she could stay in Ireland and not return to Astana. His guards were sure he would end her life right there, but he didn't. You see, I believe he loved Mother almost as much as I love my Ana. And so, he begrudgingly settled on her terms but demanded she returned once she was with child."

Penn took a sip of tea. "Every month Dmitri visited mother when she was most fertile. His time with her was brutal and not something I cared to see, so during those days, I lived in the fort my Ana had repaired. One month, to distract him, Mother told him she believed my friend was from the compound. Knowing Sarkov Industries needed a Scythian sample for research, father ordered me to bring him some of Ana's blood. As a reward, I would be allowed to stay in Ireland until I turned twenty-one. If I didn't bring him a vial within the month, he would murder my Ana in front of me and force me to take my place as his rightful heir that night."

Stephan cleared his throat. "I'm sure having little choice in the matter, you agreed."

Penn smirked. "You knew my father well. I convinced Ana to participate in a blood oath. She said they had something similar in her culture, and so we mixed the two rituals and created our own. She taught me a few Scythian words as part of her culture. I took a vial of blood as part of ours."

"But blood oaths only call for sharing of blood, not collecting it," Stephan said.

Penn raised a brow. "I know that, but my Ana didn't. She trusted me so much she never questioned it. She just smiled and held out her hand. It was after I sliced my palm and pressed it into hers that we swore to always be together."

"And what happened next?" Stephan sat on the edge of his seat, his eyes intense. It was so very rare their leader spoke more than a few sentences at a time, and what he revealed now gave light to so many unanswered questions.

Penn picked up his tea and glanced at Stephan. "I became very ill with fever. Mother stuck me in an ice bath and thought I might not make it through the night. She saw the slice across my palm and called my father, fearing foul play. A doctor arrived within the hour, and the next thing I knew I was being shuttled to the airport and flown to Astana. I managed to keep the vial with Ana's blood hidden so that if I died no one would know I had it with me. We reached the fortress before dawn, and father gave me something that kept me alive. I'm not sure what happened, but when the fever broke something within me had changed. My father didn't intimidate me as he once had, and I no longer feared death. When father came to check on me and ask about the blood sample, I made a few demands of my own. I'd give him the vial, and I'd willingly take my place at his side, something I'd fought since I was a child. The only stipulation was that no Drahzda was allowed to touch my Ana and that he assure her safety. Father must have sensed the difference too because he agreed. When I was well enough, I returned to Ireland, promising that I would go through Drahzda training in my twenty-second year.

"Was your Ana affected as well?" Stephan asked.

Penn glanced over. "What do you mean?"

"It's obvious that her blood was the cause of your illness. Did your blood affect her the same?"

"The doctor said it was a virus that nearly took my life. The fact that I no longer feared confronting my father I attributed to fate."

Stephan stood and picked up the tray. "You know you're lucky. I don't think anyone who has been exposed to Scythian blood has survived."

"Are you saying I'm too weak to have my Ana's blood flow through these veins?" Penn's voice rose as hysteria threaded through him.

Stephan's eyes flashed with fear. "Absolutely not. You are the leader of the Drahzda. A man to be respected and revered."

"Do not patronize me!" Penn threw his plate across the room. "Get out! Get out before I strangle you with my bare hands!"

Stephan backed away, muttering apologies. The crash of breaking china and screams echoed in the hall and he quickly closed the door.

Sergei glanced at Stephan. "What did you say to him now?"

"It doesn't matter. What's important is that I think I understand what happened the summer he almost died."

"Oh?"

More screams and crashes bled into the hall. Stephan shuddered. "Get in touch with Vlad and have him interview any doctors and scientists that were ordered to the fortress that summer. And then I need to speak with the council."

Sergei reached into his pocket and pulled out his phone. "Finally. With Ana on the cusp of remembering, let's hope someone can shed some light before the entire Scythian army follows her back here."

"If everything goes as it should, the Society will believe Ana dead. But if we're wrong and they attack, we pull back and head for the fortress."

"I've got men planning for that very thing, although traveling with Ana would put our forces at risk. Still, if we made it back to Astana we might stand a chance if they invaded. But in this place?" He looked up from the screen. "We won't last the night."

Nya walked into the dining hall, keeping her smile firmly in place. The tables still held the same formal dishware and floral arrangements, only this time the males were dressed in official uniforms, and the champions wore gowns. She looked at her table, seeing five strange warriors waiting for her. After Jax's little bombshell she really wasn't in the mood for the Scythian version of speed dating.

Jax walked past, and she stiffened. Her eyes tracked him as he joined Giovanni, Killian, Luka, and Aren at one of the white tables along the perimeter.

"Are you ready, Anya?" Victor placed his palm on her hand resting on his arm.

Voices droned around her as they wove through the hall until they found her table. The males stood, introducing themselves, but she wasn't paying attention.

The pressure in her chest ached.

Jax hadn't left the academy in four years, not once. He told her he'd be here to help her through the Trials, but since he'd been declared as an official candidate he hadn't taken part in the sparring session—and now he was off to Russia.

If she chose him, would Jax end up being like her father, always putting the Society first?

While she didn't want a male who demanded she give more than she could, she didn't want to be discounted and ignored either.

Victor pulled back her chair and nudged her. She sat down barely noticing the warriors doing the same. Waiters milled about, filling crystal goblets with sweet wine and water.

She glanced around the room, her gaze landing on Jax again. He was the only Tova she'd ever met, but if their reputation had a stereotype, Zander would be it. Hard. Cruel. Insensitive. Even if she were brave enough to choose Jax, she'd be under Zander's authority ... so would her *vahna.* Just thinking about it had her breaking into a sweat.

Giovanni chatted with Aren while Luka watched Tor circulate the room. Killian spoke to the server filling his glass, but Jax kept his eyes on her.

She looked away. What in the hell had come over her, telling him about her stupid pieces? She should have kept it to herself. But ever since the championships, he had slipped through her defenses. The more time they spent together, the more she spilled her guts about nightmares and insecurities. Maybe it was a good thing he was leaving. She needed to keep some distance.

A chime rang overhead, and the warriors at her table stood while new ones took their place. The soup was served, but Nya kept her hands in her lap, not bothering to pick up the spoon.

"Anya, it's a pleasure to see you again."

She glanced up at the copper-skinned warrior in front of her, his dark eyes shining.

The silence stretched and the smile slipped from his face. "I met you this afternoon. I'm Pacha Supay, a warrior from the Andes Mountains."

"Of course. Please forgive me. It's been a long day."

"I'm glad I made an impression." His droll remark had her smiling for the first time that night.

She met his open gaze. This was the type of male she'd always thought she'd end up with—someone kind, who wouldn't want more from her than a few offspring. They could part as friends, or maybe they'd stay together and live independent lives under the same roof. That idea had kept her sane the past four years. She'd be an idiot to abandon it now. Maybe she should just give in and release Jax before he went to Russia.

But her stomach dropped at the thought of letting him go.

"Interesting day on the sparring field," Pacha commented as he set down his spoon.

Nya blinked, forcing her mind to focus on the warrior in front of her. "I guess you could call it that."

He laughed, his eyes gleaming. "Yes. I'd say watching you spar with a Tova definitely falls under the interesting category. I look forward to seeing you again, Anya." The chime sounded overhead, and Pacha stood. His dark eyes swept over the dragon guarding her empty mark. "Shame. His eyes should be citrine."

Nya watched him walk away. She glanced at Victor. "Why citrine?"

"The original Incans worshiped the sun god. Citrine's golden color makes it a most valued gem in his culture."

"Oh."

Five new warriors sat at her table. She closed her eyes as the soup was taken away and a salad appeared.

Good Lord. How many courses were they going to serve?

CHAPTER TWENTY

"Goodnight, Dr. Ramova," Nya woodenly replied, focusing on putting the key in the lock. God, dinner was brutal. Now the only thing she wanted to do was take a hot shower and go to bed. She needed some alone time to figure out what in the hell she was going to do.

She opened the door, but Victor followed her in and closed it behind him. The lock clicked in place.

Nya froze. "What are you doing?"

"Part of my mandate is to counsel you after every major affair. I think we can both agree today counts as such. Now, let's have that chat, shall we?"

His hand rested on her back, and she shied away. Victor ignored the reaction and led her across the room to the sitting area by the closet.

"I thought it would be easier to speak here. But if you wish, I can ask for one of the smaller conference rooms. I will tell you the seats there are quite uncomfortable."

"This is fine," Nya muttered. She sat in one of the plush chairs, while Victor found the other. He crossed his legs and settled in, waiting for her to speak.

"Something's been bothering me all day."

Victor's brow rose. "Oh?"

"Where were the reporters? This afternoon and tonight at dinner, I mean." Her voice sounded small, and Victor reached over and took her hand.

"The media is strictly forbidden during formal affairs. And, by law, no one in the foyer this afternoon can discuss what happened because the Chancellor declared your past is classified. There may be rumors about your parents involving you in something as a child, but nothing else."

Nya relaxed a little. "Well, at least that's something."

He squeezed her hand before letting go. "Yes, it is. Now. Onto an easier subject. How did you enjoy meeting the uncommitted?"

"I liked seeing the warriors on the sparring field. Well, except for Zander."

"And tonight?"

"Honestly, I don't remember much about the conversations in the dining hall."

"What about Pacha?"

Nya shrugged. "He's all right, I guess."

"Well, then. Let's discuss your official candidates. Are you sexually attracted to any of them?"

Nya folded her arms across her chest. "You've seen my file. How would I know?"

Victor settled back in his chair. "Come now. Even though you haven't had much experience in this area doesn't mean you haven't been physically drawn to someone. Chemistry plays a big part in choosing an equal. It's the reason we procreate, and it helps partners resolve their conflicts. If you are sexually attracted to Jax, Killian, or any of the others, I see no reason why you shouldn't explore it."

He watched emotions play across her face as her eyes flitted around the room, finally settling on the bed.

"I don't want to talk about attraction."

Victor crossed his legs and put his hands in his lap. "All right. Let's move on. You didn't know Penn was Sarkov's son."

Nya shook her head. "No. Penn's last name was Karimov. I knew he hated his father, but when his dad came to the village, Penn made sure I stayed away."

"Karimov was his mother's maiden name."

"How could I not have known the Drahzdan Tsar's name was Penn?"

"He took over after his father died four years ago. You've been squirreled away at the Academy with little access to outside news sources. And even if you did know, there is more than one Allos named Penn."

"Like that makes me feel any better. Will you tell me what happened?"

Victor studied her for a moment. "A few years before the USSR dissolved, the Drahzda invaded outlying communities they knew had hidden priceless artifacts from the communist regime. While in a Kazakhstani village, Dmitri Sarkov came across a young woman, Elena Karimov. It is said her beauty captivated him, and he kidnapped her that night. Within the year, she bore him a son.

"According to our sources, Elena took precautions to make sure she had no more children, and she protected Penn as best she could. However, when the boy turned twelve, his father insisted that he start training as the next leader of the Drahzdan Empire. At thirteen, he was to be branded a soldier and sent to their top facility by the Kara Sea.

"Knowing Penn's artistic heart and having heard the horrors of what Drahzda training involved, Elena became desperate, fearing her son wouldn't last a day. When a blizzard hit the region, she ran her car into the river, faking their deaths, and fled. The Society had operatives watching the fortress, and they came upon the wreck. Posing as good Samaritans, they helped her and the boy escape to Ireland, and that's when Alexandra ordered your father to keep tabs on them."

"My parents would never have let us become friends. Unless ..." Her voice died as she connected the dots. "They knew."

A million memories of her and Penn flashed through her mind, cataloging the times her father happened to appear when she was showing too much of her Scythian strength, or when a discussion became too personal, or when she forgot and started speaking Dacian instead of English. Their fort was the only place she and Penn were truly alone, and that was because no one knew of it—not until her father followed her the night he'd found them together. "They spied on us, didn't they? Did they bug my clothes?"

Victor's calm expression never changed, and Nya's head fell back against the plush seat.

"Why would my parents allow me to be friends with Sarkov's heir? I was only ten when I met him. What could they have possibly discovered?"

"This is a discussion for Gia and Ike." Compassion warmed his eyes. "But I can be there to help if you'd like."

"Thanks," she muttered.

"Now." He reached into his breast pocket and pulled out a pair of reading glasses and a notepad. "I'd like to discuss this latest flashback."

Nya took a deep breath and held it before slowly letting it go. "I remembered Penn. Only he wasn't the Penn I knew."

Victor slid his glasses into place. "Explain, please."

Her gaze moved to the bed as her thumb worked furiously over her palm. "Growing up, Penn was loving and kind, and he knew me better than anyone. The Penn in the last two flashbacks wasn't the boy I knew. He was a monster."

"And which do you think is accurate?"

Nya hesitated. "What do you mean?"

Victor glanced up. "The mind is a most fascinating thing, Anya. It has the ability to protect us from traumatic situations. Sometimes we suppress memories, other times we alter them. And so, my question is this: Out of the two perceptions you have of Penn, which do you think best represents him? The boy from your youth, or the man from your memory?"

"Why does he have to be one or the other? I suppose he could be both."

"Yet, according to Dr. Nickius, you consistently reject the idea Penn was something other than your friend."

She rubbed her forehead. "I'm not rejecting the idea ... well, I am. I mean ..." She grew flustered. "Look, you didn't know Penn. He was a good guy. He accepted me, even though I was so different from him. We shared secrets; he made me laugh. We even made a pact—" she stopped midsentence.

Victor kept his eyes on his notepad. "How so?"

She looked away. "How so what?"

"You know well what I'm asking. How did you and Penn make a pact?"

Nya fidgeted with her dress. "It's been a long day. Can we talk about this tomorrow?"

Victor sat back. "What you fail to see is that right now I hold all the cards. As your psychiatrist, I could call the Rovni Council tonight and inform them that you are not mentally fit to finish the Trials. You would then be shipped back home to Ireland to shoulder Lucian Savva's mark." Victor leaned over and patted her leg. "Don't worry. Your mother has assured his lineage goes back to the Celtic warriors, and he seems a nice enough fellow."

She scowled. "That's blackmail."

"No, Anya. That's reality." Victor set his pen back on the pad and looked down. "The pact you made with the young lad. Explain."

Nya glared for a moment before leaning back in her chair. "It was a few months before I turned seventeen. Penn's father started visiting his mother, and Penn hated the man. That summer, his father stayed longer, and Penn practically lived in our secret fort. He became obsessed with protecting me. No matter how many times I told him I could take care of myself, he didn't believe me." Nya glanced at the bed. "One day we argued about it. I told him we'd always be friends, no matter what, and Penn asked me to prove it. The Allos had a ritual called a blood oath that swore fealty to another. He asked if we had anything like that in our traditions, and I said we did. Knowing how important equality is to me, he suggested we take a little of each and create our own. That night, I taught him the Dacian chant that went with our ceremony, and we cut our palms and then held hands, something they did during a blood oath."

Victor's fingers tightened around his small pad of paper. "Did you teach Penn our language?"

Nya grew uncomfortable. "Just the words for the ritual. Nothing else."

"What else did you tell Penn about the Scythians?"

She hesitated. "He thought we were Celts who kept ancient practices alive. He knew my father and mother went away on missions, but I told Penn they worked for Ireland's G2 Intelligence agency."

"And what of your obvious physical abilities?"

"Penn used to say that I must be some secret science experiment, like a test tube baby or something, because I was so strong, and my cuts and bruises always healed within a few hours where he took a week or two."

"That day, when you initiated the *Epona*, did you tell Penn of its significance?"

"Why do you think I chose the *Epona*?"

Victor looked over the rim of his glasses. "It's the only ritual in our history that requires blood." He looked back down. "I ask again, did you tell Penn of its significance?"

Nya rubbed her palm. "No."

"And how did he react after it was over?"

She thought for a moment. "He didn't feel well, and then I didn't see him for about a month. But when Penn came back he was more, I don't know, intense. That's when he started working on the docks."

"Ah, and your father caught him in your backyard and sent him on his way."

"How do you know about that?"

Victor shook his head. "It doesn't matter. What's important is that Penn changed after the ritual, yes?"

She stared at the bed. "I never thought about it, but yes. I guess that's when things changed."

"And did it not occur to you that it might have something to do with your impromptu ceremony?"

Nya scoffed. "Oh, come on. Don't tell me you buy into the mumbo jumbo crap. It was a few Dacian words so Penn would stop being a worry wart."

"No, Anya. It was a sacred ceremony in which you shared your blood with an Allos."

"What?"

Victor took off his glasses and pinched the bridge of his nose. "Do they not cover basic Scythian biology at the U.S. Academy?"

"Of course they do."

"Then explain what happens if someone of our species shares blood with an Allos?"

Nya met his gaze. "I'm not sure."

He put his glasses back on and placed pen to paper. "It's usually lethal."

"But Penn wasn't hurt." She ran her palms up and down her lap. "I mean, come on. We're all human. And it wasn't like he took a pint of my blood. If anything, there might have been a drop or two at the most."

"Anya, while Allos blood does nothing to us, Scythian blood acts like a virus, attacking their cognitive systems. Since the 1800s we've blamed any accidental contact with the rabies disease. No Allos has been exposed since World War II, at least none the Society is aware of."

She blanched. "Are you saying that my blood turned Penn into what he is today?"

"I doubt it. But I would like more information on the matter." Victor placed his pad and pen on the side table. "Close your eyes."

Confused, Nya glanced up from her hands. "What?"

"We're going back to the day you swore fealty to Penn."

"I don't know ..." Jax was the only one she trusted enough to do this regression thing with, and even then, it was difficult.

"It's only a relaxation technique to help you recall your memory, nothing more."

"That's all?"

He raised his hand. "Warrior's honor."

She sighed and closed her eyes.

Victor's voice became a soft lull, caressing her ears, enticing her as he coaxed her into a trancelike state. Her hands stilled, palm open, and she was vaguely aware of him stroking her scar.

The odd thing was, it didn't bother her.

His voice floated overhead. "Excellent, Anya. Let's go back to that day. You were in your fort, teaching Penn the words he needed to say. And then what happened?"

Nya's voice came from somewhere in the distance. "Penn had a pocket knife. He insisted on running the blade over a candle flame first so it would be sterile. He cut his palm, and then I cut mine."

"And then you pressed your palms together?"

Nya hesitated. "No."

"What happened after you cut your palm?"

"Penn had a little glass container with him. He placed it on the edge of my hand and squeezed, collecting blood in the vial before fastening the top and then putting it on a string around his neck. He said not to tell, but he wanted to keep a part of me with him. And then we pressed our palms together."

"Raise the hand you scored that day."

Nya raised the scar-covered palm.

Victor counted to ten, and with each number, she floated back to reality.

"You've done well, Anya."

She opened her eyes, and he put his pen and pad in his breast pocket.

Guilt knifed through her. "I didn't remember Penn taking my blood until tonight."

"You were just a *vahna,* and you trusted Penn. Although it concerns me that you never questioned him."

She wrung her hands. "The vial couldn't have held more than a few ounces of blood."

"Did you ever find out what Penn did with it?"

"I think he said he dropped it on the way home and it broke, but I can't be sure." She looked away, deep in thought. Her thumb found its way to her palm, circling furiously over the scar.

"Please share your thoughts."

She took a breath. "I just remembered something else. I made Penn a silver bracelet."

"And what did this bracelet look like?"

Her shoulder's slumped as she looked down. "It was a single spire dragon."

Victor glanced at Nya's arm. "The same symbol used to protect you until you shoulder your rovni's mark. Interesting."

She glanced at him. "I loved Penn but as a friend and not as an equal."

Victor patted her knee. "I know. But the significance of the gift can't be overlooked. Still, I'd like to wait until after the Trials to explore this further." He took off his glasses and placed them in his pocket. "It's late, and morning will be here soon enough. Get some rest."

CHAPTER TWENTY-ONE

The Chancellor stared at the top three monitors, which now showed an exhausted Anya pacing in front of the bed after her session with Dr. Ramova. Even though Alexandra could see the room from every angle, there was no sound. She should have anticipated Victor petitioning the council to remove all listening devices. He claimed they needed a safe place for their sessions, and the council agreed.

Idiots.

Her eyes skipped along from camera to camera, watching Victor make his way toward her suite. From his set jaw, he had something to share. And it didn't look good. Alexandra picked up her tumbler and took a healthy swig.

She waited until he passed the guards at the end of her hall before turning from the monitors.

A sharp knock sounded in the silence. Alexandra tightened the sash of her wine-red robe as she made her way to the front room. She opened the door.

Victor pushed his way through without so much as a hello and headed straight for the liquor cabinet. Pulling two crystal glasses from the shelf, he poured them drinks and handed one to her.

Alexandra took a seat in the nearest chair. "What has you so worked up that you felt it necessary to disturb my downtime?"

His eyes cut to her. "Don't pull that with me, Alexandra. You and I both know you were watching Anya's monitors, cursing the fact that you couldn't hear what she was saying. You probably tracked my progress until I reached your private quarters."

Her cheeks heated. "Get to the point. Why are you here?"

"Penn had a sample of Anya Thalestris' blood. *Before* she was taken."

The Chancellor's tumbler froze midair. "You sure?"

He threw back his drink in one smooth motion before getting another. "Positive. And that's not all. Apparently, Nya performed the *Epona* ritual with Penn."

She waved her hand as if to dismiss the idea. "Impossible. Penn would have to know Dacian. And the completion of the ritual involves intercourse. Nya is still a *novo*."

"She taught him the words to speak, and the ritual only states they share blood. The original Amazons were the ones who placed a cut on the male's penis so his pain would equal his romni when he took her for the first time. Nya and Penn sliced their palms."

Alexandra reached for a silver case on the side table. "So he was exposed?"

"Yes, but Nya insists it was only a few drops. How he survived remains to be seen."

"Do we know how long he had the blood before she was taken?" She took out a hand-rolled cigarette and lit it.

"I estimate eighteen months, two years, tops."

She stared at the red ember on the end of her cigarette. "The timeline would explain why the United States and certain parts of the Middle East began heavily investing in clone research."

Victor's stoic expression hid the emotions churning within. "If you have proof these countries are working with the Drahzda, it'll change our open policy with both regions."

She took another drag, the smoke curling around her face as she spoke. "Right now, it's too circumstantial. Sarkov Industries are one of the pioneers in genetic manipulation, and their prints are all over the U.S. and Middle East's classified human cloning projects. Scythian blood gets into the wrong hands, and we very well could be waging war against ourselves."

Victor wearily rubbed his eyes. "Anything else?"

She stood. "Nothing I can share at the moment."

He stood as well. "Do you mind if I check the security cameras? I'd like to make sure my candidate is resting."

The Chancellor smirked. "Of course. But if the female is anything like her father, she'll be sparring with her candidates in the bedroom before putting them through their paces on the field." She started toward the other side of the room, where her private chambers were. "I'll see you in the morning."

Nya wanted nothing more than to crawl into bed—and then she remembered the last time she'd fallen asleep she dreamed of her hand being nailed to the deck of a ship.

And didn't that make her want to snuggle down and count sheep?

Even though exhaustion had set in, maybe she'd take a shower ... and after that, a little light reading ... or she'd find the gym.

She stripped out of her dress and unpinned her hair, letting it fall to the small of her back. Left in nothing but a bra and panties, she rummaged through the built-in drawers, bypassing silk and lace in hopes of finding some good old-fashioned cotton pajamas.

A door hinge creaked from the other room. She froze.

What the hell? It was well past midnight—whoever was in her room had to know she'd be here. Maybe they thought she was already asleep.

She silently cursed as she spotted her satchel next to her bed. Ducking low so they wouldn't see her reflection in the mirror, Nya grabbed the small jar of ceremonial oil from the dresser before finding a silk scarf in the bottom drawer.

Wrapping the scarf around itself, she created a makeshift sling and placed the jar in the center pocket. Still crouched down, she swung the scarf by her side, gathering momentum as she rounded the corner. A tall frame and broad shoulders had his back to her as he closed the door. He turned, and Nya let go of the scarf. The oil hit the floor with such force it shattered.

"Shit, Jax. I could've killed you."

He froze, not saying a word.

"Won't you get in trouble if you're caught with me? Wait. Has something happened to my parents?" Panicked, she started toward him.

He stepped back. "We never finished our conversation, and we haven't started your desensitization sessions. Where are your clothes?"

Nya put her hands on her hips. "I was trying to find some pajamas when you came in. And how did you get in anyway? Victor locked the door when he left."

"Victor was in your room." His voice turned deadly.

"It wasn't as if I invited him. He insisted we talk after everything that's happened today."

"Tell me you weren't wearing that when he debriefed you."

"Of course I was," she answered, distracted as she looked down and realized she was practically naked.

"I'll kill him." His hands clenched into fists.

"Wait … You don't understand." She sidled closer to the closet. "I wasn't … well, yes, I was wearing this, but I had my dress on, too." Flustered, she crossed her arms, making her breasts protrude from their cups. "So, you want to desensitize me now? I thought Victor had to be present."

"Not quite. And isn't there a robe or something … anything for you to put on?" Jax kept his gaze on the wall.

She stopped edging toward the closet and faced him. "No one asked you to come to my room. And if I'm so damn hideous why don't you withdraw as one of my candidates?"

Surprised, his gaze met hers. "You think I'm not attracted to you."

"According to Zander, Tovaris don't follow the rules, they take what they want. Yet before we came to Carpathia, you were involved with the female in town, and you never treated me as anything more than a patient. Not to mention that now the Trials have started, you're leaving in the middle of the first round. You do the math." She headed toward the sitting area.

Jax lunged at her, spinning her around and then wrapping her in his arms. One hand splayed between her shoulder blades while the other rested on the rounded flesh above her legs. He pulled her close, allowing her to feel the thick bulge pressing on her stomach.

"This is why I need you dressed." He ground into her.

Wide-eyed and speechless, all Nya could do was blink.

Jax's voice grew husky. "I've wanted you for years, but you needed a counselor, not some half-crazed Tova throwing you over his shoulder and claiming you as his mate. And I would tell Alexandra to kiss my ass and stay at the Trials, consequences be damned, but this mission affects us both, and that I can't ignore."

"What does that mean?"

"Never mind. Just know that once this is over, I promise I'll tell you everything." Jax buried his nose in her hair. He inhaled deeply and then groaned. "Your scent is driving me crazy, has been all night. And then seeing you like this. God, Vtachi." He swiveled his hips into her like he couldn't help himself. "You can't stand in front of a Tova wearing a few scraps of lace. A warrior has only so much control, and mine is almost gone."

He gripped her hair in his fist, forcing her to meet his gaze before he leaned in and kissed her. Nya's heart raced as his tongue explored her mouth, searching as if he wanted to know every part of her. Aggressive, hard … possessive. There was nothing gentle about it, only sheer raw need.

Passion flooded that empty feeling in her chest, and she lost her breath. She whimpered and pulled away, gasping for air. Jax tipped her head back farther, exploring her neck, kissing and licking spots that made her shiver.

"How do you do it?" she whispered as he ran his thumb under the curve of her breast.

"Do what?"

"Make me feel so alive." She tensed at her unexpected honesty, but her words seemed to have the opposite effect on him.

A deep groan rumbled in his chest as he unhooked her bra, tossing the delicate lace behind her. She shuddered as his teeth raked over the sensitive skin under her jaw and nibbled down her neck, exploring the soft hollow of her collarbone before running his tongue along the edge of her heritage tattoo.

His lips brushed her shoulder. "I feel the same, but you're so much more to me than this. You've taught me to search for the meaning beneath words, that music's true beauty is found in its silence, and often the smallest scars carry the most pain."

The air swirling around them grew warm, humid, as his palms traced the contour of her ribs dipping into her waist, and then flaring slightly at her hip. He ran his fingers over soft, lace-covered curls, swirling and searching until they found the warm flesh beneath.

Everything within her focused on the raw pleasure as he nudged and stroked her. She fumbled to grab his shoulders so she wouldn't lose her balance.

Nya slowly inhaled in wonder as his scent mingled with hers. She arched her hips forward, trying to contain the dull ache blooming there. Jax's nimble fingers continued their sweet torture while the rough wool of his sweater chafed her sensitive breasts.

"Jax," she whispered, pulling up his shirt and exploring deep reefs of muscles on his lower back. Her fingers dipped beneath his waistband, traveling around his hip before grazing his lower abdomen, wrapping around his hardened flesh.

Jax froze at her touch. He softly cursed as he pulled her hand away and placed it on his chest. He took in her flushed face and half-lidded gaze, and his eyes warmed with compassion. "I'm sorry. I shouldn't have let it get this far."

She stared at him, trying to get her breathing under control. She didn't understand.

He brought her hand to his face and kissed her palm. "I know how to stoke a female's fire, Vtachi."

"Congratulations." She stiffened and tried to pull away.

Jax refused to let her go. "That came out wrong. What I meant was that I want you to choose me because I'm your equal, not because I can make you melt."

Her cheeks heated as she looked away.

His voice became gentle. "You've never known what it is to feel passion. You're just now opening your eyes to the possibility of any relationship." He ran his fingertips up and down her spine, and she shivered. "Touch, sexual pleasure, it's all so new to you. I want you to be sure it's me you want, not just this."

Her stomach dropped as realization hit. "This is part of the therapy, isn't it?"

Jax kept his hold. "In a way. You're doing much better than I expected."

She closed her eyes. God, she was such a freak. For a minute, she thought he wanted her—really wanted her. "Well, what did you expect?"

He ignored the sarcasm and kissed her nose. "Having a meaningful conversation while you're practically naked is something I've dreamed of, only I thought we'd be doing this in bed after shouldering each other's marks. I hate that I have to leave."

Goosebumps peppered her skin. "Let me go, Jax."

He hesitated, but eventually, his hands fell to his sides.

She turned from him and headed toward the bathroom, needing some space.

Something deep inside wailed at the thought of Jax leaving, the strength of it made her heart ache. She wanted to run to him, throw her arms around his neck and beg him to stay. But Jax was a Tova, and she couldn't stand the thought of him seeing her as weak.

She found a robe, donned it, and tugged the sash tight around her waist.

They stood there, each studying the other.

"Why are you here, Jax?"

He rubbed the back of his neck, his expression weary as loneliness flashed in his eyes. Nya had an urge to wrap him in a protective embrace.

His expression became that cool shrink face he usually wore. "We still haven't fully discussed today. Were you okay with the others touching you?"

Her shoulders slumped. "I attacked Zander, so we'll count that as a no."

"But you lost it because he pissed you off, not because he touched you, right?" His biceps bunched like he wanted to hit something.

"I'm not sure. What are you getting at?"

"I'm the only male that's ever been this close to you."

Her frown turned into a scowl. "So."

"I think it's important for you to explore your options." His voice darkened.

Insecurity bloomed, and she crossed her arms in front of her chest. "One minute you say you want me as your romni, the next you're encouraging me to get physical with someone else. Don't you find that strange?"

Jax's fingers dug into his palms. "Strange doesn't even begin to describe it. But I know I'm right. You must go into this eyes wide open. You need to be sure."

The insecurity exploded to doubt.

Tovas were ruthless. If Jax wanted her, he would have taken her years ago. And yet, here he stood, just minutes ago he held her in nothing but her panties, and now he was encouraging her to, 'explore her options.'

Didn't that speak volumes?

Her chin quivered, and she turned away, pretending to look out the window. "So, this is your way of fighting for us—encouraging me to see others while you walk away?"

"Vtachi, no." He stepped behind her, wrapping his arms around her, his lips finding her ear. "I am fighting for us, but it's complicated." He kissed the side of her face. "I know what I want. Now it's up to you to decide if you feel the same."

Moonlight streamed through the forest, creating a silhouetted canopy against the cloudless sky.

Nya blinked back the tears. "Have you spoken with Victor about this? Does he agree with you?"

Jax rested his chin on her shoulder. "From a psychological perspective, yes."

She closed her eyes and concentrated on his scent, the feel of his arms around her, the way his five o'clock shadow prickled her cheek.

"Vtachi?"

Taking in his scent one last time, she pulled away, avoiding his perceptive gaze. "All right. If you want me to explore my options, I will."

"It's not what I—" His phone rang. He pulled it from his pocket as he softly cursed. "I have to go."

Silence settled around them as they walked to the door. Nya reached for the knob, but he gently pulled her hand away, placing it over his heart instead.

"Trust me. Look at these other males, try to see them as a mate. I'll be back, and then I'll prove that I'm your equal."

Her breath hitched as she wrapped her pinky around his. "Staratsa, Jax."

Before he could reply, she turned and headed toward the bathroom.

Penn looked at the single spiral bracelet that adorned his wrist. A dragon's head on one end, the tail on the other. His Ana had given it to him the day they shared their blood. Penn had the good sense to hide it until the night his father died, but it had been on his wrist ever since.

Pain had been the only consistency in his life. It grew worse when he thought about his brief time of freedom before the Drahzda discovered he and his mother survived the crash and had fled to Ireland.

After he'd gone through the Phoenix conditioning, he'd learned that killing eased the heat flooding through his veins. His father started him out with low-life thugs and drug lords who strayed from the rules. But he quickly moved up the ranks and finally was given a squadron to hunt Scythians. After his first kill, his father was well pleased, and so he took advantage of Dmitri's good mood and broached the subject he had been waiting to discuss. He wanted to go back for his Ana. It was the only family dinner he thought of fondly.

"I don't care if you have a Scythian whore, son." Dmitri filled his glass with wine. "But you'll never take one for a wife." He set the bottle down.

Penn smiled. He'd abide by his wishes for now, but when Dmitri died, Nya would become Ana Sarkov before they planted the old man in the ground. "I'll keep her as my mistress then ... but you agreed. No other Drahzda may touch her."

Dmitri frowned, deep in thought as he took a roll and sopped up gravy from the roast, stuffing it in his mouth. "All right," he said. "I'll abide by my word. But since you're bringing her here, I have a few conditions."

Anxiety ran through Penn. "And they are?"

"We get more blood samples, and I question her first. After we have extracted what she knows of the Phoenix project, she's yours."

Penn sat back in his chair. "You will personally assure she survives the questioning?"

"She may be weak, but she'll live." Dmitri cut his meat before pointing the knife at Penn. "And boy? You start a war over this, and it will be more than your life's worth."

That day, Ana officially became his. Penn's body stirred as he anticipated their first night together. Oh, Penn could have taken her when she was drugged and shackled. But he wanted more, and the years apart made that need almost unbearable. He endlessly fantasized about it ... her glossy black hair fanning across feather pillows as her beautiful blue eyes and lush lips sparked with need. Her body tone, fit and lush, waiting for him to possess. Yes, she was intelligent, but she'd learn to mind her tongue. And yes, she was strong, but Penn had ways of keeping her physically weak. After all, he was the man. It was unnatural for a woman to be more powerful. But once she learned her place, they would have a good life together.

Jax buckled his harness to a carabiner in the cargo hold of a Scythian military transport plane. They taxied down the runway, and he wedged himself between large crates secured with netting. Memories of last night played vividly in his mind.

He finally got to taste his Vtachi, feel her warmth, watch her eyes glaze as pleasure roared through her. God, he ached just thinking about it. Their chemistry was off the charts. But as much as we wanted to be all over her until they no longer knew where he ended and she began, sex wasn't all he wanted. Not by a long shot.

He wanted intimacy—he craved it, actually. He wanted the entire Scythian world watching as he defeated Nya in the arena and then he claimed her as his equal. He wanted to shoulder her mark, and then remove her arm cuff and ink her with his crest. And then he'd take her back to that ridiculous room they had her in and place a symbol meant just for her above her heart. He'd carry her to that bed and look into her eyes as he took her for the first time. And then in the morning, they would go, just the two of them, to a place far from Carpathia. He'd coax her to open up, share her thoughts and fears, and he'd do the same, giving her his every insecurity and dreams for the future. In time, they'd connect on all levels, which, God willing, would develop into an *intima* bond.

His phone beeped, and he pulled it from his pocket. Victor's name appeared on the screen, and Jax frowned as he read the text.

> Nya remembered giving Penn a sample of her blood before she was taken, but that's not the worst of it. Zander's been tracking the Drahzda, and they're heading toward Russia. Inform Ike. I've been monitoring Alexandra's secretary's correspondence. This morning, she canceled your return flight home. Use alternative methods and get back here as soon as possible.

Jax cursed and hit the side of the crate with his fist. First Ike and Gia need him on a mysterious mission during his trials, and now Sarkov was headed their way. His gut screamed the two were somehow connected.

How the hell did Penn get her blood? And why was the Chancellor risking him not being there for the first round's closing ceremonies? Surely she knew Zander would protest if they tried to disqualify him.

The plane hit turbulence, and Jax braced himself against the crate and the belly of the aircraft. A growing sense of unease rippled through him. He checked his watch and cursed again. It would be a few hours until they landed, and then he'd be on a train and then another flight. God help him if the Fourth Gen's Commander wasn't waiting when he finally arrived.

Someone better have answers, and soon.

Nya took a left into a small alcove beyond the library's main entrance. White and black checkered tabletops stood in rows, chess pieces already arranged, ready to play. She found the farthest corner and settled in.

Scythian young loved chess, but full-fledged warriors rarely played, which was why she chose the spot to meet her candidates there instead of the foyer.

The light shifted from the door as someone else entered the room, and Nya silently cursed. The uncommitted followed her everywhere, and she wasn't in the mood to deal with more males. Honestly, her mind was still on Jax.

"This seat taken?"

Nya looked up, relieved to see Xari grinning.

"Bet you thought I was another male come to hound you into watching him on the field.

Nya shrugged. "Something like that."

Compassion warmed her friend's eyes. "You thirsty? I brought water."

"Thanks."

Xari took a seat, shifting the pieces off the board. She handed Nya a clear bottle before she uncapped her own and took a sip. "By the way, your candidates are on the way. I gotta say that Killian is an amazing warrior."

"Yes, he is." Nya rubbed her forehead as a dull ache settled behind her eyes. "What about you? How are your Trials going?"

She sighed and took her cap between her thumb and forefinger, spinning it, sending it dancing across the squares. "I have no clue. How do they expect us to choose someone in two weeks? I like Erik, but we don't really have a lot in common. And he's so withdrawn, serious. The others aren't much better."

They watched the cap slow until it finally wobbled then stopped.

"Are you attracted to any of your warriors ... you know, sexually?"

Xari glanced up. "Yeah. Three of them. Although Erik is the only one that smells like heaven."

Nya picked up Xari's cap, setting it off again, watching it turn to a blur as it whirled in a circle. "Well, that's something."

The cap slowed. "What about you? I know you're attracted to Jax, and the Italian seems like he'd be fantastic in bed. But what about the American?"

"Jax is, well, he's Jax. Giovanni would be a great rovni. And Killian's Scottish, actually. He's nice ... there's a connection that could grow. I just don't know."

"And what about the other two?"

"Aren's the one that pulled me off Zander, and Luka is a Greek warrior. He can cook, but I haven't been around him enough to know anything else."

Xari grinned. "He's one of the mop-headed twins, isn't he? I think it was his brother that kept pestering me the night they arrived. They're cute, but I'm not sure either of them would be considered your equal."

Nya shrugged again. "I like that he's so easy going. They seem carefree. Don't think I've ever seen that in a warrior before."

The humor left Xari's eyes. "Yeah, you could use a little carefree in your life."

Nya picked up the cap and put it between her finger and her thumb, sending it around the marble again. "Can I tell you something?"

"Always."

"Last night Jax came to my room."

Wide-eyed, Xari leaned in. "Oh?"

Nya kept spinning the cap while the whole story spilled out.

"He's trying to do the right thing, Ny. I think it's stupid, but as you said, Jax is, well, Jax. I'm sure there's some psychological mumbo-jumbo he knows that we don't."

"I don't know. Maybe I should let him go." Nya spun the cap again.

Xari snatched it off the table. "Not a good idea."

"So, you think I should keep him?"

She tossed the little bit of plastic in the trash. "I think you should do what Jax asked and trust him. He's never let you down before."

Nya sighed.

Xari patted her hand. "Just don't do anything rash. Once you let a warrior go, you can't get him back. Remember that."

Four large males darkened the doorway, and Xari stood from the table. "Looks like your candidates are here. I've got to go anyway. I'm meeting David in a few."

Nya smiled. "The Canadian?"

"Yep. He smells nice, too." Xari winked, stood, and walked away.

CHAPTER TWENTY-TWO

Ike and Gia huddled in the small concrete building that served as the Scythian airport. Russia had entrusted the Scythians to secure this area for their space program, which made this unassuming ribbon of asphalt one of the most protected places in the world. A cargo plane came into view, and Gia tensed.

"Once he sees, he'll understand why we asked him to come," Ike said, putting his arm around her.

The roar of the approaching engine grew louder, followed by screeching tires. As soon as the plane stopped, Jax bolted from the cargo hold. He jogged across the tarmac and threw open the door.

"What in the hell is so important that you've called me away from the Trials, leaving your daughter at the complete mercy of a pack of fucking wolves!"

The servicemen coming in behind him froze, shocked that anyone would speak to one of the Chancellor's advisors and the head of Fourth Gen in such a way.

Gia started toward the exit, expecting him and Ike to follow. Jax hesitated. He glanced at the warriors openly watching them before he followed her out the door.

Gia waited until they were in the lot before she spoke. "Dr. Nickius. I would not have asked you to leave if it weren't important."

"What is this about?" Jax's voice lowered as a few warriors passed by.

"There's something we've discovered, and Nya should know before she chooses her rovni."

They stopped in front of an all-terrain vehicle.

Gia got in the passenger side, while Ike slid behind the wheel, and Jax opened the back door.

His phone buzzed as he buckled his seatbelt, and he pulled it from his pocket.

> Update: No nightmares last night, and this morning's sparring session with the uncommitted had a few warriors standing out, especially that Incan, Pacha. Still, she didn't request further interaction. She's eating lunch with Killian, Luka, Aren, and Giovanni now.

Jax's shoulders eased as his head fell back against the leather rest. Only four warriors at her table meant he hadn't been replaced. However, she could release any one of her candidates, including him, at any time. He hated being two countries away, sitting on pins and needles. Every time his phone buzzed he was afraid it was Victor saying Nya had chosen someone else.

"So, this is what you call fighting for us—encouraging me to see others while you walk away?"

He glared at the back of Gia's head. If he lost his Vtachi because of her parents, he didn't know what he'd do. The Tova in him wanted to watch them bleed out slowly, but the psychologist knew Nya would get hurt in the process.

When he demanded the *Zvaz*, his brothers thought it too risky to dedicate his future to a female who might not claim him back. But they didn't understand. Losing his Vtachi would be like losing the only bright thing in his dark world. She grounded him in a way even he couldn't understand, much less explain. He felt it the first time he watched her spar.

Dust billowed as they sped along a dirt road. No one had spoken since they left the airport, which was fine with him. The only thing keeping him sane was Victor's texts, which came every few hours.

"Are we almost there?" he grumbled, shifting in the backseat for the hundredth time.

"Not much farther."

Ike's gruff voice had years of training kicking in, and Jax leaned forward. "You seem upset."

"We made a mistake putting the Society's needs over that of our *nata*. If I could go back and change things, I would."

The confession put Jax on edge. Since he'd known the Thalestrises, neither of them had expressed remorse. "What's done is done. Right now, let's concentrate on what's best for Nya."

Gia turned in her seat. "And if it's best for her to find a rovni that isn't so close to all this ugliness? If she would be happiest with someone as far from the frontlines as possible—would you still say the same?"

"Who she chooses for her rovni is out of your hands." Jax looked out the window, and heavy silence settled around them.

The forest gave way to barren fields as Ike turned onto a cobblestone lane. Large gates hung from broken hinges. Weeds and vines grew over crumbling turrets as they rounded what used to be a palatial circular drive.

"Why are we at an abandoned castle?"

Gia's breath hitched as they pulled to a stop. "Because, Dr. Nickius, this is where they kept and tortured my *nata*."

Nya still hadn't been cleared to spar, so instead of participating, she watched the uncommitted compete in hand-to-hand combat. Pacha made a point of stopping by to say hello. Even though she was impressed with him and a few other males, she'd decided to keep Jax, Killian, Giovanni, Aren, and Luka as her official candidates.

Xari was right. She shouldn't do anything rash. For now.

Four of her five warriors stood as she entered the dining hall, waiting for her to join them for lunch. It felt like a week had passed instead of just one day since Jax left. Silverware clinked on plates, and conversation buzzed as she made her way to her table. The Trials were starting to take on a routine. Apparently, round one meant an early breakfast before heading to the practice field to watch the uncommitted spar. Then there was lunch, followed by time with her official candidates. Yesterday they had walked around the lake, stopping to see who could skip the farthest stone. It had been a fun activity as her males tried to one-up each other. By mid-afternoon, Nya finally had enough of the testosterone surge and started toward the arena, challenging them all to an Urumi competition. The first four rounds she kept the lead, but on the last strike, Killian made an impossible move, edging her into second place. He tossed the razor-sharp whip on the ground before whooping a war cry and throwing his arms up in the air in celebration. Nya bit back a smile, and he scooped her up and twirled her around, laughing, telling her he'd be happy to give her lessons after she'd shouldered his mark. All cameras pointed to the far end of the field, recording the scene, and she was relieved when they finally left the area. As soon as they got back to the consulate, Luka had reserved time in the kitchen for the two of them where he taught her how to make baklava.

Today another one of her warriors would step forward, claiming some quality time.

When she and her official candidates were together, they treated her like she was part of a unit, but alone they became potent males searching for their mate, which always left her leery.

"... *Just keep an open mind, Vtachi.*"

"I apologize for being late." Nya sat down, and they followed.

Killian's eyes raked over her tired features. "I'm sure the uncommitted slowed you down trying to impress you, right?"

She smiled. "I did spend quite a bit of time watching the warriors who specialize in the Urumi. I'll admit some have impressive skills."

Killian's eye sparked at her not so subtle jab. "I can challenge them if you wish."

"That won't be necessary." She winked. Her eyes swept across the table and fell on Jax's empty seat, and the smile slipped from her lips. Why would he ask her to consider someone else if he wanted her for himself? It made no sense.

She scanned the crowd until she found Xari. Her purple-tipped hair fanned across her cheek as she leaned in, saying something, and the entire table erupted with laughter. Nya's gaze flitted from table to table, observing the other champions. The buzz of conversation warmly hummed through the room as Amazonian warriors engaged their candidates. They seemed happy to be here, ready to find an equal so they could create a lasting bond and further the strength of their kind.

"*Your loyalty to Jax is clouding your decision.*"

Those words rang in Nya's ears as she played with her food. Maybe

Victor and Jax were right. They were the freaking shrinks, after all. Maybe her wanting Jax had more to do with feeling safe.

"Anya," Victor mumbled. "Are you all right?"

She looked up to five sets of eyes staring at her. "I'm sorry. My mind drifted. You were saying?"

Their compassionate, caring gazes caught her breath. Four warriors. Some of the best in the world were at her table, wanting to claim her as their equal. Wanting to bear young with her, create a life with her.

And she couldn't get out of her own fucking head to keep track of the conversation.

Her fingers trembled as she grabbed her goblet and took a drink of sweet, white wine.

If Jax wanted her to keep an open mind, so be it.

She sat up straight and pulled her shoulders back, squarely looking at each of the males. "Aren, tell us more about Africa."

Aren's keen dark eyes glittered as he explained the beauty of his village. "Aside from the Drahzda stirring up civil wars in the region, our biggest threat is pollution."

"We have the same issue in parts of the U.S." Killian joined the conversation, explaining a project the Appalachian compound was working on that helped filter out excess chemicals in natural springs.

Aren set his fork down. "I'd like the name of the *Suveran* in charge. Perhaps we can help one another."

A server cleared their dishes before bringing out the traditional fruit for dessert.

"What, no more baklava?" Killian smiled at Nya. "After last night's dinner, some of the uncommitted asked what we did to deserve such a treat. When I told them our champion made it, they were even more jealous."

"I'm sure they were." Nya's dry tone.

Luka covered her hand with his. "It was your sweet touch that made it so delicious. I'd cook with you any day."

Killian settled back in his chair. "We'll be sure to invite you to America sometime. I'm sure Ny would love to stay in touch."

The others chuckled, but their laughter died away as a warrior neared the table.

"Tor?" Nya's eyes widened as she glanced from one twin to the other. "Wow. I almost didn't recognize you."

Tor's skull showed through his buzz cut, which was as short as his five o'clock shadow. He ran his palm over the stubble on his scalp. "I got tired of explaining that I wasn't the twin Anya Thalestris picked. Instead, I was the one stupid enough to try and stop her from kicking a Tova's ass."

Nya set down her wine glass. "I'm sorry. I didn't mean to blindside you like that."

"Don't apologize. I should have known better." He lightened his tone. "Besides, this look is a lot sexier, don't you think?"

Nya smiled. "Short hair does make you look older."

"I am older, you know."

Luka groaned. "Two minutes. You're older by two minutes."

"Still makes me the big brother, doesn't it?" Tor grinned.

Victor picked up his coffee cup. "God save us from sibling rivalry."

Tor lowered to his haunches so he could speak to Nya eye to eye. His voice deepened as intense emotion flashed in his eyes. "I'm sure I broke some protocol by interrupting your time with your official candidates, but I wanted you to know. My baby brother might not be your most obvious choice, but he's a good male, a great warrior, and loyal to his last breath. He's worthy to be your equal."

Nya's expression sobered. "I'm sure he is."

Tor patted her knee and winked, easing the mood. "Besides, you know you want to be my little sis."

He tipped his head to the males at the table, grinned, and sauntered away.

Luka groaned. "I had hoped he wouldn't come over. Until now, we've done everything together. We hadn't considered the possibility that one of us would go on without the other."

Nya sighed. "I know what you mean. Xari isn't my twin, but she's my best friend. I couldn't imagine one of us being back in the States."

Victor raised an eyebrow. "Let's not bring that up again."

Giovanni and Killian chuckled.

Luka's eyes glittered with that playfulness she loved. "At least the better looking of the two is still in the running."

"Not for long," Killian muttered.

Giovanni waited until Nya had finished her fruit before he stood. "Are you ready?"

She took a deep breath before accepting his hand. Sometimes the way he looked at her reminded her of a male lion circling a pride of females in heat.

Keep an open mind, Vtachi.

The marble foyer gleamed as sunlight streamed through tall windows. Nya glanced at Giovanni's classic features as they made their way out of the consulate. He was a good male. Strong, passionate, intelligent. He would be patient with her. Kind. And she knew she'd never let him in, which was what she wanted.

Wasn't it?

CHAPTER TWENTY-THREE

Weatherworn plywood stood guard over most of the castle's doors and windows, thistles and vines covered the walkway and crumbling stairs. Half-constructed scaffolding leaned against the southern wall, giving notice that renovations were underway. Several Fourth Gen units surrounded the perimeter while Ike and Gia made their way to a low-lying window. It didn't take long for Ike to trip the release wire they'd put in a few days before. The plywood swung from the rotting window frame, and Ike turned his broad shoulders and ducked inside. Gia wasn't far behind. Jax took one last look around, searching the densely wooded perimeter before hitching his leg over the window's casing. He pulled the warped wood back in place.

Without a word, they switched on their flashlights and headed for the door, traveling in single file, Jax mindful of stepping only where Ike and Gia had. The ballroom opened to a large foyer. Two rusted suits of armor stood guard at the bottom of a sprawling walnut staircase. Ike took the stairs two at a time until he was on the second landing. He opened the first door to his right.

Jax's heart sank as he took in the plastic sheets covering the walls, ceiling, and floor. Sunlight fought through the thick lining, it's hazy light surrounding a single hospital bed. Leather restraints hung from its metal frame. Surgical supplies, still in their packaging, lay on top of a metal cabinet. Two rolling stools sat under a stainless-steel desk. Wires hung from the wall, obviously once the home of a computer or some other technology.

The room looked like a makeshift surgical suite. Jax looked down and almost dropped to his knees.

Next to the bed was a pair of dirt encrusted jean shorts.

"I bought those for Nya when she was sixteen. They were so worn I thought she'd thrown them out." Gia's hollow voice came from behind. "She must have had them on the night she was taken."

Jax's hands trembled as he shucked off his pack and set it aside. God. He wasn't naive. He'd known the worst of war—had been part of it a time or two. But seeing that scrap of filthy material brought reality crashing in around him. He took in the restraints, the plastic, the medical supplies, and his imagination conjured up horrific images of Nya struggling, vulnerable and at the hands of someone she once trusted.

He lowered to his haunches, running his finger across the stiff shorts, and his pulse sped as anger swept through him. To be restrained, not able to defend herself or fight back, was a Scythian's worst nightmare. His knuckles whitened as he grabbed hold of the shorts.

"Leave them." Gia's voice turned husky. "The Drahzda will know they're missing."

Ignoring her, he folded the material and placed it in the pack's front pocket.

"Jax, you really shouldn't—"

"He's left them here like some fucking shrine!" His anger finally gave way to rage, and he stood and faced the two people he hated almost as much as Sarkov. "Every time he sees them he thinks of taking them off of her. Touching her. Enjoying her pain. I don't give a shit if he knows … leaving anything of hers in this place is a monument that he overpowered her, dominated her, forced her to submit like some helpless Allos."

Gia's shoulder's slumped. "We hadn't thought of that."

"Yeah. I'm sure you didn't." Jax counted to ten. It wouldn't do any good to tell them what shitty parents he thought they were. Now wasn't the time. "Why are we here, Commander?"

Ike cleared his throat. "Fourth Gen has been tracking the Drahzda interaction with the Middle East's Voyager project."

Jax tilted his head. "What does human mutation research have to do with Nya?"

"You know about the program?"

"Four years ago, my last mission was taking care of two Drahzda genetics physicists that were working on human mutation and cloning. Before they died, we extracted information that Scythian blood had been used to further the technology."

Ike wearily scrubbed his face with his hand. "It was my unit that requested your help. I suspected they were using Nya's blood. The Tovaris confirmed it."

Jax's lips thinned to an angry line as he remembered the mission. Had he known, he would have followed Zander's plan and killed the bastards slowly.

Gia started across the room. "Until this week, we believed most of their study focused on mutation in an attempt to make the Allos stronger and faster. But new evidence shows that might not be the case."

She knelt down next to a silver object that looked like a small propane tank. "Do you know what this is?"

"No." Jax's voice became gruff as his imagination ran wild.

Gia unscrewed the lid. "It's the Allos version of a cryogenic storage unit. We found a partially destroyed vial, which we took back to the lab."

"And what does this have to do with Nya?"

Her chin quivered. "The vial held a Scythian ovum."

Dread coursed through Jax as he looked away. The only female to ever be captured was now in Carpathia with Victor. "Can they create clones from Nya's eggs?"

Gia hesitated. "It's possible. But the egg we found was left intact, which leads me to believe they wanted them for a different reason. We've never considered artificial insemination. Allos sperm isn't durable enough to naturally impregnate a Scythian female. But if science forced the issue?" Her knuckles whitened as she gripped the container. "We just don't know."

Horrified, Jax froze. "Are you telling me you think that bastard wanted to create half-breeds with Nya using artificial insemination?" The thought sent him into a tailspin.

Gia looked empty, haunted. "After her abduction, we had a specialist examine her while she was still under from the hand surgery. Blood samples showed she'd been given high doses of fertility drugs, but her hymen was intact. The doctor had no idea why she'd been injected, but there was mention of the possibility of harvesting eggs, even though there was no physical evidence that such a procedure had taken place."

"There would be no physical evidence if Nya had already healed, or the other injuries masked the site." Jax paced like a tiger in a cage. "Had no one thought of that?"

"The physician did." Gia pulled away from Ike, her voice became eerie, quiet. "He ran several blood tests when Nya was on her menstrual cycle, and we followed up with an internal ultrasound when she started the academy. He was concerned at some of the findings, but we had no conclusive evidence Nya's eggs had been taken until now. I contacted him yesterday. He still believes she can conceive, as long as she doesn't wait too long to start the process."

How could Gia calmly sit here and discuss this like it was nothing? Jax glared at them both. "I have to get back."

"Gia." Ike's jaw ticked as he stepped forward. "Check with the team and make sure the perimeter is secure."

Her stoic gaze met his.

He softened his tone. "Satellites show a large convoy of trucks on the way, but Fourth Gen staged a lorry accident, which will have northbound traffic tied up for hours. I need an update. Go on. We'll meet you at the truck."

She nodded and started toward the door. Ike kept silent, listening to her footfalls echo down the stairs and into the ballroom before pulling out his phone.

"Gia's on her way down. Give us ten minutes."

"What's this about, Commander?" Jax asked.

Ike disconnected the call, swiped to another app, and typed in a passcode. "There's something you need to see. You and I both know we could have taken care of this with a secured conference call. But *I* needed to see you. Gia doesn't know—it would destroy her."

He stepped closer so Jax could see the video loading on the small screen. "I encrypted a copy and then destroyed the original. I've shown this to no one, not even the Chancellor." He pressed play. "From the timestamp, the video was taken mere days before Dmitri Sarkov died."

The grainy picture cleared, revealing a lavish room with shackles on the wall. Blood dripped down the arms of the small frame that hung there. Ripped shirt, swollen face, and filthy shorts, her chin rested on her chest as her raven hair fell in front of her like a curtain of death.

The voice of Dmitri Sarkov came from off camera somewhere. "I'll ask you again, Anya Thalestris. What do the Scythians know about Phoenix conditioning?"

Nya's head rolled to one side as if she were trying to gain momentum to hold it up. Her eyes, so full of pain, hatred, and determination, looked through strands of tangled hair.

"Fuck. You."

"The Society doesn't deserve such loyalty. Even a jackal looks after his young, but your father led me right to you. And still, you refuse to betray them, though you've endured pain that would have killed the strongest of men."

Betrayal flashed across her face as she forced her head to stay up. "That's because I'm not a weak Allos."

"Yet you are the one pinned to a wall like an insect on a board. Who's weak now?"

She smiled, her eyes nothing but chips of hate. "Take off these shackles and let's see how brave you are."

"What do the Scythian's know about the Phoenix?"

She gritted her teeth, defiantly glaring back at him.

"Have it your way."

Nya's eyes shifted as a man wearing a surgical mask and gloves appeared at the edge of the frame. He held up a large syringe, filled with thick, gelatinous liquid.

Sarkov's voice chuckled. "Let's see how fearless you are after the Phoenix has taken flight."

Nya whimpered as the man with the mask came forward. Chains rattled as she struggled to break free. The man pushed her head to the side and plunged the needle into her neck.

"If she lives, my son can choose her triggers. That is his reward for bringing her to me."

The man with the needle ran his finger down the side of her face, his eyes just inches from hers. "Welcome to the Drahzdan army."

Nya's screams rang as the video faded to black.

Jax locked his knees. "Where did you get this?"

Ike's finger shook as he swiped the screen closed. "There was a mass exodus from the Drahzdan fortress in Astana. Only a skeleton crew of servants remained. I sent in a team to infiltrate and sweep the place, looking for anything that might be substantial. They found a shattered camera in one of the main rooms, and this was one of the videos recovered."

Jax's mind whirred with thoughts, trying to find a thread of hope. "We don't know if Phoenix conditioning works on Scythians. After the Trials, we'll run tests. She can still recover."

Ike's eyes, hollow with despair, found his. "Have you ever seen the Phoenix at work?"

"No."

"Once, before we went to Ireland, I was ordered to engage a Drahzdan cell trying to sabotage a Turkish nuclear power plant. We set up surveillance around the perimeter. As Sarkov's mercenaries arrived, one of the men must have questioned the commander, because the entire unit stopped a few yards from the gate. The captain calmly walked back to the soldier, uttered a few words, and the man fell to the ground screaming in agony. We found his body the next morning in the exact spot that he dropped. Blood streamed from his ears, eyes, and mouth. Coroner's report said the man literally boiled from the inside. That's what Phoenix conditioning can do."

"Damn it." Jax glared at the other man. "If I would've known this I never would've left Vtachi. Is there anything else? Anything at all?"

"There's one more thing."

Oh, God. What now?

Ike scooted between the hospital bed and plastic lining the large window. He pulled the thick sheet back, revealing a small mark on the window seal.

Metal against wood screeched as Jax pulled the bed farther from the wall and bent down to inspect it.

Scratched in the wood was the Dacian symbol for enemy alongside a crude shaped Scythian crest.

"She also scratched a message to me in the basement. I'll send you pictures, but I'm not going back there. She's telling us that this is the place of our enemy."

Jax rubbed the back of his neck. "Or she's trying to tell us that Scythian's are the enemy."

Ike's gaze flew to Jax. "That's impossible."

"Is it? Then why is Alexandra so obsessed with Nya's memory?"

Ike stepped away from the wall. "It's a security issue. You and I both know if Nya broke during interrogation it wouldn't be good for our side." He turned back to Jax. "And what you're suggesting is ludicrous. Alex is Pumpkin's godmother. She hid Nya's abduction because she wanted to protect my daughter's reputation. Some of the elite might not understand what happened, which would ruin her chances for finding her equal."

Jax bitterly smiled. "You haven't watched the news, have you?"

Ike swallowed. "Not in the past few days, why?"

"Zander baited Nya, and she attacked him. The cameras were there."

Desperation flashed in Ike's eyes. "Is she all right?"

"A Moor pulled her off Zander before he got to his feet, so yeah, she still has all her teeth if that's what you're asking."

"Alex implied that our old Trial footage had resurfaced. It upsets Gia, and so I've made sure to stay away from the media."

"Awfully damn convenient, don't you think? I guess she also didn't mention that a part of Nya's memory resurfaced when *Alex* confronted Vtachi about the attack. The warriors that overheard her telling me Penn was the one who captured her exploded with questions and accusations, which had the Chancellor retreating to her chambers."

"No. Alex didn't mention that either." Ike frowned.

Jax shoved the bed back to its original spot. "Damn it, Ike, think. Nya's memory is returning, and the Chancellor sent the only person that can get through to her to another fucking country."

Ike's nostrils flared. "Nya is the last of Ares and Otrera's line. No way would Alex jeopardize her like that."

Disgusted, Jax started toward the door. "Past behaviors predict future decisions. You've put the Society above everything else, including your family, your entire life. The Chancellor knows this. If Nya died, you'd be heartbroken, but you and Gia would eventually have another child. And if that didn't work, I'm sure you'd find a female of good breeding and have a bastard or two. Everything in your past predicts it. And so, I ask again—just how certain are you the Chancellor won't sacrifice Nya if she felt it was necessary?"

"I'd stake my life on it."

Jax shook his head. "The question is, are you willing to stake Nya's? Because I've got to say, I'm not. But I guess that's the difference between us, isn't it? In the end, you'll do what's right for the Society, but I'd turn my back on everyone, including the Tovaris if it were best for her."

Giovanni made idle conversation as they passed a horde of reporters. Mercifully, the media could only follow them as far as the path that led to the stables. He took every opportunity to graze his fingers here, or whisper a caress there. Nya knew most females would have melted into a puddle by now, but his soft touch did nothing but ramp up her anxiety.

Jax hadn't contacted her since he left. What if something had happened to him?

"… and that's how I picked them. Which one would you like, Dea?" He smiled as he pulled her to a stop, waiting for an answer.

"I'm sorry. What did you say?"

His smile slipped a little. "I asked which of the stallions you would like."

"I'm fine with either, really."

Giovanni grew quiet, and Nya inwardly cursed. So much for keeping an open mind. She took his hand, determined to do better. "I apologize. My thoughts keep wandering."

He glanced over his shoulder at the cameras trained on their backs. "I admit the media is a bit distracting."

"I hoped it would die down by now."

He grinned. "You are the first in years to bring a Tova to his knees. What had you so enraged that you went against the doctor's orders?"

No way was she telling Giovanni Zander had called her Penn's sloppy seconds, but she had to say something.

"The Tova's Suveran insulted me. I reacted as any warrior would."

Whinnies rang ahead as two stablehands brought out the horses, one speckled gray and another black. Nya thanked them and chose the dappled steed.

Giovanni watched her mount the horse, his eyes traveling up her thighs to her hips, then breasts before stopping on her face. "I see you've ridden before. Our compound has a stable that houses everything from Thoroughbreds to Irish Draughts. After I've shouldered your mark, we'll ride often if you like."

Nya eased her horse into a canter without replying. She glanced over at the Italian and sighed. Giovanni might be a little over the top, but he was kind. And since lunch, she'd basically ignored him.

She slowed to a trot. "What was your childhood like, and how did your parents meet?"

Giovanni smiled. "Ah, my Dea is finally curious. This is a good thing." Italian rolled off his tongue like warm honey. "Mama and Papa met here, at their Trial. Although theirs was a rocky start."

Clouds rolled in, cooling the air, and Giovanni pulled his horse to a stop.

"See, Mama was in love with another and made sure he was one of her Chosen. But in the end, Papa defeated the other male."

Nya's hands tightened around the reins. "That must have been difficult. What did they do?"

"They honored the contract and went through the tattoo ceremony that evening, and then father claimed his romni's body that night."

Nya squirmed in her seat. "That's not what I meant. How did your father deal with your mother being in love with another?"

"Ah." Giovanni smiled. "Well, Papa worried that she would never accept him, but he was determined to love her as much as she would allow. His patience paid off, and my mother now sees the joy of finding her true equal, even though she was heartbroken when she first shouldered Papa's mark." He reached over and took her hand. "Understand, Dea. If I am strong enough to claim you, I will not let you go. My parents found happiness, and we will, too. Our young will grow up surrounded by friendship and love. Of that, I have no doubt."

Nya swallowed past the lump in her throat. Her upbringing had been so different from his. She was born out of an obligation to continue Ares and Otrera's line. Her parents never laughed, and they moved so much that Nya never had the chance to make friends, except when they settled in Ireland and she met Penn.

She patted his hand. "You'll make a great rovni and father someday, Giovanni. I know you will."

He pulled away as they both heard her unspoken words.

Just not with me.

CHAPTER TWENTY-FOUR

As soon as the guards opened the castle's front door, Penn stormed through. Light arced across the dilapidated foyer, and Sergei held up his hand, motioning for everyone to stop.

"What is it?" Stephan whispered.

"I'm not sure, but something is off." Sergei softly spoke into a band on his wrist, and a team of soldiers poured in from the front, some surrounding Penn while others ran up the stairs and through the hall to the back.

"You're paranoid," Penn growled, pushing Stephan out of the way. "I'm going to the containment room."

Stephan kept up with his quick pace as Sergei cursed and jogged ahead. They made their way down the back steps and into what used to be the dungeon. Penn stood outside her cell, looking at the mattress on the floor, the place where she first discovered her life had changed. He had to admit, he was surprised by her reaction. He thought she'd embrace her new life, not fight like hell to leave it. But in the end, it didn't matter. She would be his. The pharmaceuticals they'd used along with intense psychological conditioning assured that she would come back to him. Submit to him. And then they could build a new empire together. One where she wielded power, usurped only by his. It was a matter of time before the world was theirs. And then she'd see. He was right all along.

Penn closed his eyes at the sweet memories of her screams, her whimpers. She. Was. Exquisite. That's what he craved. Her, helpless. Begging. Needing him just to breathe.

He perused the room. The place looked as it had the night they brought her in. He inhaled, taking in the pungent smell of urine, mold, and dirt. God. A part of him hated that he had to contain her with chains, make her suffer that way. But breaking her body was the only way to break her spirit. And once he did that, she'd be his forever. An unpleasant step, to be sure. But oh, so necessary.

"Sir, the men cleared out most of the top floors last night so the restoration team can start at dawn."

Penn nodded that he'd heard, his eyes still fixed on that mattress. She'd managed to kill one of her guards before they tranquilized her enough to shackle her. He could have taken her then, but forcing the issue wasn't what he wanted.

He wanted her to bow to him, to understand her place was under him, serving his needs as a real wife should. He would decide what was best for her. And she would depend on his control. That was the Drahzdan way, as it was meant to be. Men were responsible for decisions—and women were content to be protected and loved.

"Sir," Stephan's voice grew soft. "I must ask. Shouldn't we wait until your Ana is back in our care? It is a risk to start on the castle right now. We have security measures in place, but if this is to be your home, we'll need to insure the entire area is secure. Renovating before we have control of the surrounding villages is dangerous."

Penn sighed, his voice eerily quiet. "Haven't we been through this? I will admit, I thought my Ana would have broken a few months after she'd been taken from me. And then she went to that nasty place in America, where we couldn't get to her. But it is no matter. Our sources confirm their therapies weren't working. She still cannot stand anyone's touch but mine. She will allow no one near her. When she is forced to find a husband, she will break and come running back into my arms, where she will take her place once and for all. It's been a long time coming, but the Drahzdan Empire is on the cusp of change. Allowing my Ana this time to struggle on her own will only make her surrender that much sweeter. And when she comes home, she'll have a castle worthy of her and our offspring."

Stephan already had a dozen women willing to surrogate their first generation. Hundreds of his Ana's eggs were safe, just waiting for his seed. And the best part? Her body would never suffer the ravages of childbirth. It would stay perfect and tight, just for him.

"But sir—"

"I said we start tonight!" Penn's shrill scream echoed off the stone walls.

The men behind them froze.

"Yes, sir," Stephan muttered. He glanced over his shoulder, and the others scrambled down the hall and through various doors.

Penn placed his hand over his heart, his mind whirring with a million thoughts. "She's close to breaking. I feel it."

Stephan hesitated. "Would you like to go in?"

Penn shook his head. "I cannot bear to be in there without her. This will be the first room we visit after we consummate our marriage. I look forward to reminding her this is the consequence of defiance." His eyes glittered as he smiled. "Her pain ... Father was right. A good woman must be strong but also know her place. Just like Mother. She proved she wasn't weak when she left Father, but once he found her and she submitted completely, only then was she truly happy. My Ana will be the same."

Stephan swallowed and kept his expression neutral. "Yes, sir."

Penn glanced back and did a double take, his eyes narrowing at a spot across the room. "What's this?"

Stephan backed up. "What's what?"

"That?" Penn pointed across the room. "Has someone been in here?"

"No, sir."

Penn charged through the threshold, past the shackles and bucket. "Then explain this!"

Stephan cautiously walked a few steps in far enough to see the clean streaks running across the grimy etchings on the wall.

"Someone has touched the markings that she made. Actually touched them!" Penn's voice rose to a hysterical pitch. "I'll gut them where they stand!" he shrieked, his eyes darting around the room as if searching for the culprit.

"Sir," Stephan's voice grew strangely calm. "I assure you. No one has been here since last week, and even then, I personally guarded this room and the extraction room when the team was securing the area for your arrival."

"The extraction room?" Penn's voice fell to a whisper as he made his way toward the door, his steps speeding to a full run. He took the stairs three at a time, bolted across the foyer and ran up to the second floor, knocking a few men out of the way. Bursting through the door, he froze. His eyes darted around the plastic-lined room, cataloging every detail, searching for evidence that someone had defiled this sacred chamber.

And then he saw it. The place where his Ana's shorts should have been. He'd removed them himself while she was still weak from the drugs they were forced to use. It had been a special time for them. Him learning the soft curves of her body while he shackled her to the examining table. The injuries she'd inflicted on several guards left her clothes filthy, but Penn didn't want them cleaned. He kept them there as a reminder that she had fought valiantly and lost.

And now they were gone. They should still be here. He left everything exactly as it was the night they extracted his future children from her body. Fury marred his face. He'd planned on renovating the place, making this a nursery for their first generation. A room full of symbolism—worthy of their future heirs.

"They know," he whispered. "They've been here."

"The Scythians?" Stephan's voice rose.

Penn's first instinct was to burn the castle to ash. He hated that someone had come in and defiled this sacred room. This was the first place his Ana learned of her future. He'd dreamed of a time when she would find her way back here. To her home. To him.

That thought cooled his temper while heating his passion.

No. He wouldn't destroy the castle in a fit of rage. This was the place they had started, and he wouldn't allow anyone to take that from them. Though they would have to now scourge this room and then possibly anoint it with the blood of those who chose to taint it in the first place.

His eyes rolled back in his head at the thought. *Yes.* That's what they'd do.

"Have the men start here, immediately. They are to work through the night, clearing away the plastic and stripping the walls to the plaster. Wash every inch with bleach."

Stephan wisely nodded and backed away. "As you wish. I'll find the foreman and tell him at once."

Penn walked over to the table, his long fingers caressing a restraint. "Soon, my love. Soon."

CHAPTER TWENTY-FIVE

Killian's eyes stayed on Nya while she roamed the vast hall. Finally, they were alone.

"I've never seen a theater like this." Nya slid her fingers along a sleek wooden bar, complete with everything from popcorn and candy to liquor and nuts. On one side, recessed lighting lit several pool tables and gaming boards, the space ending in a curved, cozy reading nook. The other held recliners, built for two, which faced the far wall that housed a large screen.

Killian came from behind. "Why don't you get some snacks, and I'll load the movie. What would you like to see?"

"How about the last in The Lord of the Rings series?"

He stepped back, needing a little space before he did something stupid, like tell her he'd known for four years she was the only female he wanted to spend the rest of his life with. "That film's been out for ages. Not much of a movie buff, are you?"

She looked away. "Not really."

He went to a touchscreen in the back of the room while she grabbed a few bottled sodas and some red licorice twists.

"Ever been to the Academy in Montana?" Nya asked as she started toward the seating area.

"Once or twice." Killian grinned.

She cleared her throat as she stopped in front of an oversized recliner built for two. "How come I didn't see you?"

"The headmistress wouldn't let me past the gates. Apparently, she was onto my game to meet you."

Surprised, she turned, watching him head her way. "You knew I was there?"

He stopped in front of her. "Oh, yeah. I knew."

Nya had become a small obsession of his after her rite of passage. He was ecstatic when he found out she'd be attending the U.S. academy. And when the CIA discovered a Drahzdan sleeper cell within fifty kilometers of Bitterroot, he volunteered to track the sons of bitches down.

That's when he saw her. Sunshine streaked a blue sheen in her black hair as she slipped through the trees with graceful speed. He'd never forget her sleek, economy of movement. He was drawn to it—that natural comfort in her own skin that only a warrior of her caliber had.

She'd just found her footing when a deep, masculine voice called, yelling something about following her to the ends of the Earth.

Killian later confirmed that young warrior was indeed Anya Thalestris, and the male with her that day was the infamous Dr. Ajax Nickius.

Nya glanced at the recliner and blushed. "I hear you're an excellent tracker."

Killian didn't give her a chance to overthink, and he sat down, pulling her with him. "Nice to know you've been asking about me."

Pink tinged her cheeks. "Apparently, you can track anything."

Her unique scent washed over him, and he settled back into the plush leather, causing her body to slide closer to his. "I'd track you to the ends of the Earth, Anya Thalestris."

Nya blinked a few times, and Killian smirked as he realized Jax had shouted that very thing to her four years ago in the woods.

"Victor seems to think I should be worried about you defeating me."

Victor is a smart, smart male. It wasn't that he doubted her abilities. Killian was sure she'd be a worthy opponent. But at the end of the day, he'd win. And then he'd shoulder her mark and bring her home where she'd finally be able to heal in peace.

"Oh, I'll defeat you." Killian kissed her cheek before meeting her gaze. His expression became grave. "But even when we're sparring, I won't hurt you."

She bristled. "I'll try not to hurt you, too."

"Good to know." His eyes twinkled.

The sound roared to life, and the lights dimmed as the opening credits rolled. Killian ran his fingertips up and down her arm, loving it when she finally relaxed. He reached over and pulled out a licorice twist.

"Can I ask why you chose this movie?" His voice rumbled above her head as he offered her the candy.

"One winter, when I was sixteen, my father came home from a mission in Russia. Something went wrong, but he wouldn't talk about it. We spent the day together watching a Lord of the Rings movie marathon, but I fell asleep halfway through this one, so I'd like to see how it ends."

Killian's hand stilled. "Did your father ever tell you what happened?"

She shook her head. "No. But I think it had something to do with the leader of the Drahzda because I heard him and my mother arguing about it that night."

His fingers resumed their trail up and down her arm.

She took a deep breath and sighed. "I didn't think I'd like this, but I do."

He smiled. He'd spend rest of his life snuggling if that's what she wanted. "I'm glad."

They fell silent, watching the hobbits struggle to Mordor.

"Frodo's a kindred spirit," Nya muttered, her voice thick as if she had been sleeping.

"How so?" Killian shifted her over until her leg rested between his.

"He suffers because only he can bear the ring." She yawned before her breathing slowed to a steady rhythm.

Killian's fingers kept grazing patterns on her back as he watched Frodo's descent into paranoid darkness, the ring ravaging his soul.

Is that how she felt about being the last of her heritage, or was she talking about something else?

She stirred, her face squinted as if she were in pain, her body twitched.

Killian pulled her closer, his hands splayed wide across her back. "Ny, it's all right. I've got you."

"Thanks, Jax," she muttered, relaxing into his hold.

Killian took a deep breath, reminding himself that Dr. Nickius had been her counselor for years. Still didn't help the urge to hunt the warrior down and challenge him to prove his worth.

Nya's hand slid over his torso as she jumped out of sleep again.

"It's okay, Ny," Killian sighed, his fingers never losing their pattern.

"I'm glad you're here," she whispered, snuggling into his warmth.

"Say my name."

She stilled. "What?"

Killian huffed. "Nothing."

Her hand rested over his heart. "I'm glad you're here, Killian."

He smiled and kissed the top of her head. "Me too."

The music swelled as giant eagles snatched Frodo and Sam, taking them back to the Shire.

"Can I ask you a question?" He pulled her closer.

"Yes."

"Why do you have a curved knife hidden on the inside of your thigh?"

Nya blushed. "I feel safer when I have something to protect myself with."

Killian grinned and pulled up his pant leg. A small holster rested on his inner ankle. "I can understand that."

"I'm sorry I fell asleep on you."

"I'm not," he whispered in her ear. "I now know what it's like to hold you in my arms. And that's worth fighting for."

"Miko, get this bucket in the air," Jax ordered.

"Calm down, Nick." Smoke curled from the end of a cigarette as the warrior smiled. She took a last drag before throwing it down and grinding it beneath her boot. "I'll get you back to your romni."

They jumped in the plane, and Jax put on his headset. "Not mine yet. And she's starting to remember."

"Zander know?"

"Hell yes, he knows." Jax glowered. "According to Doc, Zander baited her until she attacked and sent him to his knees."

Laughter echoed as the engine roared to life. "Damn, I'd have given anything to see that. Sounds like you got a good one."

Jax smiled for the first time since he'd left Carpathia. "Yeah, I do."

The Asian warrior put on her headphones. "Then let's get you home."

Propellers whirred as the two-seater taxied down the runway. Jax took a deep breath, his thoughts settling on his Vtachi. He was stuck in

Carpathia the night Nya was rescued from that cargo ship. But after Jax demanded the *Zvaz* ceremony, Zander ordered every Tova who participated in the mission to keep their mouths shut.

Now he understood why. Most Tovas settled for a solitary life, taking carnal pleasure wherever they could, knowing they'd have little more than that. Both male and female Tovaris usually had bastard children raised in compound homes or possibly by extended family. It was an accepted practice, as Tovas were usually too busy dealing with the worst the world had to offer. Revenge, hatred, death. These were things that came easily to a Tova. But love—much less an *intima* bond—was scarcely seen and was coveted above all else. When one of them found their equal, they protected it with all they had.

By ordering everyone to keep that night on the docks a secret, Zander had given Jax the opportunity to get to know Nya without the baggage her parents had caused, nor the bullshit that accompanied being the last line of Ares and Otrera.

After Jax beat the shit out of his leader, he might just thank him.

"Storm's moving in."

Miko's voice blared through his headset, stirring him from his thoughts. He glanced at the thick clouds burgeoning the sky.

Jax's lips thinned. "Fly through it."

"Sorry, Nick. Not in this field hopper. But I've radioed Zander, and he'll have a train waiting. Best we can do, but it'll be late before you reach the consulate."

He scrubbed his face with his hand as thunder rumbled in the distance. "It beats waiting on Alexandra."

"You got that right." Miko chuckled and started her descent.

They'd just landed when Jax's phone buzzed. Miko stepped out of the plane, leaving him alone.

"Where are you?" Victor's voice was nothing more than a quiet hush, and Jax had a feeling he was squirreled away in some corner of the castle, not on the grid.

"We hit weather on the way back. Zander found a train. I'll be in by morning. How's she doing?"

"She and Killian watched a movie."

Jax thumped his head on the back of the seat. "He held her, didn't he? He held her while she slept."

"Nick. This is all part of the process. You know that."

"What about the Moor? Should I be concerned?" The hair on Jax's neck prickled as his question was met with silence.

"I'd put him in equal measure with Killian," Victor finally hedged.

Jax watched as the rain started pelting the windshield. "I can take Killian."

"I'm sure you can. But this Moor has impressive Silat skills."

"Good to know."

"Was your trip productive?"

Jax rubbed his forehead as the image of Nya's bloody frame shackled to a wall flashed in his mind. "More than I wanted."

"Interesting. You've discovered new information?"

"Have you seen the new research on mind control?"

Victor paused. "Of course. The Allos are most susceptible, but if the Drahzda combined the technique with pharmaceuticals, it would cause anyone to be in a highly suggestible state."

"It would also be a reason why a warrior doesn't remember certain events until a trigger unlocks their mind."

"If we force the issue, she could enter a deep level of psychosis, or fight it and completely break down. Is this your theory as to why the Drahzda didn't kill Nya as soon as the Tovaris boarded the ship?"

"It's possible, although I believe Penn never thought they'd be discovered in the first place. I believe he put her through hell, and when she wouldn't break he took her home to watch her parents die and her compound burn. Penn wanted her at her most vulnerable so she would submit willingly to him. He must be more delusional than we initially thought because he never planned for an attack. Anyway, there's evidence to suggest he planted a trigger deep within her psyche which would cause her extreme pain until she went back to Sarkov."

"Extreme pain?" Victor's voice rose in surprise. "No pharmaceuticals could have such an effect on a Scythian."

Jax hesitated. No one knew that she'd been injected with the Phoenix, and he wanted to keep it that way. At least for now. "It's just a theory, but one I'd rather not test while I'm away."

"What aren't you telling me, Nick?"

Jax closed his eyes. "There's too much information, and I've got to catch a train. But know this. Sarkov himself set the triggers."

"Interesting," Victor said. "Touch being the most obvious."

"It's promising that she's overcome it." Jax shifted the phone as he unbuckled his seatbelt. "But I think the deepest triggers would have to do with desire, passion, or pleasure. Tell me, what do you think her physical response is to the other candidates? Other than me, is she sexually attracted to any of them?"

Victor hesitated. "We'll discuss it when you get here. Safe travels, Nick."

Rain pelted his face as Jax opened the plane door. He flipped up his hood and jogged across the tarmac, trying to block out the thought that his Vtachi might prefer another warrior over him.

CHAPTER TWENTY-SIX

Frost covered the windshield, making the remote castle seem like mottled shapes of clay. Gia had parked the SUV between the broken rampart and a clump of evergreens. The vehicle's dark color blended with the landscape, making it damn near impossible to see from the road.

Ike kept silent, his mind racing with images from that video—the betrayal in his sweet *nata's* eyes as Sarkov taunted her, Nya struggling as a needle plunged into her neck, her scream as the images went black. Thank God, his romni hadn't seen it. At least one of them could hold out hope.

"When she finds out, I don't know if she'll ever forgive us." Gia blindly stared ahead.

He reached over and covered her cold fingers with his broad palm. "We have to have faith that she will."

The roar of engines hummed in the distance, growing louder as lights filtered over the road. Dust billowed around a convoy of cargo vans and box trucks as they sped toward the castle. Gia grabbed the binoculars and leaned forward, wiping condensation off the windshield. "They're here."

"What are you up to, Sarkov?" Ike watched the first two vans pull around the broken circular drive. Their doors slid open, and Drahzda soldiers jumped out with automatic weapons, securing the perimeter. The next row of vans came to a stop, and others hopped out and started unloading supplies. A few minutes later, several buses pulled up with what appeared to be workers, most likely from a local village. Drahzda soldiers ordered the men in rows, handing them tools and hard hats before directing them up the stone steps and into the foyer.

"Why the rush?" Gia's voice shook as she handed over the binoculars. "They've had this property for a while. Why start renovating now?"

Ike focused on the flurry of activity, Jax's words coming back to him.

"... *Penn's banking that Nya will break and come back to him on her own. That's why the Drahzda are on the move. The sick bastard wants this to be their new home.*"

He shifted the binoculars, focusing on the leader by the door. "My bet is Penn wants to establish his own identity. The Astana Fortress was his father's legacy. This will be his."

"He could have done that four years ago."

Ike glanced over. "He would have spread his resources too thin if he had."

More trucks poured in from the main road.

He leaned forward, his eyes squinting through the lenses. "Text Jax and fill him in."

Surprised, Gia stared at his profile. "What about Alexandra?"

Ike said nothing.

Gia placed her hand on his arm. "You suspect something, don't you?"

He took in Gia's pale complexion and desperate eyes. "Let's hold off a while on the Chancellor."

She took out her phone and texted Jax. "And if she calls and asks about what we've found or anything about Jax?"

"Tell her as little as possible."

Nya stirred to someone knocking at the door. She stumbled out of bed and turned the knob, still only half awake. "Xari, really. I've got another half an hour ..."

Her voice fell away as males crowded the hallway. Victor shouldered through, his eyes assessing her bare legs and messy hair, wearing nothing but an oversized shirt. The warriors pressed in for a better look, and Nya stepped back.

Victor glanced over his shoulder. "She'll be ready within the hour. Until then, I suggest you make your way to the practice field."

Dumbfounded, she just stood there as Victor closed the door.

"I'd say that went well, wouldn't you?" His gaze stayed resolutely on her face. "Get dressed. We have work to do."

"What the hell is going on?"

He sighed. "A rumor surfaced last night that you have released Dr. Nickius as an official candidate. The press picked it up, and now it's all over the net."

She rubbed her eyes. "Who in the hell would do something like that?"

Victor raised a brow. "I suspect one of the uncommitted is upset that a Tova is taking a precious spot as an official candidate, and yet he hasn't been seen in days."

"Does anyone know Alexandra ordered Jax to Russia?"

"I can't be sure, but judging by the consulate's response of 'no comment,' I'd say the matter has been deemed classified. If that's the case, you may have to make a statement this afternoon to appease the council."

"What does that mean?"

He watched her rub her thumb over her palm. "It means you may have to give them five candidates that are physically here."

Horrified, Nya shook her head. "What? No. Jax is mine."

"I'm sure he'd agree," Victor dryly said.

"I meant he's still one of my official candidates."

He waved his hand, brushing her comment away. "Let's call it a Freudian slip and move on, shall we?"

A knock sounded in the room.

"I ordered breakfast. Put some clothes on." Victor strolled toward the door, and Nya scrambled to the closet to find something suitable to wear.

What a nightmare. If the council forced her to name someone other than Jax, what would she do? Once a champion released a candidate, she wasn't allowed to choose him again.

If push came to shove, she'd threaten her dear old godmother. If Alexandra hadn't told the Rovni Council, she sure as hell wouldn't want the media to know that Jax was on a mission, either. It would cause a shitstorm, but Nya would be damned before she allowed politics to push her into a corner. She had the right to choose. And she still wanted Jax.

Armed with that decision, she grabbed the only comforting thing she could find—black jeans, a matching turtleneck, and her rugged boots. She took out her Velcro strap and secured it below her knee before sheathing the small knife to the inside of her calf. Running her hand over the triple spire arm cuff that wound around her upper arm, she hoped Jax hadn't seen the news. The last thing he needed was a distraction.

But it would be helpful if he'd hurry his ass back to the consulate.

The scent of bacon wafted through the room as she made her way out of the dressing area.

"All black. A bit Tovarian, don't you think?" Victor raised a brow.

She sat down, grabbed a bagel, and slathered on some cream cheese. "Like I care."

Victor smiled. "Which will impress the warriors more. You really know how to work this, don't you?"

Nya's bagel stopped midair. "What do you mean?"

"Think of it, the challenge you present. You are the last of Ares and Otrera's line. The *nata* of a female who sits on the Chancellor's council and whose father is the commanding officer of Fourth Gen. If they could take you from Jax, the only Tova that has entered the Trials in decades, and claim you as their equal, what a victory that would be."

Nya's mouth went dry, and she dropped her bagel on her plate. "I hate this."

Victor sat back. "Why, Anya? Most Amazons would love to be in your shoes. And yet you look as if you are being tortured."

She glanced at him. "Strange choice of words, Doctor Ramova."

"I see we're back to formalities."

She started to rise from her chair, and Victor held up a hand.

"We're not done yet. Sit. And please, eat something."

She flopped back down, and Victor crossed his legs as if to stay a while. "The past few days have given you a chance to get to know your candidates."

"Yes. And?" She tore off a piece of her bagel and stuck it in her mouth.

"Are you satisfied with the warriors you've chosen?"

Nya sighed. "Just get to the point, Victor."

He leaned forward. "I suspect the uncommitted will be out in full force this morning, demonstrating their abilities. It is prudent that you observe all the candidates with the eyes of an Amazonian warrior looking for her equal. When you declare your Chosen, there is no going back."

Nya closed her eyes. "This is crazy."

"No. This is tradition. And you would do well to respect the Trials as they are the reason our species exists."

Dread iced through her as Jax's words came back.

Keep an open mind, Vtachi.

What in the hell was she going to do?

CHAPTER TWENTY-SEVEN

Penn stood at the end of the parapet, just behind the castle's tallest spire. Saws and hammers drummed beneath his feet as hundreds of workers started in the upper rooms. He'd been there well before dawn, watching the road, hoping against all the odds the serum had finally taken its toll and his Ana was on her way home.

"Sir," Stephan spoke to his right, and Penn ground his teeth together. It would do no good to throw his assistant off the ledge. Stephan had been the longest to survive in this position. Good help was hard to train.

"What is it?" Penn kept his eyes on the road.

"As you have requested, the extraction room is now completely sanitized, and the plaster is being repaired as we speak. Everything in that space has been taken out back and burned. Would you like the workers to join the others on the top floors, or would you rather they start restoring the plaster and windows in the foyer?"

"Have them concentrate on Ana's and my suite. That will be the first set of rooms needed."

"Yes, sir."

Stephan slowly backed away.

Penn rested his elbows against the low wall that protected the parapet. The constant pain brought on by the Phoenix serum subsided as he remembered confronting his father on Ana's treatments. She'd already undergone two weeks of conditioning that would have killed any man. And yet, amid the screams and whimpers, she never betrayed her kind, never uttered a word about her father or the chancellor, never spoke of anyone in the Society, even after she'd been injected with the Phoenix. Dmitri finally reached his limit and ordered Ana's death, but Penn had endured enough of his father's tyranny.

When he burst into the room where Dmitri met with his council, no one thought a thing of it. They all knew how he felt about Anya Thalestris. Penn's one condition for bringing her to Dmitri was that no one, Drahzdan or Scythian, would ever be allowed to touch his Ana again. Only Penn would know what she looked like unclothed. No one else would smell her sweet scent or feel her soft flesh.

He reminded the council that Dmitri had decreed that very thing mere months ago. His father stood, stating that he had not gone back on his word. He promised Penn would be the only one allowed to touch Nya, and no one had. She had been beaten with whips and canes, and when she was sedated or moved, his men used gloves. Dmitri was an ethical man, after all. And so, it would only be fitting for his son to drive the knife through the young Scythian's heart.

Penn's blood blazed at the order, making it difficult to stand.

No one questioned it when Penn walked toward his father, pleading with him to reconsider. The guards hadn't moved as he stepped closer, his hands placed together in supplication, begging Dmitri to change his mind.

The Drahzdan Tsar laughed, calling his son weak, and Penn thrust his hands forward, lunging straight for Dmitri's neck, the tips of his fingers crushing his father's windpipe. Before the Drahzdan guards even blinked, Penn had grabbed his father's head and whipped it from side to side, efficiently snapping his neck in two.

Embracing the hell blazing through his veins, Penn stood over Dmitri's lifeless body and let out a primal yell that reverberated down the corridors of the fortress.

Yes, Penn smiled, his thoughts turning to the present as he looked at the road. The time his Ana had insisted he learn Scythian defense had taught him well.

By Drahzdan law, the minute Dmitri died Penn became the new ruler. Which meant no one could touch him. Penn viewed it as the ultimate justice.

That night, after he publicly had Dmitri's council executed in front of the Drahzdan Army, Penn ordered the troops to swear fealty to him. Those that hesitated were thrown on the blazing pyre that already engulfed the dead. The new regime quickly replaced the old, and within the week Penn had his commanders in place. He took his Ana from the Astana fortress, and they made their way across Russia—to the castle that would become the head of the new Drahzdan Empire. One that no longer relied on Phoenix conditioning alone.

Yes, his sweet Ana would return, and he would remind her of the time before the blood fires. A time when, in their innocence, they learned to love.

Memories of Ireland took their toll as heat roared through him, reminding him that Dmitri had chosen his triggers well. Cursing his father for the thousandth time, Penn's hand shook as he reached into his pocket and pulled out a vial. He popped a few pills under his tongue, closed his eyes, and quieted his mind, allowing the meds to soothe his raging body.

He'd need to conserve his strength. Soon, his Ana would be home.

Aren rested his hand on the small of Nya's back as he led her across the foyer toward the front doors. He stopped several times, speaking to warriors that milled in and out of the dining hall. Nya nodded at the right times, not really paying attention.

It had been a hellish day with Victor taking hidden passageways and back corridors to avoid the press. She'd eaten meals with her official candidates in a secured conference room, and Xari was the only one other than her males allowed to speak with her.

They finally made it through the foyer, and Aren opened the front door. Lights blinded them as bulbs flashed from all directions.

"Anya Thalestris, have you released Dr. Nickius as an official candidate? And if so, which warrior has taken his place?"

"Anya, have you spoken to your mother about the move? Is she the reason you've released the Tova?"

"Anya! Will you consent to an interview before the ball tomorrow night?"

Aren held up his hand, and the reporters fell silent.

"This is my official time with my champion." His voice rang with a thread of annoyance. "I'd appreciate it if you would respect the rules of the Trials. If you will excuse us."

Aren nudged her forward, and Nya kept her head high.

God, she hated the media. They had been the reason her mother struggled with doubt. Nya had watched similar scenes like this her entire life as reporters questioned if her mother was the best choice for the last of Otrera's line. And every fall her father's final round was like some sick sports reel they splashed over every Scythian channel. The most scandalous trial of the century was followed by the first broadcast of the shocking news that the infamous Ike Thalestris had settled for someone other than a champion. Year after year, the constant barrage acted like water over stone, slowly eroding Gia's spirit until she was a mere shadow of her former self.

Nya would be damned if she'd do the same.

Aren led her away from the consulate and into the night.

Fresh anxiety rolled over her like salt on a wound.

Why hadn't she thought of it before? No matter who became her rovni, the press would never leave them alone. But if it was Jax? God. He was just as notorious as her father.

The media would be relentless, much less Zander who would never let her forget that she was the reason for that big scar across this face. Even though he openly approved of the match, privately, he'd probably spend the rest of his life reminding her she wasn't strong enough to be a Tova. Eventually, Jax would start believing it, too.

A cool breeze brushed across her face as Aren guided her farther into the woods, towards the planetarium.

"Penny for your thoughts." He wove his fingers between hers.

Nya's cheeks flushed, and she was grateful the trees blocked the moonlight. "It's nothing."

"Oh, I think it's something all right. I'm guessing it has to do with the one candidate who isn't here."

She sighed. "I've seen Jax almost every day for four years. He's been an instructor, counselor, and friend. He's helped me through things—I'm close to him."

"Ah." Aren led her past the path that led to the stables. "And are you attracted to him, as a female is a male."

Nya kept her eyes forward. "Yes."

They came to a clearing, and Aren gently turned her to face him.

"Attraction is a response to pheromones and physical personal preference. Nothing more. Are you attracted to any of your other candidates?"

Nya swallowed. "It's different, but yes."

"Are you attracted to me?"

She grew quiet. "I think so."

He stepped closer, his scent wrapping around her.

"Do you know why the Moors choose to stay among their own when finding a romni?"

The question surprised her. "No."

His fingers slipped through her hair. "It isn't because we're an exclusionary culture, or that we find differences sexually unappealing. Scythian Moors view love differently."

Nya's shoes sunk into the soft earth. The rain had finally cleared, but heavy gray clouds still hung low in the sky. "How so?"

"The Allos are shallow, hunting for love as if it were the ultimate prey. Or they resent love, seeing it as unjust because it finds only those that cannot appreciate its beauty."

Nya raised a brow. "That's rather cynical."

Aren smiled. "Yes, it is. But most Scythians believe that love doesn't exist at all. It's a manifestation of awareness and the mind's way of making sure we procreate."

"And that's rather scientific."

Aren's smile grew. "Yes, it is."

He curled his fingers around the dip of her waist, and they started forward again. "Moors, however, believe in love so deep it can form connections that transcend consciousness."

"You mean an *intima* bond?"

"Both Maori and the Moors call it something else, but yes."

"And is that what you want—to find someone who shares more than just their mind and body?"

Aren took her hand and brought it to his chest. "I had it once, and until recently I never thought I'd find it again."

A small crease appeared between her brows. "But you can't create a bond like that with just anyone."

"True. There has to be chemistry between the partners to achieve that deep of a connection. But, like is drawn to like. And my tribe, my people, we have a saying. A love received demands love returned."

Nya's breath caught as he stepped closer. "So you think love is a choice."

"Absolutely. Attraction creates a connection that grows when we trust another with our deepest insecurities and strongest desires. Exposing oneself in such a way allows our mate to seep into the hidden places of our heart. It's a profound link which lasts a lifetime. And that connection develops and becomes something more—something spiritual."

"Oh." Nya's voice trailed away. If that's what Aren believed, then there was no way she would equal him in matters of the heart. Yes, she was attracted to his strength, but as she'd already told Jax, she doubted she'd ever be able to give that much of herself to anyone.

He nudged her forward. They made their way down the path and through the trees. A dome-shaped silhouette appeared in the distance. They ascended the planetarium steps, and he unlocked the door.

"In you go."

Nya stepped through the threshold. Aren walked past and placed the keys on the welcome desk.

The glass dome revealed a cloud covered sky, and Nya sighed. "Not sure tonight's the best night for star gazing."

Aren smiled. "That's where you're wrong. Take a seat."

A group of recliners, much like the ones in the theater, stood in the center of the room. Aren went to a control panel while Nya sat in one of the oversized chairs. A few seconds later, everything went black, and Aren settled next to her side.

"Relax and look at the universe." His deep voice rumbled as he pressed a button and the seats reclined.

The darkness around them melded into the Milky Way, pouring over the curved walls and onto the floor. Orchestral strings softly played as a shooting star blazed across the dome. The images slowly rotated, giving Nya the sensation they were floating in space.

"This is fantastic," she whispered, afraid to break the spell the place had created.

He put his arm around her, pulling her close so her head could rest on his shoulder. "I'm glad you like it."

They settled into a peaceful quiet, and the music swelled then ebbed as the galaxy floated above them. Aren shifted his body until he rested on his side, his lips grazing a tender spot on her neck, his braids brushed across her chest as he nuzzled close.

She stiffened. "Aren, wait."

His beautiful ebony skin gleamed in the limited light, his thumb tracing over the dragon spire arm cuff guarding the place where an empty mark stood.

"Why? You're an Amazonian warrior, searching for her rovni. I am a Scythian Moor looking for his mate. Why shouldn't we explore if we can connect on a physical level? My people would welcome you, Anya. You would have a tribe, one that loves in a way western cultures don't understand."

She shifted so she could see his eyes. "What do you mean?"

"Even in Scythian societies, Western Civilization is obsessed with conformity. It makes them comfortable when they can put others in certain categories. But both the Moors and the Maori accept warriors for who they are without the constraints of norms. There is no judgment, no criticism. Just acceptance."

Nya eased back a little. What would it be like to openly admit you couldn't remember a part of your past and just have people accept it?

He softly kissed her lips. "The point of the Trials is to explore the possibility of a future with one another. I want you to enjoy our time together. We'll never know if this can work unless we try. And if you end up with someone else, at least you'll have this memory of me."

She took a deep breath and tried to settle back into his arms. This was what Jax had asked of her—to experience new things so she'd really know what she wanted. A true Amazon wouldn't think twice about interacting with a prospective candidate this way.

He ran his fingertips up and down her bare arm. The whisper-soft touch combined with the music and scenery and Nya's reality shifted to nothing but sensation, lulling her into the pleasurable space between relaxation and slumber.

Aren waited until she settled before he turned, bearing his weight on his forearm. He leaned in, circling his nose around her pulse then kissing her neck.

She shied away at first, but his touch was so gentle, so caring, that eventually her muscles relaxed and her bones turned to jelly. The music swelled, the constellations above them shifted, bringing her focus on a series of stars she'd never seen.

"What's that?" Nya's breath caught as he nibbled on a tender spot behind her ear.

Aren didn't look up, but continued his pilgrimage. "The newest pictures from the Society's telescope." His tongue circled the dip where her neck met her shoulder, his lips making their way downward as his hand tucked beneath her breast. "Scythians have known for years that we are part of a multiverse, not just a universe. Makes our lives seem insignificant, doesn't it?"

She didn't answer him. Couldn't. Her mind, her heart and her body were at war. Being touched this way felt amazing, but as she closed her eyes, all she could see was Jax—his smile, memories of the way he always challenged her, how he read her like a book, didn't take any of her shit.

Confusion surged, and she stiffened. Aren's fingers kept circling her flat abdomen, tracing around the small indent of her belly button.

"I know this is new to you, Anya, but try and clear your mind." He grazed his nose down her neck until his lips were centered between her breasts.

She tried to relax as Jax's voice echoed in her thoughts … *Keep an open mind, Vtachi.*

Aren shifted, his heavy leg nestling between hers. "Focus on here—now. I offer you my respect, honor you with my touch. You, in turn, honor me by accepting my affection."

This seemed wrong. How could she physically feel pleasure from one male while thinking about another?

And why did she feel like she was betraying someone entirely different in the process?

Nya fought to stay quiet as he nipped and nuzzled, traveling up her neck until he found a place that seemed particularly sensitive. He gently bit the tender skin and then soothed the spot with his tongue.

The lights above swirled in celestial patterns as violins crescendoed in a sweet symphony.

The blood pounding in her ears turned painfully hot, and familiar panic flooded through her.

"Penn, please. This is wrong. You know it."

Rope had been replaced by shackles, the cargo hold had turned into a palatial room, a camera recording the horrid scene.

Penn came forward, his hand palming her breast.

"Shhhh, my love. It'll be fine. You'll see."

"Let me go," she said, trying in vain to jerk away from his touch.

"This isn't easy for me, either." Penn's breath brushed over her face. *"Watching you suffer. But it's the only way I can have you. Just tell father what he wants, and then we can be together. I promise."*

The memory came back in a rush. Her blood raged as if her veins were on fire. She pushed on Aren's chest.

He leaned up, his eyes searching hers. "Anya, what is it?"

Her thoughts jumbled in a mass of past and present. Aren's gentle black eyes fused into merciless hazel, his dark skin melded to pasty white. Fury, rage, and, most of all, a deep-seated need to escape gripped her. She took a ragged breath, hoping to calm the urge to punch Aren in the throat and then run. She hadn't experienced the reaction since Jax taught her control.

Oh, God. It was happening again. She didn't want him touching her. She didn't want anyone touching her.

"Nya, have I done something wrong?"

Her body went rigid as Dmitri Sarkov's voice echoed in the distance.

"Lexi. Yes, I have things well in hand." The guttural rhythm of muffled Estonian bled through the door. *"Yes, yes, I understand. Even though my son is an idiot, we still have a deal, no?"* A pause. *"No. I cannot give you back the girl. She is a gift for Penn. I promised him long ago."* Another pause. *"You have my word. She'll be well cared for. Leave her with us, and the cloning research stops immediately. And Chancellor? Stay out of Russia."*

The memory faded, and Nya's mind raced. It was no secret Alexandra was born in Estonia, but no one knew she was a traitor.

Nya wasn't safe. No one was.

Aren sat up and clicked the remote. The music stopped, and the constellations faded as the house lights came on. "Nya, what is it? What's wrong?"

She batted his hands away like they were covered in spiders and then jumped up from her seat. "I can't do this. I'm sorry, Aren."

Before he could say anything, she ran.

CHAPTER TWENTY-EIGHT

Sweat trickled down Nya's face as she walked back to her room. She stumbled a few times, ignoring the servants asking if she was all right. Her emotions had always felt detached, like some distant illusion.

Now they were nonexistent.

She no longer felt anger, not even hatred. It was like she'd turned into an objective observer, viewing her life like a scientist would a bug under glass. Her mind whirred until she boiled her life down into three universal truths.

Her parents were asshats that dangled her in front of the Drahzda like a piece of meat.

Penn was never her friend; he was an evil bastard that now commanded the Drahzda.

And Alexandra had betrayed the Society.

But she didn't trust anyone enough to tell them what she'd remembered. Well, Xari. But Nya would never drag her into this shit. Victor was lead counsel for the Society, which meant he couldn't be trusted. And daddy dearest had taught her early on that a good Scythian warrior was loyal to the Society no matter what, which meant telling any of her official candidates would be too risky.

Which left Jax, and he wasn't around.

What about the Tovaris? They were openly aggressive with the Senate on many issues. But Zander hated her, and besides, she had no idea how deep his ties to the Chancellor went.

She stepped into her room and locked the door.

God, she was hot. She looked at the over-the-top room, dripping with curtains, and wondered where in the hell the thermostat was in this place.

Crossing the space, she opened the windows. A light blinked from the top of the seal, probably alerting the council that her room was unsecured, but right now she could give a shit.

The curtains billowed as a breeze blew in, and Nya tipped her head back, allowing the cold air to brush against her.

That was better.

She shucked off her shirt as she headed toward the shower. Tomorrow night was the ball, which signaled the end of the first round.

Peeling off the rest of her clothes, Nya left them on the floor before she cranked on the shower and stepped beneath the spray. Tepid water pelted her skin, and she hung her head and closed her eyes, her hair streaming in front of her face like a river of despair.

There were too many holes in her memory. Jax's keen dark eyes drowned out all other thoughts, his voice echoing, calmly reminding her to think and not react.

Why wasn't he here?

She shook off the thought and allowed memories of their many sessions to lull her into a calm state.

The water cooled the top of her head, and she concentrated on the night she was taken.

"*I like you helpless, needing me,*" Penn whispered. "*Once you stop fighting, things will be better. You'll see. I'll worship you, cherish you, and treat you like a queen.*"

Nya took measured breaths as rage bubbled under the surface. The Allos always thought the same. In their world, females were a weird mix of something weak that needed protecting and yet worshiped at the same time.

She had only remembered the tip of the iceberg, and she had a feeling she wasn't going to like what she saw when her mind finally released its secrets. Nya was right when she told Jax she'd been conditioned. Penn's obsession with her must be the key to finding the triggers, but that could be anything from a childhood memory to a name.

Leaning against the shower wall, Nya thought of all the times she'd remembered something. Her first memory came after Victor had gotten into her personal space … and after the surgery, maybe the drugs triggered that one. She felt threatened when Alexandra confronted her, that, combined with her horrid tobacco stench, triggered the memory of Penn on the ship. But the strongest memory by far was when she was with Aren.

Great. So her triggers were obviously being touched by a male, feeling threatened, foreign scents, oh, and sedatives.

She rubbed her forehead as hopelessness spread through her. She'd been fooling herself into thinking there was some way out of this, hoping that eventually, she'd find some semblance of normalcy.

Hopelessness bloomed to despair, and she dropped to the floor and hugged her knees to her chest. Whoever ended up as her rovni would have to deal with all this shit. And when word got out about her abduction, the Society would publicly support her, but privately her entire family would be shunned. She had been taken by the Drahzda and left tainted, unclean.

She couldn't do that to any of her candidates, especially Jax. They deserved a future better than the one she could offer them. What in the hell was she supposed to do now?

Maybe setting out on her own was the only way out of this mess.

Victor made his way down the hall, his instinct screaming something wasn't right. To hell with it, he'd go against protocol and check on Anya. He was, after all, her guide.

Ambling through the crowded foyer, he maintained an air of ease. As there were no formal affairs scheduled for the evening, the press mingled among the warriors, and they stopped him, demanding answers about the ever-elusive Ajax Nickius. With the stealth of a seasoned politician, Victor's linguistic gymnastics were impressive. It wasn't until he made his way outside and past the fountains that tension settled around his shoulders and he picked up his pace.

The distant rumble of a motorcycle had him shifting direction. Gaslights lined the narrow path that led to the old carriage house, which now served as a garage.

He waited for the motorcycle to come into view, and he breathed a sigh of relief when he noted the familiar frame sitting on the seat.

Jax dismounted and threw the kickstand down before pulling off the helmet. "Waiting for someone, Doc?"

"I heard Siva's bike. Either she decided to go against orders and leave her territory, or she let you borrow her baby."

Jax grinned. "She has two months left before Zander lets her off her leash. Not sure why his panties are in such a wad. She took out an entire Drahzdan team."

"Yeah, and she burned down a weapons factory while doing it. A factory the Chancellor wanted to be searched before it was destroyed."

"Well, that explains it then." Jax stared at the bike. "She'll have my balls if I don't bring it back."

"True."

Jax tilted his head, noting the tension in his mentor's voice. He crossed his arms and leaned against the seat. "Why are you waiting out here?"

Victor hesitated. "I was heading to check on your little bird, but I heard you coming and thought you might want to join me." His eyes glanced toward the woods.

Jax followed his gaze; the planetarium's dome shone in the night sky. "After such a long ride, a walk would be perfect."

They stepped off the path that led to the planetarium and into the woods. As soon as they were away from security cameras and the threat of reporters, Victor stopped in the middle of the field.

"How is Vtachi?"

"When I last saw her, she was all right, but I can't shake the feeling something's off."

Jax started forward, taking a sharp left, cutting through the woods in a direct path to the domed structure. They came through the tree line to find Aren sitting on the planetariums front steps, his forearms resting on his thighs as he stared at the ground.

"What happened?" Victor asked, jogging to catch up with Jax.

Aren's brow rose when he saw the two warriors standing a few feet away. "I'm not sure. One minute we were doing well, the next she was like a zombie. Strangest thing I've ever seen."

"What were you doing when her manner changed?" Victor pulled out his phone.

Aren met Jax's gaze. "Let's just say I was showing her how enjoyable being a part of my tribe could be."

"Sonofabitch," Jax cursed, taking a step toward the Moor.

"Were you aware that she's a *novo*?" Victor's voice stayed calm as he stepped between the warriors. "And did she share that it's been only recently that she's learned to accept a male's touch?"

Aren scrubbed his face with his hand. "I knew she was innocent. As for the other, I'm not sure what you mean."

Jax clenched his jaw. "When Nya started at the academy any touch would send her into a rage. The past four years have been an exercise in helping her control the response, but it wasn't until last week that she learned to accept instead of just tolerate it."

Aren took a deep breath and wearily exhaled. "I watched her eyes when she confronted the Chancellor in the foyer. Tonight, she had that same look ... like she did when she remembered being on that boat."

Jax groaned. "I should've never left."

Aren stood, and the three warriors headed back through the trees.

The large stone building came into view. "I knew I was going too fast. Should've never pushed her."

Jax scrubbed his face with his hand but Victor was the one to speak.

"You didn't know. And I'm sure a good night's rest will be just what Anya needs."

They veered left toward the back of the consulate, taking the servant's entrance instead of risking a confrontation with the press.

Aren muttered something about seeing them both in the morning, and he walked away.

Victor blocked Jax from leaving the mud room. "You can't go bursting into her room again. Too many are watching right now, and she doesn't even know you're back.

"She remembered something," Jax whispered, his eyes glancing at the ceiling, looking for cameras.

Victor motioned him to follow, and they went through the kitchen and into a small conference room. "This area is secure."

"I can't wait, Doc. I won't. I've already let her down, and she needs me right now."

"Let's at least see if she's all right before you go off half-cocked and tip your hand." Victor reached into his coat pocket. "Here. I've patched the video streaming from her room to my phone." He swiped the screen a few times and then handed the device to Jax. "Here's the live feed."

Jax watched Nya come from the shower in nothing but a towel, her hair dripping wet. Her stilted movements were so different from the way she usually walked. She lost the bath sheet and sat naked, scooping her hair to one side and brushing it to its end.

Jax scowled. Damn it. What was she doing? She knew the room was wired, someone would be watching. It wasn't in her nature to be an exhibitionist.

"I'll take care of the video once we're done here." Victor looked away.

Nya set the brush down and slipped under the comforter, turning her head away from the camera.

Still. Jax had never seen her so still.

"Something's wrong. I'm going to her right now."

Victor took his phone back and straightened to his full height. "She's mine to counsel."

"Damn it, Doc. Don't do this."

His voice softened. "I don't want to give Alexandra the weapon she needs to have you disqualified."

"Let her try." Jax's voice lowered to a menacing growl.

Victor put his arm around his friend's shoulder. "Trust me. I'll watch her through the night. You go. Get some rest, and we'll deal with things in the morning."

CHAPTER TWENTY-NINE

Diaphanous curtains billowed as a frigid breeze blew through the open window. Goosebumps peppered Nya's skin, and she rolled over, dissecting the odd sensation of outwardly being so cold while heat pulsed from within.

Weak sunlight brightened the dismal sky, signaling the dawn of a new day.

Physically exhausted and emotionally numb, she made her way to the dressing area, ignoring the constant aches in her muscles and joints. If she didn't know that Scythians were immune to Allos viruses, she'd swear she had the flu.

She stumbled in front of the mirror and took a hard look. Hives splotched her neck and torso, leaving angry patches of raised welts. A permanent flush graced her cheeks and the bridge of her nose, bringing out the dark circles blooming under her eyes.

She grabbed a blue turtleneck and a pair of black jeans.

Thank God Victor hadn't shown up last night demanding a recap of her time with Aren.

A soft knock sounded from the front. Nya groaned, heading toward the door.

"Victor, I don't want to talk about …" her voice stuck in her throat as she looked into familiar dark velvet eyes.

"Vtachi." Jax's voice held such longing and a quiet desperation.

She took in his five o'clock shadow and rumpled clothes. His eyes sparked with sheer need, and she blinked back the tears.

He reached for her. Memories of Penn flooded her mind, and she stepped back.

"When did you get here?"

"Late last night. I wanted to come to you then, but Victor didn't think it was a good idea."

She glanced down the hall. "Probably for the best. I'm sure Alexandra has her eyes on me."

He reached for her again, this time pulling her in for a tight hug.

"God, I've missed you," he whispered, his lips grazing her jaw.

His touch eased the heat running through her, and for just a moment she gave in, melting into him.

Footsteps echoed down the corridor, bringing her to her senses and she tensed.

Jax put a little space between them, his eyes boring into hers. "Are you okay?"

She ignored the question. "How was your mission?"

"Complicated."

She leaned back against the doorframe. "Well, I hope everything turns out all right."

"It might be rocky for a year or so, but I have faith it will work out in the end." He placed his palm on her cheek. "You're too warm."

"I'm all right." She pulled away. "We should probably head down to the dining hall. The others will be waiting."

Jax kissed her forehead before he wove his fingers through hers. "You should know, your official candidates met with the press late last night."

They started down the hall.

"Oh?"

"Yes. The Chancellor felt it best to address the growing controversy as soon as I got back."

"What did you tell the press about where you'd been?"

"That I had been working with a patient in the ward as a personal favor to the Chancellor."

"And they bought it?"

Jax smirked. "It seems so."

"Shouldn't I have been there?"

He stopped at the top of the stairs. "Probably, but Killian and I argued the point the news would be less sensational if you weren't there to field awkward questions."

"Oh, okay."

Silence, mired in distance, surrounded them as they made their way to the dining hall.

Her other four candidates stood as soon as she entered the room. Nya let go of Jax's hand and pasted on a smile.

She hugged Killian, Giovanni, and Luka before facing Aren. He stood, his eyes askance, not meeting her gaze.

She stood on her toes and pulled him close, straining to whisper in his ear. "I'm sorry."

Surprised, Aren's gaze found hers. "I believe I should be saying that to you."

"Last night wasn't your fault."

The others uncomfortably shifted in their place, but Nya ignored them. "I promise. This one's on me."

The least she could do was try and ease his guilt—she'd be damned if a fine male like Aren spent his life blaming himself for something he didn't do.

Aren's hands gripped hers as he held her gaze. "Next time, you lead."

She looked away. There wasn't going to be a next time. Aren deserved better. They all did.

"Sounds good," she said, squeezing his hand before letting go.

Jax assessed her every move as she rolled her head from side to side before taking her seat.

Nya guided the conversation with endless questions about the press conference, making sure no one ventured into the sensitive waters regarding her time with Aren. Her candidates answered in soft voices, their worry obvious. After the last plate had cleared, the crowd thinned, and champions headed to the arena.

"I'm afraid we part ways here." Nya stood. "I'm expected on the field to watch the uncommitted spar for the last time, and then my team has requested I meet them early."

Killian set down his cup. "That's odd. Did you question why the change in schedule?"

She shrugged. "No. They cleared it through Victor, though."

All eyes pointed toward her guide, and he stood, his shrink expression firmly in place. "Yes, well. If you'll excuse us, I'd rather go through the kitchen, so we aren't hounded by the press.

Chairs scraped across the mahogany floor as everyone stood. Killian, Giovanni, Luka, and Aren hugged her in turn.

Jax hung back, following Nya and Victor out of the dining hall and into the corridor. They stopped in a small servants' area that held several custodial closets.

"No more than five minutes, Nick." Victor turned and walked into the washroom.

Jax's fingers gently enveloped her hand, his thumb finding her scar. "Talk to me, Vtachi."

"What is there to say?"

He leaned in, his voice became husky and warm. "I'm sorry I left. I should have defied Alexandra's orders, consequences be damned. But I'm here now. Please, talk to me."

Her heart stuttered as she stared into his deep, intelligent eyes. God, she wanted to rely on him, she really did.

Dmitri's deep voice rumbled in the back of her mind ... *She is a gift for my son. I promised him long ago ... Leave her with us, and the cloning research stops immediately.*

Defiled ... tainted.

She rubbed her forehead as her chin quivered. "It doesn't matter now."

Jax's palm caressed her shoulder. "Of course it does."

She looked up, her heart aching at the sight of him. "I did what you asked and kept an open mind."

Jax swallowed a few times. "And?"

A tear streamed down her cheek. "I should have run."

The quiet confession sent Jax reeling. What the hell happened last night? "Damn it, Vtachi. That's not true, and we both know it."

"Everything all right, Ny?" Killian stepped from the shadows.

Jax glared at the other warrior. There was a reason Killian's call sign was Ghost. Right now, he just wanted to the warrior to disappear.

Nya wiped her eyes. "Yeah. Everything's fine."

Killian crossed his arms as he leaned against the doorframe. "Doesn't look like it from where I'm standing."

She met his gaze with a watery smile. "Really. I'm okay. Thanks, though."

He glanced at Jax and then focused on her. "You need me, you know where I am."

Victor came from the bathroom just as Killian walked away. He cleared his throat. "Are you ready, Anya?"

"Yes." Nya searched Jax's face like she was trying to memorize every feature. "I'm sorry. For everything."

They watched her weave through the kitchen's stainless steel workstations and head out the back door.

"She's choosing someone else, isn't she?" Jax's voice turned husky.

"She hasn't expressed an interest in any other warriors." Victor clapped his hand on his friend's back before they headed outside.

Blades of light cut across the cobblestoned lane as the sun broke through the clouds.

"Why does Nya's team want to meet with her early?" Jax asked as they neared the arena.

Victor smirked. "You forget that I create her schedule, which means I've built in some time for a session before dinner."

"She won't be too happy."

"She'll adjust."

They watched Nya pass through the coliseum's arched entrance. She never looked back.

Jax's heart sank. "Get to the bottom of it, Doc."

Victor's eyes became grave. "She's a loose cannon right now. I have no idea what she remembered with Aren nor how she's processing it. I know it goes without saying, but I cannot manipulate the situation. I won't give her an opinion on whom she should choose, nor will I betray her confidence. Not even for you, my friend."

"I wouldn't have it any other way."

Nya didn't wait for Victor to join her. Instead, she headed straight toward the center of the sparring field. Males dipped and jabbed as they tried to bring the other to the ground. The past few days the arena had taken on an intense frenzy, and today was no different.

"Anya." A copper-skinned male looked up from his fight and motioned for his partner that he needed a break. He jogged to where she stood. "I thought that was you."

Nya's eyes sparked in recognition. "Pacha. How are you?"

He smiled. "I'm better now that you're here."

She took a deep breath but her emotions stayed close to the surface.

"Would you care to walk with me?" Pacha held out his hand.

Nya hesitated before she took it. "All right."

They passed the target field, and Pacha sighed. "My culture teaches true happiness is found when we focus on *what is* instead of concentrating on *what is not.*"

She rubbed her forehead. With all the shit she had going on, she didn't need riddles right now. "Pacha, I already have my—"

"Hear me out, please." He squeezed her hand. "All week I've seen you concentrate on what you didn't have. The Moor throwing you off kilter, you struggling to find something in common with the Italian, your attraction for the Scotsman, and then feeling guilty about it because he wasn't the one you wanted. The Tova leaving when he should have stayed."

She stopped and pulled her hand from his. "You were the one that leaked the rumor to the press."

"I was tired of watching you cover for a warrior who put a mission above the needs of his prospective mate."

"How in the hell do you know all this anyway?"

He took her hand again. "Because I watch with the eyes of my ancestors."

"What does that even mean?" She spoke through clenched teeth.

His dark eyes gentled as he smiled. "It means I see you, and I understand. I meant no malice toward the Tova, I only wanted you to see there are other options."

She took a deep breath. "I'm listening."

"Tonight, if you find you need a way out, consider me. Our mating can be whatever you want it to be. I will abide by your wishes." He grew near, his musky smell a combination of virile male, earth, and sunshine. "Know this. My tribe lives among some of the most rugged terrains. We still have villages the Allos know nothing about—even the Tovaris haven't been able to find them. You want time away from this world, we'll head into the Andes Mountains and not come out for years, the Society be damned."

Her brows rose as she kept his gaze.

"Anya, I'm another option. One that doesn't require that you sacrifice a future to escape the past."

He brought her hand to his full lips, kissed her knuckles, then walked away.

Dumbfounded, she just stood there. How did he know?

"What was that about?" Victor came from behind.

"Nothing. Pacha and I were talking."

Victor frowned. "Never underestimate his kind. They are as elusive as they are intelligent."

"I think I've seen enough." Nya's eyes flickered back to the Incan.

Victor studied her for a moment. "As you wish. Your lunch will be delivered to your room, and you'll have time to rest before your team arrives."

She doggedly made her way toward the front of the arena with Victor following closely behind.

"Chancellor, there's a call for you on line two."

Alexandra looked up from her report. "Who is it?"

"Wouldn't say, ma'am. When I asked, he said he's coming to collect what is his. Said you'd know what he was talking about."

Alexandra blanched. "I'll be in the War Room, and I'm not to be disturbed."

The warrior tipped her head and walked away.

The Chancellor hurried through the monitor room and into the inner chamber where the retinal scanner stood. Red light swept across her vision, and a moment later the tumblers clicked in place. A hidden panel slid open, and she crossed the threshold and waited for the door to close behind her.

She picked up the phone. "This is Alexandra Vasilica."

"My dear Chancellor. The last time we spoke I was but a child."

Alexandra's hand shook as she fumbled in her pocket for a smoke. "I want nothing to do with you."

"Why? You'll find it much easier to deal with me than Dmitri."

She lit the hand-rolled and took a big drag. "I highly doubt that."

He sighed. "Lexi, I—"

"Don't call me that."

Penn chuckled. "Why not? My father referred to you often that way. He was, after all, your *friend*, was he not?"

Silence.

Penn took a deep breath and sighed. "Oh, Lexi, I know all about your time with Dmitri. Surely you haven't forgotten the summer you rebelled against your Society. Imagine what the Senate would say. Their fearless leader whoring herself out. It would be bad enough if it were with a common Allos, but the Drahzdan Tsar? Why, I'm sure they would love that, now wouldn't they?"

She closed her eyes. "What do you want?"

"Exactly what I told your assistant. Four years ago, you took something from me. And now, I'm taking back what is mine."

"She was never yours, and the answer is no."

"I'm not asking for permission, Lexi. This is merely a courtesy call. As we speak, my men are getting in position to extract my fiancée from your consulate."

"That's impossible. No Drahzda could get on Scythian soil, especially during the Trials."

"And yet, we have. My Ana will be back home within a day or two. Do what you must, but if I were you, I'd spin the situation to my advantage."

"And how am I supposed to do that? Tonight, Anya will declare her Chosen. There is sure to be a media firestorm if she doesn't show. Not to mention the entire Scythian world is watching. When it comes out you've taken her the Senate will demand we go to war."

Penn chuckled. "And Scythians are supposed to be the intelligent ones. I'll wait until after your precious ceremony. When we come for her, leak the break-in to your press. We have an expendable team nearby for you to capture, which you will report as a failed terrorist attempt on the trials. You'll look like the hero, and the alleged attack will serve as a nice distraction."

"And when she doesn't show for her first official sparring session with her Chosen?"

"Surely you can make something up that seems plausible. You are, after all, the leader of the entire Society."

Alexandra grew quiet. "She doesn't want you, you know."

"You're wrong." Penn's voice became aggressive. "My Ana loves me. She always has."

The silence stretched as Alexandra's mind raced. She hated being cornered. "I can't let this happen. Not again."

"I have footage of you in Dmitri's bed."

"Release whatever you want. I'll have our experts say the film was doctored—the Senate will believe it is nothing more than an attempt to discredit me."

"And while you are calming the firestorm and smothering conspiracy theories, I'll take my Ana anyway and then put all our resources on the cloning technology we've been sitting on for years." Penn's voice gentled. "Lexi, work with me as you did Dmitri. Together, we could fight the injustices of the world. The Society could make great strides in getting terrorism under control while I spend my time solidifying the Drahzda's hold on Mother Russia. The world is a delicate balance of political maneuvering, you know that. We are on the brink of humanity imploding on itself. Let's not add a war between the Drahzda and the Scythians to the chaos."

Alexandra remained silent as she took another deep drag off her cigarette.

Penn sighed. "Come now. Surely you see the benefits? Think of the good you could do. It's the foundational belief of your Society, is it not?

To better humanity through knowledge and strength?"

"Not if it means a world regime with a Drahzdan Tsar at the helm." Smoke rolled out of her mouth as she spoke, and she ground the last of the hand-rolled into a crystal tray.

Penn's voice grew dangerously soft. "Scythians are known for their logic. Surely you understand one of your females isn't worth jeopardizing your entire race. Especially now, when Anya Thalestris is of little use to you anyway. The chances of her naturally procreating are slim. Help me this one time. Keep my Ana's rescue from your Senate, and in exchange, the Drahzda will leave you in peace."

Alexandra's knuckles whitened as she gripped the phone. "For how long?"

"Until your legacy is through."

"And the cloning research?"

"Will be buried for generations to come."

The Chancellor stood and went to the window. Hundreds of spectators milled about, making their way to the stadium. A *nata* rode on her father's shoulders while her mother held his hand. They disappeared under the arena's arch, the Society's anthem started to play, and the muffled cheers rumbled through the glass.

The Trials had been going on for thousands of years, bringing forth the best of their race. Sacrifices must be made so future generations could thrive. And as for her legacy? Hell, she'd made so many mistakes. First the debacle at her trials, which still haunted her to this day. And then that stupid decision to share a little Scythian technology with a few companies that were known for their global outreach. She had hoped the Allos would use the new capabilities to improve the lives of those suffering, but the corporations hoarded the breakthrough, and their profit margins were now in the billions, throwing the global economy into a tailspin. Her reign had seen the rise of the Drahzda as well as the birth of new Allos terrorist factions, which were just as dangerous and ruthless as any adversary their culture had faced. And under her watch, the Society had lost more warriors in the last fifty years than in the previous fifteen hundred combined. She'd be damned if the entire Scythian race fell, too.

Penn's voice broke through her thoughts. "Decide, Lexi. Which story will be reported in your news tomorrow? Will it be a piece about how your warriors discovered a hidden Drahzda terrorist cell and saved the Trials, or will it be that you had a torrid affair with Dmitri Sarkov and Anya Thalestris was abducted right under your nose?"

Damn it.

Tradition. Honor. Valor. These were the things Scythians wanted to see during the trials, not the last of Otrera's line being taken from them.

And an all-out war wasn't something they could afford right now.

"One warrior dies on Scythian soil, and I'll go to the press myself."

"Noted."

Her shoulder's slumped as she hung up the phone. She turned from the window and grabbed the crystal decanter and a glass.

CHAPTER THIRTY

Nya's team stood by the door, each with the same awed expression they had last time. A mineral salt bath had helped with the hives, but Nya still insisted on wearing her hair down. The French woman, Brigitte, braided a wreath around her head and wove jasmine through it, the white flowers matching her dress.

"Nya glanced at the clock. "Why did you request to meet me so early if we were going to finish a few hours before the start of the event?"

"Beg pardon, your guide set the time, not I," Brigitte said.

The door opened, and Victor sauntered in. "Thank you for your service to the house of Otrera. That will be all."

Nya scowled as he calmly ushered out her team, closing the door and locking it behind them.

"What the hell is the meaning of this?"

He ignored her tone. "Come. We have much to discuss."

She took a deep breath. It would be pointless to try and get out of it. Victor was like a pit bull with a bone. "Lead the way."

He crossed the room to the sitting chamber and took his seat.

Nya found her spot and rested her hands on her lap, her thumb nowhere near her scar. "Now what is it you would like to discuss?"

"Let's start with your time with the Moor."

She didn't blink. Never moved. "What about Aren?"

"He seems to think your little tryst in the planetarium may have sparked a memory."

"Not at all." She squarely met his gaze. "I became overwhelmed. I've spoken with Aren about it, and we've moved on."

He took in her relaxed shoulders, her motionless hands and unwavering gaze and sighed. "Are you sure that's all there is?"

"Yes. Now was there anything else?"

"Jax. He's back from his mission."

Her eyes flashed with pain before she schooled her expression again. "Yes, and I'm happy to see that he made it back in one piece."

"You were worried that he wouldn't?"

"Dr. Ramova—"

"Victor."

"The Chancellor wouldn't have asked him to leave his Trials had it not been something big. That alone would lead to the logical conclusion that danger was involved."

"You've avoided discussing your feelings on the matter of his leaving in the first place."

"There's nothing to talk about. He was ordered to go."

Victor kept his eyes locked on hers. She calmly gazed back.

"Fine. Let's move on to the warrior you spoke with today."

"Pacha. He's from the Andes Mountains."

"He seemed interested," Victor commented, pulling out his glasses.

"He was. He offered me another option. One I'd never considered before."

Victor reached for his pad and pen. "Which was?"

"He said I didn't have to sacrifice my future to escape the past."

Victor scribbled something across his pad. "And how did that make you feel?"

"Tempted." The word left her lips before she could stop it.

Victor's pen stopped midsentence, and he looked over the rim of his glasses. "Surely all your time with Dr. Nickius has taught you that running doesn't solve anything."

"Disappearing would, though."

He placed his pad and pen on the side table and leaned forward. "No, Anya. The Incan is wrong. The only way to embrace your future is to face your past. Deep down, you know that."

Nya turned away. "Are we done here, Dr. Ramova?"

Victor sighed and leaned back in his seat, picking up his pen and notepad. "Not by a long shot."

A few hours later a haggard Nya and an extremely frustrated Victor emerged from her sitting room. She had endured two hours of the good doctor's endless questions and constant prodding. The male had tried everything, but she'd managed to get through the session without breaking down and telling him that she might not pick Jax for his own good and Alexandra was a traitor.

Warriors crowded the corridors as they made their way down the stairs and into the dining hall. Nya glanced at Xari's table. Her stunning purple dress was at odds with the scowl marring her face.

"Something's wrong," Nya veered toward her friend. "I'll be right back."

Victor took her elbow, stopping her. "The press is here."

"I thought they weren't allowed to take photos of formal events."

"The only exemption being the naming of the Chosen and the final rounds."

Nya glanced around the room, noticing the sleek camera drones silently hovering in each corner, a small light blaring as they all pointed toward her.

She forced herself to smile, and Victor directed her toward her table. "Might I suggest catching up with Toxaris after you've both declared your Chosen? It seems unlikely she'll be candid and open at the moment. And we all know how frustrating that can be, now don't we?"

He raised an eyebrow, but Nya ignored the jab.

"What does it matter? The press will still be here after dinner."

"Not exactly. They're only allowed to film the champions making their declarations and then entering the consulate. The celebration afterward is off limits."

Why in the hell hadn't she realized the entire world would be watching when she declared her Chosen?

It was probably because she'd grown up in a household that never watched the Trials.

Jax focused on Nya as soon as she entered the room. Her tense shoulders and Doc's worn expression must have meant the session didn't go well.

She glanced at the drones and notably tensed. Ah, Victor must've informed her about the press joining them for dinner.

More pressure for his Vtachi. He hated that.

Her eyes flitted to a warrior along the wall, and he winked.

Jax tensed as he watched the interaction. The male's dark skin and tribal costume told of his South American heritage. Incans were almost as brutal as Tovas, only they were one of the few Scythians that chose to isolate themselves from the rest of the Society. Rarely did they leave their villages and venture into the world.

"Here she comes," Killian muttered. Everyone at the table stood.

"Otrera couldn't have been as stunning as Dea," Giovanni said.

"She does look like a goddess tonight." Luka fidgeted with his sash, making sure it was straight.

Killian's jaw clenched at the comment, obviously not liking the other two ogling her any more than Jax did.

Aren looked away.

Jax took a deep breath, reminding himself for the thousandth time that this was all part of the process. Once Nya shouldered his mark, and he hers, everyone would know they belonged to one another. God willing, this primal urge to tear out the other warriors' throats would finally go away.

"Good evening, sweet Dea." Giovanni stepped forward.

Her eyes darted to the Incan as Giovanni leaned in and kissed her on her cheek.

The others followed suit, and each time it was the same.

Jax finally stood and made his way toward her. He completely blocked her view of the male by the wall. But instead of leaning in for a sweet peck on the cheek, he placed his hands on her shoulders and tugged her to him. His fingers dug into the spiral dragon guarding the empty space on her arm as he brought his lips to her ear.

"I don't know what in the hell is going on in that complex head of yours, but I'm half tempted to haul your ass out of here, even if you're kicking and screaming."

She pulled back, as her eyes sparked back to life. "Go ahead and try."

Jax kept her gaze, watching that spark grow dim. God. The last thing his Vtachi needed was his aggression. He groaned and kissed her shoulder.

"Apologies. Where's a cliff to scale or a ravine to jump when you need it?"

Something between laughter and a sob sounded as Nya leaned her head on his chest. "You have no idea how many times I wished for the same thing."

He nudged her chin up until her eyes met his. "I'm right here, Vtachi."

She took a deep stuttered breath, her voice barely making it past her lips. "But you deserve better."

Jax frowned as she turned and took her place at the table.

What the hell was that about?

Hammers pounded over the buzz of a circular saw as Sergei passed by Ana and the Tsar's suite. This was insane. These men were tearing out walls and using hidden passageways, and they hadn't been thoroughly vetted. There wasn't time. Hell, he had to double Penn's guard to keep him secure. Drahzda soldiers were expected within a few days, but that didn't help his men now. They were stretched too thin.

They'd take a serious hit if the Scythians attacked before the other units arrived.

He headed up the stairs to the parapet, Penn's favorite spot of late. The Drahzdan leader had been tense, which usually ended with someone either being punished or put to death. But not this time. This time he seemed to turn inward, withdrawing from the activities around him.

Sergei waited until he was in Penn's periphery before speaking. "I've ordered six more units to come into the area. Three will infiltrate the villages we've not yet taken, and the remaining three will stand guard outside the perimeter. The units should be here by the week's end."

Penn nodded that he had heard and kept his eyes toward the road. "I'd like your counsel."

Sergei's brow rose. Stephan was his right-hand man, and Sarkov had a roomful of advisors. In all the years he'd known him, He'd never asked for any advice.

"It would be my honor."

Penn glanced over before focusing back on the road. "Stephan and his men are in Romania. By the time the sun rises, my Ana will be on her way home."

Sergei stayed silent and nodded.

"Will our forces be ready if the Scythians attack?"

He chose his words carefully. "I'm sure our men will be up to the task. If I remember correctly when you brought your Ana to Astana the first time, we prepared for an invasion, and yet it never came. They have the same leader, yes?"

"The Chancellor has not changed, not even after Chevnia."

Sergei scoffed. "Maybe they are not as strong as we fear."

"My father had her under control. I have the same leverage."

Sergei smiled. "That is a good thing."

Silence settled as a breeze whispered through the trees.

"I used that to taunt Ana, you know." Penn rested his arms on the stone wall. "When I set her triggers, I kept reminding her that she'd been abandoned by her own kind and they weren't coming for her. It was working until the fertility specialists came to harvest her eggs, and then something changed."

Sergei kept his stoic expression firmly in place. "Stephan mentioned that you've sent for the scientists that helped with the procedure. Do you think there is an issue?"

Penn shoulder's slumped. "Yes. At the time, I didn't make the correlation. But looking back now? Now I just don't know."

"If you don't mind my asking, what was different?"

"For one thing, her will became iron. She no longer cared if she lived, but if she died, she wanted to take me with her. And she seemed stronger and healed faster than before. We needed to do something, so we set sail for Ireland. If I destroyed all that she had, she'd break. It was the only way. I discovered that she needed constant pain to remain manageable, and so before we made port, I shackled one hand to the railing and put a knife through the other, pinning it to the floor. It was the only thing I could think of to assure she didn't get away. I wanted her to watch the compound burn."

"That was the night the Tovaris took her."

Penn stood, his gaze left the road and landed on Sergei. "Yes, I still hear her screams calling out for me as they carried her away. The blood fires must have been brutal because I've never heard such a sound before or since. I'd defended her as best I could, but my guard was either dead or fighting when the warriors made their way to us. I had been shot but managed to escape by jumping overboard. And then he took her, the Tovaris leader took my Ana from me. Keeping close to the hull, I tracked her screams, hoping to rescue her when they made it to water. And then the screaming just stopped. I searched the dock and saw a warrior hand her slumped body to her father. At first, I feared the pain was too great, and she had died. But then she stirred, putting her arms around his neck. I wanted to invade that night, but we had lost too many, and I was injured. They sank the cargo ship, and what was left of our crew managed to survive until we were rescued."

"It may not seem it, but her being taken may have turned out for the best." Sergei kept his voice soft. "It gave us much needed time. Time to reorganize the troops and prepare this part of the region for you."

For once, Penn didn't lose control and fly into a rage. "I've thought that as well. The Drahzda are stronger than ever, and the hatred in the region has increased our numbers significantly. It is time for my Ana to come home."

CHAPTER THIRTY-ONE

Dinner had been something short of torture as Nya silently plowed through eight courses. Her males followed her lead and stayed quiet as well. Cameras panned from left to right, sweeping across conversation and laughter before settling on her table, which was silent as a tomb.

Mercifully, the traditional fruit dessert was served, and she set down her fork. Victor placed his napkin on his plate and stood, waiting for her to join him.

They wove through the other champions enjoying their dessert, and Nya idly wondered if their leaving early seemed strange.

Not that she really cared.

Light gleamed across the marble foyer, its onyx Scythian symbol mocking her as she walked across the floor. Her official candidates followed close behind, their somber footsteps echoing in the vast hall.

Victor opened the front door and calmly escorted her down the stairs.

"This is a perfect night for a Choosing." He smiled as he took in the crisp clean air. "Don't you think so, Anya?"

She ignored him and rolled her head from side to side. They strayed from the cobblestone path and headed into the woods. Solar lights hanging from tall trees left soft splotches of light along the narrow track. Night owls hooted as a gentle breeze blew, the chill causing Nya's bare shoulders to pebble like gooseflesh.

They neared a clearing, and Nya's steps faltered. Thousands of candles lined the perimeter, their pure white light flickering and dancing in the wind. Wooden benches, darkened and worn, stood row after row, angled toward an amphitheater at the front. Mounted cameras nestled on low-lying branches, their tell-tale red light blinking off then on as technicians checked the equipment. The semi-circular dome reminded

Nya of her last round of the championships, where Jax held her in the fog-laden arena.

She found it hard to breathe.

Memories of Jax's body settling on hers as he whispered it was all right—they'd get through this together.

We got this, Vtachi.

God. What she would give for that to be true.

They descended the steps, growing closer to the amphitheater's center. Victor stopped at a bench that held her family's crest. She glanced behind her, surprised her candidates hadn't followed them down.

"I've asked for a few moments," Victor said, taking in her expression.

She tried to smile. "Want to give me some last minute advice?"

"No. I want to say goodbye."

Stunned, Nya gasped. "What?"

"I'm afraid this is where we part ways, Anya. Our time together is through."

"Why now?" Her voice grew thick with tears. God. She never thought about going through this without Victor. He'd been with her since she got on that damn plane. "And why didn't you say something this afternoon?"

He raised a brow. "Would it have made a difference in our session if I had?"

She sighed. "Probably not."

His blue eyes gentled as he patted her hand. "The role of the guide is to ease your path until you have found your Chosen. You have no need of me once that is done." He stepped back and let her go. "During the ritual, your candidates will sit on this bench, and you will join the other champions on the platform. The females have been placed in order from lowest to highest ranking, so I assume you will have a while until you are called. Once you have declared your Chosen, you will exit the stage from that side, and your males will leave the way we came in. You will then meet them in the ballroom. I should warn you, the Chosen celebrations usually last until dawn."

Oh, God. This was actually happening. She reached out and clutched his arm. "Stay."

He patted her hand before pulling away. "I'm sorry, Anya. I can't. I must check in with the council before the ritual starts, but I'll be at the ball if you would like to say hello. Now, if you'll excuse me."

That hollow feeling engulfed her as she watched him walk away. Why did every male she depended on leave?

Her warriors started down the aisle.

Luka, Giovanni, and Aren came forward, each taking a moment to remind her why they were compatible as equals.

Numb, Nya thanked them for honoring her with their commitment.

Killian was next, and the emptiness eased. He stepped forward and ran his thumb across her cheek. "How you doin', Ny?"

"Not so great, if I'm honest."

He placed his hands on her upper arms, his palm covering the blank space above the dragon cuff. "You know, I've been thinking about hobbits."

She half smiled. "Yeah? Why?"

His gray eyes became intense. "You said Frodo was a kindred spirit. And if that's true, remember that he suffered because he was burdened with the ring. But it didn't destroy him."

Her eyes filled with tears. "He set out to save the Shire, and it had been saved, just not for him."

Killian's eyes widened as he realized she quoted one of Frodo's last lines from the movie … right before he boarded a boat, never to return again.

He pulled her close. "Damn it, Ny. What the hell is going on?"

She took a deep, unsteady breath. "It's nothing, really. You should take your seat."

Killian bent down and pressed his lips against her forehead. "If you need me, you know where I am."

She sadly smiled. "I know."

Jax openly watched the exchange, his eyes solely focused on her. Nya rolled her head from side to side as she did earlier, and he sighed.

"Vtachi." He stepped forward, taking her hand in his, rubbing his thumb across her scarred palm.

Her empty eyes met his, and he pulled her into his arms.

"Whatever you're planning, please don't do it." His gruff voice whispered as he rested his lips on the base of her neck.

She shivered. "I should go."

He pulled back, his eyes desperate. "Please, Vtachi. I need you, and you need me. Together, we got this."

She rested her hands on the sides of his face, gently bringing his forehead down until it touched hers. Her chin quivered as she kissed his lips. "You have a great heart, Ajax Nickius. A fierce, wonderful heart. Never forget that."

She let go and stepped back.

Jax's desolate gaze followed her as she walked away and found her seat on the stage.

The breeze swept through the amphitheater swirling leaves around empty chairs like some playful ghost. Nya sat alone amidst weatherworn wood and muted, flickering light. Numb, she blindly stared forward in a daze as warriors started filtering in from the forest, the candle's glow softening their harsh features. The breeze whispered through the trees again, and Nya found it strange the darkened forest seemed calm, as if this place had witnessed the ritual thousands of times and had grown accustomed to the Scythian's presence.

Her eyes fell on her males.

Jax and Killian sat side by side, both straight and tense. Giovanni and Luka leaned back as if they didn't have a care in the world. Aren rested his forearms on his knees, his eyes cast toward the ground.

Five incredible warriors. None of them deserved to have their heritage sullied by her past. But they also didn't deserve to be humiliated in front of their entire race while she chose a complete stranger either.

The benches slowly filled as one by one, the champions took their place on the stage. The crowd stood, their thunderous applause echoed through the night as Alexandra stepped onto the stage. She dipped her head in acknowledgment before crossing to the observation box on the other side. Her amplified voice blared across the crowd as she introduced the Rovni Council, thanking them for such diligence in honoring the traditions of their race. The council took their seats in the twelve chairs behind the Chancellor, leaving the champions front and center on the stage.

Quiet shrouded the amphitheater. Not a soul moved.

"Sophia Luna." The Chancellor's voice rang through the silence.

The female next to Nya stood. She made her way to the podium.

"Declare your Chosen."

Her voice shook as she named her first male, waiting for him to stand and make his way out of the amphitheater. There was no celebration, no applause. Only respectful silence for a long-standing tradition that had been credited with the birth of their race. She called her next male.

Nya's stoic expression remained frozen in place, although internally she started to panic. She thought she could do this. She really did. But after last night? No way would she drag any of her males into this shitstorm.

"Alyonna Pavlaski."

A champion from the other side of the stage stood, and sweat beaded on Nya's brow.

Damn it, all roads led back to Penn, didn't they? Jax was right. Her childhood friend was the root of all her problems.

An idea whispered in her mind. She could hunt Penn down. Turn the tables and strap him to a wall, make him explain. And after she'd killed him and his henchmen, she'd turn her eyes toward the Chancellor.

Her heart settled as she took a deep breath.

Yes. It was time to finally listen to her instinct and run. It wasn't the best timing, but if she took off during the second round at least she wouldn't have to saddle one of her males with someone who had been damaged by the Drahzda. She blindly stared forward as the next champions were called, her mind formulating a plan to escape.

"Toxaris Romaine."

The name startled her from her thoughts, and Nya glanced at the empty chairs surrounding her.

Xari walked to the podium. Her voice rang out clear and sharp as she called out warrior after warrior, each one standing and walking the long aisle back toward the consulate.

She turned and winked at Nya before leaving the stage.

Nya rubbed her thumb across her palm, her eyes darting from exit to exit.

"Anya Thalestris."

Her knees shook as she stood. Dread wrapped its icy tendrils around her heart, and she started toward the podium. Empty rows surrounded her warriors in the front, the uncommitted were seated in the middle and the press and spectators toward the back.

"Declare your Chosen." Alexandra's voice blared from overhead, and Nya shivered.

Pacha stood, drawing her focus to the back rows. Hushed disbelief whispered through the crowd, and Jax turned in his seat, his eyes narrowing to slits.

"I'm another option. One that doesn't require that you sacrifice a future to escape the past."

Nya shook off the memory and looked back at her row.

"Luka Romano."

Her amplified voice echoed through the trees, and Luka grinned as he stood and walked up the aisle.

"Giovanni Rossi."

Giovanni blew her a kiss as he stood and shuffled down the row.

"Aren Maori."

Aren's gaze flew to hers as if he were surprised. Grimly, he stood and made his way past her last two candidates.

"Killian McCrae."

Killian slumped over, resting his forearms on his thighs. He took a deep breath and smiled, his relief practically radiating off him in waves. He clapped Jax on the back before making his way off the bench.

She took in Jax's tense frame, his deep brown eyes boring into her as if he could see her very soul.

She swallowed as she looked away, her eyes finding Pacha. He subtly nodded to her, encouraging her to say his name. Nya's heart pounded in her chest. The Incans were elusive, exclusionary. It was possible that Pacha could help her hunt Penn down and find some answers. And then Jax could go back to that woman in the valley. Raise his young, find happiness in the arms of a female that didn't carry a wagonload of baggage wherever she went.

She could protect him, save him.

"Declare your final Chosen, Warrior." The Chancellor's voice blared overhead.

She found Jax's deep brown eyes, so intense and passionate. *You and me, Vtachi. We got this.*

Her chin quivered, and she closed her eyes.

"Ajax Nickius."

Nya stepped from the podium and bolted off the stage.

CHAPTER THIRTY-TWO

The moon hid under grey clouds, and Nya was grateful for the surrounding darkness that kept her from prying eyes. She started toward the consulate.

God, her life was a mess. For a split second, she honestly considered calling Pacha's name. But she couldn't do it. Jax meant too much to her. She'd never humiliate him that way.

Not that he wouldn't be any less humiliated when he woke up tomorrow to find her gone.

Shit. She should have followed that instinct a year ago. Now her only hope was to hide somewhere along the Bulgarian or Serbian border and wait for a way to make it to the Astana fortress.

No way she was stepping one foot into Russia.

Didn't matter, though. Either way, eventually the Tovaris would catch up to her, but hopefully, she'd be able to fake her death by then.

"There's my favorite champion."

Nya crouched, ready to attack.

Xari grinned as she came out from the shadows.

"You scared the shit out of me. What are you doing standing out here alone? Shouldn't you be at the ball?"

Xari chucked Nya's arm. "Nah. I wanted to wait for you. I'm kind of surprised no one is with you."

Nya looked back at the distant glow surrounding the amphitheater. "Apparently, we no longer need guides, so I have no idea where Victor is."

They started forward again. "Yeah. Can't say I was sorry to see my guide go." Xari glanced over. "And Jax?"

The path grew narrow as the forest became dense, and Nya snapped a leaf from a nearby sapling. "I'm sure he's headed back to the consulate with the rest of them, but I didn't wait. I kind of ran out on him."

Compassion swam in Xari's eyes. "I thought we were past that."

Nya sighed and changed the subject. "So, what had you so riled at dinner? Is it the reason you're here waiting in the dark instead of drinking champagne?"

"Erik and I had a fight, and now I'm not sure what in the hell I'm doing."

"What was the fight about?"

Xari took a deep breath. "It started before dinner when he said we needed to talk. We didn't get the chance until after the ritual. I told him when we first met that I wanted to move back to the States, and he said he'd go with me. But now that he's one of my Chosen he's changed his mind and wants to stay here, in Carpathia."

Nya frowned. "That seems manipulative."

Xari threw her hand up. "I know, right? And then David, you know, the Canadian, he's so sweet and kind, at least to me. But he's utterly ruthless on the field." Her eyes sparkled as her words sped up. "And he has already established in his Canadian compound, which is just over the American border."

"So what's the problem?"

"It's just … well, I had it in my head that Erik was the one I wanted. But as I get to know him, I don't know if he's right for me after all."

Nya turned them around, leading her friend toward the stables. It had been so long since they had a minute to themselves. "That's what the second round is about. You're supposed to be able to see if you're a match. Can David take Erik? Would he fight for you?"

"I'm not sure," Xari said.

"Well, can you defeat Erik and take him out of the equation?"

"Again, not sure. But if I can't, I think David can. At least I'm hoping he'll want to fight for me, anyway."

Nya had a taste of what the Chancellor might have gone through all those years ago. Having faith that Ike would defeat anyone he was up against only to have him purposefully lose. The betrayal must have been incredible.

"Ny?"

She brought her thoughts back to the present. "Sorry. Just thinking through the options. What about the other three? Are they good candidates?"

Xari shrugged. "I think I can take them, but I don't know. Maybe I should let them win and see who really wants me."

Nya shook her head. "And then you may get stuck with someone who isn't your equal. I think that would be worse than living on separate continents."

Xari sighed. "True. What am I going to do?"

Horses whinnied up ahead, and the moon peeked through the clouds. Nya stopped at the edge of the field that led to the stables. "Well, you can come live with me. We'll raise our young together like some weird lesbian wannabe's."

A twig snapped to the left, and Nya stopped. "What was that?"

Something whistled past her head. Xari gasped and stumbled back.

"Run." She feebly tried to push Nya away as she fell to her knees.

Pain exploded below Nya's ear, and she stumbled, falling next to Xari on the ground.

She brought her hand up, her fingers grazing a dart sticking from the side of her neck. Her sight swam out of focus as she tried to pull herself up.

Military boots came into view. "Leave the other."

A man, dressed in camo, reached for Xari, and Nya's foot met the side of his head. He dropped where he stood.

Someone cursed, and then she felt the sting of a needle pierce her arm as everything went black.

Victor stood at the edge of the amphitheater as Jax came out from the trees. "I take it she chose you instead of the Incan."

Jax smiled. "She chose me. Although she gave me a heart attack before she finally called my name. Why are you here? I thought we agreed you'd be waiting for her in the foyer."

"She never showed."

"Sonofabitch." Jax started down the champion's path, his eyes scanning the forest. "She's going to run; you and I both know it. But I didn't think she'd be reckless enough to try it tonight."

Victor's phone buzzed, and he pulled it from his pocket. "Yes ... No, I have no idea where Toxaris is." A pause. "Really? Yes. Keep me posted. No need to alert the Chancellor. Not yet, anyway. Call me as soon as you hear from her. And Erik? Thanks." He hung up and started scrolling through his apps.

"What the hell's going on?"

Victor kept his eye on the screen. "Apparently, Erik, one of Toxaris' Chosen, had a bit of a tiff with her. She was upset and took off."

"You sure she's missing?"

"According to Erik, she went to the restroom. He waited for a while before he finally went in to check on her, and she was gone."

"I don't have a good feeling about this."

Victor pulled Jax to a stop as he held up the screen. "I've patched into the security feed from the consulate's front steps." He scrolled back until Xari entered the building. They fast forwarded until Xari came from the side of the building and headed back down the champion's path.

"She must be waiting for Nya."

Victor looked at the consulate and then at the screen. "They must be headed to the stables. They shouldn't be too far ahead of us."

Jax started jogging down the way, followed closely by Victor.

Dark cloth shrouded a female body that lay on the narrowed path.

"Oh, God. No. No, no, no ..." Jax bolted to her. Blond hair gleamed in the moonlight as he rolled her unconscious body over.

Victor knelt and inspected the dart jutting from her neck. "Perfect aim—nowhere near the carotid or the spine." He eased the dart from her skin and put it in his pocket.

Jax picked her up as if she were a ragdoll. Xari's head lolled over his arm as she tried to stir. "We'll take her to the infirmary. Dak still on call tonight?"

"Yes. Every Tova assigned to the consulate is on duty, especially in the hospital wing."

"Zander's doing or yours?"

"Does it matter?" Victor veered them toward the right, and they skirted in and out of the treeline. "The point is Dak will take care of her and make sure she's all right."

Xari stirred.

Jax tightened his grip as he leaned close. "Did Nya do this?"

"No." Xari forced out a whisper like she was screaming. "They took her."

He brushed the hair from her eyes. "I'll find her and bring her back. I promise."

Relieved, Xari's head fell against his shoulder as her eyes rolled back in her head.

"Let's go." Victor's fingers flew over his phone screen. "Zander's alerting the Tova now. They're covering all roads out. And Jax. If we think there's cause and we can find a way, he's authorized Dak to give us the prototype."

Jax's hands tightened around Xari as he quickened his steps. "About fucking time."

They ran to the servant's entrance at the back of the consulate, Jax staying in the shadows while Victor took the lead.

Victor's phone rang again, and he growled as he swiped the screen. "I'm a little busy here, Alexandra."

"We have two downed warriors at the back gate and, apparently, a hurt champion. What the hell is going on?"

Victor motioned for Jax to move and they started up the second set of steps.

"I have no idea what happened to the guards, but Toxaris fell and hit her head. We're taking her to the infirmary so she can be seen." He hung up before the Chancellor could respond. "We're getting ready to have company."

Jax the entered the hall leading to the infirmary. "I'm sure she's already tracking us. The place is wired."

Victor swiped his phone and entered a code. The red lights above the cameras' lenses stilled.

"Nifty trick," Jax said.

"Been saving it for a rainy day. It won't take her team long to figure it out." He pushed open a set of double doors and turned to the guards.

"No one gets in. No one."

The warrior touched his fist to his chest and blocked the entrance.

They hustled into an empty room. Golden hair fanned across the pillow as Jax laid Xari on the bed. An orderly shuffled around him and started her IV. He stuck a few leads on Xari's chest and checked the tablet he'd had tucked under his arm. Satisfied with whatever he saw, he laid the tablet on a rolling cart before he walked out the door.

A female entered, her gun metal gray eyes a sharp contrast to her short spiked black hair. "Didn't want to see you tonight, Doc."

"Dak, glad you're here." Victor held up the dart. "You know what they used?"

"Hear the unit's going dark."

She took it from him and held it to the light. "Not sure. We're testing it now."

Jax swallowed a few times. "You think it's lethal?"

She placed it in her pocket. "The guards they brought in haven't died yet, so I'd say no." She picked up a syringe from a nearby tray and plunged the needle into Xari's IV bag. "This should counteract most drugs. I'm keeping her overnight to make sure, though. Give it a few, and you'll be able to talk to her."

"We're burning precious time." Jax paced at the end of the bed, torn between needing information and wanting to find his Vtachi.

Victor's thumbs flew across his screen again. "I'm contacting Killian and the others. They'll be waiting by the fountain. We'll leave as soon as we can."

Another text popped up and Victor scowled. "Damn."

"What is it?"

"Erik and the rest of Xari's Chosen are on their way."

Jax stopped pacing. "The press gets wind of this and they'll slow us down."

Dak grabbed tablet from the tray. "I'm on it."

"Wait up. I need a minute." Victor followed the doctor out of the room.

"Jax ..." Xari mumbled, opening her eyes. "They've got Ny."

He grabbed her hand. "I know. Listen, your Chosen will be here soon. The Chancellor's been informed that you hit your head, and the doctor is checking on you now."

Xari leaned back on her pillow and closed her eyes. "I take it this doctor is a Tova?"

"Yes."

She glanced up at the camera, which was stuck in an odd position with its light off. "Got it. Now, tell me what really happened."

"Tranquilizer dart."

"Lethal?"

"We don't think so."

"Thank God. And Ny?"

Jax's expression became ruthless. "The Tovaris are already searching, and I head out as soon as we're done here."

"But why would the Drahzda attack tonight? And why Ny?"

Jax's voice became nothing but a menacing whisper. "Because ten years ago Ike and Gia Thalestris used their daughter as bait to lure Sarkov's son into telling them a bunch of shit about the Drahzda. Ike, conceited bastard that he is, thought he could protect her. He was wrong, and she was taken. Horrible, unspeakable things were done to her—things she couldn't recall until recently. I'm sure by now Vtachi has remembered every second of the hell they put her through."

Xari struggled to sit up. "Give me five, and I'll be ready to go."

"No." Jax retook her hand. He had to tread carefully here. Xari was now a full-fledged Amazonian warrior, and it was her born right to defend her own. No Scythian male would ever disrespect a female by telling her what to do. He took a deep breath and kept his voice calm. "If you go with us, the press will have a field day which will put Nya in more danger, and there won't be anyone at the consulate to keep tabs on things here."

Xari's voice rose. "Surely the Chancellor is going to declare war. The Trials will be suspended."

"No alerts were sent out when the back gates were compromised."

Xari's eyes widened. "You think she's covering it up?"

"You and I both know it's impossible for a Drahzdan team to get on Consulate grounds. And until now they've never left Scythians alive."

Victor came back into the room and handed Jax a small glass vial.

"Will it be missed?"

"It officially has never been here."

Xari struggled to sit up. "What's going on?"

Victor ignored her, his intense gaze never left Jax. "Only if you trust her, and be sure she knows the consequences."

"Jax?" Xari's voice grew stronger as frustration threaded through.

"Wrap it up," was all Victor said and he walked away.

The mattress tipped as Jax sat down. "You and I may not agree on everything, but a common bond we share is our loyalty to Nya. The Tovaris is walking in blind on this mission—we don't have the information we need."

She sat up. "How can I help."

Cool glass grazed her fingers as Jax slipped a vial into her hand. "This is one of the last remaining prototypes of a serum created by Chem Warfare. It's a pharmaceutical designed to suppress the Phoenix while unlocking a soldier's mind. The intellects and warriors tested it on Scythian volunteers. It was extremely successful in that the subjects were unable to lie and couldn't withhold any information. Unfortunately, it was too strong for the Allos, and the researchers decided to go in a different direction. After the Chevnian riots, Zander confiscated the last case before it made its way to the incinerator."

Xari looked down at the small vial. "It looks like water."

"It has no taste, no odor, and you'll have about thirty minutes to get information before the victim becomes unconscious. If you find a window of opportunity, use it on the Chancellor."

Xari's fingers wrapped around the glass.

"Before you agree to this, understand the consequences. If we don't have concrete proof of any wrongdoing on the Chancellor's part, she'll remain in power."

"Which means no one will be able to help me if I'm caught."

"You could be executed for treason if the mission doesn't go our way. Alexandra is brilliant in the political arena." His voice deepened as he leaned in. "And know the effects of the prototype are stronger when combined with alcohol. Some subjects they tested didn't even remember what happened to them."

She fell back against her pillow, her eyes darting aimlessly as her mind raced. "So I need to get her drunk and then use this on her."

Jax smirked. "That won't be as difficult as you think."

Angry male voices bled down the hall.

"Looks like Erik's here." Jax stood.

"Wait. Nya doesn't show tomorrow the press is going to go ballistic."

Jax's voice became hurried. "Vtachi isn't feeling well and has left the ball. Tomorrow morning Dak will notice the leg injury has developed another infection. The media will be informed that she's back in the hospital, but due to a fear of exposure only her Chosen are allowed to see her."

She scoffed. "The way Scythians heal, no one's going to believe it."

"They will if Nya's best friend backs up the story."

Xari tucked the vial in the folds of her blanket and nodded. "I can do that."

"One other thing." He glanced at the door as the voices got louder. "When we go, you'll be the only one at the consulate who knows what really happened. Bide your time and try to get the information we need. If all hell breaks loose contact the Tovaris. I'll text you Zander's number. Whatever you do, stay safe and don't be reckless. If you can't find an opportunity to use the prototype, don't risk it. We'll find another way."

"By God, I'll have someone's head if you don't let us in!" Erik's voice bled through the door.

Xari hooked her pinky around Jax's. "Staratsa."

He squeezed her finger before letting go. "Staratsa."

The door burst open, and Erik bolted in, followed closely by four others. "What the hell are you doing here, and what happened to my champion?"

"I'm sure Xari will explain everything. If you will excuse me."

The males barely acknowledged Jax as they rushed around the bed, each wanting to make sure their Champion was all right.

The cameras whizzed back to life.

"Dr. Nickius?" Xari's voice made it over the grumblings of the warriors surrounding her.

Jax stopped and looked over his shoulder.

"Tell Ny I hope she gets to feeling better. I'll be busy all day tomorrow, but I'll try and stop by if I get a chance."

"I'm sure she'd appreciate it," Jax said just before he closed the door.

CHAPTER THIRTY-THREE

Nya stirred, her head pounded, and her mouth felt like it had been stuffed with cotton. Disoriented and pissed off, she grumbled as the hard floor beneath her jostled and swayed. Someone had placed a thick wool blanket over her, and she wrapped it around her shoulders and sat up, resting her cheek against a cool wall, trying to ignore the queasiness rolling through her.

Dread washed over her as she took in her glass-paneled prison. Judging from the toggle bolts lining the sides and top, the walls were several inches thick and most likely bulletproof. A few feet beyond stood corrugated steel.

A train whistle screamed from somewhere in front of her. She was trapped in a glass cage on a freight car in the middle of who-the-hell knew where.

She searched the four glass walls. Wait ... where was the door?

Her heart sank as she glanced up. Hovering overhead was a steel hatch, a vent for circulation, and a hole that held a hose.

God only knew what they planned to do with that.

Red lights blinked in the boxcar's upper right-hand corner as a camera whirred to life.

"I see you're up," a deep Russian voice rumbled from a speaker above.

"Who are you?" She tucked her knees against her chest and grazed her palms over her thighs, hating she wasn't wearing her leathers.

"It's disheartening to think you could forget me so easily, Ana Sarkov. After all the time we spent together."

"You must have me confused with someone else. The name's Anya Thalestris."

"You'll soon remember your true identity, I'm sure." He chuckled. "In the meantime, we'll be switching rails in a few hours. I'll bring you some food then, and if you need to use the restroom, we'll lower down a bucket. I apologize for the crude conditions, but it can't be helped."

"You're fucking kidding me."

"It won't be for long, you have my word. And then I'll protect you until you arrive home safely. Unfortunately, the castle has not been fully restored, but we've been working round the clock to make sure your suite is fully prepared."

Her eyes raced from corner to corner, trying to find some weakness. What castle? "How long until we get to there?"

"Ah." The man chuckled. "I'll be sure to let Penn know you are anxious to see him. I spoke to him earlier, you know. While he is overjoyed to finally have you back, he's distressed at the thought of any Scythian male touching you inappropriately. Shame on you, Ana. It is unbecoming of the Tsar's future wife. He feels it necessary to remind you of the consequences of such betrayal."

A chill ran down her spine.

"Don't worry, Ana. It'll be over soon. And then we'll put this unpleasantness behind us. Until then, Penn has asked you enjoy a little music."

She slammed her eyes closed, rocking back and forth. "No, please…"

"Rest well, Ana Sarkov."

A hundred deep Russian voices echoed off the steel walls. In an instant, a dam broke in Nya's mind, and her blood turned to liquid fire. Horrid memories combined with the blaze, and she threw her head back and screamed.

Light bled from the monitors, each sharing a different story. Some told of late night trysts in darkened stairwells, others of warriors socializing in open areas. But what held Alexandra's undivided attention were the three monitors on the bottom row that recorded the front of the consulate's drive.

The Chancellor had alerted the press of a breach of security in the back entrance, and like good little puppets they packed up their gear and headed out.

She couldn't have timed it more perfectly. The media had just left when a large passenger van rolled up and screeched to a stop. A few moments later, four of Nya's Chosen started hauling boxes and bags out of the consulate and tossing them in the vehicle.

She leaned back as the front doors burst open and Jax came out like a demon from hell. The others finished loading and hopped in, but Jax just stood, openly staring into the camera as if he knew she was watching.

He pulled out his phone, his finger sliding across the screen, and the hair on the back of her neck prickled as a chime went off in her pocket.

Alexandra cleared her throat and brought her phone to her ear. "What can I do for you, Counselor?"

"I've informed Toxaris that Nya is not well. We are taking her back to the hospital as I fear she may be experiencing complications from her wound. Her Chosen have decided to stay by her side."

"A testament that her candidates are males of worth. And I'm sorry to hear Anya is injured again." Alexandra's hand shook as she reached for her cigarettes.

Jax clenched his jaw, his intensity radiating through the screen. "Nya's condition will not allow visitors, and so I am sure you will alert the media of the situation."

"Of course."

"One more thing. If I find out you had a hand in this, you'll die knowing the meaning of pain."

Alexandra took a deep drag. Smoke billowed around her face. "Don't threaten me, Counselor."

"I'm not threatening. If you took part, I will make sure you die." He hung up the phone before she could respond.

Alexandra turned from the monitors and headed for the liquor cabinet.

Jax hopped in the van's passenger seat and slammed the door.

Victor raised a brow. "Please tell me you did not just threaten the leader of the Scythian world."

"No threats, just a Tova making a promise."

"As I thought." Victor smirked and started down the long gravel drive, the van's lights flooding the darkened road. They turned onto a smaller lane, heading deeper into the forest. "Let's hope one of her minions didn't record the call."

"I don't give a damn if they did."

"Threatening the life of the Chancellor is an offense punishable by death."

Jax shifted in his seat as he buckled his belt. "She wouldn't be stupid enough to put me in front of a tribunal, and we both know it."

"I've got new intel." Killian's voice came from the back. He leaned forward, his phone's light brought out the harsh planes of his features. "Twenty minutes ago Alexandra sent an entire squadron to an undisclosed location but allowed a slew of reporters to tag along. Apparently, they found a Drahzda cell, not fifteen kilometers from here. The Scythian News is now running a live feed, and they plan to go the traditional route and show their executions at dawn. According to my partner at the CIA, the Chancellor will be holding a press conference afterward, giving details about a failed Drahzdan terrorist attack."

Luka leaned over to see Killian's screen. "She knew they were going to take her. We're all pawns in her game."

Jax stared out the window at the ink-stained sky. "We may be forced to play by her rules for now, but the game is about to fucking change."

CHAPTER THIRTY-FOUR

Nya seized twice before the music mercifully stopped. Hoarse from hours of screaming, she didn't know how much longer she could take it. After the last seizure, the pain started affecting her eyesight, and a red haze now tinted the barren metal walls.

Hideous laughter echoed in her mind as the first night on the Drahzdan ship played over and over in her head.

"Penn. This is wrong. You know it."

"Shhhh, my love. It'll be fine. You'll see."

Six men with thick gloves held her down while shackles were latched on her wrists. She strained as Penn came forward.

She managed to get a foot free before the last shackle was latched on her ankle. A sickening crunch sounded as she whipped her leg, her foot smashing against the side of Penn's face. Another soldier rushed toward her, and she thrust her heel into this throat, sending him to his knees. Wildly kicking, again and again, she struck anyone who came near while she strained to break free. Two more men dropped, but a third came from the opposite side, tackling the lower half of her body and pinning her to the wall. The others dove, scrambling to get the manacle around her ankle. Everyone smiled as they stepped away.

Penn stepped close, wiping the blood from his mouth and nose. His breath warming her chin. "You may hate me now. But once you see the future I have planned, my sweet fianceé, you'll thank me." He brushed the hair from her face. "Now, try and get some rest. You won't be able to break these chains. I've made sure of it."

He tried to kiss her lips, but she jerked away.

Penn growled and turned to his men. "No one touches her but me."

The freight box jolted, bringing her back to the present. Something creaked overhead, and the entire car listed as it was hoisted in the air. Nya scrambled back, tucking her body into a corner, knees to chest, her feet pushing against the glass floor so she wouldn't tumble as it shifted and swayed.

The box eased down, jarring her as it landed on solid ground. Men shouted from one side and then the other.

Estonian. Dmitri Sarkov's native language.

Metal groaned as the back latch opened. Light flooded in, and Nya squinted, holding up her hand to shield her eyes from the harsh glare.

"Ana Sarkov. It's good to see you again." A stocky Allos came forward, his greasy black hair slicked back from his face. "The trip seems to be taking a toll, but I have no doubt you will recover once you are in Penn's arms again."

She grimaced as memories flooded her consciousness. This sonofabitch was Penn's right-hand man. "Fuck you, Stephan."

He stepped closer until he was a few feet from the glass. His muddy brown eyes glittered as he smiled. "Now, that's no way to speak to an old friend. I see the music wasn't as soothing as I had hoped."

Nya glared, refusing to look away. A Drahzdan soldier scaled the metal rungs running alongside her clear prison. He hopped on the roof, his worn soles squeaking on the glass as he made his way to the latch. Metal tumblers clicked until they fell into place, the top hatch opened, and a boxed lunch dropped next to her.

The hatch locked into place before the soldier walked back to the rungs and slid down the rails.

"I seem to remember you like turkey on rye, am I right?" Stephan smiled.

Nya shoved the container with her foot and kept her eyes on him.

"Do you need to use the facilities?"

She said nothing.

Stephan moved forward and knelt down beside her, the thick, transparent barrier the only thing between them. "I strongly suggest you try." His voice softened as if he cared one way or the other. "If you don't, you'll have to hold it until we reach Moscow. Unfortunately, I won't be able to come check on you. We'll be switching from rail to road. Too risky. But don't worry. I've taken care of everything." He stood and stuffed his hands back into his pockets. "Now, do you need the bucket or not?"

Hatred glittered in her eyes as she kept silent.

"Have it your way." He started toward the light, his voice bouncing off the harsh, metal walls. "Eat, or the music comes back on."

The door closed, and she hung her head as darkness smothered her once more.

Alexandra sat in the now empty briefing room. It had been a hellish morning. How she managed to keep Nya's abduction from the media was nothing short of miraculous. The compound security tapes had been erased before Victor and Jax left the grounds, but she'd spent the rest of the night personally splicing in old footage to fill the time stamp should someone notice. The Drahzdan cell that was found and accused of attacking the compound had been executed at sunrise while the Scythian world watched, a slew of reporters recording the whole affair. Of course, a press conference followed where Alexandra fabricated an elaborate plot involving explosives in the arena during the final round. This, naturally, segued into the sad update that Anya Thalestris was back under doctor's supervision. Her heartfelt wishes for the Thalestris family went off like a charm, and the news that Anya's Chosen had decided to stay by her side was met with quiet admiration. Toxaris was the only champion who attended the media circus. Afterward, the young warrior happily spoke to reporters, spouting off memories of her and Nya's time in the academy. Her support and convictions were impressive.

Either the chit believed the story, or she was a hell of a liar. Alexandra couldn't figure out which.

The other Amazonian warriors took the news of Nya's hospitalization with a collective shrug. They kept their focus on finding their mate, and, thanks to Toxaris, Alexandra encouraged the press to interview the other champions. After all, equality must prevail.

Her phone buzzed. Ike's name flashed across the screen. She reached for her tumbler and threw it back, letting the whiskey calm her. How had it gotten so bad that she'd started drinking before noon?

"Ike."

"I've spoken with Jax. If Pumpkin isn't back on Scythian soil by tomorrow, there'll be hell to pay."

"The Tovaris are going dark, so I'm sure everything will be resolved soon." Alexandra circled her finger around the rim of her glass.

The line grew quiet. "You remember the night before our final round?"

Alexandra's glass froze midair as a lump formed in her throat.

"I think about it sometimes," Ike said. "Us sneaking off into the woods. I would have taken you right then if you would've let me. Planted my seed and forced my claim, the consequence be damned."

Pain etched across her face, and she finished her drink.

"You stopped me, though. Still didn't keep me from taking all I could, did it?"

"Ike—"

"And just before dawn, as I held you in my arms, you whispered that you loved me. You vowed I was the only male for you—that you'd never be able to create an *intima* bond with anyone else. Do you remember?"

"We swore we'd never speak of it," Alexandra whispered.

"But we should have. I should have apologized and tried to explain. Alex, I never meant to hurt you. That night was more about me trying to prove we could work. I was young and stupid and confused. I know you won't believe me, but I didn't go into the third round intending to lose. It wasn't until we were on the field I realized sexual chemistry wasn't enough."

She slumped in her chair. "Why are you bringing this up? It happened years ago."

"Because all this time I've felt so damn guilty." Ike's voice became gruff. "Guilty that I had encouraged your feelings, even though I knew deep down I didn't feel the same. Guilty that because of me, you never fully bonded with your mate. Guilty the footage of our final round still circulates years after our Trials. And because of that guilt, you've been invited to events meant only for family and close friends. Even Nya's rite of passage made international news because you were the first to strike ink on my *nata*—not her mother, which was her right, but you."

Wearily Alexandra set her tumbler down. "What's your point, Ike?"

"I thought including you in my life would atone for the way I treated you. But I now understand just how wrong I've been. Promoting me, elevating Gia to your council, keeping Nya in the forefront of the Society, all of it has been a ploy, hasn't it? We're nothing but pawns in a game where you decide who wins and who dies."

She reached for the whiskey and filled her tumbler again. "That's not true. You know I love Anya as if she were my own."

"I used to believe that, but not anymore. Now I think you're using Pumpkin to exact your revenge."

The color drained from her face. "Ike, no. I lo—"

"Which is why I'm officially giving notice." Ike's voice became aggressive. "After this mission, I'm stepping down as Commander of Fourth Gen. Gia's already alerted your executive assistant she's resigning as well."

Stunned, Alexandra's stomach turned as she struggled to find the right words to say.

"Oh, and Chancellor?" His voice turned deadly. "I'd make sure Nya makes it out of this alive because if she dies, the line of Ares and Otrera ends with her."

The phone went dead, and Alexandra threw her tumbler across the room.

CHAPTER THIRTY-FIVE

Bile rose in Nya's throat as she tore off a small bite of sandwich and shoved it in her mouth. The rye bread felt like sawdust, but no bathroom meant no liquids. Something whirred in the quiet, and she glanced at the camera in the far corner.

Fucking Stephan. Bet he loved watching her squirm.

She leaned back and rested her head on the glass wall. Using meditative techniques Jax had taught her, she allowed her mind to wander back to Carpathia. God, she hoped Xari was still alive. And what about Jax, Killian, and the rest? Did they know she'd been taken, or had Alexandra told everyone she'd finally cracked and bolted for the hills?

Wouldn't put it past the bitch.

Nya had more questions than answers, but at least she understood why Penn did what he did.

"My mother almost ruined her marriage the day she took me and ran away. I cannot allow that to happen to us, and so I've made it impossible for you to do the same. The Phoenix lives within you, and if you betray me, you will burn. Do you understand, my sweet?"

She now knew she'd been injected with the same serum as the Drahzdan soldiers, put through the same hell, but it didn't seem to affect her as it did them. Her mind had protected her, for one thing. When Zander took her from the ship, the Phoenix raged through her. Every pulse had sent fresh fire through her veins, and at that moment she'd prayed her heart would stop beating. The night Zander freed her from the boat she must have gone beyond her natural threshold of pain, and her brain shut down.

But her mental capabilities were superior to the Allos, and even now, with the Phoenix taking flight, excruciating as it was, she still had control of her thoughts, her actions. But Penn once mentioned there were nine levels of conditioning. He laughed, saying Dmitri had fashioned them after

Dante's Inferno and his nine circles of hell. She had no idea what level the Russian music triggered, but every hour she survived it gave her hope because the serum's effect seemed to be lessening.

She leaned forward, tucking her knees to her chest. Her mind slipped into the place between awake and slumber, and she created a mental timeline of the shit she'd been through.

Penn kidnapping her … Dmitri Sarkov and that damn serum … And … oh, God …

The plastic lined room.

She forced herself to remain still. Visions of being tied down, fighting while doctors sedated her. Penn touching her, promising a bright future. And then the pain as they'd taken her eggs from her.

Panic choked her, and she fought the urge to attack her cage in a desperate attempt to flee.

A new breed of human. A hybrid race. That's what he wanted. The best of both to rule them all.

What if he'd already done it? What if he greeted her at the castle's door with a babe in his arms, one that had his nose, but her eyes … her Scythian heritage?

She couldn't live with that, but would she be able to murder innocent young simply because their father had forced them into being born?

Shivering, she ran her hands up and down her arms, trying to warm them from the seeping cold. Her fingers grazed the triple spire dragon still wrapped around her arm. Tears blurred her vision as she thought of the empty place it guarded.

Even if she made it through this, she'd never shoulder anyone's mark. The small ember of hope for a normal life, one where she could give the dragon to her little warrior as a gift for making it to the Trials, had turned to ash. But she'd keep this cuff on her arm until she breathed her last as a tribute to Jax—the one who'd kept her sane the past four years.

Sudden longing to see him, to have his arms around her one last time, surged from within. Her blood blazed through her veins as her heart thumped painfully in her chest. Nya whimpered and curled into a ball, her hands gripping her head as she pressed her temples with her palms. Her mind raced, and she tried to breathe through it while searching for the cause and effect of the Phoenix.

"Ana? Are you well?" Stephan's concerned voice blared from the speaker.

She ignored him while her mind latched onto an image of a lone field next to a stream. For years she questioned why this meadow, the one with her and Penn's secret fort, would be in her nightmares. But now she knew.

This was the only place she had willingly let Penn touch her, kiss her. He must have used the memory as a way to pull her back from the Phoenix fires when he set her triggers.

Something hissed overhead, and a bitter scent misted down, but she barely noticed as her mind latched onto another memory.

"No one is allowed to touch you, my sweet Ana. The blood fires will come if they do. Your pleasure is mine and mine alone. Do you understand? You belong to me now."

Her eyes grew heavy, and she slumped to the side.

That's why she reacted so violently when a male touched her. Her subconscious knew the pain she would endure if she became sexually aroused. Aren's passion had sparked in her that sense of panic, and yet, Jax's touch gave her pleasure and made her feel alive. Why?

Her arms felt like lead as she struggled to pull the blanket over her.

Her eyes drifted closed, and she groaned. It was because when Penn set her triggers, he couldn't use what she had never experienced—that's why Jax was different. What she felt for him went far beyond passion, deeper than lust.

Somewhere along the line, she'd fallen in love with him.

Sunlight filtered through worn curtains as Victor and Nya's Chosen quietly sat around the old farm table. After a long flight, they'd driven through the night and then spent the majority of the day trudging through heavily wooded terrain. Killian's contacts confirmed the CIA had secured a cabin and a few hundred acres after Sarkov industries had bought the castle on the next parcel over.

Jax had to give it to Killian's unit. They'd been instrumental in assuring the surrounding acreage stayed protected under an international initiative to save Russia's dangerous wildlands. Of course, none of it meant shit if his Vtachi didn't make it out of this alive. She'd been gone for over twenty hours. If they didn't hear something soon, he'd go crazy. He rolled his head, trying to loosen the tension in his shoulders.

The movement caught Victor's attention, and he glanced up from his tablet. His astute eyes took in Jax's harried appearance. He stood and made his way into the kitchen where he gathered a stack of plastic cups and a bottle of vodka. Setting down the cups, he poured each warrior a drink.

"Thanks," Killian muttered.

"*Tova, loyalnost, sila.*" Victor raised his glass in a traditional toast.

Jax tipped his cup toward his friend, repeating the Tovaris credo of Brothers, Loyalty, and Strength. It was the center of who they were, the very meaning of the symbol branded on both of the male's chests.

The others held their glasses in tribute, though none were stupid enough to utter the doctrine.

"I thought you were the only Tova psychologist working for the Society." Aren tossed back his drink.

"I work *with* them—big distinction. And Victor's Tovaris roots aren't widely known. It tends to intimidate his patients."

"You know what bothers me most?" Luka said, changing the subject. "Why now? The Drahzda must know how reckless it is to take Nya during the Trials. Why not snatch her when she was at the academy?"

"They tried." Killian's statement plunged the room into icy silence.

"Come again?" Jax leaned forward, his voice dangerously soft.

"Four years ago, I was the lead tracker in an op that involved capturing a Drahzdan team outside Bitterroot Montana."

Jax scowled. "Why the hell wasn't I informed?"

"Because the U.S. had given control of the mission to the Society, and the Chancellor ordered it stay classified. We found them ten miles from the Academy before taking them out."

Jax tapped the table. Victor poured him another drink. "The Tovaris should have been notified."

Killian shrugged. "I suggested the same, but the CIA Scythian commander informed me the mission never happened. I let it go."

A soft knock on the door had everyone on their feet and reaching for a weapon. Jax crept across the room, staying away from the light. He peeked out the window and groaned.

"Who is it?" Killian took his Glock from its holster.

Jax straightened up and opened the door. "Chosen, meet your potential in-laws."

Nya's body ached, her tongue felt two feet thick, and why in the hell was that music still playing in the background? She gritted her teeth and tried to accept the blaze roaring through her veins. The sensation was painful as hell, but at least she'd stopped seizing.

Confusion whirled as she stretched, sinking into something soft and warm and ... not moving.

Wait. Where was she?

Her heart plummeted as she opened her eyes. A familiar coffered ceiling stretched overhead.

She was back in that godforsaken castle.

Her fingertips brushed against her silk dress, and she breathed a sigh of relief. At least no one had stripped her of her clothes this time.

God, she hated this place.

Her head rolled to the side as she squinted, trying to focus.

Muted lamplight glared across another glass wall, which cut the room in half. The bed and bathroom were on her side, but a sitting area, complete with floor to ceiling windows and antique furniture were on the other. The music stopped, and her blood mercifully cooled.

Jax's deep, gentle voice caressed her mind. *You and me, Vtachi ... we got this.*

Nya drew strength from his memory as she struggled to sit up. She knew she wouldn't make it out of this place alive, but that no longer mattered. A new reality took hold as she swung her feet over the side of the bed. Her life was no longer about continuing Otrera's line. It was about saving the Society. She'd make sure Penn didn't use her genetics to create a hybrid race.

Kill Sarkov ... find the eggs ... destroy the Chancellor. She ran the words over and over in her mind, a mantra that grew stronger each time she silently repeated it.

She'd start by looking where it all began—in that plastic-lined room.

Few knew that Penn used to visit her at night through a passageway hidden behind wooden paneling. She had no idea how many corridors were buried within the walls, but she was sure if Penn wasn't in the room where he'd stolen her eggs, he'd be somewhere close by.

Yes. Keep the priorities. Find a way to get to that room. Kill Sarkov … find the eggs … destroy the Chancellor.

Tumblers ticked as the door beyond the glass wall opened. Stephan's stocky frame cast a deep shadow as he stepped into the formal sitting area. Nya doggedly ignored the pain and locked her knees. No way she'd face the bastard sitting down.

"I thought I would find you huddled on the floor. And yet, here you stand, bold as brass. How are you able to fight the Phoenix?"

"Superior genetics."

Stephan's lips thinned. "The Tsar's conjugal visits begin tonight. Your maid is coming to help you prepare."

Hatred flashed in her eyes as she kept his gaze. "I'll never be Ana Sarkov. You more than anyone should know that."

Stephan stepped closer. "At least consider the possibility. These past four years Penn has invested heavily in your future. And while the talk among the old guard is the Tsar has become weak, they don't understand that you were meant to create a new destiny."

"I won't submit, not to Penn." She grew strangely calm.

Stephan pressed a button on the wall. "Next year, I'll remind you of this discussion. It should be interesting to see what you have to say then. Oh, you should sit down—unless you want to end up on the floor."

She wanted nothing more than to wipe the smirk off his face, but mist filtered from a vent high overhead, and she stumbled, her legs barely making it to the edge of the bed before they gave way.

"The Tsar is eager to finally take what is his. Serve him well if you wish to survive. And then maybe we can put all this unpleasantness behind us."

The last time she was here, Penn touched her for hours, making sure she remained aware of what was happening but drugging her so she couldn't move.

"Rest well, Ana."

The mist turned to a fog, and Nya rolled, so her face stayed buried in the soft comforter. She remained stock still, taking shallow breaths, allowing the bedding to serve as a filter. The minutes seemed like hours, but even though her arms felt like lead, and her legs stayed at an odd angle, dangling to the floor, she never lost consciousness.

Finally, the fan overhead came to life, clearing the fog away.

Voices bled from the hall, and she completely relaxed and kept her eyes closed. The door clicked open, followed by a series of beeps and then another click as the inner glass panel gave way.

"Oooh, she's as lovely as a rose." The English lilt of a woman's voice sounded dangerously close, and Nya forced herself to stay limp.

"Chosen, I'd like to introduce Ike and Gia Thalestris." Victor's calm demeanor did nothing for the tension running rampant in the room. Disgust and judgement etched on their faces, Nya's Chosen stood shoulder to shoulder and glared at the couple.

"You may not like me, but as an Amazonian warrior I demand your respect." Gia shouldered her way through the males and crossed the room.

Ike dropped a rucksack by the door. "Let's concentrate on getting Anya back, and then you can condemn us to hell."

Jax closed the door as Gia set a small projector on one end of the table. With the press of a button, the old Formica turned into a touchscreen. "Here are the castle's original blueprints." A few more touches and a satellite image popped up. "And this was taken four hours ago."

Hundreds of workmen milled around the outer perimeter. A large flatbed, loaded with a boxed car, stood by the front steps.

"How many men are Drahzdan soldiers and how many are common Allos workers?" Luka asked.

She shook her head. "We don't have a head count yet. But we do know the Drahzda have hired construction crews from as far as Moscow, and satellites show several large Drahzdan convoys heading this way."

Giovanni's phone beeped. "Excuse me." He left the table.

"I say we go in guns blazing." Luka pointed to the back of the castle. "And we start here."

Victor shook his head. "The Tovaris aren't in place yet. And even if they were it would be a bloodbath."

"Not to mention Penn Sarkov, sick fuck that he is, will have a contingency plan that no doubt will end with Nya being in a lot of pain." Jax's voice darkened. "As much as I hate waiting, we find a way to get in and out before anyone knows we're there."

"We believe she's being held here." Gia swiped across the northern wing, zooming in on a section along the second floor. "Which means we split up."

The room grew quiet as Jax stepped forward. "Should you take the lead on this one? Killian's our best tracker, and I—"

"No." Gia's voice turned soft, deadly. "It is my right. I claim vengeance in the name of my *nata*."

Everyone stopped as her words rang in the room. Victor placed his fist over his heart. "So be it."

All eyes turned toward Gia, and she took a deep breath. "Victor, you'll join Zander and the rest of the Tova's and secure us a way out of here once we've rescued Nya. Ike and Jax, find my *nata*. Luka, Giovanni, and Aren will defend the perimeter while Killian and I track Sarkov." Her voice became high, tight. "I should have killed Penn years ago, but I didn't, and Nya paid the price. I won't make that same mistake again."

Jax cleared his throat. "We'd have a better chance of getting Nya out first if we had a way to the roof."

Giovanni came back in the room. "I agree. And I believe I've found a way." He scooted between Gia and Aren to enlarge the image so the southern parapet covered the table. A black chute cascaded over the outer wall and into a large, encased dumpster.

"According to our sources, the old plaster from the second floor was covered in black mold. The construction engineer felt it best to contain it, and so they're bagging the debris and then dumping it through this chute into the enclosed container below. As soon as we discovered they were looking for a mold removal company, the Italian forces sent in Allos who are Scythian loyalists to help. They're changing out containers this afternoon, which means if we can get into the dumpster, we can scale up the chute and be on the roof in a matter of minutes."

Gia rubbed her chin. "How sturdy is the plastic?"

"It's heavy gauge with reinforced spiral wiring, which will serve as a ladder. It'll have to be well timed. The Tsar has the construction crews working around the clock. The chute will be used in shifts."

Jax looked out the window. Thick clouds hung low in the sky. "Unless it's raining, which means the crew will stay indoors."

Thunder rumbled overhead, and Victor clicked off the projector. "I believe that's our cue."

CHAPTER THIRTY-SIX

"It's been an hour, and she's still out of it." The woman's voice floated overhead.

"She shouldn't be." Frustration darkened the male's tone, and Nya forced her body to remain lax. Sergei. The bastard was head of Sarkov's guard. He would be third in line to die—right after Penn and Stephan.

"Poor dear." The woman touched Nya's head. "They had her under for hours before she got here, and now this. It'll be a wonder if I can get her into the bath, much less the waxing table."

The Allos had weird rituals about plucking and shaving specific parts of a woman's body, but Amazonian warriors had little body hair to speak of, and Scythian males didn't care about such trivial things anyway. Still, Penn would want her buffed, powdered, and polished for his pleasure. He'd want her scented and lotioned, soft and submissive, primped with stained lips, and cloying perfume like an Allos woman would be.

She couldn't stand the thought, but if it gave her time to gather her strength and find a way out of this mess, she'd let them shave and wax whatever they wanted.

"She's not as harmless as she looks." Sergei's voice turned harsh. "Be careful. These *things* are strong."

"Don't call her a thing." The woman's defensive voice dropped to a hushed whisper. "Besides. Penn might be listening."

Sergei hesitated. "You haven't seen her kill a soldier with one foot. I have." His tone became businesslike. "Now, there's an alarm by the bathroom door. Just push the button should you need help. Can you get her undressed and in the tub by yourself?"

The woman scoffed. "And if I can't, would you like to tell the Tsar that you helped bathe his beloved Ana?"

"Of course not." The bed dipped as Sergei sat next to Nya. Her listless body rolled toward him, her side brushing against his hip. Warm breath swept across her face.

"What are you doing?" The woman panicked.

"Making sure she's really under."

Something grazed Nya's cheek, and she forced herself to remain still.

"I believe you're right." Sergei stood, and Nya rolled back. "The sedative must have been too strong so soon after her journey here. I'd planned on giving her something so she wouldn't be able to kill you where you stand."

"Penn will have you drawn and quartered if she isn't at least coherent by tonight."

He paused. "I'll send a few maids in to help."

The woman bristled. "The Tsar chose me personally for this task, and I'll not be disappointing him. Besides, the others aren't allowed on this floor, you know that."

"Then I'll send for Penn."

Panic threaded through Nya, but she managed to remain calm.

"He doesn't want to see her until tonight," the woman warmly chided. "He said it'll be like unwrapping a gift he's been looking forward to for four years."

Nya couldn't help but tense at that, but she quickly covered it up with a soft groan and forced herself to relax again.

"Looks like she's coming around, best be getting on with it," the woman said.

Nya flinched as a large palm dipped beneath her knees, and another made its way around her shoulders.

Sergei's deep voice grumbled just above her face. "I'll get her into the bathroom, but then you're on your own."

He lowered her into the tub and started the tap. Cold water rushed onto her silk covered legs.

"I'd planned on stripping her first." Frustration bit through the woman's voice.

"You can do that here. It'll make it easier anyway. Oh, and braid her hair. The Tsar wants to unbraid it himself."

Bile rose in Nya's throat. When they were young, Penn spent hours playing with her hair. He couldn't get past the silky texture, yet each strand was as strong as twine.

The water warmed, and air stirred as Sergei stood. "I'll be back within the hour. Have her in the bed by then. I've set a syringe on the nightstand, just in case."

"Yes, sir."

"You know her trigger if she gets out of hand?"

"Of course."

"And don't forget to set the security alarm. It'll be more than your life's worth if she manages to escape." His voice trailed away, and then the door clicked closed.

"One time," the woman grumbled. "I forget an alarm one time, and I never live it down. I swear that man ..." She kept mumbling to herself as she bustled around the room, collecting soaps and lotions and God knew what else.

Warmth seeped over Nya's thighs as the water rose. She tipped her head to the side, weakly groaning as her eyes opened to slits.

The woman's kind gaze met hers, and she patted her shoulder. "Don't you worry, Ana. The sedative will keep you docile as a lamb. There's no need to fight me, you know. I've worked for the Sarkov family for years. Penn and I were friends, well, that is before his mother took him away. He'll treat you right if you let him."

Nya's lids floated closed, her mind racing through her memories of Penn when they were little. He did mention a few times having one other friend. She was older, though ... what was her name? Mindy ... Molly?

The woman hoisted Nya up to a sitting position, hiking her dress up to her torso and pulling it off over her head. Her bra was next.

Something pinged in the room.

"Millie, how is my Ana doing?"

Nya forced herself to stay still as Penn's voice echoed off the harsh tile walls.

Millie ... that was it. Penn once said she was the only other person he trusted.

"She's as beautiful as you said she'd be. And she's still out like a light."

"Will she be ready?"

"If Stephan stops pumping her room full of sleeping gas, she will."

A few moments passed before Sarkov answered. "I'll speak with him. A situation has arisen that requires my attention. I'll be later than planned, but I expect to enter our suite with my Ana warming our bed."

"Yes, sir. I'll have her tucked in as snug as a bug in a rug."

"Make sure her hair is —"

"In one braid down her back. Yes, we've gone over this, Penn." Millie's voice warmed as if she were appeasing a child. "She'll be well rested for you with her beautiful hair just the way you want it."

The room went silent, and Millie sighed, shifting closer to the tub. "You're a lucky girl." She brushed back Nya's hair. "As the Tsar's wife, you'll live in a palace and want for nothing. You'll be waited on hand and foot, protected, coddled, and adored." Longing deepened her tone. "A lot of women would give anything to be in your shoes. It's every girl's dream."

Nya's eyes shot open as her hand lashed out, wrapping around the woman's neck. Pulling her so close her lips rested against the woman's ear.

"It's my fucking nightmare."

Millie struggled, but Nya brought up her other thumb and pressed down hard on the woman's neck. Millie's eyes rolled back in her head, and she slumped over the tub.

Standing as quietly as possible, Nya lowered the older woman to the ground. Water gushed as she turned both taps to full and unplugged the drain. The constant rush of water filled the room as Nya stripped Millie down to her bra and panties. She whipped the silky sleeveless red nightgown over the woman's head, tugging it past her waist before threading her arms through the matching robe.

The older woman started to stir, and Nya flipped her on her stomach and stuffed a wet washcloth in her mouth. She shoved her knee in the middle of Millie's back and tied her hands with the silk tie from the robe.

"Fight me, and I'll snap your neck," Nya whispered in her ear. "I don't want to kill you, but I will if I have to. Now, what is it going to be?"

The maid stilled.

"One sound, one movement, and you die. If you know anything about Scythians, you know I'm not bluffing."

Tears trickled down Millie's face as she watched Nya grab her uniform and put it on. The black pants were a little large, but thankfully the Allos woman was taller than most. Nya tucked in the roomy shirt before securing the entire thing with her belt. She pulled her black hair into a bun, thankful for the ridiculous lace cap that was part of the maid's uniform.

Nya felt like she'd been run over by a truck, but at least she was getting her strength back. She looked at the woman cowering on the floor and bent down, taking her hair out of its tight bun.

Shit. Millie's mousy brown hair would be a dead giveaway. Not to mention it wasn't nearly as long as it needed to be. Nya took a towel and dipped in under the running water until it was sopping wet. She wrung it over Millie's head, darkening her color.

Better.

She tossed the towel into the corner before braiding the maid's hair and slipping it under her robe.

If she kept the lights low, maybe it wouldn't be too obvious.

Nya shoved her feet in the woman's shoes before bending back down. "Now. Millie, is it?" Nya looked into her eyes.

The other woman whimpered.

"Sarkov's a bastard. He's probably going to murder you and not think a thing about it. But if he knew you were conscious and didn't call for help he'd make you suffer, killing you slowly instead. I don't want that on my conscience, so I'm really sorry about this."

She thumbed the woman's neck again, noting the bruise blooming there. Within seconds the maid went lax.

Nya turned off the water and hoisted Millie's arm over her shoulder while keeping hold of her waist. Head down, she opened the door and started toward the bed. Her strength hadn't fully returned, but she realized she could use that to her advantage. The video feed would show one woman in a uniform struggling to get another woman across the room. Nya flipped the side lamp off and pulled the duvet back. She lowered Millie onto the bed and pulled the covers up to the maid's neck.

Millie groaned, and Nya grabbed the syringe from the side table, plunging it into her arm. The woman went utterly lax.

Bile rose in her throat, and Nya swallowed a few times as she adjusted the woman's braid, tucking it between the pillows.

Eyes to the ground, she calmly walked back to the bathroom. It took everything she had not to bolt from the place, but she gritted her teeth, forcing herself to move slow and easy as she gathered the wet silk dress and towels. Picking up her sandals on the way out, she turned the knob.

Relief flooded through her as the door clicked open. She focused on the security pad near the glass wall, thanking God the system had an 'alarm on' button instead of using a code. Knowing Sarkov, she wouldn't have been surprised if the thing took a thumbprint or retinal scan.

Clutching the towel and her leathers to her chest, she opened the outer door—and stepped into a hallway full of Drahzdan soldiers.

"Finally, I get you to myself. I thought breakfast would last forever." Erik took Xari's hand, bringing it to his lips for a soft kiss.

Distracted, she searched the great hall. Erik had suggested a walk around the lake, and now she regretted saying yes. How in the hell was she supposed to find an opening to drug the Chancellor while trudging through miles of frigid forest?

"It's a relief to have the first round behind us, isn't it?"

She nodded. "Uh huh."

Alexandra entered the room, and Xari's eyes narrowed as she watched the bitch warmly smile and speak to the surrounding warriors. God. The female was lethal like a snake and could slither out of anything. Information wouldn't be enough. What they needed was tangible proof. But how to get it?

"Xari?"

"Hmmm?"

"You're regretting your decision about me, aren't you?"

She finally gave Erik her full attention. "What?"

His expression turned grim. "You're regretting choosing me, aren't you?" He scooted closer. "Listen, about staying in Carpathia. I didn't mean to mislead you. If you can't be happy here, we can try another compound."

She stood and took his hand. "I don't regret choosing you."

Erik's eyebrow raised as he stood as well. "You sure? Because this right here ..." he motioned between the two of them. "This feels like regret."

Xari glanced around. "Let's go. We need to talk, and I hate feeling like people are listening."

They left the dining hall and started across the foyer to don on their hats and gloves. Xari opened the front door and brushed off the reporters loitering on the steps. They stayed quiet as they made their way into the forest. The leaf-carpeted path led to massive trees that stretched overhead, boughs tangling together, creating an arch high above them. Rays of light filtered through, spearing the forest in random patterns. A golden eagle screeched in the distance, making the silence between them seem louder. Erik kept hold of her hand, giving her time to mull over her thoughts.

"Please tell me what's wrong," he finally asked.

She snapped a twig off a tree, rolling the leaves between her thumb and forefinger. "I've just been distracted, that's all."

"You've fallen in love with David." Erik suddenly stopped. "Haven't you?"

"No. It's not—"

"Listen." He turned to face her. "I know I'm not as good with words as he is, but when I'm around you I can't think clearly. And we have this strange connection, you know?" He put his hands on her waist and rested his forehead against hers. "Even though I'm serious and you're quirky. I follow the rules, and you look for the exceptions. I'm quiet, and you're a chatterbox. It's like we are opposites, but we still make sense." His voice grew uncertain. "At least, we do to me."

She pulled him close and rested her head on his chest. "We make sense to me too."

Erik smiled. "Yeah?"

"Yeah." She tugged him forward and they headed for the lake. The path ended a few hundred yards from the muddy bank. They walked to the water's edge, watching the light play off the ice-laden cattails.

"I spoke with a friend of mine who's a Tova at the hospital," Erik said.

"Oh?"

"He informs me that Nya is doing well, although when I checked there was no record of her being admitted."

"I'm sure it's an oversight, with the Trials going on and all."

"Not possible." Erik took her hand. "Retinal scans are taken as soon as someone is seen, any medical information is then collected and stored into the mainframe."

She swallowed. "Maybe they never officially discharged her."

"Or maybe that's why you're so distracted."

Her cheeks flushed. Erik was one of the best warriors at the Consulate. She wouldn't be able to fool him for long.

"Why don't you trust me?"

His question stood like a barrier between them, and she looked away.

"Xari." Erik put her hand over his heart. "If you can't trust me, trust this. I won't let you down."

She leaned forward, resting her forehead on his chest. "I need your help."

"Finally." He kissed the back of her head. "What is it that you need?"

"A recording device. One small enough to go undetected yet can hold hours of conversation."

Erik frowned as he tipped her chin up to meet his gaze. "That's a tall order."

"That's not all. It must be capable of sending information to someone else, and I need it as soon as possible."

His voice lowered to a rough whisper. "Are you in trouble?"

"No. It's nothing like that."

"I take it you need to record something in one of the consulate's secured rooms. Something sensitive."

She tensed. "It's a possibility, yes."

Erik kissed her lips. "I have a friend in Counter Intel. I'll see what I can do."

Nya swallowed her panic as she slipped away from the door, briefly glancing at Sergei at the end of the hall. Boots scraped on marble as the soldiers shuffled forward, their dark-rimmed collars telling that she'd stumbled into a meeting of Sarkov's top men. Sergei's thick Russian voice carried over the group, giving them their orders for the night. She tucked her chin to her chest, hugging her wet clothes like a lifeline. Muttering Russian apologies, she slipped past, hoping like hell the soldier's kept their gaze on their commander. The crowd thinned as she wove through the back of the group. Every step distancing them eased the tension in her gut.

Sergei stopped speaking as if he had noticed something. Nya picked up her pace.

"Millie, did you have any trouble with Ana?"

Several soldiers chuckled, but Nya kept her back to him and shook her head.

"Do you have her clothing?"

She barely heard him through the pulse pounding in her ears. She nodded and held up the dress and sandals.

"Very good. Take them to my office. I'd like to make sure no one's tracking her."

Nya glanced over her shoulder as she neared the end of the hall.

Sergei tilted his head, his eyes narrowing as if he knew something was different but couldn't figure out what it was. "On second thought, I'll take her clothing now."

Panic gripped Nya's chest; her mind raced with options.

Boots thundered up the stairs, and Nya pressed against the wall as a team of soldiers ran past.

"Sir, the sensors in the southern region have gone off."

Nya turned the corner and started toward the stairs.

"Are you sure it isn't a herd of deer again?"

"I've already sent a team. They've found boot prints along the boundary leading to the Forest Preserve.

Sergei let out a growl. "Damn it. Send a squadron. Double the security detail, especially in this hallway. I'll see to Ana."

Nya gave up any pretense and ran. If she were still in the open when Sergei figured out the woman in the bed wasn't her, she'd be outnumbered. Even rested and at full strength, she wouldn't be able to overpower an entire squadron.

She had to get to the plastic lined room, find out what happened to her eggs, and, hopefully, kill Penn before Sergei discovered she was gone.

A man covered in plaster dust loomed ahead, and she slowed her stride, keeping her distance. The room she sought was just beyond the second-floor landing.

Fresh air brushed her face as the hall widened, opening to a large balcony. A balustrade stretched across the landing, following the walnut stairs that wound to the first floor below. Sweat beaded on her brow as she hurried across the open area, praying that no one would find it odd a maid was on the second floor. She stopped as she got to the other side. The room that had tortured her dreams lay just a few feet away.

The castle's door flew open, startling the construction crew working on the baseboard and crown molding. Four men trudged dirt and mud on the newly polished floor.

"I'll gut the entire team like fish if they've let Scythians on my land!" Penn's voice echoed from below, and Nya dove for the knob and rushed inside.

She eased the door closed. Paint fumes tinged the air, stinging her nose. Floor to ceiling windows lined the entire back wall, allowing weak evening light to angle through the room. Nya's stomach churned as she took in the space.

Sunny yellow paint had replaced plastic lined walls. Mahogany floors gleamed beneath her feet while Scythian lettering, elegantly written in gold, ran under the crown molding. She gasped in horror as she recognized their meaning. Even though some of the letterings had been re-ordered for the sake of design, she could still make out the Dacian apology she'd etched in stone to her father so long ago. Three chandeliers hung from the coffered ceiling, hand-painted cherubs hovered around their bases. Her gaze dropped from overhead, and bile rose in her throat as she counted the row of mahogany bassinets, each accompanied by a rocking chair and changing table.

Eighteen. Oh, God. Nya's eyes swept from one side to the other, and reality took bitter hold. Penn had created a nursery out of the room they used to steal her Scythian heritage from her.

How fucking poetic.

What if it was too late? What if some *woman* already carried her young? How could she even begin to deal with that? Scythian blood acted like a virus to the Allos. Surely they wouldn't be able to carry a Scythian fetus to term?

Unless Penn's scientists had discovered a way.

Adrenaline kicked into overdrive, and Nya started shaking. She needed to kill Penn. She really did. But if he died too soon, they may never discover what happened to her eggs.

Several male voices murmured in the hall as workers passed by, and Nya's gaze shot around the room. The closet doors stood unhinged against the far wall. The space must have been recently created because the plaster had not yet dried and the shelves were stacked on the floor, waiting to be installed.

"Is the nursery finished?" A man's voice bled through the door. Nya spotted an empty box near the closet and ran across the room. She flipped the box over and squatted down before she placed the box over her head. It barely fit her frame.

"Yes, I'm sure you'll be pleased." Another deep voice rumbled as they stepped into the room.

"What about the closets?"

"The dehumidifiers will be here as soon as the secret suite is finished. Should be tonight."

"The Tsar wants the closets done and stocked before his Ana sees the space. They will be spending a few days together to get reacquainted. But there'll be hell to pay if it isn't finished by Sunday."

"I'll see that it's done."

The footsteps softened as the men walked away. Nya clenched her cold hands together. Time was running out, and she had no game plan. No path. No resources. No backup. And apparently, the servants knew her triggers.

Fantastic.

CHAPTER THIRTY-SEVEN

Penn whistled as he made his way down the hall. Stephan had assured him the woods were being thoroughly searched. And he'd settled the matter of one of the villages protesting their presence. A team of the best soldiers were sent to bring the villagers to heel. Being the great leader he was, Penn had allowed his men to claim one of the village women for their own as a reward for a job well done. And if the women were married? His soldiers made sure they were widowed before they were shuttled onto a bus and carted away.

Granted, it was an unusual move in this day and age, but his men needed a token of his affection. After all, he now had his Ana, and it only seemed right his most loyal had the same pleasure of finding a good woman to warm their bed at night.

The uprising and the sensors in the woods had put him behind schedule, but it was of little consequence. One of his battalions was a few hours from the castle, the other three would be arriving within the week. They had enough land to build barracks for the upper guard, and they would use the village stupid enough to question his authority as a place to house their servants.

The hairs on the back of his neck prickled as he stopped at the top of the stairs.

Why was it so quiet?

Sergei came from Ana's suite. He grimaced as he walked toward his leader.

"Has something happened to my wife?" Panic threaded through his tone. Maybe they had been too heavy handed on the sedative.

Sergei shook his head. "I checked on your Ana after Millie tended to her, and then again just now. The lights were off, but she is resting."

Penn scowled. "I specifically asked that Millie leave the side table light on so the cameras could see if Ana was in distress.

Sergei swallowed. "I'm sure everything is fine."

Penn bolted through the door. Tension eased from his face as he saw the curve of a hip and a shoulder in the bed, a braid tucked between two pillows.

Sergei came from behind. "The sedative can cause headaches. I bet the light hurt her eyes, and Millie kept the lamp off to ease her pain."

Penn rubbed the back of his neck. "Yes, that must be it."

"I'll ring for some Nurofen."

"That won't be necessary. The bathroom medicine cabinet is fully stocked."

Sergei tipped his head in a bow. "Very well."

Penn turned toward the glass door and put in his code. "See the cameras are turned off. And no one enters this room unless I request it."

"As you wish," Sergei said. "Enjoy your time with your Ana, my lord. I'll take care of the rest."

The outer door clicked closed as the inner glass panel slid open. Penn stepped forward and shucked off his shoes. He took his time undressing, wanting the anticipation of finally having his Ana in his arms to last a few minutes longer. Going to the bathroom, he grabbed a quick shower and donned a pair of sleep pants. The rasp of a match strike sounded in the quiet as Penn lit several pillar candles throughout the room. Her skin would be so beautiful in the soft, warm light. Lust painfully ached through him as he slipped under the covers, his large palm covering the rise of her hip.

The minute he touched her he knew something was wrong.

Penn rolled to his side and flipped on the light before he roughly shoved the woman lying next to him flat on her back.

Millie's eyes were half open, her slack mouth drooling around a wet cloth.

Enraged, Penn screamed as he jumped off the bed and hit the alarm. Sirens wailed in the night.

Erik waited for Xari at her door, watching her saunter down the hall. He pulled her into his arms as soon as she was in reach, making a production of kissing her long and hard. His hand swept under her sweater, cupping the side of her breast.

"Change in the bathroom; what you need is here," he whispered as his finger nuzzled between her breast and the bra's cup. "I've texted directions on how to sync it to your phone."

Xari stood on her tiptoes, hugging him tightly. "Thank you. I'll never forget it."

"Oh, I know you won't. I'll remind you every year we celebrate our marking anniversary."

Xari pulled back and grinned. "I'm starting to like that idea."

Erik kissed her neck, making his way back to her ear. "Finally. It only took a covert mission and a device that could get us charged with treason to do it." His whisper turned gruff. "You're worth it, though. I'd walk through fire for you."

Xari's breath caught as she met his intense gaze. He kissed her one more time before walking away.

She opened her suite's door, locking it behind her, and headed toward the bathroom. She placed her phone on the counter before shucking off her shirt. A small black object, no bigger than a pea, was wedged between her bra and skin. She sat on the side of the tub and opened Erik's text. The device could hold up to three hours of audio. Xari set it to automatically start recording as soon as it was activated. Whatever information she discovered would send once her phone found a signal.

But who to send it to? She scrolled through her texts looking for Gia's information, but when Jax's last message rolled onto her screen, she smiled. She'd forgotten he had sent her Zander's number. Making sure the recording made it into the hands of the Tova's leader was perfect. She'd also send it to Victor. She needed a backup and Jax would be solely focused on finding Nya.

If all went well, she'd use the prototype to give the Tovaris evidence that linked the Chancellor to this entire mess.

She grabbed the third and final dress in her wardrobe and shucked it on, thanking God almighty that she'd never have to endure another cleansing ceremony again. Slipping the small glass container down her front, she nestled it between her cleavage and her bra. Xari stared in the mirror, inspecting the places where the recording device and vial were hidden. The neckline of the dress softly draped across her chest in silky spills before gathering on one shoulder, creating dips and shadows along the soft contours of her breasts. No one would suspect she was hiding a thing. Satisfied, she took a deep breath and headed down to the dining hall.

No sooner had she made her way to her table, Alexandra sauntered in, crystal tumbler in hand. She wandered around the tables, chatting with the champions while finishing off her drink. Another was brought as she continued making her way through the room. She'd finished off the second before she managed to circulate to Xari's table.

"Toxaris. It's wonderful to see you've recovered from your ordeal."

"Thank you." Xari smiled. "I'm just sorry Nya isn't doing as well."

Alexandra's calculated smile didn't reach her eyes as she motioned for a server. "May I join you for dinner?"

"We'd be honored."

An extra chair was quickly rushed out, and Alexandra sat as the room followed en masse. The first course was brought out, and the conversation flowed. As soon as the Chancellor's glass was less than half full, Xari motioned for the waiter, encouraging to be generous in his pour.

Erik's what-the-hell-are-you-doing expression had Xari wondering if she'd overstepped her bounds, but she remained the perfect host, directing the conversation and changing topics when the need arose, all the while making sure the waiters kept the Chancellor's glass full.

Alexandra became animated as the night wore on, and a ruddy blush ran across her cheeks and over the bridge of her nose. She seemed to find something David said particularly funny because she openly laughed as she ran her hand up and down his arm.

"I enjoyed your press conference." Xari set down her spoon. "Since I've been here, I've discovered an interest in public relations. And you, my Chancellor, are the master."

Alexandra smiled, cradling her glass to her chest. "You're too kind, young warrior. In our Society, it's crucial that hard issues such as terrorist attempts remain transparent."

"Yes, Scythians value the truth above all else," David commented.

"I agree." Xari sat back as the waiter took her plate.

Alexandra studied the young warrior. "Truth. Its realities are often harsh and cruel, but necessary, is it not?"

Silence fell over the table, and David cleared his throat and looked at his watch.

"I believe we've lost track of the time."

"It does seem to fly when in good company, doesn't it?" Xari placed her napkin on the table.

Alexandra set her glass down with an uncharacteristic thump. "You are a charming host, Toxaris. If you don't mind, I'd like a word in private."

Erik stiffened. "Begging your pardon, Chancellor. The press is waiting in the arena for their first official interview with the champions and their Chosen before the opening ceremony of the second round."

Xari put her hand on his arm, her fingers digging into his uniform. "I'm sure we won't be long. I asked the Chancellor to keep me updated on Nya's progress."

Alexandra stood, keeping her hand anchored on the back of her chair. "Yes, and that's what I intend to do. Chosen, your warrior will meet you in the arena."

Xari briefly linked her pinky around Erik's, squeezing and then letting it go before she stood and followed the Chancellor out of the room.

They made their way up the stairs and past her personal guard in silence.

"What a lovely home," Xari said as soon as they entered the suite.

Alexandra grunted in agreement, her hand grazing along the backs of the furniture as they crossed the living room. They passed through the security room, and Alexandra nodded at the Amazonian warrior watching a wall of monitors.

Xari grew leery as they started down a darkened corridor.

"Wait," Alexandra muttered, resting her forehead on the wall. The retinal scanner raced over her eye before a green light flashed and a hidden panel slid open. She swept her arm wide. "Join me, please."

As soon as they passed the threshold, the door closed, leaving them in silence. Xari felt like a mouse trapped by a cat. "Why did you need to see me?"

"I haven't had the opportunity to speak with you privately since your accident."

Xari's expression became unreadable. "It was nothing. I'm fine."

"Still, I'd like your account of what happened."

Xari ran her hand across her chest as if she were scratching her shoulder. She pressed the small listening device taped to the underside of her bra strap, hoping like hell the thing worked. "Nya and I were walking along the path, discussing an argument I had had with one of my Chosen when I fell and hit my head. When I came to, Jax informed me that Nya had helped me to the infirmary, but the doctor there noticed she didn't look well. When they discovered her temperature had gone back up, they admitted her again."

"And you remember nothing from the time you hit your head until you awoke in the infirmary."

Xari shrugged. "The physician said that was normal with a concussion."

"I had an interesting conversation with the head of security today." Alexandra turned, resting her back against the door.

Xari raised her brows. "Oh?"

"Apparently, you've been very vocal about expressing concerns for Nya's wellbeing."

Xari took a deep breath and sighed. "Seeing Otrera's exhibit in the museum made me miss my best friend. I worry about her."

The Chancellor thoughtfully shook her head. "As do I."

Xari looked around and whistled. "This is the war room, isn't it? I've heard about it, but I've never even seen a picture. Isn't this only supposed to be used when Scythian security is threatened?"

Alexandra crossed the room and flopped into the nearest seat. "I see you paid attention in your government classes. It's the only place that I have complete privacy. We wouldn't want anyone to construe our conversation as some conspiracy."

Xari circled the large oval table, her fingers grazing the smooth dark wood. She stopped in front of the alcohol. "Would you like an after-dinner drink? Brandy, perhaps?"

Alexandra rubbed her forehead. "I'd love one."

Xari stood in front of the decanters, blocking Alexandra's view. Her hands shook as she slipped the vial from its hidden place between her breasts. Thick liquid trickled down the side of the snifter as she emptied the vial before slipping it back down her dress. She picked up the crystal decanter and the glasses and brought them to the table.

"You're a little young for a digestif, don't you think? After all, we wouldn't want you stumbling into the arena to address the media."

Xari grinned as she poured. Brandy splashed into the snifter, mixing with the liquid already there. She swirled the glass, watching the amber alcohol race to the rim. Handing the drink to the Chancellor, she smiled and then poured one of her own. "My father was born in Belarus. I was practically raised on the stuff. And it's been a long day."

Alexandra warmed the alcohol between her palms. "Yes, it has."

Heat rushed through as Xari took a sip. "I do apologize if my concern for Ny came off heavy-handed. I know you must be worried sick, too— you being her godmother and all."

Alexandra rubbed the glass against her bottom lip before she took a healthy drink. "She's like a daughter to me, you know."

Xari placed her snifter on the table and faced the Chancellor. "I knew you must be close by the way she admired you—talked about you all the time. You only had sons, right?"

An Amazonian's greatest blessing was the birth of a daughter.

"That's correct." The Chancellor grimaced. She downed the last of her brandy, and sighed.

Xari's eyes sparked. "I'm sure you're extremely proud of them."

"They lived with their father growing up, but yes. My sons are fine males."

"Commander Thalestris said as much."

Alexandra's breath caught as her glazed eyes looked up. "Really? You spoke with Ike?"

"After the Championships, I joined them for dinner. The commander told me how close the two of you were and how relieved he was that you would be here to watch over Ny."

Alexandra closed her eyes, as if she were in pain. "I tell you, I'd give anything if Anya could be here. Anything."

The statement rang in the silence and Xari wanted to lash out and call the female a liar. But she'd have to be careful. The audio file being recorded must sound like a conversation, not like the Chancellor had been drugged and was being interrogated.

"You know," she finally said. "I bunked next to Nya for four years. Did you know she talks in her sleep? Sometimes the others would complain, but I didn't mind."

"Oh?" Alexandra glanced up from her drink, sounding like a baleful cat.

"Yeah. We never understood why she had such horrid nightmares, waking everyone up screaming something about being nailed to a ship or rolling around gripping her stomach like someone had just ripped a knife through her."

Alexandra's hand shook as she brought her glass to her lips. "She's been through quite a lot."

Xari swirled the amber in her snifter. "Yeah, she has, but none of us understood why until now. I overheard Myrina talking about it the other day."

Alexandra's expression grew wary. "How many warriors were in your barracks?"

"Oh, over the course of four years, I'd say about thirty or so. I'm sure they all remember."

"God," Alexandra whispered, rubbing her head.

"You know, one night she dreamed of you." Xari took a sip of brandy. "At first, I thought it was because of you being her godmother and all. But then she mentioned Sarkov ... something about a promise ... and that you needed to stay out of Russia."

Alexandra's eyes rounded in horror as her knuckles whitened around her glass.

Xari leaned in, her voice threaded with steel. "What was she talking about, do you know?"

The Chancellor's lips thinned to a white line like she was struggling to keep them closed.

Xari's tone softened. "You can tell me the truth."

"I had nothing to do with Dmitri and his plan to take over Russia," she finally blurted out. "And I never thought they'd steal Anya from her family."

"I'm sure you didn't. You thought of Nya as a daughter, and Ike trusted you to keep his *pumpkin* safe."

The Chancellor brought her empty snifter to her chest, hugging it like a lifeline. "Ike's resignin' from his post, d'you know?" She squinted as her words began to slur. "Gia's done the same. And Penn's threatenin' to go to the Senate, all because of a mistake I made almos' thirty years ago. The summer I met Dmitri I had no clue who he was … I thought he was jus' some Allos I'd toy with to piss off my father." She sighed and closed her eyes. "But Sarkov knew who I was. And hell, I've been paying for it since."

"Is that all?"

"Ike's hell-bent on never seeing me again." She rested the snifter's cool glass against her cheek. "I've loved him for over twenty-five years. Twenty. Five. Years. Even after he humiliated me in the arena and then shouldered someone's mark beneath his bloodline. Even after *he* was blessed with a daughter while *I* was given sons. And now this. It isn't my fault Penn's obsessed with Nya. An' how in the hell was I supposed to know that the Drahzda would use her blood to further that damn Genesis project?" Her voice grew desperate as her bleary eyes met Xari's gaze. "It isn't my fault."

Xari sat back in her seat, looking at the wreck of a washed-up warrior teetering on the edge of destruction.

"Is there anything else I need to know?"

"I had to do it."

"Do what?"

Alexandra wearily rubbed her forehead. "Sacrifice Anya for the greater good. If Penn gets her, the Drahzda leave us alone. Don't you see?" Her voice broke as she closed her eyes. "I had no choice."

The Chancellor's head bobbed a few times before she slumped over, her chin resting on her chest.

Xari replaced Alexandra's snifter with her own before picking up the empty glass and heading toward the door. The panel slid open as soon as she drew near, and she let out a sigh of relief.

She passed the warrior watching the monitors. "The Chancellor has asked not to be disturbed."

"I'll let her guard know," the female said, her eyes not leaving the flat screens on the wall.

CHAPTER THIRTY-EIGHT

The moon peeked through the clouds as Nya's Chosen trudged through dense woods. Aren, Giovanni, Victor, and Luka soon broke from the group, planning to draw any Drahzda on guard away from the back of the castle. Gia led Ike, Jax, and Killian to the south, her quick even strides pushing them to keep up.

She took little notice as Ike stayed by her side. She hadn't spoken to him since she'd taken charge of the mission. Her mind raced with impossible situations. Everything from being forced to kill her daughter, or, worse yet, her own grandchild.

The thought left her bitter. If she made it out of this alive, she would take Nya away, and they would live as outcasts. Her *nata* wouldn't have to find a rovni unless she wanted to, and Ike could have his precious Alexandra and the Society. Hell, she should have done that years ago.

They stopped at the top of a small hillock overlooking the courtyard. Gia waited until Killian, Victor, and Jax caught up. Several metal containers lined the castle's back wall.

"There," she tipped her head toward the long black tube stretching from the parapet to the dumpster below. "Ike, Jax, you'll head that way. Killian, where do we start?"

The warrior closed his eyes and took a deep breath, his brow furrowed in concentration. "He's here. I can sense it." He pointed to a servant's entrance, just beyond the dumpsters. "We'll enter there."

"Gia." Ike stepped close.

His gentle voice, so warm and loving, made her leery.

He ran his finger down her cheek. "Please. Let me go with Killian. Nya will need you when we find her."

She jerked away from his touch. "It is my right. I will avenge my *nata*."

Ike's eyes lost their warmth as he stepped back. "Be careful."

She turned from him, and she and Killian slipped through the trees and into the night.

Victor's phone buzzed, and he reached into his pocket. His brow furrowed as he swiped the screen.

"What is it?" Giovanni asked.

They stopped in the middle of a dense copse of evergreens. "Not sure." He held the phone to his ear, his eyes growing wide.

Luka stepped forward. "Have they found her?"

Victor smiled. "It's not from Jax. It's Toxaris, and she's left us a gift." His phone buzzed again, and he scrolled to another incoming text. "Interesting. Zander got the same message."

Sirens blared and Klieg lights exploded to life, flooding the castle's perimeter in blinding light.

The warriors hit the deck, scurrying for cover.

"So much for the element of surprise." Killian ducked behind a tree.

"I hope to God that's not because of us," Giovanni muttered.

"We'd be dead if it were." Aren peered through binoculars. "I bet Nya's escaped."

Victor kept low and crept back into the shadows. "Damn it, we can't wait for Zander now. The Tovaris are still thirty minutes out, and that's a lifetime when a Drahzdan battalion is breathing down your neck."

Luka shifted closer. "Nya won't last that long."

"Then we'll give her the distraction she needs." Aren shucked off his pack. He zipped open the front pocket and pulled out several small blocks of green clay.

"Well, that should shake things up a bit." Luka grinned.

Aren grunted in agreement as he placed the putty at the base of a tree. "I've got a few more, which should hold us until Zander gets here." He took out a small device and pierced the clay before throwing a clump of wet leaves over the explosives. "We have ten minutes before these trees turn to toothpicks."

Aren zipped up his pack, and the warriors ran, skirting the fringe of lights flooding the open field.

Nya stayed crouched under cardboard as the nursery door opened. Soldiers dipped in, then out, checking that no one was there.

Luckily, the dimwits never gave the upside-down box in the closet a second thought.

Hidden in plain sight. At least, for now. Someone eventually would think to do a better search of this room, but she'd be damned if she'd be there to see it.

"No one gets through the front gates. And for god's sake, lock that door. If the Scythians are here, we don't want them anywhere near the nursery."

The door slammed shut, muffling the rest of what he was saying. A bolt snicked in place, and Nya closed her eyes, straining to hear if someone had been locked in with her.

Nothing but silence.

The box scratched along the floor, and she silently cursed as she tipped it forward. She peeked from beneath a corrugated flap. Relief surged through her. She was alone. There'd be no reason to waste energy killing a grunt over being in the wrong place at the wrong time. A box cutter and putty knife lay just a few feet away, and she picked them up and made her way past the bassinets lining the wall.

Rich mahogany paneling loomed before her, and a shiver ran down her spine as hideous memories surfaced. Penn opening the panel that served as a hidden door, its small hinge creaking in the dark. Her pulse drummed in her ears. The hours Penn spent with her alone in this room were some of the worst memories she had. He'd drone on and on with his vision of their future, petting her in sensitive places while she was shackled and defenseless.

She should cut off his hands before he died to teach him how wrong it was to touch someone without their consent.

The thought had adrenaline pumping through her veins, and she dropped the wet clothes by an antique armoire. Running her fingers along the wainscoting's raised frame, she found the hidden latch and pulled. The metal lever released before it snapped off, and she silently cursed. Now she wouldn't be able to secure the panel closed.

Dirt, must, and the scent of damp rock swirled through the passageway as air rushed in.

Nya stepped through and closed the panel as best she could. Dozens of doors lined the right side of the darkened hallway, the left remained riddled with boxes. Frustrated, she scrubbed her face with her hand.

It never occurred to her that the passageway would be full of other hidden panels. It would only be a matter of time before she opened one with a roomful of workers or Drahzdan soldiers. And the more doors there were, the less secure she became. Anyone could come strolling through, and if she were caught now, Sergei and his merry band of tranquilizers would just slow down the process of killing Penn.

She tucked the box cutter into her waistband at the small of her back and left everything else behind.

Stopping by the first panel, she rested her ear against the cold wood. Silence.

She opened the panel a crack. A closet.

Shit.

She scanned the corridor for places to hide as she crept toward the next door.

A thunderous explosion shook the walls, and Nya dropped to her knees and covered her head.

What the hell was that?

The gentle patter of rain accompanied Jax, Ike, Gia, and Killian as they made their way to the edge of the courtyard.

Gia stopped before the tree line thinned. "Aren's getting ready to light up the woods, which will serve as our diversion."

"If they don't find a way to kill the halogens, it won't matter. We'll be like fish in a barrel out here," Killian said.

An explosion rocked the night, and the Klieg lights flickered a few times before going out, leaving the warriors blanketed in sweet darkness.

"Quick, over there." Jax pointed to the dumpsters close to the kitchen's entrance. "It'll be tight, but we can make it."

He bolted from the forest, the others following close behind. They dove between the large metal containers just as the lights buzzed back to life.

The warriors crouched low, ducking in the shadows as the rain grew heavy, slanting through the bright beams of light.

"Damn it, we're pinned down," Killian whispered.

Jax peeked around the back. "We're in luck. The lights are angled, so we have shadows that will serve as cover."

Wind whistled through the trees as a storm blew in.

Ike turned to his romni. "And what about you and Killian?"

Gia bristled. "We'll manage."

Ike gripped her upper arms. "You listen to me," his voice became gruff. "You're too far in your head for a mission. Stay here. Killian can track Sarkov and contain him. He'll bring him to you if that's what you want."

Her eyes hardened to stone. "You really think I'm so weak that I need to stay safe while someone serves Sarkov to me on a silver platter?"

"That's not what I meant." His voice grew desperate.

She pulled away. "I'm no longer your concern, getting our *nata* out of this place is."

The lights flickered a few times before going off again. Killian edged closer to the castle. "This might be our only window. We have to go."

Shots rang in the distance.

Ike whipped out his phone. "Zander and the Tovas are here."

The servant's entrance burst open as construction workers poured out, running from the battle raging in the front.

Jax glanced at Ike. "It's now or never."

Ike's grip tightened around Gia's arms. "Listen, I—"

"For the love of God, go," Gia practically hissed, pulling from his grasp and following Killian toward the front of the dumpster.

Ike hesitated before following Jax. They slipped around the back of the dumpster and through the shadows, passing a few large steel containers until they came to the last one cocooned in a protective tarp.

Jax pulled a knife from his boot and made a clean cut along the plastic covering the dumpster's edge.

"She'll be fine," Jax said, pulling the plastic and then cutting again. "It's you I'm worried about."

The comment had Ike's full attention. "I'm focused on the mission."

"You better be." Jax took the lead, slipping between the metal and plastic. He reached up, grabbing the top of the dumpster and hoisting himself over the side.

Blackened damp plaster softened the fall, and dust plumed as Ike landed next to him.

"I'll go first." Ike grabbed the bottom of the chute, finding the spiral wiring.

The rain turned torrential, and Ike stopped a few feet from the top of the parapet as workers scrambled to get inside.

Heating and air conditioning units stood a few yards away, and Ike took cover behind them. Jax scurried out of the chute and ducked low, making his way across the roof.

Rapid gunfire echoed through the woods as Ike caught up with him. "Once we get inside, we'll head away from the secured area in the north wing."

"Nya's not hiding, she's hunting. She'll head straight into the devil's lair."

Ike frowned. "She'd never go after Sarkov on her own."

Frustrated, Jax glared at the male. "Seriously, Commander. Do you know your *pumpkin* at all?"

Ike looked away. "All right, then. You lead."

Jax started forward, his voice aggressive and low. "Vtachi will want answers before she kills Sarkov. The most logical place to start looking is in the room on the second floor, where we found her shorts."

Metal railing lined a hatched door, which lay in the center of the flat roof. Jax motioned for Ike to cover him as he released the lever and pulled. The door sprung open, revealing a long narrow staircase, ending in a construction grade metal exit. Stone walls guarded the narrow staircase.

Light streamed under the door's crack at the bottom. Jax started down the stairs as Ike climbed in after him, closing the roof's hatch in place.

They took the stairs two at a time and Jax opened the door as if they were supposed to be there, followed closely by Ike. The sounds of war bled through the large stained-glass windows, which were nestled in wells large enough to create alcoves lining the wall. Boxes lay scattered and open along the corridor as if an entire squadron had come through and ripped the place apart.

Ike grabbed a carpenter's belt laying atop some discarded tools and hitched it around his waist. Jax shoved a painter's hat on his head, and they started toward the staircase, making their way to the second floor.

They had reached the open area that overlooked the foyer when another explosion rocked the castle.

Jax crouched low against the far wall and ran, hoping like hell that all the Drahzda had been called to fight Zander and the Tovaris.

Ike rattled the knob before he growled in frustration. His muscles strained as his knuckles whitened, and he twisted the knob with all this strength. The metal groaned in protest before the lock gave way.

They hustled through the door, closing it behind them.

Jax flipped on the lights, then froze. "What the fuck is this?"

CHAPTER THIRTY-NINE

Lights flickered along the abandoned corridor as Gia raced up the servant's stairs, and Killian silently cursed. She'd been like this since they'd left the cabin.

Ike was right. Gia wasn't in the right headspace for a mission.

Scattered boxes littered the top landing, and she stumbled, slowing her stride.

Killian grabbed her arm, pulling her into a darkened corner. "Damn it Gia. Get it together."

She tried to jerk away, but his grip tightened.

"You've been reckless since you took control of this mission. You may not care if you get yourself killed, but Nya will. And she doesn't deserve a lifetime of guilt because her mother was murdered by the Drahzda. After all the shit she's been through, she doesn't need that, too."

Gia's harsh expression flashed with regret. "You're right. I'll be more careful."

"Not good enough." Killian released her. "Until we find Sarkov, I'm taking the lead."

He didn't wait for a response as he started down the hall. Gia had led them to the third floor, wanting to sweep from the top on down. But his instincts screamed that Sarkov wasn't up here.

They were wasting precious time.

Weatherworn wood stretched along an endless corridor. Large window alcoves ran along the outer wall. Their wells so deep they cleverly housed narrow broom cupboards along the sides of the niche.

Dark silhouettes loomed in the distance, and Killian held up his hand. Gia stopped. He waved, signaling for her to hide in the closet. She followed the order, opening the narrow door and silently closing it behind her. Soldiers started down the hall as the latch clicked closed.

Killian slipped behind a stack of boxes.

"We've already checked this floor." A deep Russian voice neared, stopping between Killian and Gia's hiding places.

"Check it again."

Four of the six men marched down the hall, each opening doors and clearing rooms as they went.

"Sir, there's nothing here."

"Sweep the servant's quarters, and if you see her, wound, but do not kill."

The men saluted and started down toward the stairs.

"Captain, it's obvious she's escaped."

A gruff voice scoffed. "Then why are the Scythians still fighting? No. If they had her, they wouldn't be engaging us."

Another explosion rocked the castle's outer wall, and plaster dust sifted from the ceiling.

"Should we abandon this mission and help fight? Our men are getting slaughtered out there."

The leader's tone became aggressive. "You really want to defy the Tsar's orders?"

The sound of a creaking hinge halted their conversation, and both soldiers turned to see a narrow closet door easing open.

Killian glared across the way. Damn it, what was Gia doing? If they called for backup, he'd have to waste more time fighting instead of tracking Sarkov.

The men stepped closer, one shoving the cupboard wide open with the tip of his automatic weapon.

A shadow shifted in the back.

The captain unclipped a two-way radio attached to his belt.

"Sergei, we have a situation. Over."

Shit.

Killian whipped out his knife and lunged. He knocked the radio out of the captain's hand before stabbing him through the heart. The man dropped where he stood. Gia sprang from the narrow space, grabbing the other soldier by the throat. She rammed him against the wall, her eyes calmly taking in the way he struggled to breathe.

Radio static echoed down the hall. "Boris, status update."

Killian smashed the radio with his heel. "Speed this up. Company's on the way."

Gia reached into her breast pocket and pulled out a syringe, ramming a small injection in his arm.

The man visibly relaxed.

"Where's Penn?"

He shook his head as if he didn't know.

Her knuckles whitened as she squeezed his neck, her other hand waving an empty vial with a needle jutting from one end. "I'll tell you a secret. See this? It's a lovely little concoction I spent years developing. It keeps your Phoenix in control." She hitched him higher against the wall until his feet dangled a few inches from the ground. "I'll ask again. Where is Sarkov?"

The soldier stayed silent.

Gia's free hand traveled over his chest and down his torso until her fingers wrapped painfully around his groin. "I can take you back to Carpathia, where we'll have years together to play." She tightened her hold, and he whimpered. "We'll start by getting rid of these. And you'll be awake for every blessed second, I promise you that."

The man's eyes widened as she leaned in.

"I can do it, too. I have a team at my disposal, they'll heal you, make sure you're nice and healthy before I visit again. After what my *nata's* been through, you'll get no mercy from me." She thumped his head against the wall, her voice becoming a mere growl. "One last time. Where. Is. Penn?"

He frantically pointed toward the stairs. "Second floor ... secret suite behind the bookshelves at the end of the hall."

Gia let the man go long enough for him to stumble to his feet.

"Thank you." Cold ruthlessness sparked in her eyes as she grabbed either side of his head, snapping it from side to side.

The man's skull hung at an odd angle as he fell to the floor.

Uneasy, Killian cleared his throat, and he and Gia made short work of stuffing the bodies in the closet and closing the door.

Water dripped from somewhere above as Nya crept along the hidden passageway. She'd checked every door, except one.

Her eyes focused on the sliver of light at the end of the hall. Her thumb furiously ran over the scar on her palm as cool air brushed across her face.

The sounds of rapid gunfire bled through the thick walls, and Nya rubbed her forehead.

Jax—he was here, she could feel it. But he shouldn't have come. He shouldn't put himself in danger for someone so tainted and unclean.

She opened her eyes, finding that sliver of light again.

He wouldn't give up until he found her, though. And she wasn't going anywhere until Sarkov died. Which meant the sooner she finished this, the better.

She started forward, slipping past the boxes and broken furniture. Her pulse thrummed in her ears as she stalked her prey.

Sarkov first. Find the eggs. Then destroy the Chancellor.

She repeated her mantra over and over, allowing her anger to flow, strengthening, until it pounded through her like a sacred drum, summoning the demons of hell.

Her lip curled as every horrid thing that Penn had ever done played in her mind. Heat pulsed through her veins, and she embraced the pain. Speeding into a run, her primal scream echoed off the walls as she kicked open the door.

The sharp crack of wood exploded in the silence as Nya burst into the room.

Her eyes widened as she froze.

Old warped planks ran in rows along the floor, the cobbled walls, fashioned with mud and straw, created soft corners and textured surfaces. Overhead, large beams formed an A-frame, complete with a thatched roof. Even their small cot, broken farm table, and two chairs stood next to the fireplace. It was a perfect replica of their secret fort.

Bile rose in her throat, and she stumbled back.

"I made it for you." Penn's voice came from the shadows.

Nya whipped around, searching.

"I did it all for you."

Something sharp pierced her arm, and the world went black.

CHAPTER FORTY

Ike's eyes never left the Dacian symbols hand-painted under the crown molding. "Why in the hell did Penn put that on the walls?"

"I think it would be obvious." Jax's frustration came through as he read her apology. "Even though Penn can't read the language, he knew the markings were important to Nya, so he chose to surround their young with them."

Jax jogged across the room and bent next to the antique armoire. Wet silk and ceremonial sandals lay on a towel. He bent down, his fingers gently caressing the silk. "Why leave this here, Vtachi?"

Footsteps thundered down the hall.

Ike dove for the door and shoved a chair under its knob, securing it in place as a squadron of Drahzda ran past. "I have a feeling it won't be long before they recheck this room."

Jax leaned against the panel, his mind whirring. "Where would she have gone from here?"

"Sarkov has to have a central command."

Jax shook his head. "He wouldn't be there. He doesn't give a damn about his men. His sole obsession is Nya, he's searching for her—or waiting for her to come to him."

"We're sitting ducks, Jax. We have to move."

"Then we'll start in this wing and work our way around." He pushed himself away from the wall.

A rusty hinge creaked as the decorative mahogany behind him shifted, it's edge coming even with its wainscoting frame. He wedged his finger between the panel and the wall, forcing it to open the rest of the way.

"That wasn't on the blueprints." Ike double-checked the chair before making his way to Jax.

"I should've known he had a secret passage to this room."

"How?"

Jax stepped into the corridor, sweeping his gaze from one end to the other. "Vtachi always sleeps with a weapon."

"So?" Ike followed him in.

"Sarkov must have come to her in the night, while she was helpless and shackled to that bed. She couldn't defend herself, and so she learned never to be defenseless, especially when she sleeps."

Ike flinched, his hands shaking as he took off the toolbelt he'd snagged in the hall.

Jax grabbed a putty knife from the belt and shoved it between the hidden door and its frame. "That should at least keep it from opening on its own."

They started down the hall, and Ike softly cursed as he noted the doors lining the left side of the corridor. I'll take this one, you start down the way."

"At least we know we're on the right track. The question is, how long ago was she here, and where is she now?"

The rasp of a match struck the silence as Penn lit an incense stick and placed it in a jar of sand. His eyes glittered in the limited light. "I knew it was only a matter of time before the Phoenix showed you the path to enlightenment. Welcome back, my love."

Revulsion hit Nya in waves as she looked up to see her wrist bound with thick rope, tied to a bracing high overhead. Four Drahzda soldiers stood in each corner of the room. "How long have I been out?"

Penn smiled. "Only fifteen minutes or so." He turned to his men. "Tell Sergei it will be his head if so much as one Scythian is left alive. Now, leave us."

Nya swallowed a few times, trying to figure out how in the hell this happened. She shifted, her wrists chafing under the thick hemp rope. The movement must have caught Penn's gaze, because he turned to watch her struggle. She stilled.

"So, my Ana is finally home." He picked up the sand-filled glass jar.

"I hadn't planned on having to restrain you in this place, but I know your triggers. I'm sure I'll be able to handle you."

She turned away as he brought the incense toward her. Smoke curled around her face like a lover's caress.

Nya's head lolled forward, and she fought to keep it up. Warily, she glanced at the incense. "What is that?"

Penn smiled as he breezed more smoke in her face. "Something that will assure you stay calm while we have a little chat." He set the incense down and clapped his hands together. "Now. Let's have it. Why did you run, Ana?"

He stood only feet away, right next to her. His tall, lanky frame shouldn't have intimidated her, and yet, she shook with deep-seated fear. He was an Allos. Her feet weren't bound. She could kill him easily, but for some reason, she couldn't move. Instinct caused the hair on the back of her neck to stand. She couldn't lie to him—something awful would happen if she did. But if she could get him talking, distract him in some way, it would give her precious time to figure things out.

"Ana, why did you run?"

She broke out in a cold sweat. "Sergei. He said some things that scared me."

Penn's voice grew gentle. "Yes. Well. I'll have to speak with him and make sure it doesn't happen again."

Nya's skin crawled as he sidled closer. She pressed her back against the cold wall.

"We need to discuss these Scythians storming the manse. Our sources have no indication the Chancellor has gone back on her word, and yet a battle rages outside our front door. Did you find a way to reach out to them?"

Nya blankly stared ahead. "Who?"

Penn's expression turned ruthless. "Your Chosen." His fingertip softly ran down her cheek. "They want what's mine."

"I don't know anything about an attack."

Penn watched her eyes as his thumb grazed her cheek. He leaned in, his lips touching hers in a chaste kiss. "You are wise to tell the truth."

Nya turned away.

He held his hands out, gesturing toward the room. "Do you like it?"

"I'm stunned you could do this so quickly."

He smiled as he crossed to the small cot. "It's amazing how far a little incentive can go when dealing with contract workers."

She stayed silent and looked at her wrists.

He kept his eyes on the makeshift bed. "Do you remember that night? I dream of it all the time. We laid right there, your soft voice panting in my ear."

She shuddered with revulsion as she wiggled her hands back and forth, loosening the ropes around her wrist. "I remember."

Penn glanced back, and she froze. He turned to the cot again, seemingly lost in thought.

"Why are you running from our destiny." Sadness and confusion seeped into his tone. "I don't understand."

The rope gave way, and she wriggled one wrist free.

Penn started pacing. "I've spent an exorbitant amount of money and time creating a future for us. I wanted our son to be here when you finally came to your senses. We lost ten fetuses within weeks of inception. But the researchers assure me they have fixed the problem, and we have at least a dozen hosts lined up for the spring."

Horrified, she froze, both hands still in the air.

He stopped just feet from her, his eyes imploring. "Don't you see? I did this all for us. We have a lifetime of love and laughter ahead. Full of children and more money and power than we could ever need. And yet, after all I've done, you still defy me." He stepped toward her and cupped her face with his hand. "Why? Is it because of these Chosen?"

She didn't move.

His expression turned dark. He leaned in and kissed her forehead. "Tell me, my sweet Ana. Have you betrayed me?"

She whimpered as her veins painfully throbbed. "In what way?"

Penn's temper flared. "Don't be dense. Did you betray me by falling in love with one of those *things*?"

Her temper flared. "I'm one of those *things*. And I'm not in love with anyone."

As soon as the words crossed her lips, she knew she'd made a mistake.

Her blood turned to liquid fire as a red haze coated her vision.

She whimpered, and Penn fisted her hair at the scalp, pulling her head back. "Did you allow him to enter your body and take what is mine?" Rage flashed in his eyes.

"No." Flames erupted within her, and Nya gripped the back of her bound hand, desperately trying to free it. Warmth trickled from her ear down her jaw, and she watched crimson droplets fall to the floor. Panic threaded through her.

"You lie." Penn muttered something in her ear, and fresh agony blazed.

Oh, God. She was going to die, right here. Bound like some helpless woman. She'd never know what happened to her eggs, and she'd never see Jax again.

The thought of Jax had memories whispering through the haze fogging her mind. His quiet reasoning as she struggled with something in a session. The way he challenged her to climb a peak, or goaded her into attacking him on the field.

We got this ...

The pain eased enough for her to think. It was impossible to reason with Penn, but his stupid Allos obsession with her virginity might be his undoing. And once she had the upper hand, she'd find out where he had taken her eggs.

She squinted, trying to focus on his face. "You're right. I do love someone, and he's taken a part of me you'll never have."

Pain flashed in Penn's eyes. "No, it's not possible."

"Jax is a fantastic lover, and I might be carrying his young right now." Agony ripped through her, but she locked her muscles in place refusing to show any sign of weakness. "I've been with him for four years, sleeping in his bed, spreading my legs for him, willingly submitting to his every whim."

"You whore!"

"Better a Scythian whore than a Drahzdan Tsaritsa."

Penn backhanded her, and Nya's face jerked to the side.

The physical pain allowed her some semblance of control, and her free hand whipped behind her, grabbing the box cutter.

Her right shoulder screamed in pain as it carried the brunt of her weight. Rearing back, she head-butted Penn and then swung the knife in a lethal arc. He ducked, but the tip of the blade caught the flesh below his eye, slicing down his cheek and along the side of his neck. His shriek echoed as he stumbled back, finding a button on the wall. Male voices blared through the room, their Russian song sending fresh fire through her body.

Nya desperately swung the box cutter toward her other wrist, trying to free it from the rope, but Penn grabbed her arm, twisting it back. The sharp blade clanged to the floor.

Blood streamed down his neck, saturating his shirt. "It didn't have to be this way. I would have protected you, cherished you. Loved you."

Nya's heart stuttered as her body fought the rage within. She grabbed his shirt, hatred marring her face. "Yeah? Well for the last time, I don't need your fucking protection, Penn."

She shoved him as hard as she could, sending him flying, his back crashing into the wall before he crumpled to the floor.

He scrambled to his feet. "You'll wish you had never defied me before this night is through."

She wildly swung her legs and arm, trying to reach him while swaying back and forth like some sick pendulum.

Penn skirted around her and headed toward the table. "I will have my future, with or without you."

Her gaze flew to Penn as a match strike rasped in the silence. A small flame burst to life, its warm glow reflecting in his eyes.

"Amazing, isn't it? How one little spark can set the whole world on fire?"

Penn grabbed her notebook he'd taken from their fort and angled the bottom corner above the small flame. The book's edge blackened, the pages curling as smoke circled toward the ceiling. Flames rippled up the cover, marring the leather with every stroke. He dropped the book onto the old farm table. Orange and yellow ran along the warped wood, licking the side of the wall.

Hazy smoke thickened the air, and she coughed as Penn crossed the room, standing just outside of her reach.

"Goodbye, my sweet Ana. Die knowing we could have been happy. But if it will ease your passing, I promise our children will never know of your betrayal. I'll tell them stories of Ana Sarkov, the sweet soul I fell in love with that eventually became my wife and their mother. They'll never know of Anya Thalestris, the Scythian whore I so easily disposed of."

Nya swung again, but the momentum sent her legs from under her, and Penn lunged, grabbing her free arm and pulling it behind her.

"My father demanded only one thing when he gave you to me—a trigger that would kill. I fought him over it, knowing you would never betray me." His voice became nothing but an angry growl. "But father was right after all. You've turned into something I never dreamed you'd be. And for that, you must die."

He fisted her hair and jerked her head to the side, whispering the words that unlocked the very hell that lived within.

Every nerve ending exploded in agony as she dangled from one arm, the tops of her feet dragging the old plank floor. Warmth seeped out of her ears, nose, and eyes, blinding her vision with red.

"Goodbye, my love." Penn disappeared in a shroud of dense, black smoke.

CHAPTER FORTY-ONE

Jax finished closing his fourth door when a wisp of smoke filtered through the air. He turned, his eyes searching. The corridor's end had turned hazy and white.

"Vtachi," he muttered, bolting past Ike and the discarded furniture.

He tore the broken panel from his hinges, and a black smoke rolled out. Heat billowed as orange flames sped along the ceiling, curling around the corner, growing bigger as they raced toward the floor.

"Nya!" Jax coughed, bringing his shirt up over his nose. "Where are you!"

Heat washed over him in waves. Something shifted ahead, and Jax ran toward a limp body strewn up from one arm, a curtain of raven hair shrouding her face.

He grabbed his knife from his boot and cut her down.

"Is she in there?" Ike's voice barely made it over the blaze's roar.

"Yeah. I'm coming out!" Jax cradled Nya to his chest as he crouched low, running through the growing blaze.

They hurried past the doors and back into the nursery.

Ike slammed the panel closed and reached for his phone.

Jax eased the bloody hair from Nya's face. Slick crimson covered her swollen features, making her indistinguishable.

"Oh, God, Vtachi, what have you been through?" Jax's voice broke as he held her close, muttering the Dacian words he'd used the past four years, hoping like hell they would help ease her pain.

"How bad is she?"

"It's not great, but she's still breathing."

A thunderous crash shook the castle, as smoke wisped from under the paneling.

Ike looked at his phone. "I texted Zander and told him we have Nya, but we can't fight our way out. The Tovaris are on their way."

Jax grabbed Nya's dress from the floor and ripped a strip off of it, wiping the blood from her face.

She stirred. "Jax ... you're here."

"I told you. I'd follow you to the ends of the earth."

She sobbed as her stuttered breath grew shallow. "Promise me something."

"Don't talk." Jax swallowed as blood leaked from her nose.

"Promise me." She struggled to keep his gaze. The whites of her eyes had become bright red, making her blue irises seem surreal.

Jax nodded. "Anything, Vtachi. Whatever you need."

She brought her hand up to his face. "Swear on the life of your Tova that you'll get them back. All of them."

Jax's voice grew husky as he placed his forehead against hers. "I swear."

Relieved, she dropped her hand. "I love you, Ajax Nickius. Never forget. I'll always ... love ... you ..." Her voice trailed away as her eyes rolled back in her head, and she lost consciousness.

Flames jutted through the crevice at the top of the panel, growing stronger until it rushed over the ceiling in a burst of light.

Panic threaded through him as smoke rolled in. He tore a swatch of her dress and loosely wrapped the cloth around Nya's head. "Damn it, Ike, we can't wait any longer. We have to go."

Wood groaned as the fire intensified. Ike kicked the chair from the knob and flung open the door.

They rushed into the hall, and all hell broke loose.

Bodies lay at odd angles, strewn down the third-floor hallway and into the stairwell. Gia and Killian had left a stream of dead Drahzda in their wake, and Gia had taken a bullet in her thigh. With Penn in her sights, she'd be damned if they abandoned the mission now.

The servant's stairs were located in the back section of the castle, which meant they had to cross several hallways.

They doggedly continued down empty corridors. Muffled gunfire sounded from outside, but the castle had become silent as a tomb.

"Sarkov must have ordered the rest of his men to the front." Killian wiped the blood from a wound over his brow.

Light streamed ahead as they reached a landing that led to the grand staircase.

A smoky haze filtered from the left, bringing with it the acrid scent of burning plastic and wood. The shelves at the end of the corridor shifted, rolling to the side, and Killian pulled Gia into the shadows.

"Stephan!" Penn shrieked as he stumbled into the hall, his palm trying to stem the blood gushing from his face. "Where the hell are you? I need my pills!"

Gray smoke trailed behind him, curling over his head as if following him out of the bowels of hell.

"Stephan!" He leaned against the wall as a door to the right burst open.

Ike and Jax stumbled out.

Penn's eyes locked onto Nya's lifeless body draped over Jax's arms, and Gia bolted between them, her uneven gate doing little to slow her down.

Ike called her name, but she didn't stop. Raw hatred pummeled through her, and her vision narrowed to the man who had caused so much suffering and pain. She wrapped her hand around Penn's throat, ramming him against the wall, but his gaze never left Jax.

"Is that the bastard that took her from me?" Penn shrieked, his eyes livid and wild as he tried to break free.

Gia's expression turned bitter. "He took nothing from you because she was never yours."

Dark smoke rolled from the nursery's threshold as flames came from the other direction, blazing over Gia and Penn's head.

"Ike, get her out of here!" Gia shouted.

Penn wheezed as Gia's grip tightened. "It won't make a difference. By morning she'll be dead."

"So will you." She cocked her fist back and shattered the side of Penn's bloody face.

His shrill scream echoed as the bone under his eye protruded through torn flesh.

"Gia, kill him and let's go!" Ike bellowed over the roar of the flames.

Penn's lips snarled in a wicked smile. "You're too late. Penn and Ana Sarkov will live on in their offspring for generations to come."

Her hand tightened, and he gasped for air.

The thunderous crash of falling beams shook the hall. A rush of embers sparked and flickered as the ceiling between Ike and Gia collapsed, the flames rushing between them in a wall of unholy heat and light.

Penn's blood ran down Gia's arm as he grew weaker.

"Nya's eggs. Where are they?" she shouted.

Penn stopped struggling as his hazel eyes became oddly peaceful. "Someplace you'll never find them."

Gia screeched as she placed her thumb over his windpipe and pushed, shattering his airway. Penn's breath gurgled to a stop before his body slumped forward.

The blaze around them became a deafening roar as orange and red licked the walls. Sweat dripped from her face, and she dropped Penn's lifeless body, watching it crumple to the floor.

Ike took his coat off, desperately trying to beat the flames. "Jump, it's your only chance!"

Gia looked at the surrounding inferno. The fire whipped and eddied, growing stronger like an ancient angry beast hellbent on consuming them both.

Her eyes, so poignant and knowing, kept Ike's as she placed her hand over her heart.

"I love you," she whispered. "I always have."

"Gia, no!" Ike's voice broke as she was engulfed in flames.

Jax crossed the foyer as crimson dripped off the silk swathing Nya's face. Killian ran ahead, taking point, and he opened the door, his eyes sweeping the horizon for signs of the enemy.

Movement along the tree line had both warriors scrambling, but it was Zander and several Tovas making their way from the forest.

"I need a medic." Jax's voice broke as he ran down the steps.

"Doc's with them over that hill. You," Zander pointed to a warrior. "Make sure they get there in one piece. Killian, you're with me."

Jax shifted Nya in his arms and followed the female Tova down the broken road and into the woods. His heart hammered, fear tightening like a band around his chest.

The trees thinned, revealing several military trucks under camouflage netting. Warriors lay on the ground in a makeshift triage center.

"Sir, are you hurt?" A medic ran toward them.

"It's Nya ..." Jax mumbled, cold. "She needs help."

The medic shouted, and two Tova rolling a gurney came from the transport and headed their way. Victor jumped out of the vehicle and ran alongside.

They stopped in front of Jax, and he lay Nya down on the stark white sheet. His fingers trembled as he peeled back the blood-soaked cloth shrouding her face.

"Nick, let me do that." Victor reached for her, but Jax shook his head.

"No. She's my responsibility. I need some gauze ... something ... I have to clean her up."

"There's some in the truck."

The gurney rolled forward, and Jax kept hold of her hand as Victor stayed by his side.

"Do you know what happened to her?"

"That bastard unleashed her Phoenix." Jax's voice broke.

Victor swallowed a few times before he spoke. "She's strong. She'll pull through."

They stopped by the medic transport, and Nya's chest weakly rose as if it were an effort to breathe.

"I know you'll want to stay by her side, but we need room to work."

The doctor in Jax knew Victor was right, but the Tova in him hated it. He brought Nya's hand to his lips. "I'll be right here, Vtachi. I'm not leaving. I promise."

Victor nodded at the medics, and they lifted the gurney and rolled it into the portable trauma center.

Smoke sifted through the forest like a harbinger of death, and Jax locked his knees so they wouldn't buckle. What if she didn't make it?

Rustling leaves stirred behind him as two warriors came from the trees, carrying an unconscious body between them. Burnt flesh blackened the warrior's arms and face.

Zander ran alongside. "Get him in an isolation chamber as soon as you can, and then get him out of here. We have a team waiting at the preserve."

The males lumbered forward, keeping the burnt warrior's arms around their necks while his feet dragged behind them. They trudged toward another vehicle a few hundred meters away.

Zander stopped next to Jax. "Crazy son of a bitch put up a helluva fight. Wanted to stay and die with his romni, but I figured your Princess shouldn't lose both her parents on the same day."

Numb, Jax stared ahead. "So, Gia didn't make it out?"

"Killian thinks she never intended to. How's your female?"

"I don't know." His gaze became tormented, hollow. "I ... if she doesn't make it ... I can't—"

Zander gripped the back of Jax's neck, pulling him close, resting their foreheads together. It was a Tovaris tradition, a sign of ultimate respect and support. "Whether she lives or dies, we stand with you. And we don't rest until she's avenged."

"She has to make it," Jax whispered.

Zander's thick arms came around him, pulling him against a wall of a chest. Jax tensed but then let himself go and hung on the Tova's shoulders.

"I believe she will." Zander's voice became gruff. "And when she does, we hunt, and we won't stop until we find what was stolen from her." Stepping back, he cleared his throat, his meaty fist resting on the brand on Jax's chest. "*Tova, loyalnost, sila.*"

"*Tova, loyalnost, sila,*" Jax muttered back.

A female rushed from the dark recess of the medic transport. "Nick, Doc needs you."

Zander stepped back as Jax scrambled into the truck.

A medic held a mask over Nya's face, pumping fresh air into her lungs.

Tubes ran from an IV hanging overhead and into her arm. Her shirt had been ripped open, EKG leads dotting her chest and abdomen. Victor had cleaned off most of her face, but blood still trickled from her eyes and nose.

"What's wrong?" Jax knelt by her side, grabbing her hand.

Victor dug through the medical supplies, desperately searching for something. "She started coming around. As soon as she opened her eyes, she struggled and then started seizing. We can't get it to stop."

Alarms sounded as a high-pitched beep turned into a scream, and Nya's body jerked and twitched as if in the last throes of death.

Victor took a syringe and plunged it into the IV.

The alarm continued.

"We're losing her." He stood and beat on the roof of the transport, and the truck rumbled to life. The transport rocked and swayed as they started down the hill.

Jax leaned close, resting his lips against her ear. "Damn it, Vtachi. Don't do this. You said you loved me. If you do, then fight."

A gurgling sound bubbled from Nya's throat. The twitching stopped.

His hand brushed the hair from her face. "You can't leave me now. I've wanted you since the first moment I saw you, standing outside the arena. I'll never forget the way you stood with your hands on your hips, so confident and proud. I couldn't take my eyes off of you. Honestly, I wondered if you were even real."

He brought her cold hand to his cheek, rubbing the rise of her knuckles across his bristly jaw. "And our first therapy session, when you refused to speak." His voice broke as he took a deep breath. "God. I've never been so incredibly frustrated and turned on at the same time. That's when I suggested we go hiking. It was either that, or I'd take you then and there."

He placed her hand over his heart. "After four years, I can't imagine a life without you in it. Come on, Vtachi. Fly back to me. I need you."

The screaming alarm turned back to a beep.

Nya stirred. "Jax …"

"I'm here." He grazed her cheekbone with his thumb. "Thank God you're back."

A sob escaped her lips. "Take me home."

"You got it, Vtachi." He kissed her forehead. "You got it."

CHAPTER FORTY-TWO

Jax lowered his axe, splitting a log in two, the sound echoing in the trees beyond.

The trip from Russia had been a nightmare. Victor and the medics stayed with them until they got to the Academy, where Cassius made sure Nya had around-the-clock care. Zander had ordered a squadron of Tova to secure the perimeter. But as soon as Nya was strong enough, Jax swept her away, to a place high in the Montana Mountains—a place he'd spent the past four years building with his own hands.

A place he desperately hoped they'd soon call home.

The surrounding rugged terrain made it difficult to get to by land and impossible to see by air. Better still, their cabin was off the Allos' grid. Even though Penn's death had thrown the Drahzda into disarray, they wouldn't be down for long. Too many were more than willing to step into his shoes, which was why Jax was glad no one knew this place existed.

He put another log on the stump and raised the axe. Over the past few weeks, the woodpile had gone from a few leftover scraps to an overflowing stack. Victor's insistence that Nya needed privacy during their sessions had Jax finding odd jobs to do outside their cabin, but he didn't mind. Hell, he'd chop down the entire forest if it helped her heal.

Nya was most at ease surrounded by nature, which is why he bought the acreage to begin with. The past few weeks they'd spent endless hours exploring the new landscape, sometimes in silence, others in free-flowing conversation.

They'd grown closer emotionally, but Jax hadn't pursued her physically. Even when he held her at night, chasing away her nightmares, he kept his touch comforting and not sexual.

The Tova in him demanded that he take her, shoulder her mark, and make her his in every way. But after Nya had asked about her parents, he knew the claiming would have to wait.

God, telling his Vtachi about her mother's death had been the worst night of his life. Nya's grief ripped his heart in two. Afterward, she seemed so fragile he wasn't sure she'd recover. But after a few days, something sparked back to life, and she insisted they watch the Scythian news.

Every media outlet that had once questioned Gia's worth as Ike's equal now praised her as one of the greatest warriors of their time. The injustice of it had Nya wanting to hunt them down and beat them to a pulp, and honestly, Jax couldn't blame her.

Scythian stem cell therapy had eventually healed Ike's burns, but even in the beginning, he hadn't allowed his injuries to slow him down. Still bandaged, he'd taken to the airwaves like a male obsessed. While he dodged personal questions, he was more than willing to talk about Alexandra's disgrace, and Nya soon realized that her father was using the media like a whetstone to a blade, sharpening the Tovaris' case against the former Chancellor. Within a week, the Senate had charged Alexandra with trial tampering and sedition. Ike's heartfelt interviews caused an outpouring of support from compounds all over the world, and the Senate had little choice but to name him as the Society's new leader.

Jax held Nya as they watched Ike's impassioned acceptance speech, vowing he would not rest until the Drahzda organization had been completely destroyed.

Soon, all eyes turned to the one thing not yet resolved. When would Nya complete her Trials?

Giovanni, Luka, and Killian remained at the consulate, waiting for Nya's return, but Aren left Carpathia after Ike's induction. He openly stated that he believed Jax was the only male strong enough to be Nya's equal, and so he withdrew from the competition. The racier channels speculated the East African Suveran no longer found Anya Thalestris desirable after learning of her history with Dmitri Sarkov's son. Aren repeatedly refuted the claim, but no one seemed to be listening.

Jax finally insisted they stop watching after a scathing report that sent the Rovni Council into a closed session to decide if Nya should choose a fifth candidate or if she could finish her Trials with four.

Jax couldn't stand the thought of taking her back to Carpathia to complete some ancient ritual, surrounded by the media while grieving for a mother she never really knew.

But the issue needed to be resolved, and soon.

Victor opened the back door, coat in hand. "Anya would like to see you now."

Victor typically spent hours with Nya, often eating dinner with them before making his way back to the compound. Thanks to his intense therapy, most of the Phoenix's after effects had been contained, although Nya would still need sessions for months, possibly years, to come.

"What's your hurry?"

His bright blue eyes glittered as he smiled. "I think you'll want to handle this one on your own. We'll talk when you get back."

Unease rippled through Jax as Victor clapped him on the back and started down the hill.

Back from where? He swung the axe, embedding it in the stump, and started toward the back door.

"Vtachi?" His voice rang through the silence. Jax stepped into the kitchen, sluffing off his boots and coat. He started through the open area that served as their living room.

"I'm up here." Nya's voice came from the loft above.

Jax took the stairs two at a time. "What's up? Are you all right?"

He froze in the doorway as music softly played. Nya had her back turned to him, opening a dresser drawer on the other side of the room. Her hair ran like a river of silk down the length of her spine, her short red robe swinging and swaying over the tops of her thighs.

He swallowed as she turned, noticing the Scythian inking set in her hand.

"Dad finally called during my session." Her voice grew thick. "The compound in Ireland is performing mom's *Nex* ceremony in a few days, and he'd like for me to be there."

Disappointment stung as he realized she was gathering her things to leave. He turned away. "I'll book a flight."

"No ... wait."

Confused, he looked over his shoulder, watching her place the inking set on the bed.

Her fingers shook as she untied the sash of her robe. Red silk floated to the floor. His dragon arm cuff glittered in the evening light.

Jax walked across the room and threaded his hands through her hair, tilting her head back for a soft kiss.

"Talk to me, Vtachi. I need your words."

She took a deep breath and slowly let it out. "I don't care about the Rovni Council, or the Society, or what anyone else thinks. You're mine, and I don't want to leave here without shouldering your mark."

Relief flashed in his eyes. "That's all I needed to hear."

He pulled off his shirt and wrapped his arms around her, loving the feel of her soft flesh pressing against his.

Nya leaned back so she could look into his eyes. "I love you, Jax."

"I love you, too." Jax groaned as he kissed her shoulder.

His fingers roamed along her tattoo that delicately trailed to her shoulder, his palm coming to rest on her upper arm. "I think I'll start here."

She sat on the bed while he opened the inking set, putting the sleek silver machine and little pods of color on the nightstand.

Nya shivered as he tugged the Scythian Dragon cuff downward, slipping it off her arm.

"I made this by hand, you know." He set the cuff on the table and picked up the machine.

Her brow rose. "Really?"

"It's the Tovaris Dragon, the strongest in Dacian lore, known for its ruthlessness. That's why Tovas wear black." Jax winked as he dipped the needles into dark ink and ran the first line of his heritage along the empty place on her arm.

"You are pretty tenacious."

He dipped the needles again, keeping his focus. "Zander calls it being pig-headed, at least that's what he said when I demanded he perform the *Zvaz*."

He started for the ink again, but Nya put her hand over his. "I didn't know. Why didn't you tell me?"

Jax shrugged. "I didn't want to pressure you or influence your decision. For this to work, you have to want me as much as I want you."

She squeezed his hand before letting it go. "You really would have spent your life alone?"

Jax dipped the tip in ink, the machine buzzed to life as he curved another line. "I've been alone since I was eight."

"Oh, Jax."

He tucked a loose lock of her hair behind her ear, his gaze never leaving those lovely blue eyes, so filled with patience and understanding. She had looked at him that same way when he shared with her about his parents' murder and the brutal way his uncle had raised him. They soothed him in a way nothing else ever had, and the past few days he'd found any excuse just to make eye contact.

She cleared her throat. "Well, you're not alone anymore."

He leaned in for a quick kiss. "When I built this cabin, I knew it would either serve as our home or be my sanctuary."

"Can't it be both?"

He grinned as he tore his gaze away from her face and started another line. "It can now."

The machine droned on as he completed his mark.

Nya tilted her arm so she could see. "Looks good."

"Yes, it does." He sat back, and a sense of peace washed over him as he looked at his symbol, forever imprinted on her body. He cleaned the spot with a special solution before scooting closer. "One more and then it's my turn."

Nya closed her eyes and leaned back as he swiped a new cloth over the flesh guarding her heart. The machine buzzed to life again. "I'm so glad we're doing this now."

He smiled. "Me too."

She concentrated on the music softly playing in the background as he continued inking, then wiping, over and over again.

"All right. I'm done. Take a look."

She shook her head. "I want to wait until yours is done so we can see them together."

Jax stood and helped her up. "Then it's your turn."

Nya changed the tip as he settled on the bed. She smiled as she rubbed cleaning solution across his chest and around his heritage mark. "Good thing I've practiced a thousand times growing up."

Jax grinned. "I'm glad to hear it."

She picked up the tool, dipping it in ink and then swirling the beginning of her design on his sternum. "I can't believe you aren't even flinching."

"You kidding? You all over me while inking my skin? I'm in heaven."

She switched inkpots and tips, and Jax kept his eyes on her, loving that she was so at ease without a stitch of clothes on. She scooted over, needing more room as she scrawled across his chest and around the mark on his arm. Finally, she sat back and wiped the ink and a little blood from the design.

Jax leaned up and kissed her before he stretched.

"One more." She swiped the flesh over his heart with antiseptic.

"This one I'm looking forward to most of all."

Nya grinned. "You say that now, but I've only sketched this design a few times." She grabbed a felt marker and drew the image first, taking her time to get the lines just right. "I can't believe you did your tattoo freehand."

"I've been waiting for you for four years, Vtachi. I could do that tattoo in my sleep."

Silence fell around them as she shaded in the design. Evening settled into night, and Jax kept still, watching that slight line appear between her brows as she concentrated on what she was doing.

"Okay." The buzzing stopped as she sat up and stretched. "I think I'm done."

"You think?" He smiled.

"Well, I'm not sure I got the bottom curve right. If you don't like it, I can try and thicken the lines, or maybe add a shadow or something."

"I'm sure I'll love it." He held her hand as he stood. "No fixing anything."

They shuffled from the bed, and Jax led her into their private bath.

He stood by the door. "You first."

She stepped in front of the mirror, focusing on the tattoo centered over her heart.

"Oh, Jax. It's beautiful."

A small falcon soared in flight, its beak nipping at the tip of her lineage mark as if it had captured the ink midflight.

"The day I tracked you down, a Kestrel kept circling overhead, and it reminded me of you. You were smaller than me, yet fierce, a predator in your own right, and you were meant to soar—just like that Kestrel. But your past held you captive, and I wanted more than anything to set you free. I could only hope that you'd find your way back to me. That was the first time I called you Vtachi."

Nya reached for him, pulling him into a hug. "I'll always find my way back to you."

Images of her, bloody and unconscious ran through his mind, and he pulled her closer. "God, I hope so."

"Now it's your turn." She pulled away, but Jax kept hold of her hand, and together they stepped in front of the mirror.

He smiled at her heritage lacing across his chest and around his mark, but his eyes widened as he focused on the symbol over his heart. Centered in the middle of a triple-spired Dragon was the Scythian's most sacred symbol, the *Kedah*. Rarely seen, the emblem encapsulated the very heart of love, it meant complete and utter respect and devotion. The original Amazon's used the *Kedah* when their equal became more than a lover, more than a sire—more than a mate. It encapsulated the idea of a love so deeply ingrained that two souls became one.

"Vtachi," Jax's voice turned gruff. "I don't know what to say."

Nya's eyes glittered as she wrapped her arm around his waist. "When I was trapped, and in pain with fire raging around me, I heard your voice, felt your presence. You were the reason I survived because we already have a connection most Scythians will never know. I look forward to creating an *Intima* bond with you."

He picked her up and carried her to their bedroom. Jax settled her in the middle of the soft mattress before scooting off the bed. He stood, his eyes never leaving hers as he unbuttoned his jeans and slid them to the floor, taking his boxers with them.

Nya's brows rose under her bangs as she took in his powerful form.

Jax grinned and crawled toward her, the mattress dipping in his wake. "Quit thinking, Vtachi. We got this."

He sank his hands into her thick hair, his lips drifted down the gentle arc of her throat before traveling to the mark meant just for her.

Nya closed her eyes, a soft sigh escaping her lips as his palm grazed the fresh tattoo between her breasts. Subtly, slowly, his whisper-soft touch stroked her pebbled, sensitive flesh, and her breath quickened to short, shuddered pants. Jax kissed her newly marked skin before traveling lower, his lips grazing, tasting, exploring the delicate indentations between her ribs. He took his time exploring every part of her, loving the way her waist dipped in before flaring into sensuous curves.

"Your skin is so soft, and you smell like heaven."

Nya brushed her fingers through his hair, muttering softly as if she found it hard to speak.

His tongue circled her belly button before his fingers plunged lower, into her soft curls and the fragile crease hidden beneath.

"So perfect," he whispered, totally absorbed in her scent, gently ravaging every part of her.

She shifted her legs, squirming beneath him.

"Jax, I need you closer."

Her husky voice had his lips trailing back up her body until they found hers. His knee parted her thighs, creating a space for himself. Resting the brunt of his weight on his forearms, he buried his hands in her hair and kissed her softly. "Keep your eyes open. I need to see you."

She wrapped her arms around him, and he held her gaze as he settled his hips closer.

"I love you, Vtachi." His breath shook as he pushed into her, breaching her for the first time.

She whimpered as her fingers ran down the deep groove of his spine. He forced himself to keep still, giving her time to adjust to him.

Lost in sensation, she tilted her head back, arching toward him as her body instinctively tightened around him.

"Oh, God," Jax whispered.

Nya kissed his soft lips, and pulled her knees up, encasing him in her strength. She ran her hands up his sculpted back, wrapping her fingers around his shoulders and holding him as she circled her hips, her body completely immersed in pleasure. Jax marveled at how completely she gave herself to him, so vulnerable yet strong, taking him as much as he was taking her until neither of them knew where one began and the other ended.

He tangled his fingers in her hair, his eyes never leaving her face as he whispered how much he loved her, how incredible she was, how happy he was that she had chosen him. With each word, his movements grew stronger, deeper.

She whimpered, her eyes rolling closed as passion swept her away. Jax's control shattered, following her, finding his release in turn.

Thoroughly drained, he fell forward, burying his face in her neck, his body enveloping hers. He took in her sweet scent, which had mingled with his own musk, and it became his life's mission to end every day just like this. He rolled onto his back, taking her with him.

Nya started to shift, but he kept his arms around her. "Not yet."

"I'm smothering you," she murmured, kissing his chest.

"No, you're not. I need you." He linked his hands together at the base of her spine, nudging into her luscious warmth. "Stay with me, just like this."

"I can do that." She smiled.

They settled into a peaceful quiet. One born of utter contentment.

"It's still possible, you know," Nya mumbled, fighting off sleep.

"What is?"

"Having young." She rested her cheek over the Tovaris brand on his chest.

Jax kissed the top of her head. "As long as we're together, I'm happy either way."

"If we're going to try, we need to start soon."

"I think we just did," he muttered.

Nya giggled. "True."

He stroked her back until she yawned and finally eased into slumber.

Yeah. Jax would never tell her how badly he wanted her to have their *nata,* a true Amazonian female, or maybe a *vina* that would carry on the male traditions of Troy—or both. Hell, he'd love a houseful if they could.

But Sarkov may have made that impossible.

He must have grown tense because Nya stirred.

Jax muttered in Dacian, and she nestled down again.

Moonlight filtered through the trees, streaming in their window as a lone wolf howled.

They'd take it one day at a time, but Vtachi was officially his, and right now that's all that mattered.

CHAPTER FORTY-THREE

Three days later Nya and Jax made the long journey to Ireland. They exited the plane, and Nya half smiled as she saw Zander standing by the entrance to the jet's hangar.

The thick scar marring the side of his face glared at her in the morning light, his eyes ruthless, angry.

She walked up to him and wrapped her arms around him. "Thank you."

Surprised, the male tensed. "For what?"

"For making sure we survived."

He wrestled her arms from his waist, gently pushing her away. "Don't get used to the royal treatment, Princess. You're a Tova now."

Nya grinned. "A Tova that kicked your ass."

Amusement glinted in his eyes before he scowled again.

Jax shook Zander's hand, Dacian rumbling across his lips. "How are you, my brother?"

"Better, now that we have the *Zvaz* behind us. I've warned the other Tova that anyone who pulls that shit again will have forty-eight hours to claim their romni or they'll answer to me. Four years is entirely too long."

Jax chuckled as they made their way to the SUV out front. "It was definitely worth it, though."

"I can only imagine." Zander raised a brow.

Nya smirked and kept her eyes forward as they wove through the lot.

A Tova waited in the driver's seat, and Zander jumped in the passenger side while Jax and Nya got in the back.

The vehicle rumbled as they drove through the village and onto the compound's private drive. They neared the gates, and Nya gripped Jax's hand as a slew of reporters rushed towards them. Camera's flashed, even though the tinted windows made it impossible for anyone to see inside.

"The Irish Suveran has forbidden the press to report on Gia's *Nex* ceremony, but that hasn't stopped those nosy bastards from hanging at the gates," Zander said.

Nya groaned. "I hate the media."

"We'll have to deal with them at some point." Jax kissed the side of her head.

"Yeah, well it fucking isn't going to be today." Zander motioned the driver forward, and the Tova hit the gas.

The gates opened, and they left the media behind. Zander's expression softened as they pulled to a stop in front of a modern cottage. "The Suveran has reserved one of the compound's guest houses for you. He thought it would be too painful for you to return to your childhood home."

Nya took a deep breath and got out of the car. He was right. There were too many memories associated with the place, both of her mother and Penn.

Zander opened the back hatch. "There is one other matter."

A dark-headed warrior with gray eyes opened the cottage door.

Nya froze. "Killian."

Zander hefted a suitcase under one arm. "As soon as Jax called to say he'd finally shouldered your mark, I went to the consulate and informed your Chosen. The others accepted it, but Killian insisted on seeing you first. Figured it was better him showing up here than at your cabin in Montana."

"Damn straight," Jax muttered. His warm palms ran up and down her arms, briefly resting on his mark. She tilted her head, and he kissed her neck before pulling away. "I'll wait for you in the house."

Jax grabbed another case from the back, and he and Zander walked away.

The warriors warily nodded hello as they passed one another.

Killian waited until Jax closed the cottage door before facing her.

"So. It's true. You've shouldered Jax's mark." He tripped over the words like they were difficult to say.

"Yes." Nya cleared her throat. "Are you staying for mom's *Nex* ceremony?"

Killian shook his head. "Can't. The American Academy postponed the start of the Claiming Season until tomorrow. My plane leaves in a few hours."

Stilted silence settled around them. For the first time in weeks, Nya's thumb found the scar on her palm.

"Jax said you were with my mother when she died."

Killian sighed. "I was. We were outnumbered ten to one, and your mother had taken a bullet to the thigh, but she refused to give up. We'd just gotten to the second floor when Penn came from a hidden passageway at the end of the hall."

Nya swallowed back the tears. "Did she say anything …" her voice trailed off.

Killian stepped forward and rested his hands on her shoulders. "She loved you, Ny. Maybe she didn't openly show it, but when we were searching through the castle, it was like she was possessed. I've never seen anything like it."

"Thank you," Nya whispered.

Killian ran his finger down her cheek, his deep voice softened to a husky whisper. "You should have come back to Carpathia. I would have fought for you."

"I know."

He leaned forward, his eyes intense. "You're happy?"

She took a deep breath. "Yeah, I am. I love Jax. I think I always have."

He stepped back, his unhappy gaze taking in her features. "Well, I guess that's that."

"I never …" Nya's voice became thick. "I know it doesn't help, but I'm sorry you're hurting."

Killian leaned in and kissed her forehead, lingering for a moment before he pulled away. "Me too, Ny. Me too."

Night settled over the compound's rolling hills, shrouding the verdant landscape in black. Gas lanterns glowed in the chilly breeze, their comforting flicker guiding grieving warriors to the rocky shore.

Nya pulled her mourning shawl across her shoulders, watching the shell of her father's former self lead the crowd to the ceremonial pyre, a small vessel cradled in his arms.

Zander's recovery team had gathered an urn full of ashes and a partially melted necklace that Nya had given her mom as a birthday gift years ago.

The ceramic vessel hadn't left Ike's sight since Zander brought it to him in Carpathia.

Her father's gaunt face held a gray tinge, his muscles seemed to hang from the bone. Nya had offered to stay, help him ease into a life without Gia in it, but he refused, saying he had already scheduled a flight back to Carpathia as soon as the *Nex* was complete.

"Dad can't keep going on like this."

Jax wrapped his arm around her shoulder. "I know, but as hard as it is to accept, he has to find his own way."

Since Gia's death, Ike had emotionally shut down. Tonight was worse—his eyes were no longer guarded and empty, but were now completely open, raw. He kept a tight hold of the urn as he neared the wooden structure jutting from the water's edge, his white ceremonial robe sweeping the ground behind his bare feet.

The moonlight reflected off the black water like a thousand teardrops glittering on the sea. Ike brought the vessel to his lips, kissing the side, rocking back and forth, muttering his final goodbyes. He stumbled in the water, placing the urn on the platform. The first spark beneath the pyre flickered in the night, the flame hissing and snapping as the dry wood caught ablaze. He fell to his knees, freezing water lapped around his waist as he hung his head and openly wept.

Nya started toward him, but Jax held her back.

"He's requested to do this alone."

She wiped her nose with the back of her hand. "I know, but he needs me."

Jax kissed her forehead before pulling her into his arms. "He does, and we'll be there for him when he's ready. But right now, he can't see past his pain."

Silent tears streamed down her face as the blazing pyre gave way, its flames dancing across the wooden pallet as the currents pulled it out to sea. Firelight wrapped Gia's urn in bright light before the platform's charred remains sank into the depths below.

Ike stumbled to his feet, his ceremonial robe ebbing and flowing in rhythm with the waves. Cobalt kissed the horizon, hinting at the dawn of a new day. He turned from the light, his feet unsteady, and stumbled back to shore. The others followed at a distance.

Nya's back nestled against Jax's chest as she looked up at the waning night sky. They watched the stars twinkling lights disappear as pink and purple bled into various shades of orange.

The last conversation she'd had with her mother flitted through her thoughts.

"Love exists, but you must let go of the past. Concentrate on the beauty around you and live in the moment you're in ... "

A tear slipped down her cheek, and she brushed it away. Someday she'd share her memory with her father as she finally understood what her mother was trying to say.

The past was riddled with pain, and tomorrow would surely bring more heartache, more war.

But in this moment, there was beauty. In this moment, she was loved. And in this moment, Nya knew her mother finally had found peace.

Her eyes stayed on the horizon, watching the sun crest over the endless sea of blue. Gulls called overhead as a chilly wind blew from the north, and she turned and looked into Jax's deep brown eyes. This life with Jax was something special, something rare, something worth fighting for.

He kissed the tip of her nose as if he sensed her thoughts. "Come on, Vtachi. Let's go home."

EPILOGUE

Headmistress Cassius's voice blared over the speaker as the wind whipped through the arena. Killian stood next to Giovanni, watching the female warriors spar. Luka had declined to participate, stating he wasn't ready for the responsibility of a romni. He wanted to wait a few more years before putting his name on the list again. David and what was left of Xari's Chosen were toward the end of the field, and Myrina's warriors watched from the other side.

A few of the males had been enthusiastic about finally having control of the process, but Killian hated it. His father had found Killian's mother in the Highland Academy Claiming Season. Their mating was a disaster.

Luckily, the upheaval in Carpathia kept the news crews busy, thank God. Killian's pride already had taken a hit, and he shuddered at the thought of the press storming the American Academy's gates.

Giovanni clapped Killian on the back. "I think I have chosen my candidates, although I do believe there is only one that matches my passion."

Tonight was the end of the first round. The Academy had catered a formal meal, and afterward, the males would declare their potential mates. The problem was, Killian had already dismissed four of the five from the initial personality analysis, and he hadn't found anyone to replace them. Not that these weren't fine Amazonian females. They were, to be sure. But for years he'd wanted Ny—obsessed about it if he were honest. And after meeting her? No way he'd settle for less. The cold, hard reality was that none of these females even came close to what he wanted—and they never would.

Giovanni kept his eyes on the arena. "So, have you heard from Dia?"

"She's on her *Amanti Azil*. Why would she contact me?"

Giovanni glanced at his friend. "After her time with her rovni, she'll call or write. You were special to her, moreso than the others. She'll want to stay in touch."

"I'm not sure that's a good idea." Killian rubbed the back of his neck. No way would he tell Giovanni that he had volunteered to become the CIA lead on a tracking mission to find Nya's eggs. Even as they spoke his team was prowling Drahzdan hotspots for information.

But his Ny didn't need to know that, and neither did her mate. Killian wanted to find what was taken from her so she could have some peace.

And maybe then he'd be able to close this chapter of his life and move on.

The horn blared, signaling the end of the sparring round. Rissa looked up, waving both arms overhead as she smiled.

Giovanni waved back. "Tonight is the night I officially name her as one of my Chosen."

"I'm afraid I won't be here to see it."

"I thought you might leave."

Hating the pity in the other warrior's eyes, Killian looked away. "I'm not in the right headspace for this."

"I've heard it gets better with time." Giovanni's eyes warmed with compassion.

"I'm sure it will."

The sun sunk below the horizon as Killian made his way out of the stadium. It didn't matter if the pain of losing Ny went away or not. In his heart, he knew she was his one chance at developing an *Intima* bond.

He may never have the future he'd dreamed of, but he'd make damn sure his life counted for something.

"The time scale for evolutionary or genetic change is very long. ... But today we do not have ten million years to wait for the next advance. We live in a time when our world is changing at an unprecedented rate. While the changes are largely of our own making, they cannot be ignored. We must adjust and adapt and control, or we perish."

— **Carl Sagan,** *Dragons of Eden: Speculations on the Evolution of Human Intelligence*

Terms and Definitions

Allos (**ALL**-ose) Scythian term for an average human.

Amanti Azil (a-**MAN**-tee a-**ZEEL**) Dacian for honeymoon.

Dacia (**DA**-chi-ah) The original Scythian homeland.

Dacian (**DA**-chi-an) The original Scythian language.

Drahzda (**DRAH**-zdah) An elite group of Allos soldiers determined to eradicate the Scythian species.

Epona (ee-**POH**-nah) Ancient Amazonian blood oath ritual, generally before a marking ceremony.

Honorarium (**ON**-oh-rare-ee-um) A designated place in transports designed to carry the dead back to their home compound.

Intima Bond (**IN**-tih-mah bahnd) Rarest form of Scythian connection that goes beyond the most profound intimacy. Allos humans cannot experience it because they lack the intellectual and emotional depth to understand it.

Kedah (**KEH**-dah) The most beloved symbol in the Scythian culture that literally means *sacred center of your soul.*

Nex (**NEKS**) The Scythian grieving ritual meant to cleanse the heart after a loved one's burial.

Nata (**NA**-tah) Dacian for daughter.

Novo (**NOH**-voh) A virgin.

Romni (**RAHM**-ni) A female equal, similar to the Allos term, 'wife.'

Rovni (**RAHV**-ni) A male equal, similar to the Allos term, 'husband.'

Scythians (**SI**-thee-ans) An evolved species of human that is stronger, more intelligent, and live longer than the Allos population.

Staratsa (sta-**RAH**-tza) A Dacian farewell meant to bless a family member or loved one.

Suka (SOO-kah) Dacian for whore

Suveran (SOO-veh-ran) A title given to the leaders of Scythian compounds or regions.

Tova (TO-va) Dacian for brother.

Tovaras (to-VAH-rahs) The darkest faction of the Scythian Society that are respected as much as the Chancellor and the Senate.

Vahna (VAH-nah) Scythian children.

Vtachi (vTAH-chee) Dacian, meaning little bird.

Zvaz (ZVAZ) Sacred ceremony in which warriors declare their intended equal before their peers.

ACKNOWLEDGEMENTS

It's not often words fail me, but there isn't a phrase or narrative strong enough to express just how much these people mean to me. My heartfelt thanks go out to the incredibly creative Corina Vaccarello, who has been with me since the very first days of purple moons and hundred-year-old Oak trees. Her unwavering friendship, support, and encouragement is a blessing beyond measure. To Mindy Ruiz, who inspires me to branch and out and grow as a writer. She, too, is immensely creative, and I'm so grateful to call her my friend. To Italia Gandolfo, agent, friend, and all around bad-ass. Her steadfast belief in me is humbling and inspires me to traverse well beyond the limits of my comfort zone. And to Liana Gardner, whose intelligence, tenacity and frankness keeps me grounded in a way few people can. You, my friend, are a true warrior.

They say to find your tribe and love them hard. I have, and I do.

ABOUT THE AUTHOR

Elizabeth Isaacs is an author and teacher who began her career as a national presenter for Resource Profiles, where she developed teacher seminars designed to foster creative brain stimulation. Moving into formal education, she helped at-risk students improve their writing skills as well as created and implemented a creative writing/blogging program that centered on teaching the 21st-century learner. Works stemming from this initiative were published online and seen in over 40 countries.

Elizabeth receives invitations to speak nationwide at schools and book clubs about Young Adult (YA) content and writing. She runs the popular Facebook group, Writers etc., which builds an exciting bridge between the publishing and Hollywood communities and reaches thousands of people throughout the world. Elizabeth has a Master's degree from Austin Peay State University, where she was trained in classical opera. She graduated Magna Cum Laude and was a member of the Phi Beta Kappa Honor Society.

Her debut Fantasy title, *The Light of Asteria*, received Honorable Mention at the New York Book Festival.

www.ElizabethIsaacs.com